PREY

KEN GODDARD

TOR

A TOM DOHERTY ASSOCIATES BOOK
NEW YORK

PREY

A Tor Book
Published by Tom Doherty Associates, Inc.
175 Fifth Avenue
New York, N.Y. 10010

Tor® is a registered trademark of Tom Doherty Associates, Inc.

ISBN: 0-812-51198-0
Library of Congress Catalog Card Number 92-20815

First edition: September 1992
First mass market printing: August 1993

Printed in the United States of America

0 9 8 7 6 5 4 3 2 1

This book is dedicated to my mother and father.

ACKNOWLEDGMENTS

My sincere thanks to Wally, Al, Roger, and Mark, for their camaraderie, their war stories, and their skill in keeping the planes in the air over Alaska.

A CAUTIONARY NOTE

There is always the chance that a fiction writer who uses his daytime job as a backdrop for creating a story may cause his fellow employees to rush to the bookstores with either delightful anticipation, nervous concern, seething anger, or outright dread. Thus, for the record:

Certain federal government-position titles are used in this story for the sake of realism. No characters in the book, however, are intended to resemble anyone who has ever held any of these titles; nor do they resemble any individual currently or previously employed by the U.S. Fish and Wildlife Service, the Justice Department, the Department of Interior, or any other agency of the government. All of the characters in this book are fictional, as is the plot.

To my knowledge, there has never been an International Commission for Environmental Restoration (ICER) or an Operation Counter Wrench within the United States Department of Interior. And as far as I am aware, the position of special executive assistant to the deputy assistant undersecretary within that department remains fictitious.

My good fellows, it's really a very simple concept. We all know that there are hundreds of deer in the forest. Which means that the King, and all his men, can kill all of the deer they want, any day of the week they want, and there will always be more. So you see, there is absolutely no reason why the game laws should apply to any of these gentle-born men, just as long as we do *our* job and make sure that the peasants are never allowed to kill a single deer.

—Anonymous Supervisory Gamekeeper
Sherwood Forest
Nottingham

HUNTER . . .

CHAPTER ONE

SATURDAY, SEPTEMBER 25TH

It began on the eve of a severe Alaskan snowstorm. Two men stepped out of their four-wheel-drive vehicle into the freezing night. Pausing under a glary streetlight to check their watches, they carefully slid fully loaded .45 SIG-Sauer automatic pistols into the pockets of their down jackets.

Seemingly alone, the men looked up and down the block, crossed the street, and entered one of Anchorage's sleaziest biker bars.

The man watching all of this from the room above the bar checked his watch. It was exactly eleven fifty-five P.M.

The late-night crowd in the High Horse Saloon was a touchy mix of bikers, fishermen, and oil-field roughnecks. One of the scruffier patrons, Henry Lightstone, sat by himself at a small corner table.

"Get you a cold one?"

Lightstone put his hand over his glass and shook the waitress off as he watched two men enter the bar through the double doors. He wouldn't have given them more than a casual glance if one of them hadn't looked like a cop. Right now, a cop was the last person that Henry Lightstone wanted to see.

He glanced down at his watch again—eleven fifty-six. He had planned that in four minutes he would resolve the problem that had been plaguing him for three months. Now he had only two options: stay in the bar and risk getting trapped in an arrest, or leave immediately—and flush six weeks of work down the toilet.

The two newcomers walked over to a wall table, pulled off their heavy jackets and set them on an empty chair. They ordered drinks from a waitress as they sat down.

Henry Lightstone leaned his chair back against the corner wall and draped his long arms across the wooden armrests, trying to look like a man who was working on his fifth or sixth beer of the evening instead of his second.

Come on, he muttered to himself, somebody *do* something.

Two minutes to go.

The waitress returned with the beers and a basket of the bar's notoriously stale popcorn. The man who looked like a cop pulled two folded bills out of his shirt pocket, tossed them onto her tray, then turned his attention back to his companion.

Lightstone watched the stunned waitress stare at the money. She hurriedly stuffed one of the bills into her low-cut tank top before returning to the bar.

Two twenties, Lightstone told himself. Four beers would have been twelve, and he didn't figure she would skim tips for a lousy five or ten.

Throwaway money. A technique used by insecure people trying to make an impression. Unfortunately, it was also a trick that undercover cops used to throw people off.

Henry Lightstone let his eyes drift slowly around the smoke-filled room. He half expected to see a five- or six-man raid team taking up positions near the rear exit, but the doors were clear.

Lightstone tried to convince himself that the two newcomers were just a couple of moose-hunting tourists grounded in Anchorage by the unexpected storm. Macho types who didn't have enough brains to stay out of places like the High Horse at eleven fifty-five in the evening.

He'd been running across guys like that ever since he'd gotten into town six weeks ago.

He watched as a biker who had been sitting at the bar walked up to the two men. He was classic outlaw: big, with a scraggly black beard, dirty hair, a torn leather jacket, and patched jeans. He crashed into the table, splashing beer on the two men.

The newcomers stared up at the black-jacketed figure with bemused indifference.

Conversations began to die out at several of the surrounding tables.

Lightstone watched the biker bring his hands slowly to his narrow hips, his right hand over the leather knife pouch on his belt. The guy who looked like a cop smiled at the biker, shook his head slightly and stared straight into the biker's bloodshot eyes. Lightstone could lip-read what he said from thirty feet away:

"Don't even think about it, asshole."

For a moment, the outlaw biker appeared stunned by the newcomer's insolence.

Two of the saloon's bouncers took up positions near the newcomers' table. One was black, the other Asian. Neither was trying to conceal the buckshot-filled saps they tapped against their legs.

The biker stepped away from the table to face the two bouncers, the fingertips of his right hand still tucked under the leather flap of his knife pouch. But then he faltered. Clearly outbluffed and outmaneuvered, he glared at the bouncers, then swaggered back toward the bar as if the episode had been a waste of his time.

A couple of the oil-field workers, who'd obviously had their fill of swaggering bikers, rose out of their chairs, intent on taking a black leather jacket home as a trophy.

Instead, they found themselves standing nose to shirt pocket with another bouncer, this one a former offensive tackle for the Raiders. Smiling pleasantly, the bouncer placed a courtesy pitcher of draft on the table and shook his head.

"Couple of bad-ass dudes," a familiar-sounding voice said next to Lightstone.

Henry Lightstone glanced up at the tall, leather-jacketed figure and motioned for Brendon Kleinfelter to join him at the table.

"You know them?"

"They come here every now and then, have a few beers, and then walk out like they don't give a shit that they look like a couple of cops."

"You sure they aren't?"

"Not according to my sources." Kleinfelter shrugged. "Far as we know, they're a couple of import-export guys looking to make some extra money on the side. Popper doesn't like them hanging around here, and he thinks he can run them out. He just keeps forgetting about Larry and Mike."

"The sap-artist twins?"

Kleinfelter nodded his bearded head.

"I assume you don't really give a shit either, since you own the place," Lightstone suggested.

"Their money's good," Kleinfelter agreed.

"Know anything else about them?"

"Why? They make you nervous?"

"Damn right they do," Lightstone said solemnly. "I didn't set aside much for lawyers this year."

"Names are Paul and Carl. At least that's what they go by around here. Way I understand it, Paul is the money man. The guy with the attitude is Carl. Figure him for the protection."

"Protection for what?"

"That's always the question, isn't it?" Kleinfelter nodded. "Did you remember to bring cash?"

"Yeah, sure," Lightstone said sarcastically. "I left it with the waitress for safekeeping."

"Just as long as we understand each other." Kleinfelter's eyes gleamed maliciously.

"What *I* understand is that I'm here to check out the merchandise. If I like what I see, I make a phone call. They give me an address, and you send a couple of people out to check the money. If everybody ends up happy, your people pick up the cash, I load up the goods, and you guys start setting up bank accounts for your old age. And if everybody *stays* happy with the deal, we start weekly pickups, five hundred pounds a whack. Is that the way you understand it?"

"Sound's right to me," Kleinfelter said. "Back room okay?"

Lightstone shrugged. "Yeah, sure. Why not?"

"Then let's do it."

Lightstone and Kleinfelter worked their way through the crowd, then stepped into a long, narrow hallway that was closed off at either end by steel doors. About halfway down the narrow hallway, a pair of support beams stuck out from either side, leaving only enough room for one person to walk by at a time. An x-ray device. No lights or buzzers went off when Lightstone walked through the narrow opening, but he figured there was a scanner and men with firearms on the other side of the doorway.

"You getting paranoid in your old age?" Lightstone asked, tapping his knuckles against the solid surface of the second door.

"It's the only way I know to *get* old in this business," Brendon Kleinfelter said as the second door was pulled open from the inside.

At least half of the floor space beyond was taken up by stacks of stainless-steel kegs and shrink-wrapped pallets containing hundreds of cases of Bud, Miller, Moosehead, and Stroh's. It was obvious that the High Horse Saloon would not run out of beer, no matter how long the winter season lasted this year.

"Nice operation," Lightstone said.

"First-class. That's the way I like it," Kleinfelter said as a man with a scanner wand came forward.

"Any objections?" the outlaw gang leader asked.

"Be my guest," Lightstone shrugged.

He held his arms up while the scanner ran under his armpits and across his chest. It registered nothing at all. Same reaction for the buttocks, hips, and crotch. No guns, no knives, no beepers, recorders or transmitters. It was only when the device was brought down along the front of Lightstone's long legs that it emitted a shrill beep.

"Right boot," Lightstone said calmly. The man operating the scanner squatted down, lifted up Lightstone's pant leg and carefully removed the loaded .38 five-shot Chief's Special from the boot holster. The weapon was handed up to Kleinfelter, who glanced at it, then looked over at Lightstone quizzically.

"You always carry a shit-ass piece like this?"

"That's right."

"What for?"

"Handy for bears," Lightstone shrugged, returning the outlaw biker's calm, icy stare.

"Yeah, right," Kleinfelter chuckled. "A thirty-eight's gonna have a serious impact on a thousand-pound grizzly. Didn't anybody ever tell you about Magnums?"

"I don't like big guns," Lightstone said. "They make too much noise, and they don't fit in my boot."

Brendon Kleinfelter gave him an evil smile, then tossed the handgun back to Lightstone, who fielded it one-handed, then slid the still-loaded weapon back down into his boot holster. The rest of the search turned up nothing of interest.

Kleinfelter opened another door, and Lightstone entered a smaller warehouse. A dozen people, most of whom Lightstone recognized from the bar, were surveying at least a hundred and fifty military ammo crates with rope handles on the sides. Standing next to a small stack of the ammo crates were the two clean-cut newcomers. The one who looked like a cop was holding a small crowbar in his gloved right hand.

"What the hell are *they* doing here?" Lightstone demanded, glaring at Kleinfelter.

"You mean Paul and Carl?" Kleinfelter asked. "They're what you might call your competition. You think you're the only guy who ever came up to Alaska looking to make a deal?"

"Are you trying to tell me I've got to stand here in front of an audience and *bid* for this shit?" Lightstone couldn't believe what he was hearing.

"That's about it," Kleinfelter told him.

Lightstone nodded toward the newcomers. "So why don't *they* have to get their nuts fried in a goddamned X-ray machine?" he demanded.

"I've been dealing with Paul and Carl for a couple of months now," Kleinfelter said. "I know a lot about them. But you're new."

"Fucking incredible," Henry Lightstone muttered.

"To tell you the truth," Kleinfelter said, "I don't think you're really going to be competitors anyway."

"Mind telling me why?" Lightstone asked.

"Take a look at the merchandise."

They all watched as Carl crowbarred open the top of the ammo crate.

"What the hell's *that*?" Henry Lightstone asked, staring into the open container.

Carl smiled. "That, my friend, is what Mr. Kleinfelter likes to refer to as Alaskan White."

"But that's a . . . a . . . ."

"An ivory carving?" Paul suggested as he picked one of the carvings out of the crate.

"I don't believe this," Henry Lightstone said.

"You got a problem with it?"

The voice behind Lightstone belonged to the biker named Popper.

Without turning around, Lightstone snarled: "Fuck off."

Then he froze when he heard the distinctive *click* of a six-inch knife blade snapping open.

Spinning to his left, Lightstone shoved the thrusting knife hand aside with his open right palm, brought his left hand up to catch the wrist, and then twisted hard.

The crack was audible above Popper's choking scream.

For a long moment, everyone simply stared.

Lightstone retrieved the open knife. Closing the blade, he tossed it to the ex-Raider-turned-bouncer, who had stepped in between Kleinfelter and Lightstone.

Catching the knife, the huge man stared at Lightstone appraisingly, as if trying to decide which limb to rip off first.

"Man, I'm *really* going to enjoy this one," the bouncer finally said.

"I shouldn't have let it get out of control like that," Lightstone forced himself to say, even though no one seemed to care about the injured biker, who thrashed on the concrete.

"Popper'll survive," Brendon Kleinfelter said. He motioned to a pair of his men, who picked the man up off the floor and carried him out of the warehouse. "The question is, will you?"

Kleinfelter was smiling, but his eyes were expressionless.

"None of this would have happened if you'd given me some kind of warning," Lightstone said.

"When Brendon offered to sell you a thousand pounds of Alaskan White," Paul said, "you weren't expecting to purchase ivory, were you?"

"Not hardly," Lightstone replied.

"I don't suppose your people have any drugs around here that you might offer this fellow instead?" Paul laughed as he turned to Kleinfelter. "Some cocaine, perhaps?"

"We could probably lay our hands on a kilo or two," Kleinfelter shrugged.

"Oh, yeah—" Lightstone started to say. Kleinfelter held up his hand.

"But it'd be kinda dumb to sell cocaine to an undercover cop."

Lightstone's knees sagged.

"Are you sure about that?" Paul asked.

"Damn right, I'm sure," Brendon Kleinfelter said. "This guy is Henry Lightstone, homicide investigator for the San Diego Police Department. Soon to be ex-homicide investigator."

Lightstone thought about the Chief's Special in his boot, but he was suddenly aware that all three bouncers were now holding baseball bats and that the eight remaining bikers had unzipped their black leather jackets to reveal an assortment of handguns.

"Homicide?" Paul said, his eyebrows raised in surprise. "I would have thought narcotics, surely?"

"No, the man's definitely homicide," Brendon Kleinfelter shook his head. "See, about six or eight months ago, some homicide dick named Bobby LaGrange was rummaging around the harbor area, trying to figure out why some two-bit hooker got herself dead. Somewhere along the line, LaGrange got the idea that some of us might have been involved, so we decided to distract him a little. That about the size of it, Henry?"

Henry Lightstone said nothing.

"And this Bobby LaGrange, I take it, worked with this fellow here?" Paul asked, looking over at Lightstone.

Kleinfelter nodded.

"I see," Paul said calmly. "And tell me, uh, Henry," the man went on, seemingly unfazed by this latest bit of information, "how much time does Brendon face if he's charged for your friend's unfortunate accident?"

Henry Lightstone decided he had nothing to lose by going along with this man's game. If nothing else, it might buy him more time.

"If Bobby recovers, three to ten," Lightstone said.

"And if he doesn't?"

"He'll fry."

"Only three to ten years for nearly beating a police officer to death? That's incredible. Don't you think so, Carl?"

"Hell of a deal," Carl nodded in agreement as he continued to rummage through the ivory statues.

"Especially when a person could get ten years and a ten-thousand-dollar fine just for selling one little carving," Paul went on, holding up the statue of a walrus. "African elephant ivory. *Loxodonta africana.* Absolutely prohibited. And, of course, Lord knows what he might get if there are any more like this." He gestured toward the pile of ammo crates.

"Ten years for *that*?" Henry Lightstone said, astonished.

"At least one more," Carl called out as he held up a carved seal.

"Oh, good," Paul said. "That makes it twenty and twenty. Oh, and did I happen to mention," he said, turning to Brendon Kleinfelter, who had a thoroughly perplexed expression on his bearded face, "that Carl and I are federal agents and that you and your associates are all under arrest?"

"*What?*" Kleinfelter blinked in disbelief.

"Arrest," Paul repeated. "You know, hands above your head, you have the right, so on and so forth."

"You are out of your fucking mind," Brendon Kleinfelter said softly.

"Like I told you, I'm with the federal government," Paul

said agreeably. "Now, if you'll all just put your hands above your heads . . ."

Henry Lightstone was still looking back and forth between Paul, Brendon Kleinfelter, and the ex-Raider bouncer with the bat when the outlaw leader suddenly came alive and reached for the shoulder-holstered 9mm Smith & Wesson under his black leather jacket.

Henry Lightstone was already lunging at Kleinfelter, and he barely saw the bat in time to duck. The hulking bouncer caught Kleinfelter square in the middle of his bearded face, knocking him head over heels in a spray of blood and broken teeth.

The biker closest to Lightstone was still fumbling for his own 9mm, but now Lightstone was back on his feet, kicking him hard—first in the knee and then in the neck—seizing his gun, then spinning around with the Ruger automatic pistol in both outstretched hands.

He was too late. A noise like a dozen coconuts cracking together ripped through the warehouse and signaled the end of the fight.

Before Lightstone's astonished eyes, six of the bikers lay sprawled out on the concrete floor, while two of the bouncers, down on their knees, were checking pulses and applying handcuffs. Two other bikers were dangling from the huge hands of the ex-Raider-turned-bouncer, who dropped each to the concrete with a loud, hollow *thunk*.

Henry Lightstone looked up at the hulking giant in disbelief.

Paul nodded to Lightstone. "Henry, let me introduce you to Dwight Stoner. Ex-offensive tackle for the Raiders." He glanced at the sprawled figure of Brendon Kleinfelter. "And also, fortunately for us, a special agent of the United States Fish and Wildlife Service."

CHAPTER TWO

SUNDAY, SEPTEMBER 26TH

At eleven o'clock on the same morning, seven hours after the Alaska White suspects had been booked into the Anchorage Police Department jail, Mike Takahara opened the door of the penthouse suite in the downtown Anchorage Hilton.

"We were about ready to give up on you two," the muscular agent said cheerfully as he motioned the two men inside, then firmly pushed the door shut. "Hey, guys, we've got company."

The three men seated at the dining-room table looked up as U.S. Attorney Jameson Wheeler and Henry Lightstone entered the room.

"Hey, Jameson! ¿Qué pasa, hombre? And Lightstone, mah man!" Larry Paxton grinned widely.

"Yep, it's that crazy fellow all right." Dwight Stoner, the huge bouncer-agent nodded, then went back to work on his dinner-plate-sized omelet.

"Ah, don't know, man, maybe he ain't so crazy after all," Paxton observed. "Dude brought a gawdamned *lawyer* with him this time."

"Yeah, but he didn't bring a very *good* one," Carl Scoby said, giving Wheeler a broad wink.

"I keep telling them that I'm either going to start being more selective about my clients, or increase my already outrageous fees, but they just won't listen," U.S. Attorney Jameson Wheeler said to Lightstone as he shook his head sadly. Then he yelled out toward the kitchen, "Hey, McNulty, how's a guy supposed to get anything to eat around here?"

"About time you guys showed up," Paul McNulty said as he poked his head through the kitchen door. He came out wiping his hands on his grease-stained apron. "Thought you might have decided to have brunch down at the jail instead. What'll it be? The McNulty Special?"

"I'll have whatever Stoner's having, only make it normal human size," Wheeler answered.

"You got it," McNulty said agreeably. Then he turned toward Henry Lightstone, who was still standing in the entryway of the spacious four-room suite.

"So, what do you think, Henry?" McNulty asked, a thoughtful expression on his relaxed face.

"I'd say this place looks more like a drug dealer's hideaway than the command headquarters for a federal undercover operation. It's also a lot nicer than where I spend the evening," he finally said.

"Yeah, I understand the PD's a little stingy on its accommodations," McNulty smiled.

"Did it ever occur to you guys," Lightstone went on, "that you *could* have told them I was a cop before you had me booked?"

"Shit. *Knew* there was something we forgot to do," Larry Paxton said to Dwight Stoner.

"Told me *you* were gonna do that," Stoner said, mumbling the words through a large mouthful of omelet.

"*Me?* Ah thought *you*—"

Lightstone turned to Wheeler. "Of course they *did* remember to tell the cops that I'd been pinched for buying illegal walrus ivory, so they'd be sure to announce it to the world when they put me in the tank with about a half-dozen shit-face drunk Eskimos."

"Oh, yeah, we definitely remembered to do that," Stoner nodded with a cheerful smile.

"So how'd the brothers react when they saw you get bailed out a few hours later by some sleazy lawyer?" Larry Paxton asked as he winked at Jameson Wheeler.

"I'd say it probably confused the hell out of them," Lightstone said. "It confused the hell out of me, too. The way

I understood it, I was supposed to dig at them a little deeper while Kleinfelter and Popper were still in the hospital."

Paul McNulty came up alongside the tall police officer, patted him on the shoulder and motioned him over to a chair next to Wheeler at the head of the large kitchen table. "Believe it or not, Henry, there really was a purpose to all of this. Why don't you sit down, have a cup of Martha's coffee, and let Scoby here fill you in? I'll whip up a couple more omelets for you and Jameson."

An hour later, Henry Lightstone finished his boysenberry pie, set the plate aside, and looked over at Paul McNulty, who was scraping out the bowl of a large briar pipe with his pocket knife.

"So when did you guys know?"

"About you?" McNulty asked.

Lightstone nodded.

"Oh, I'd say it was about four weeks ago," McNulty told him.

"That's about the time I first met Kleinfelter at the bar," Lightstone said, embarrassed by the sudden realization that he'd been made from day one.

"That's when," Dwight Stoner mumbled through a huge mouthful of pie.

"Don't feel too bad about that, Henry." Larry Paxton smiled sympathetically. "Once Stoner worked his way into the High Horse as a bouncer and then got us our jobs, we started running makes on anybody who ever said more than three words to Kleinfelter. We got curious about you when Mike over here hit a brick wall trying to track back on that Mastercard you used to rent the Honda."

"Yeah, had to spend the better part of a weekend peeling back all the protection layers on that computer of yours," Takahara complained good-naturedly.

"What computer? I don't—" Lightstone started to say, then it hit him. "You guys broke into the *San Diego Police Department's* computer? Christ, that thing's supposed to be *protected!*"

"No big deal." Mike Takahara shrugged, "I cheat."

"I see," Lightstone said, nodding slowly as if he understood the situation, which he didn't.

"Having a guy like Mike along on an operation makes it real difficult for the bad guys to hide," Larry Paxton commented. "Otherwise we wouldn't put up with the little runt. Him and his goddamned egg-rice, seaweed shit. Enough to make a grown man puke."

Lightstone looked over at the Asian agent and judged that at about six-one and no less than two hundred and ten pounds, Mike Takahara was maybe an inch shorter and twenty pounds heavier than Paxton. The covert team's idea of a runt.

"Power of the computer age," Takahara grinned. "You just watch. Microchips and robotics are gonna make you field guys obsolete yet."

"Already made *me* obsolete," Lightstone commented sourly. "Doesn't make much sense to spend a couple of months setting up a deep cover if assholes like Kleinfelter can tap into a goddamned police comphuter any time they want."

"Kleinfelter tap into a computer?" Takahara laughed out loud. "Come on, give me a break. It'd take those idiots a week just to find the on-off switch."

"Then how was he able to figure out I was a cop so fast?" Lightstone demanded.

"Probably because Stoner told him," Mike Takahara said matter-of-factly.

"Stoner did *what*?" Lightstone exclaimed, blinking his eyes in shock and then turning his head slowly to stare at the huge ex-bouncer.

Dwight Stoner looked up over the remnants of his pie and nodded his massive head in confirmation.

Lightstone sat in silence for a long moment and then turned back to McNulty. "Any particular *reason* why you guys decided to set me up so I could get my ass blown off?" he asked quietly.

"Actually, there was," McNulty said in a perfectly calm and reasonable voice. "We had Brendon pretty well lined up for the big sale, and we were all set to take him down; but then he started getting suspicious. Didn't want to show us his stock, and he kept sending that little asshole Popper and his buddies around to give us a bad time, see how we'd react. Then all of a sudden you show up, hot on the trail, all by yourself, nice cover, determined to work your way in."

"The perfect distraction," Carl Scoby nodded. "Stoner supposedly checks us out, gives us a clean bill, and then lets Brendon know that he's got a cop on his ass. All of a sudden we look real good."

"And then Larry steps in with the Alaska White scam, which Brendon thinks is a really funny idea," Takahara added. "Stoner follows up by telling Brendon that he wants to be the one who knocks you off 'cause he's never got to kill a cop before, which pretty well lines it up for you to be there at the buy."

"And gives me a real nice opportunity to save your butt," Dwight Stoner finished.

"Which *you* put into jeopardy in the first place," Lightstone reminded.

"Yeah, exactly. Kinda poetic, huh?" the huge ex-Raider bouncer smiled.

"Think I'm going to make friends with a couple of pro linebackers," Lightstone said after a moment. "Maybe Lawrence Taylor and Carl Banks, for a start. See if I can get those guys to work you down to my size."

"LT and Carl? Couple of pussies. No problem," Stoner grinned happily.

"So," Lightstone went on, "Mike the Hacker here tracked me back to the PD through the computer, and that's how you found out about Bobby and figured I was running a Lone Ranger operation, right?"

"No, actually we called up your captain and asked if he knew where you were," McNulty said. "Naturally he had no idea, since you hadn't bothered to check in for about six weeks. We got the impression that if we'd found your body facedown in a ditch, he wouldn't have been all that upset."

"That's probably right," Lightstone muttered glumly.

"Typical brass," Dwight Stoner nodded as he gratefully

accepted another piece of boysenberry pie from Martha Mc-Nulty. "We got the same problem."

"Which reminds me," McNulty said, ignoring the slight on his supervisory status, "Bobby is doing fine. Came out of the coma a couple of weeks ago, wanting to know where the hell you were."

"You're kidding?" Henry Lightstone exclaimed, his eyes widening in a mixture of delight and relief.

"Nope, honest-to-God truth," McNulty said. "Doctors seem to think he'll be fine. Just needs to rest up, stay off his feet for a couple months. His wife and kids said to say hi. They seem to think a lot of you."

"You talked to Mary and the kids?"

"We wanted to get an idea of who we were dealing with," McNulty explained as he sipped his hot coffee. "You have an interesting reputation among your fellow officers."

"'Interesting.' That's a pretty good description," Mike Takahara grinned.

"Exactly," Larry Paxton confirmed. "See, the thing is, we figure we've got one hell of a group here, as far as federal undercover teams go. In fact, to paraphrase one of our infamous ex-secretaries of Interior, what we've got is one genuine black, namely, me; one more or less genuine Asian," he nodded over at Mike Takahara; "a gimp," another nod toward Stoner, "and a guy who, as you mentioned, looks an awful lot like a cop." A final nod over at Carl Scoby.

"But what we really lack, what we really need to round out the team . . ." Mike Takahara continued.

". . . is a truly crazy fellow," Dwight Stoner finished with a satisfied smile.

Martha McNulty reached over and filled Lightstone's cup with more of the steaming hot coffee. "I think," she said quietly, "they're trying to ask if you'd like to go outside and play with them." She patted him on the shoulder.

"You mean this is some sort of interview?"

"More or less," Paul McNulty acknowledged.

"We've found that police officers don't usually make good wildlife investigators," Carl Scoby explained. "The cop types always want to control a situation, put everybody on the ground, take away their guns, that sort of thing, instead of going along with the flow . . . like you did with those fellows in the drunk tank."

"You guys monitored the cell?" Lightstone asked.

"We usually let Jameson do all that sneaky-peeky stuff," Scoby shrugged. "Helps him maintain that sleazy image."

Lightstone looked over at the U.S. Attorney, who smiled back, nodding his head.

"And then, too, you don't run across all that many cops who are willing to take on thirty-six outlaw bikers single-handed," Larry Paxton added. "Sort of a Don Quixote with a death wish. We like that in a guy."

"Yeah, especially since we've got plans to take on some fairly serious characters in the next few months," Mike Takahara said.

"*Serious* characters, as opposed to wimps like Kleinfelter?" Lightstone said, trying hard not to smile.

"Serious enough," Larry Paxton said. "Senators, congress-men, high-level bureaucrats, federal judges, CEOs, lawyers, cops. The kind of guys who can make an agent's life downright miserable."

"Guys who don't think the laws apply to them. Guys who don't like to lose," Carl Scoby added.

"The thing is," Paul McNulty finished, "we don't like to lose either. Which is why we're looking to bring on another man who can be flexible in a tight spot. Balance out the team. Maybe give us an edge in the likely event that we run into somebody with serious connections."

"Like the boss said, a crazy fellow," Dwight Stoner agreed. "The game is bunnies and guppies. Big playing field, shit pot full of rules and no referee. Last guy still on his feet wins."

Stoner paused for a moment and glanced around the table. Then he looked back at Lightstone with a serious expression on his meaty face.

"You wanna play?"

CHAPTER THREE

SUNDAY, DECEMBER 2ND

The cat had been aware of their presence for almost a half hour before he finally chose to show himself, silently pushing his massive head through the concealing sheath of yellow-draping flowers and broad mango leaves to verify with his eyes what his far more sensitive ears and nose had confirmed long ago.

There were five of the upright human creatures now—four in the tree and one on the ground.

If a Bengal tiger could have smiled, this one would have done so.

Taken from his mother and his native India in his second season, the huge male cat had endured six long and frustrating years of captivity at the hands of these creatures.

Six long years of living in narrow, confining cages, with little else to do but pace back and forth and snarl at his hated captors. Waiting for the chain-link barriers to finally give way against his savage bursts of rage. And watching as the fragile humans winced and cowered back in spite of themselves, their eyes widening with instinctive fear as the cage wire bulged outward, yet held once again.

He had suffered those six years with implacable patience, waiting for that one moment—the moment that had occurred less than an hour ago now—when the massive steel door was suddenly winched up to reveal a long, narrow, open-ended runway that led out to a wide expanse of brush and trees, and a barely remembered freedom that had been the driving force of the Bengal's very existence for all those many years.

And when that moment arrived, the Bengal had paused for only a brief second before lunging out onto the sawdust-covered ground, his incredibly powerful muscles tensed, his terrible claws extended, and his fearsome teeth bared in a deep-throated and spine-chilling roar as he searched with fierce yellow eyes for the first human creature to make the fatal mistake of trying to drive him back into the hated cage.

Several of them had been there, watching his release from the security of a high, restraining fence, and he had stared at each one with a savage hopefulness.

But none of them had been so foolish as to climb over the fence and stand in his way, and so now he was free . . . to hunt, to kill, to tear apart the fragile, upright creatures, one by hated one.

"There he is!" Lisa Abercombie whispered, all too aware that her normally calm and authoritative voice was choked and raspy with a nervous excitement that she hadn't felt since her childhood.

"Where?" Dr. Reston Wolfe and Dr. Morito Asai whispered simultaneously.

"Two o'clock, in the mangoes," Abercombie responded in a forcibly controlled voice, her hands trembling slightly as she brushed her dark, shoulder-length hair away from her sweating face. She refocused the low-powered binoculars.

They were perched twenty-two feet off the ground in a tree with a forty-inch main trunk whose secondary branches were at least twelve feet off the ground, and surrounded by enough waist-high oak planking and iron bracing to stop a rogue bull elephant. The cat knew they were there, so there was no real point in trying to keep their voices low anyway.

But because the observation platform that had seemed so high and secure earlier that morning now seemed unacceptably fragile and much too low to the ground, the urge to be as silent as possible was instinctive.

What made it worse was the chilling sense that the six-hundred-pound Bengal hated each one of them personally.

Each of them had seen the glint of purposeful rage in the cat's furious yellow eyes as he lunged his massive body into the steel mesh again and again, trying to tear through the chain links.

"I see him," Dr. Reston Wolfe nodded, once again glancing nervously over at Tom Frank's bolt-action .416 Weatherby Magnum rifle propped up against the far wall of the platform. Wolfe could still feel the strength of the beams that had been so reassuring that morning, but at this moment, more than anything else, he wanted that Weatherby Magnum rifle in his hands. Wolfe understood now, in a way that he hadn't understood before, that twenty-two feet of height and oak wood barriers wouldn't begin to stop the fiercely dangerous creature that remained partially hidden in the mangoes, staring up at them with those cold, deadly, and absolutely merciless yellow eyes.

As if sensing the human creatures' fear, the big cat opened its jaws wide, exposing its glistening yellow-white incisors, and roared. The thunderous and primeval sound reverberated through the trees and sent cold chills down the spines of the four treetop observers.

It was probably just as well that Dr. Reston Wolfe didn't know that his career, and his life, were in the hands of a woman who savored the intensity of a risk-filled adventure. Because if he had known, and had truly understood the forces that motivated a woman such as Lisa Abercombie, he would have been forced to recognize himself as the sacrificial goat. And *that* would have been more than a self-centered and self-serving bureaucrat like Wolfe could have tolerated.

Two years earlier, a strikingly beautiful grass-roots campaign worker from Riverdale, in the Bronx, had used her Italian father's considerable political connections to broker her way into an exclusive "power loop" of wealthy and influential Northeastern conservatives. She could finally say what most of the party elders were afraid to even think.

"Gentlemen," she had begun in her characteristically forceful voice, "you know and I know goddamned well that the United States of America has squandered its birthright."

Several pairs of watery eyes had blinked, and the room had suddenly grown still.

"We have become a second-rate economic power," Abercombie had continued, "and are certainly heading toward third if we don't do something about these *damnable environmental terrorists* who are crippling our critical industries."

The subdued applause had suggested that, her point made, she should quickly conclude so that the professionals in the room could get back to business.

But Lisa Abercombie had come too far to stop now.

"And if we *are* going to do something, instead of just clipping our goddamned coupons," she had said, her eyes filled with rage, "we damn well better do it *right now*, while those coupons are still worth something!"

The room had gone deathly silent again.

And then, to the shock of every man present, Lisa Abercombie had described not only what *could* be done, and *how*, but also why she was the woman who should be allowed to pull it off.

All she needed were money and contacts—and the authority to use them as she willed. She would take all the risks and get the job done. Those coupons would continue to reflect the wealth and authority of the Northeastern conservative power structure.

With that, Lisa Abercombie had excused herself from the meeting, leaving phone numbers where she could be reached during the next seventy-two hours.

The debates that followed were tense and emotional. Dozens of private meetings held in electronically swept rooms were dominated by arguments. Decisions were made and reversed in an atmosphere of chaos.

Three days later, Lisa Abercombie had found herself on the seventh floor of the Main Interior Building in Washington, D.C., being sworn in to the newly created position of special executive assistant to the deputy assistant undersecretary for internal affairs of the Department of Interior.

The position had not required the approval of Congress. It was one of those vague Washington titles that would basically allow her to maintain anonymity within the department. This was considered crucial to Lisa Abercombie's secret, but now official, mission: to establish a fully operational covert entity within the executive branch of the federal government.

The entity would be called the International Commission for Environmental Restoration. The suitably vague name, strung of popular D.C. buzz words, had been concocted by Lisa Abercombie herself, who particularly liked the resulting acronym.

ICER.

Suddenly aware that she could lose it all, right now, here on this platform, Lisa Abercombie's eyes flashed with rage as she swung her head around and glared at Wolfe.

"Reston, this is insane!" she hissed. "I want you to stop this before someone gets killed."

Her words were insistent, but Wolfe could sense the underlying excitement that had already drawn her attention back to the distant mango tree and the Bengal.

This is what you asked for, boss lady, he told himself, forgetting his own fear for a moment. *You wanted to see what it means to be a real, honest-to-God risk-taker, someone who really puts it all on the line. And now you know.*

He wanted to tell her that, but he didn't dare, because Lisa Abercombie might fire him on the spot. He wasn't willing to risk *that* much. Not when all the power and influence he had ever dreamed of were within reach.

"There's nothing we can do," he said instead.

"You can go down and kill that damn thing before it finds Maas," she retorted, her hands trembling as she stared through her binoculars at the huge feline head. "We can't afford to lose him. Not now. Take Tom's rifle and—"

"No dice. The rifle stays up here with me," Tom Frank interrupted. "That was the agreement. As long as that cat's on the ground, this rifle stays where it is."

"I know what we agreed to, but the circumstances have changed," Abercombie tried to argue, unable to turn her eyes away from the huge cat. "That creature is going to come up here after us. Look at him. You can see it in his eyes."

"They tell me he can't climb very well," Frank argued in a voice that lacked conviction.

"Who told you they can't climb very well?" Lisa Abercombie demanded. "You bought this thing from a traveling circus one week ago. What the hell do you know about Bengal tigers?"

"If he tries to get up in this tree, I'll drop him," Tom Frank said in what he hoped was a calm and reassuring voice. He was thinking about the fifteen thousand dollars he had been guaranteed to set up this bizarre confrontation. Fifteen thousand would get him out of trouble with the IRS this year. But he knew he'd never see a cent of it if he failed to live up to his end of the contract.

Tom Frank had been running his Texas hunting ranch for almost eleven years now, and he figured that at one time or another, he had faced down just about every kind of dangerous animal there was. Or at least that was what he told anyone willing to listen to one of his whiskey-enhanced stories.

But Tom Frank had to silently admit that he had *never* before released a creature like this on his ranch. And despite his genuine expertise with the high-powered .416 Weatherby Magnum, he wasn't at all sure that he'd be able to stop the huge male Bengal with the one shot he'd be lucky to get off. Part of the deal that he and Gerd Maas had agreed to was that he would keep his bolt-action rifle unloaded during the entire event. The only rounds he would be allowed for the Weatherby would be three copper-tipped cartridges in elastic loops over the right breast pocket of his shirt.

Before they had climbed the ladder, Maas had actually checked the magazine of the rifle to make sure it was empty, and had patted him down for extra rounds. "Just to be sure that all is clearly understood," the tall, white-bearded Maas had whispered in his guttural German accent, winking cheerfully as he did so.

Three goddamned rounds, Frank swore silently. As if the amount of ammunition he carried really mattered. He knew full well that if the Bengal decided to charge the platform, it wouldn't matter whether he had three rounds or a hundred and three.

There wouldn't be any chance for a brain shot. He'd have to go for the neck to paralyze, or for the shoulder for a breakdown shot. And in either case, the cat would be climbing fast, so the best he'd be able to do would be to point-shoot and pray.

One shot to put it down. And if he missed, the cat would be on them. Unless he broke his contract and fed all three of the Magnum rounds into the Weatherby's magazine and chamber right now.

The trouble was, Tom Frank was far more afraid of Gerd Maas than he was of the Bengal.

"Doctor Asai," Lisa Abercombie pleaded, but Dr. Morito Asai just grunted, focusing his binoculars on the Bengal's fearsome eyes.

Asai was the only one on the platform who would willingly allow himself to be drawn into the depths of the Bengal's scornful hatred. He was the product of sixteen generations of Japanese samurai. Of the four, he alone truly understood the forces that drove Gerd Maas to seek out and confront death in such a terrifying manner.

Then the cat began to move. It was crouched down and approaching them slowly. Tom Frank was already reaching up toward his shirt pocket when the yellow eyes suddenly turned away.

"Oh, my God!" Lisa Abercombie breathed, feeling the icy chill travel up her spine as she watched Gerd Maas step out of the woods less than fifty yards from the Bengal.

Tom Frank blinked in disbelief.

"Where the hell's his rifle?" Frank whispered as Maas took two more steps to clear the last of the overhanging branches.

"No gun," Dr. Morito Asai said softly, smiling in anticipation as he held his binoculars tight against his high cheekbones. "His reputation is well earned. He has just bow, knife, one arrow."

"*One* arrow?" Frank sputtered in disbelief as he, Wolfe, and Lisa Abercombie fumbled for their binoculars. "Christ Almighty, that bastard's trying to commit suicide!" He started to reach for the Weatherby, but found Dr. Asai standing in his way.

"No gun." Asai shook his head firmly. "No gun, or we no pay. Very important."

"Screw your money and screw your suicidal contract," Frank snarled. He began to go around the slender Asian but staggered backward as Dr. Asai stopped him with a casual wrist block. Then, in a motion too quick to follow, Asai quick-handed the Weatherby up and over the platform's wooden ledge, letting it drop twenty-two feet to the ground.

The Bengal reacted instantly to the sound, shifting to face the platform, tense and alert. Its yellow eyes took in the swirl of dust surrounding the fallen weapon, then shifted upward to the four pale faces high in the tree. Growling low in its throat, the huge cat took three smooth, gliding steps toward the tree, then blinked and snarled as though it suddenly understood that there was no immediate threat from that direction. The threat was on the ground.

The Bengal slowly swung its massive head to face the single creature standing alone and upright in the clearing. It opened its fearsomely toothed jaws in a loud, menacing roar that promised a quick and horrible death as soon as the upright creature turned to run.

Instead, Gerd Maas simply smiled.

Enraged by the fearlessness that the cat's primitive brain correctly interpreted as threatening, the Bengal launched itself into a full, snarling charge, teeth bared and claws fully extended.

Gerd Maas stepped forward into the charge, extending his bow and drawing back against its eighty-pound pull with his right hand to bring the shaft of the arrow tight against his cheek. He was still smiling. He waited with inhuman control until the charging cat was less than twenty feet away and coming down on its front paws to prepare for the last fully extended leap that would put it onto its prey.

Then, as the Bengal brought its rear legs under its body and lunged upward, its snarling jaws open in a feral rage, Gerd

Maas let out a pent-up scream and released the broadhead arrow, sending the blurry shaft right into the huge cat's open mouth. The tiger's momentum was not broken. Maas used the bow in his left hand to deflect the Bengal's slashing right forepaw. He clenched his sheath knife in his right hand, and with its sharp, scalloped edge, cut across the tendons of the cat's extended paw.

Then, still reacting to his carefully honed survival instincts, Gerd Maas completed his roll to his left and crouched down, the bloodied knife extended and ready.

The Bengal lay sprawled chest-down, its massive head turned to the side, its eyes still glaring their hatred. Its fearsome paws were thrust forward, twitching in the blood-splattered dirt.

The razor-sharp edges of the wide broadhead had severed the cat's spine just below the base of the skull. The bloodied triangular blade and five inches of the blood-streaked titanium shaft were visible now, sticking out from the back of the Bengal's neck like a gruesome mast.

Smiling gently, Gerd Maas—a man with an international reputation for hunting, killing, and satisfying his craving for the ever-addictive sensation of facing death—knelt down in front of the still-trembling Bengal and laid a firm, steady hand against the cat's broad, sweat-soaked head. He waited, silent, intent, contemplative, until the last traces of the cat's un-yielding courage finally dissipated.

Fully sated then, Maas stood up, recovered his bow and knife, and began to walk slowly back to the platform tree. He knew that when he got there, a numbed and shaken but thoroughly *alive* Lisa Abercombie would tell him that he had been selected as the assault group leader of Operation Counter Wrench.

And because the money involved would enable him—for many years to come—to satisfy his fearful compulsion to confront death, Gerd Maas would make every effort to act as though he cared.

CHAPTER FOUR

SUNDAY, JUNE 2ND

The Chareaux brothers had been trying to line up the kill for almost two weeks now. But it was the seventh game of the NBA Western Conference Finals, so Henry had been emphatic that they understand about Sunday.

Any other day, any *other* Sunday for that matter, no problem. All they had to do was to get a fix on the target, give him a call, and he'd be out the door with hiking boots, cammo and survival gear, a twenty-eight-hundred-dollar bolt-action McMillan Signature Alaskan rifle, a Zeiss 3–9x variable scope, and fifty rounds of .300 Winchester Magnum jacketed soft points all packed and ready to go.

But not *this* Sunday.

Marie might be a problem, though, Henry realized. She had spent the last two months working overtime and trading shifts to get five days off in a row. He was supposed to take her to the Helena National Forest for a long-promised backpacking trip along the continental divide.

So it was all a matter of timing now—no matter whether she managed to get off early from her last shift of the week or worked late and called after the final buzzer.

After it would be nice, he thought as he waved his hand over the steaming Belgian waffle iron and then raised the lid and forked the golden-brown almond waffle to the plate. Very nice indeed, but hardly likely, he reminded himself as he poured thick, hot blueberry sauce over the steaming waffle. He'd discovered that having an emergency-room nurse for a girlfriend was just about as bad as being a homicide cop, especially when it came to making plans for days off.

Timed to perfection, the perking coffeepot rumbled one last time and then fell silent.

Henry Lightstone wasn't the least bit surprised to hear the phone ring just as the referee lofted the ball for the tip-off. The jarring sound caught him with a mug of steaming coffee in one hand and a forkful of waffle in the other, forcing him at last to make a decision. Basketball or Marie. One or the other, and he was probably going to have to decide right now. He stared into his coffee cup. It should have been an easy decision, because Marie Pascalaura was the best thing that had happened to him in years. The incredibly sensuous emergency-room nurse of Hispanic and American Indian descent preferred long hikes, tent-and-shovel camping, and slow dancing over almost everything—except sex.

And most important—despite her career—she wasn't the least bit concerned about the guns.

"Hello," he mumbled through his mouthful of waffle, forcing his voice to remain casual as he watched Drexler steal a bad pass from Scott.

"Henry Lightner, please?"

The voice, instead of warm and lively, was jarringly cold, whispery-hoarse, and all too familiar.

"Yeah, this is Lightner. Who is this?" Lightstone asked, trying to stall for time.

"Henry, surely we know each other too well for such games? I call you today to tell you the most important thing—that it is time to go. My brothers and I have found him."

The voice had shifted in tone, now vaguely French, decidedly Cajun, and discreetly mocking.

"Hello, Alex." Lightstone responded cautiously, because Alex Chareaux was known to be a coldhearted kill-freak who had lulled more than one victim to a horribly slow death. His pressed-linen suits, his slickly combed long black hair, his gentle phrases, and his silk-smooth Cajun charm belied his favorite passion: traditional French-Indian combat. The confrontation required each combatant to clutch a razor-sharp frog knife in one hand and the opposing end of a large white handkerchief in the other, while they fought to stay alive without letting go. The femoral artery, right at the point where the groin and upper leg intersect, was the target of choice, because—as a Louisiana warden had explained to Lightstone—you could stand there and watch the life fade from a man's eyes while the spurting arterial blood turned the clothes of the two adversaries a bright red.

It was said by those who had experienced the horror of watching Alex Chareaux fight that the fiery glaze in his dark, reddened eyes was a permanent result of staring at too many piles of blood-soaked white linen burning hot and bright in the midnight darkness of the humid Terrebonne swamps.

But the incredible part of the Chareauxs' reputation was that Alex Chareaux was considered by far the most civilized of the three Chareaux brothers.

Henry Lightstone had decided long ago that he wouldn't mind at all if he never met the other two. He felt mildly disturbed by the realization that he had never really severed his long, depressing association with psychopathic freaks, even though it was over ten months since he'd worked his last homicide case. Lightstone shook his head slowly and then hit the record button. All that Special Agent Henry Lightstone could really do now was to play his character and see how it flowed. Alex Chareaux was an exceedingly dangerous individual who, more than anything, loved to play with things before he watched them die. It was very important to listen carefully to what he said.

"Henry, I know. This was supposed to be a special day for you," the whispery-hoarse voice chuckled sympathetically, "but who among us can ever say how fate will play her hand, no? My brothers, they searched all the night and all the day looking for that one special creature who would best satisfy your needs. I know today is your Sunday, but when he appeared, it was as though fate herself had smiled on us all. What could I do?"

There was a silent pause.

"Henry," he went on quietly, "if you do not want him now,

I will understand. He is yours first, as we agreed, but we have other clients who would be happy to take your place. You understand, surely, that there are not so many like this one that we can just let him go."

"What's he like?" Lightstone whispered, unable to help himself because he was fully in character now, and this was what he got paid for. And besides, Alex was right. Henry Allen Lightner, wealthy businessman, sportsman, and safari hunter par excellence, had been waiting for this one for a very long time.

"I am telling you straight, Henry. He is Boone and Crockett, without question. So obvious, it will not even be necessary that they make the measurements."

"Wow," Lightstone whispered.

"He is an amazing creature, Henry," Chareaux went on. "Huge and terrifying. Even Sonny, I think, is a little afraid of him. When you see him, you will understand."

"Where?" Exactly the question Henry Allen Lightner should be asking, because he would be salivating. Lightstone knew the man all too well. He had created him, and lived him for six months: an ex-jock from San Diego State University with a bachelor's degree in marketing, a decent stake of family money, and a kickback friendly attitude that masked the true disposition of a game-player who was willing to go for the jugular to make a deal. Lightner had moved to Montana and made his fortune in record time. But deep down inside, he was an aggressive, greedy, and dedicated killer. A man who would pay almost anything to fill up all the empty spaces on the basement walls of his secret trophy room.

"He is just north of Yellowstone now, a few miles east of Gardiner. My brothers, they spotted him in the park about an hour ago, but he kept moving, so it took them a while to get to a phone," Chareaux added.

"You found him *inside* the park?" Lightstone blinked in genuine surprise.

"But of course, Henry. Where do you think the big ones live? Outside, where they can be killed by any penniless fool with barely the money to buy the bullets and a tag?"

"So you guys moved him out?"

Alex Chareaux laughed. "They are smart, these creatures, and I think they know that the park is their sanctuary. But," he added conspiratorially, "they have no real sense of boundaries, so you see, it is not so difficult after all."

"For Christ's sake, Alex, that place is crawling with park rangers and federal agents. Are you guys out of your living minds?"

Really into character now, Lightstone nodded, because Henry Allen Lightner was extremely worried about getting caught by the Feds. He'd made that very clear at his first meeting with Alex Chareaux and had continued to emphasize it during their subsequent conversations.

And now, after weeks of work, he just might have the bastard.

It was better than he could have hoped for, and at the same time, far worse, because Yellowstone was about two hundred and twenty-five miles south of Great Falls, which meant a good four-hour drive even if the roads were clear. Which they weren't, Lightstone knew, because the radio stations had been putting out storm advisories all morning.

Lightstone felt his chest tighten as he realized that the only viable option was to fly down to Bozeman and then rent a car and pick up Highway 89 at Livingston.

"You should not worry about these federal people, Henry," Alex Chareaux advised cheerfully. "My brothers and I have been outsmarting them since we were little children. You have heard the story, of course, that most of the federal judges are chosen from the lowest ten percent of the law-school students?"

"Oh, yeah?"

"I am told that it is absolutely true," Chareaux said. "But even if it is not, I can assure you that none of these federal judges or prosecutors or policemen are so smart that you need to be concerned. They are simply people who have neither the brains nor the ambition to find honest work, so they take it upon themselves to hinder the honest work of others."

Under normal circumstances, Lightstone might have enjoyed the idea of egging Alex Chareaux on, but he really wasn't paying all that much attention to the outlaw guide now. Mostly because he was desperately trying to figure out some other way to get down to Gardiner without having to go up in an airplane during storm-advisory conditions.

He hated to fly. Absolutely hated it. From Henry Lightstone's decidedly nervous perspective, modern airplanes were made up of thousands of complex parts, each of which had to work perfectly in order for the plane to continue to fly extremely fast so that it wouldn't fall out of the sky.

"Yeah, well, that's fine of course, unless we *do* get caught," Lightstone said. "I'm the one who'd go to the goddamned state pen for the next twenty years."

"Actually, it would be a *federal* prison, Henry," Chareaux corrected. "And only for ten years at the most. But none of that matters, because you and I are going to do this together, and we are *not* going to get caught. You have my word on that. After all, for what do you think we charge you so much money?"

In spite of himself, Henry Lightstone smiled.

Henry Allen Lightner had a reputation for snap decisions and aggressive action. He was also gutsy enough to have made just over four and a half million in his multifaceted business deals; smart enough to have kept a goodly part of it away from the IRS; and self-serving enough to indulge himself with some of the nicer things that money could buy. All in all, he was exactly the type of client that had made Alex Chareaux and his brothers very wealthy, and increasingly greedy over the past few years.

"What about the locals? Anybody see him?"

"Sonny and Butch are with him, but they're staying back because he is very edgy now," Chareaux spoke. "Perhaps he knows you are coming. Sometimes they can sense that sort of thing, you know. Especially the big ones."

"Really?"

Very nice touch, Alex, Lightstone nodded approvingly. A gentle ego massage for all those born-again clients who were always trying to forge an emotional link between themselves and their intended prey, but were still just a little bit nervous about spending the next ten years in a federal penitentiary.

"Oh yes, I am almost certain of that, Henry," Alex Chareaux said, carefully reinforcing the point. "They are funny that way. Absolutely fearless, but incredibly sensitive also. That is why it is so important that they die well. We owe them that."

Hemingway, Lightstone smiled. Christ, how could Lightner resist?

The point being, of course, that he couldn't. Henry Allen Lightner, moderately wealthy businessman, infamous slayer of the great ones, and proud teller of even greater tales, was hooked.

"Amazing."

"I think you will cherish the memory of this one, Henry," Chareaux agreed. "He has a younger one with him. A thousand pounds perhaps. Too small for your trophy room, of course; but I think he will try to protect her, so you must be quick. The shot must come fast, and be well placed."

"Is she part of the deal, too?" Lightstone asked eagerly, vaguely discomforted by the ease with which the words seemed to flow from the warped soul of his borrowed persona.

The voice on the other end of the line hesitated for a moment, calculating.

"A significant bonus certainly if he is coerced into a charge," Chareaux said finally. "Perhaps an extra two thousand for the charge, but no more than that."

Lightstone remained silent, and Chareaux went on quickly. "It is a shot that only a handful of men ever experience and live to tell about, Henry."

"But you will be there, too, just in case . . ."

Lightstone had been careful to include a few well-chosen flaws in Henry Allen Lightner's persona. Henry Allen Lightner, the young and wealthy Great Falls businessman, was just a little too tight with his money to play the role of a big spender, and perhaps a little too cowardly to stand and face a full-grown grizzly all by himself.

For that, he would need the spine-bracing presence of a

Cajun coon-ass swamp boy who had faced death a thousand times from the day he could first stand.

"But of course," Chareaux replied immediately. Lightstone thought he could detect a trace of contempt in the guide's well-controlled voice. "But only to watch for others. Your meeting with the dark one is a private affair, Henry. My brothers and I will be there, certainly, but I can tell you now that you will neither want nor need us on that day."

. . . *if you have any balls*, Lightstone understood the implication.

"Are you sure no one else has seen him?" Lightstone whispered. What he really wondered was if anybody would spot the Chareaux brothers. The Louisiana Department of Fish and Game was eager for their arrest in any way possible.

According to the dossiers that Paul McNulty's Special Operations team had put together, Alex, Sonny, and Butch Chareaux had been born and raised in the backwoods bayous of Terrebonne Parish. They had been taught to shoot by their maternal grandfather, who—despite a thirteen-page rap sheet—truly believed that the illegal killing of wild game was an honorable way to make a living. The boys took to killing wildlife like ducks to corn bait.

Their motto was "If it flies, it dies." They eagerly killed any fish or animal they could, limited only by the number of shotgun and rifle rounds they could steal in a week. When the local fish and game authorities finally decided that they'd had enough of the Chareaux brothers, Alex, Butch, and Sonny were wakened at three o'clock one morning and quietly escorted across the state line with six .357 Magnums pressed solidly against the back of their long-haired heads. They were politely offered a chance to emigrate.

North, south, east, or west, it didn't matter as far as the Louisiana Department of Fish and Game was concerned. Given the well-earned reputation of the Fish and Game Department for being serious about protecting the state's wildlife, the Chareaux brothers had wisely chosen to move on. But six months later, two of the "relocation" wardens were discovered facedown in the Terrebonne swamp, with numerous deep cuts crisscrossing their arms and chests.

And when further examined by the coroner, it was determined that both of the officers had had their femoral arteries severed.

In spite of some very emotional testimony, a local magistrate had come to the interesting conclusion that there wasn't enough evidence to warrant an extradition order on the Chareaux brothers for murder. But the way the teletype read, in the event that any law-enforcement agency in the country *ever* managed to obtain a felony arrest warrant for Alex, Butch, or Sonny Chareaux, the Louisiana Department of Fish and Game would be more than happy to provide a team of four volunteer officers to kick the door.

"They said they saw no one else, but it is of little consequence, because we will be in and then out, so very fast."

"So where do I meet you?" Lightstone asked agreeably.

"I have made reservations at the Best Western in Gardiner. Room one-oh-two is yours. I'll be next door, in one-oh-one."

It was a canned deal all the way. Chareaux had known where the target was—in a cage ten miles east of Gardiner—for the last five days, but Lightner wasn't supposed to know that.

All of which meant that either they were playing with him—holding off until just before the game started—or they still didn't trust him.

There was also a third possibility: that they knew he was an undercover agent and intended to kill him.

And the thing was, he couldn't just be serious. He had to convince them that he was *dedicated* serious. That was the key. They had to believe that he was one of those truly driven hunter-killers who would do damn near anything to expand his illicit trophy collection, or he would never pull it off. And a truly driven hunter-killer would be focused on only two things: the target and the kill.

There was a brief, ominous pause.

"Henry, it is now or never," Alex Chareaux said flatly. "You know how our system works. This one—the one you have dreamed about all your life—is yours, but you must decide now. Do you *really* want him? You must tell me."

"I want him," Lightstone said. He sighed one last time and then nodded. "I'm in," he whispered. "See you in Gardiner."

CHAPTER FIVE

The ritualistic killing of the fearsome Bengal by Gerd Maas turned out to be a pivotal event in the life of Lisa Abercombie and Dr. Reston Wolfe, although neither of them had any sense of that at the time.

It was only six months later, in an isolated cedar log cabin several hundred miles west of Tom Frank's hunting ranch, that the emotional aftereffect of that terrifying day finally began to surface.

There, Lisa Abercombie—a thirty-six-year-old woman with icy political savvy, visceral determination, and very special connections to a White House advisory team—did something that was completely out of character.

Without warning or hesitation, Abercombie suddenly reached under the massive six-sided wooden table, rubbed Dr. Reston Wolfe's upper thigh, and smiled.

"I'm very impressed, Reston," she whispered in a voice that was both firmly authoritative and discreetly enticing, giving his thigh a little extra squeeze before bringing her discernibly warm hand back to her lap. "You've made incredible progress since I was here last."

Wolfe started to say something—anything at all—but discovered that his mind had gone completely blank. For a long, embarrassing moment, Dr. Reston Wolfe could only blink his eyes and stare.

Then, mercifully, Abercombie reached over and patted his hand in a more traditional bureaucratic greeting that finally got Wolfe's mind back in gear.

"That's all right," she whispered, the warmth of her words reflected in her smoldering dark eyes. "You look like you could use a long vacation far away from here."

Wolfe, feeling very much like a love-struck fool, decided then and there that Lisa Abercombie was the most provocative woman he had ever met.

"It's been a long eight months," he nodded, feeling his entire body surge with barely controlled lust as he forced himself to concentrate. "But getting off by myself is the last thing I want right now."

"You're eager to get started, aren't you?"

Wolfe desperately wanted to believe that Lisa Abercombie was aware that her words were loaded with double meaning.

"To tell you the truth," he said honestly, remembering the press of her hand, "I can hardly wait."

"I assure you that the entire committee feels the same way," she said quietly.

Wolfe looked around the huge conference room that was filled with equipment, weapons, files, and the twelve men and women he had brought together as a team.

His team.

His operation.

Reston Wolfe envisioned himself leading Gerd Maas and the rest of the ICER assault group into action while Lisa Abercombie looked on with . . . what?

Admiration?

Affection?

Desire?

Or maybe even . . . passion?

"You know what you've done, don't you?" Abercombie asked, snapping Wolfe back to the present.

"What's that?" He blinked away the images that were too absurd to even think about. Especially not now. Not here.

"You've made ICER a reality," Lisa Abercombie said, her eyes glowing with an emotion that Wolfe had never seen before. "These people," she gestured out across the room, "that *you* selected and brought together are going to have an impact far beyond anything we have ever imagined. They are going to realign the industrial revolution, literally change the course of history. And all because of *your* efforts. You should be incredibly proud of what you've done here."

Dr. Wolfe nodded and smiled, shamelessly basking in the warm glow of Lisa Abercombie's praise.

"It's been a team effort all the way. You and I both know that," he said, deliberately making direct eye contact. He remembered the expression on her face when she had knelt down and stroked the hot, sweaty fur of the Bengal, her dark eyes glazed as she stared at the glistening broadhead sticking through the back of the Bengal's bloodied skull.

He'd seen the blood-lust in her eyes, and he knew now just how he'd . . .

One of the resident caretaker staff walked up to the table and whispered something in Lisa Abercombie's ear.

"I have a phone call," Abercombie said as she got up from the table. "I'll be right back."

"I'll be here."

He watched her walk across the room, her snug jeans providing a thoroughly distracting view of her well-toned torso.

Reston Wolfe knew full well the inherent dangers of trying to establish a relationship with a driven woman like Lisa Abercombie. Yet he simply could not resist the temptation. And it wasn't just the fact that Lisa Abercombie was a beautiful and alluring woman, like so many others who were readily available in Washington.

What he *couldn't* overlook was the political and bureaucratic clout that Lisa Abercombie possessed and exercised in a manner that belied her youth and overwhelming physical charms.

What it all boiled down to were two very distinct and separate possibilities.

If Operation Counter Wrench was successful, then he and Abercombie would become wealthy, powerful, and influential beyond comprehension. If it all failed, he would be either a hunted felon or, more likely, dead, buried, and forgotten.

All in all, Wolfe, told himself as he remembered again Lisa Abercombie's hand on his thigh, it was worth the risk.

Lisa Abercombie followed a staffer into a small office, where he pointed out a complex-looking console phone sitting on a small wooden desk. There were three rows of yellow-tabbed buttons in the center of the console, one row of blue tabs above them, and a single red-tabbed button in the upper right corner. The red tab was blinking.

"Line one," the staffer said.

"Fine, thank you," Lisa Abercombie nodded. She pointedly waited until the staffer had exited the room and closed the door before reaching for the phone.

"Abercombie," she responded in a gruff, neutral voice.

"Lisa?"

"Al, how are you?" Lisa Abercombie smiled, her voice softening with genuine pleasure as she sat down in the thickly padded chair. She pressed a tab on the console marked "Secure" and watched as a small green light began to blink, confirming that the two-point link was secure from taps or traces.

"I'm fine. How are *you* doing? I understand that you've had some adventures these last few weeks."

"Nothing as exciting as crewing for a deranged skipper in the Gulf Stream," Abercombie replied, referring to the sailing trip that she had taken with Albert Bloom during the previous summer. Intent on consummating their intricate political relationship in the luxurious suite of a Freeport hotel, they had sailed straight into the teeth of a sudden and unexpected tropical storm that nearly sank the thirty-six-foot skiff. They had fought the storm for almost sixteen hours, losing the engine and trying to stay afloat with sea anchor, rudder, and torn sails, when suddenly the surging winds and waves and dark clouds had given way to an unlikely calm that left them collapsed in their safety harnesses, soaking wet, shivering and exhausted.

Somehow they had been able to maneuver the boat into the

shelter of a small cove, where they dropped anchor and staggered down into the shambles of the main stateroom ready to collapse. Instead, they had found themselves caught up in a frenzy of survival-enhanced sexual passion that continued on intermittently through the night and well into the next morning.

They had never made it to their luxurious hotel suite, and had never regretted it for a moment.

Al Bloom laughed easily. "I'm sitting here in my office, getting ready for a one o'clock appointment on the Hill, and now I won't be able to concentrate on a damn thing."

"I have a similar problem," Lisa Abercombie said. "Perhaps we should get together to discuss it."

"Unfortunately," Bloom said, "Senator Talkins has expressed an interest in doubling the budget for ICER."

"You mean our *official* budget?"

"A seven-and-a-half-million-dollar increase. Isn't that nice?"

"No, it's not," Abercombie said fervently, all thoughts of sex immediately forgotten. "For God's sake, Al, we've got commitments for at least five *billion* from the private sector. And more on top of that if we need it. At this stage, any kind of add-on from Congress, no matter how small, will just attract attention. And that's the *last* thing we need right now."

"Yes, exactly," Bloom agreed. "But one thing we *do* need is more contingency support, and Talkins is just the man to handle some of the more sensitive inside maneuvers."

"In exchange for a good-sized contribution to his campaign fund?"

"Precisely," Bloom said.

Lisa Abercombie hesitated, and the finally said: "I hate to say it, but I think it's worth it."

"So do I, but not if it means taking on one of his people."

"He's asking for that?"

"Yes."

"No way," Abercombie said firmly. "This one's too touchy to be run by committee. You know that. And besides, it's ours."

"I'm glad you feel that way, because that's exactly what I planned to tell him," Bloom said. "But that's not really why I called. We may need to advance the start date for Counter Wrench."

Lisa Abercombie blinked in surprise. "But I—"

Bloom interrupted her. "We just received an interesting report from one of our internal sources. It seems that there may be an alliance forming among the primary opposition groups."

"Earth First! and Greenpeace are linking up?" Lisa Abercombie whispered in a quiet, shocked voice.

"As well as Headwaters, Wind/Rain/Storm, and Le Natur. It seems that the environmental terrorists are finally getting some professional advice."

"We expected that," Lisa Abercombie said, forcing her voice to remain calm as her analytical mind raced.

"Yes, of course we did," Bloom agreed. "But not this quickly. How soon can you be ready?"

"The entire assault group is here now. It's just a matter of completing the briefing and determining the priority of the assignments," Abercombie said. "I would say two days at the outside."

"Give yourself three, just to be sure. We are dealing with very emotional people who are suspicious of everyone. I think that a few judiciously placed rumors should keep them from forming their alliances too quickly."

"Albert, you're malicious," Abercombie laughed. "Just my kind of guy."

Bloom chuckled. "What about the training situation?"

"Training won't be a factor. Not with these people. All we have to do is get them coordinated, aim them at a target, and then turn them loose."

"Intelligent, self-guided, counterterrorizing missiles. The ultimate weapon." Bloom nodded in satisfaction. "They will go through those self-righteous bastards like a hot knife through butter."

Lisa Abercombie shivered at the vivid memory of the bloodied and horribly sharp triangular blade sticking out of the back of the Bengal tiger's massive head.

"And they won't even know they've been cut until it's much too late," she whispered.

"No, they won't," Bloom agreed. "Tell me, does Wolfe still think that he made the final selections?"

"I'm sure he does," Abercombie said confidently. "We spent several hours going over the lists, but the choices were pretty obvious since I yellow-highlighted the relevant points. I only had to make a couple of gentle suggestions to keep him on track."

"Does he still think he's in charge?"

"That was what you wanted, wasn't it?"

"Reston Wolfe's a good man," Bloom said. "Right family background, good contacts, good political instincts, willing to be a hard ass when he has to be."

"But not very smart, and therefore expendable as far as this project is concerned," Lisa Abercombie finished.

"You must never forget, my dear, that we are *all* very expendable as far as this project is concerned," Bloom said. "But I think everyone on the committee agrees that Reston is a special case. If it weren't for his extremely useful connections . . . speaking of which, how is your, uh, side project coming along?"

"It's progressing nicely. Do you want a full report?" Abercombie teased.

"Good Lord, no," Bloom chuckled. "I don't think that I could stand to hear about it right now. Tell me later."

"I'll do better than that," Abercombie promised.

"Yes, I'm sure you will," Albert Bloom sighed, and then turned serious. "Listen, my dear young friend, please make sure that you *never* forget one thing. What we're doing is extremely dangerous. You must be firm in maintaining absolute control, but above all else, you *must* be careful. Do not make any mistakes."

"Don't worry, Skipper," Lisa Abercombie said in a soft, seductive voice. "You taught me what to do. Anybody gets in our way, we go right over the top of them."

"That's my girl. I'll call you soon," Bloom said, then hung up the phone.

* * *

Dr. Reston Wolfe, newly appointed executive director of ICER, had thought long and hard about where the all-important first meeting of Operation Counter Wrench should be held. There could hardly have been a more ironic choice than the very jewel of protected lands, a site whose very name was synonymous with care and trust and hope for the future.

Yellowstone National Park.

Because the potential risks were enormous and the potential rewards beyond imagination, enemy surveillance had to be avoided at all costs. In this respect, Whitehorse Cabin was a good bet. Set off by itself on a high, wooded hillside, surrounded by huge clearings, the cabin was supposed to be impossible to approach in the daytime without being observed. It was further isolated within a two-and-a-quarter-million acres of federally protected wilderness. Dr. Wolfe was not one to take chances, however. He had the authority *and* the means to clear the grizzly bear range of any campers, hikers, biologists, and the like who mistakenly believed that they had a right to go out and enjoy their wilderness whenever they chose to do so.

The means were simple. He designed a crucial scientific experiment that would investigate and resolve, once and for all, the potentially lethal conflicts between bears and tourists.

As announced by ICER, the project was to be directed by a blue-ribbon task force of twelve internationally recognized experts who would clear the bear range of all nonparticipants for a period of no less than six months.

Government biologists who chose to grumble or question the expertise of these unknown experts were notified that they had suddenly become eligible for long-sought-after foreign travel, with all of the per-diem perks allowed by law. In effect, they were bought off in style.

To confirm that Whitehorse Cabin was absolutely secure, Dr. Wolfe asked Lisa Abercombie to use her White House connections to obtain the temporary services of a crack Special Forces reconnaissance team. Seven men arrived by helicopter the next morning and quickly demonstrated their professionalism by managing to sit through a one-hour briefing without once cracking a smile.

In fact, the only time that any member of the reconnaissance team ever *did* smile was when the team leader, a clean-cut lieutenant who looked more like an eighteen-year-old high-school quarterback than a twenty-four-year-old professional killer, walked up to Wolfe after the briefing, shook Wolfe's hand, grinned, and said: "Piece of cake, sir."

Eight hours later, after six failed attempts with varying types of electronic sweepers and camouflage gear, the frustrated recon team members were forced to admit that they couldn't get within a half-mile of the cabin without tripping at least a dozen of the five hundred and twelve computer-monitored sensors that dotted the hillside and clearings.

It was then that Wolfe explained to the soldiers that the detection system in question had been installed by another team of military experts, this one from the National Security Agency. He went on to describe the sensors as being so sensitive and discriminatory that the computers receiving the data could instantly trace the pathway and determine the biomass of any animal with a heartbeat greater than a field mouse's.

Although initially irritated by Wolfe's game-playing, the members of the Special Forces team felt better when they were shown blueprints that described the extent and sophistication of the intrusion system. And when questioned further, they quickly agreed that a covert approach on Whitehorse Cabin in the daytime was out of the question.

It just wasn't going to happen.

They did suggest, however, that they would like to try a night approach, despite the fact that they were in the middle of the largest wild grizzly bear habitat in the lower forty-eight states. If anything, the idea of having a real, live enemy out there seemed to give the aggressive young soldiers a heightened sense of purpose.

Five hours later, at precisely 0200 hours, the recon team made its first and only night attempt on the Whitehorse Cabin, using light assault weapons, third-generation night-vision goggles, and a considerable array of electronic sensing gear.

Aided by a predicted cloud cover, an unexpected fog, and the incredible sensitivity of some of their latest gadgets, the highly motivated reconnaissance team managed to get within a respectable quarter-mile of the cabin before one of them activated the biological sensors of a twelve-hundred-pound grizzly that happened to be both territorial and grouchy when disturbed.

The end result was the expenditure of fifty-seven rounds of .223 military hardball; one dead female grizzly; one very large, slightly wounded and extremely annoyed male grizzly; two severely mauled soldiers; and one thoroughly shaken team leader, who politely but firmly declined to make a second attempt at night.

As a result of that trial run, Whitehorse Cabin was judged to be secure. All involved were quick to agree that Dr. Reston Wolfe, director of ICER and primary architect of Counter Wrench, had chosen well.

CHAPTER SIX

"What do you *mean*, all flights are booked?" Henry Lightstone demanded.

"We can get you out on the first flight tomorrow morning," the reservations clerk offered. "You'd be landing at Bozeman at nine thirty-seven."

Henry, it is now or never. You know how our system works. This one—the one you have dreamed about all your life—is yours, but you must decide now.

They've already failed to show up at two scheduled meets.

Possibly because they had their own scheduling problems, but far more likely because they still didn't trust him. And he knew they had other hunters on their string, so he didn't dare push them too far or they'd be gone.

So he had to do exactly what Henry Allen Lightner, the wealthy Montana sportsman with an unsated lust for yet another record trophy kill, would do.

Either that or lose his first undercover investigation as a federal agent.

"No, I'm sorry," he said. "Tomorrow morning would be too late. What about another airline?"

"I'll be happy to check for you, sir, if you'd like."

"Yes, thank you."

As he waited, Lightstone tried to calculate moves. That was not easy, though, since Alex Chareaux was by far the least predictable individual Henry Lightstone had met in his life.

"I'm sorry, sir, but there are no other flights to Bozeman until tomorrow morning."

"Could you put me on stand-by?"

"Certainly, sir, but we already have a waiting list. You would be . . . let me see, number eight."

"What about taking a couple of hops? A roundabout route?" Lightstone tried, anxious now because he knew what McNulty would suggest if he couldn't find himself a commercial flight.

Carl Scoby or Larry Paxton.

Both of the agents were licensed pilots, but only for Super Cubs: the small, slow, underpowered, but nonetheless reliable two-seater planes that the Fish and Wildlife Service biologists used for monitoring wildlife populations.

To Henry Lightstone, the small planes looked like something one of Paxton's teenage boys might have built in their garage over the weekend. Paxton had taken him up for a ride one day. Lightstone had wedged himself into the backseat of the Super Cub for a few claustrophobic moments before advising the black agent-pilot that he'd just as soon go jump off the roof of the airport tower. Get it over with quicker and save the government a couple of gallons of gas in the process.

But Paxton, Scoby, Dwight Stone, and Mike Takahara had

been persistent, and Lightstone had finally agreed to go up for a short orientation flight. Two hours later, after receiving at least a dozen threats on his life from the backseat, Paxton had brought the plane back in a wing-swaying, multibounce landing that he later admitted was not one of his best because he'd been laughing so hard.

That had been on a nice, calm day, Henry Lightstone reminded himself, shuddering at the memory.

Lightstone reassured himself that McNulty would never let them put a Super Cub up in this kind of weather. It would have to be a bigger plane. At least a 737.

The reservation clerk was back in less than two minutes. "Sir, I can route you through Missoula with a stopover at Butte."

"And that's on a seven-thirty-seven, correct?"

"Uh, yes sir. The flight out of Great Falls is on a seven-thirty-seven, but you'll have to change planes at Missoula, and we're experiencing weather advisories—"

"What kind of plane would I be changing to at Missoula?"

"Oh, let me see. That would be a Metro Three jet prop."

"You mean a *small* plane?"

"Oh, they're not really *that* small," the reservation clerk chuckled understandingly. "The Metro Three has eighteen seats and two engines."

A small plane, Lightstone thought. Jesus!

"What time would I arrive in Bozeman?" he interrupted, not wanting to hear anything more about the Metro Three.

"Approximately seven-thirty this evening."

"I see. Thank you anyway."

Henry Lightstone closed his eyes and shook his head slowly as he hung up.

He waited for a few seconds, then dialed the familiar number and let it ring four times.

"Hello?"

"This is Henry. I've got a problem."

He explained the situation to his field supervisor.

"I could send Carl or Larry down in one of the Cubs, but

they're both in Nebraska," McNulty said. "Never make it there in time."

Henry Lightstone smiled.

"So what do you think?" he asked, making an effort to sound disappointed. "Call Alex and try to reschedule?"

"No, don't do that yet," McNulty said. "I think you're right. If you back away now, you'd probably lose him. Give me a few minutes. I'll call you back shortly."

McNulty would arrange it, no problem, Lightstone knew. It was McNulty who had registered Lightstone into the federal government's Criminal Investigator's School and Special Agent Basic as a U.S. Custom's agent trainee. Sixteen long weeks in Glynco, Georgia, had taught Lightstone how federal officers enforced federal laws, handcuffed suspects and read them their rights (as he expected, pretty much the same as every other state and local cop).

Along about week fifteen, it occurred to Lightstone that he had learned almost nothing about fish or wildlife.

"Look at it this way," McNulty had suggested. "You'd know a duck if you saw one, wouldn't you? Let's say it's four o'clock in the morning and you're in a swamp, maybe waist-deep in water, and you're sneaking up on a couple of guys sitting in a duck blind."

"Yeah, what are they doing, selling coke?"

"No, just sitting there in the blind, wrapped up in blankets, drinking coffee, and waiting for daylight so they can start killing ducks."

"And I'm standing in waist-deep water, freezing my nuts off and watching these assholes drink *coffee*? Am I out of my mind?" Lightstone had asked, incredulous.

"No, you're a federal agent of the United States Fish and Wildlife Service, and you're looking to nail these guys for multiple violations of the Migratory Bird Treaty Act."

"So what is it, a capital offense to shoot a duck at sunrise?"

McNulty shook his head. "Actually, a misdemeanor, but only if they go over the limit. Which you won't be able to prove unless you count the number of ducks they shoot. So what you're going to have to do is stay out there in the swamp until, oh, I'd say until about eight or nine in the morning, ideally behind some cover, and count drops."

"Drops, as in dropping ducks?"

McNulty nodded. "And while you're doing that, you're going to be keeping detailed notes on the approximate location where each duck falls, the time, the sex, the species involved . . . and on the apparent hunter."

"With my waterproof pen and paper," Lightstone had smiled agreeably.

"Which reminds me," McNulty had added as Lightstone's amused smile turned to laughter. "Assuming that you've searched all around the swamp in about a fifty-yard radius, and all through the blind, and you haven't been bitten by a snake or an alligator, and you haven't found anything that looks like a duck, what else are you going to be looking for in the way of evidence?"

At that point, Henry Lightstone had stopped laughing because it suddenly occurred to him that his supervisor might be dead serious.

"I don't know," he'd shrugged. "Feathers? Duck shit?"

"Okay. And what are you going to do if you can't find any feathers or duck shit anywhere around the area?" McNulty pressed.

"Then I'm probably going to figure that the stupid sons of bitches haven't the slightest idea of what a duck looks like either," Lightstone had replied with unrestrained sarcasm.

"There you go." McNulty had shrugged in apparent satisfaction. "Sounds to me like you've got the basics down just fine. I'll have Mike send down a couple of ID books with pictures, get you a little better oriented to the critters. In the meantime, you just make sure you pass those final exams and get that badge. It's about time you started earning your keep around here."

Those last words spoken by McNulty three months ago still echoed in Henry Lightstone's mind.

It was those words, and pride, and a strong personal conviction that he really *did* need to earn his keep—by taking on homicidal idiots like Alex Chareaux and his brothers, even if it meant getting into a goddamned flimsy airplane—that kept Henry Lightstone waiting on the phone.

Ten minutes later, McNulty was back.

"I've got the man you need, close by with a plane all fueled up and ready to go. Name is Len Ruebottom. Nice fellow, family man, hell of a pilot."

"Ruebottom? Is he one of us?" Lightstone asked. "Name's not familiar."

But that didn't necessarily mean anything, Lightstone knew, because during the entire six months that he'd been employed by the federal government, the only Fish and Wildlife Service agents that he had ever met face-to-face were the members of McNulty's Special Operations team.

Paul McNulty seemed to want it that way.

"No, he's actually one of the new agent-pilots," McNulty said. "I made arrangements to borrow him from the Portland regional office for a while. Plane and pilot are ours for as long as we want them, long as I pay all the expenses."

"You're sure the guy can be trusted?"

"Halahan will make sure Ruebottom keeps a lid on. Unfortunately, he's still green when it comes to investigative work. Tends to want to do everything by the book, which is probably why he's so good at keeping airplanes up in the air."

"Have I ever mentioned to you that I hate to fly?" Lightstone asked.

"You'll get over it. Have to if you're going to stay in this outfit. Think you can handle Ruebottom?"

"Do I have any choice?"

"I could always send you to flight school," McNulty shrugged.

"Ruebottom sounds like one hell of a guy," Lightstone said quietly. "We'll get along just fine."

CHAPTER SEVEN

As intended, the conference table was the immediate focus of attention for anyone who stepped into the huge, log-walled meeting room of Whitehorse Cabin.

The slabs for the large, six-sided table had been cut from a two-hundred-year-old sequoia redwood. The rough-cut boards had been trucked to a pair of master carpenters in Bend, Oregon, who had spent six months carefully measuring, planing, joining, and then finally hand-finishing the six individual pieces so that they formed a virtually seamless hexagonal surface precisely thirteen meters between any two opposite corners.

To Dr. Reston Wolfe, executive director of ICER, the table represented image *and* substance. It had cost the financial backers of ICER a bundle, but as far as Wolfe was concerned, it was worth every penny.

Sitting alert at the designated head of the table, Wolfe scanned the huge conference room, savoring the massive rock fireplace, the six-by-eighteen-inch support beams, the over-stuffed chairs, and the original artwork on the log walls. Thoroughly satisfied, he waited while two members of his carefully screened staff finished clearing away the plates and silverware.

A thick stack of sealed folders and envelopes was set before each of the guests. It was only after the doors were quietly pulled closed behind the two staffers that Wolfe's gaze shifted to the thirteen men and women seated around the huge table.

"I hope the breakfast was to your satisfaction."

There were polite murmurs of approval. Wolfe had expected

no less, since the iced king crab and fresh shrimp for the omelets had been flown in fresh from Anchorage and New Orleans that morning.

"In that case," he said with quiet firmness, "we will return to business." He noted that the three groups continued to sit apart. In the middle, the Germans—Maas, Günter Aben, Felix Steinhauser, and Carine Müeller; to the left, the Japanese—Asai, Kiro Nakamura, Shoshin Watanabe, and Kimiko Osan; and to the right, the Americans—Paul Saltmann, Arturo Bolin, Roy Parker, and Corrie James.

They didn't trust each other yet, Wolfe realized, knowing that *that* would have to change before he and Abercombie sent them out on a mission, where there could be no room for failure. It would be up to Maas, the assault-group leader, and his two primary assistants Asai and Saltmann, to forge the necessary links. And they would have to hurry, he reminded himself, because there wasn't much time.

"We spent the better part of yesterday providing you with some of the tools necessary for you to carry out your mission," Wolfe began, comfortable in his role as project director. "Clothing, cash, credit cards, as well as the means to access houses, land vehicles, air transportation, and virtually any other resource you might need."

Wolfe paused for effect.

"Later on this evening, we will distribute a wide range of firearms and other weapons for your use."

As Wolfe fully expected, the topic of weaponry drew the complete attention of everyone in the room.

"I realize that given a choice, you would prefer weapons with which you are intimately familiar. I certainly understand your reasoning. But here I must emphasize a crucial element of our operational planning.

"As far as we are concerned," Wolfe said as he looked around the room, "all weapons used in Operation Counter Wrench are disposable. In the event that it ever becomes necessary for one of you to use *any* weapon against *any* opponent in the field—and by this I mean not only firearms, but also knives, arrows, clubs, darts, et cetera—that weapon is to be wiped down for fingerprints and then destroyed or discarded at the first opportunity. The same goes for any related ammunition, magazines, and expended casings to the extent possible and practical. This is the only way we can be sure that a projectile, an explosive, or an injury cannot be traced back to our operation.

"For reasons that I hope are obvious," Wolfe placed the palms of his hands on the table for emphasis, "*that must not happen with Operation Counter Wrench.*"

Knowing the background of some of the group members, Wolfe had expected some sort of negative reaction to this announcement, but all he received were a few silent nods of approval.

"Because of this policy, we have not only stockpiled several dozen replacement weapons for each of you, but we have also made certain that the make, model, and manufacture of these weapons vary considerably. Here again, we are making a determined effort to avoid patterns that law-enforcement investigators traditionally use to link suspects to victims or crime scenes.

"To aid you in familiarizing yourself with these weapons," he went on, "you will be given full and unrestricted access to the state-of-the-art training facilities we have constructed on the Whitehorse Cabin grounds. These facilities include underground firing ranges, combat simulators, advanced robotics. The staff we have hired to design, equip, and run this facility is the absolute best."

That comment caused considerable murmuring among the ICER assault group members.

"You will be given access to your weapons and some of the automated firing ranges beginning this evening," Wolfe said. "Meanwhile, it is now time to explain to you exactly what the mission of Operation Counter Wrench is, and what we expect from each of you."

In spite of Lisa Abercombie's political connections and the extensive technical and military skills possessed by the other individuals sitting around the table, at this moment Dr.

Reston Wolfe truly felt that *he* was the one in charge, and he liked that feeling.

He could also feel Lisa Abercombie's eyes on him from the far back of the room, and he liked that, too.

"Your specific assignments," he said, his confidence growing with every passing moment, "are described in detail in the sealed folders before you. I want you to read them carefully. But not now."

Wolfe was pleased to note that not one of the twelve assault group members had reached for his stack of folders and envelopes. Instead, each watched him with a quiet and easy patience that suggested a strong sense of discipline and training. He liked to think of himself as a leader of such men.

"There will be time to read this material this afternoon and this evening," he went on, "and we will discuss it at great length tomorrow afternoon. I have a few other matters to address at this time.

"First, as you know, you are all posing as highly specialized biologists. You have been given the necessary background materials, passports and visas, and should have no trouble in maintaining your specific identity. If you are *ever* queried about your work, please remember that you need only respond in meaningless generalities. You are working on a government project that has certain biological sensitivities, none of which you are free to discuss. I might add that a little bit of bureaucratic arrogance—but not too much—is always a nice touch.

"Which brings us to your real work." Wolfe paused to look at each of the twelve faces.

"To begin, I would simply remind you that you were selected for Operation Counter Wrench on the basis of your technical expertise and previous experience, with specific emphasis on your military skills. We have considered these skills very carefully in making the team assignments, which, as I said, are in the folders before you.

"The basic plan is for ICER to operate as an assault group made up of three teams, each team being comprised of one German, one Japanese, and one American. While we may need to vary the team composition from time to time, the German member of each team will always function as the team leader. Accordingly, they will report to Mr. Maas, the assault-group leader, who in turn will report to me."

Wolfe gestured across the table to Maas, who responded with a brief nod of his white-haired head.

"Technical support," Wolfe went on, "in the form of surreptitious entries, electronic monitoring systems and counter-measures, photo and video surveillance, computer access and transportation, will be the responsibility of the Japanese member of each team, with Dr. Asai functioning as the technical support coordinator."

Dr. Morito Asai responded to the mention of his name with a formal nod.

"Intelligence, in terms of data gathering, analysis, and dissemination to the other team leaders, will be the responsibility of the American member of each team, with Mr. Saltmann functioning as the intelligence support coordinator."

Wolfe gestured toward the curly-haired, well-built individual who looked far more like an advertisement for Golds Gym than an intelligence analyst.

"And finally, should anything go wrong during the course of our activities, as things inevitably do," Wolfe added with a knowing smile, "it will be the responsibility of the American members of each team to provide the necessary covers, escape routes, and what we might describe as appropriate distractions."

There were a few nods, smiles, and murmurs of approval around the room, although Wolfe noted that Gerd Maas was now staring at the muscular, curly-haired Saltmann in a cold and reflective manner.

"Having said that much," Wolfe went on, deliberately lowering his voice to underscore the perception that he was in charge, "I would remind you that Operation Counter Wrench was not, and I repeat, *not* designed to be a military operation. At least not in the sense that you are accustomed to. Operation Counter Wrench is a covert operation. We will have to take aggressive action, but we will never do so openly. Every action we take will be from a point of concealment, hidden from the eyes of the world. If we are to succeed, nothing can *ever* be traced back to any of the people in this room.

"In effect, all of you here today will be the hidden warriors of our operation—the ones who will confront our enemies and cause them to destroy themselves with their own weapons."

"Dr. Wolfe."

The voice had come from the far end of the table, and Wolfe turned to look at the blond West German, who seemed perfectly comfortable sitting next to Gerd Maas.

Günter Aben, Wolfe nodded, immediately recognizing the face from the file photos and remembering the summary notations under the photo. Aggressive, fearless, and extremely deceptive in his mannerisms. Excellent covert operator. Can't ever tell what he's thinking. Good man. Ruthless and lethal. Controllable only by someone he respects.

Someone like Maas.

"Yes, Günter?"

"Dr. Wolfe, you make the nice image that we are the hidden warriors who will use deceit as our primary weapon," Günter Aben said, his youthful face open and smiling. "But you do not tell us who this enemy is that we are to deceive."

"Yes, an excellent question," Wolfe smiled. "Our enemies. Who are they?"

He looked around the room as though expecting someone to raise a hand, but no one moved.

"Greenpeace, for one," he said, answering his own question. "And Earth First!, and any of the other environment activists. No—" he paused, holding up one hand in a theatrical gesture "—let's use a more accurate word for these people. Call them what they really are.

"*Terrorists.*"

Wolfe let the word flow from his lips as if he savored its very pronouncement. The word itself seemed to echo throughout the quiet room, or at least in the minds of the people who sat there, silent and listening.

"For you see," he went on, caught up in the dramatic flow of his oration, "that is *exactly* what they are. Driven, emotional people who don't hesitate to use fear, uncertainty, and distortion as a weapon to force their will on an entire unsuspecting world.

"Our countries, Japan, Germany, and the United States, have been the most powerful in the world, because our businesses and our industries have been able to compete from a position of strength. But we in the United States are now threatened by an inability to compete. Our businesses and factories are being choked to death by needlessly restrictive rules and regulations put forth by the environmentalists and voted in by a brainwashed public. A public that simply won't understand what they've done until they no longer have their cost-effective cars, and lifesaving air conditioners, and freezers filled with food.

"And what we must all understand here," Wolfe went on, "is the fact that the United States is not alone in this. You need only read the newspapers to find that the environmental groups in Japan and Germany are not far behind.

"So what all of this comes to," Wolfe finished, his voice brought back to its normal pitch, "is the simple fact that these self-righteous entities, well-meaning as they might be, simply *cannot* be allowed to bring the industrial might of the free world to its knees."

For a long moment the silence in the room remained inviolate, until it was finally broken by the familiar, cheerful voice of Günter Aben, the quiet, deadly one.

"So we are to destroy the Green Movement, is that what you are saying?" Aben asked.

"We will not directly destroy them," Wolfe corrected. "That would be counterproductive. What we will do is to divert their resources, disrupt their plans, cause divisions where they are trying to create alliances. In effect, altering their public image and destroying their *effectiveness* by exposing them for the self-righteous and self-serving bastards that they really are."

Wolfe looked down at the table for a brief moment and then brought his head back up to stare out at the group.

"A few moments ago I suggested to all of you that these

environmental activist groups are, in fact, terrorists. Now, in that same line of thinking, I would further suggest that you look upon yourselves as counterterrorists."

"But with no official standing," interrupted a voice, cold and foreboding.

Gerd Maas, the German assault group leader, sat with an imperturbable expression on his white-bearded face.

Wolfe felt his throat constrict. Much as Wolfe hated to admit it, Maas scared him half to death.

"That is true. This is not an official government operation," Wolfe said, swallowing hard as he felt the uncontrollable numbness spread down his limbs.

"Perhaps I can expand on that answer," Lisa Abercombie said in a forceful voice from her seated position.

All eyes in the room shifted to the strikingly beautiful woman.

"I believe that Dr. Wolfe would agree when I say that this *is* an official government operation," Lisa Abercombie said, acutely aware that Gerd Maas was staring at her with his cold blue eyes. "It is not, however, officially *sanctioned*."

"I do not understand the difference," Günter Aben said matter-of-factly.

"The difference is simple," Abercombie said. "You are living in a federal government training facility, and you are being directed by Dr. Wolfe, who is a federal government employee. You will also have access to a wide range of federal government equipment and supplies as necessary.

"*However,*" she went on firmly, "because of the extremely sensitive nature of this operation, the United States Government *cannot* and *will not* acknowledge your existence. I am sure you can understand why this would be necessary."

"Does the United States Government know what we are doing?" Gerd Maas demanded in his glacial, penetrating voice.

To Lisa Abercombie, it was like having a bucket of ice water suddenly thrown in her face, and it was all that she could do not to flinch.

"Yes," she answered, forcing herself to remain calm and controlled.

"All the way to the top?"

Like Dr. Reston Wolfe before her, Lisa Abercombie could feel the fearful chill spread down her spinal cord, but to her credit, she hesitated only briefly before answering.

"No."

"Who is responsible then? You?"

"Myself, and a coordinating committee, yes."

"But this coordinating committee will not be involved in direct operations, correct?" Maas pressed.

"Yes, that is correct."

For perhaps thirty seconds the room remained deathly quiet. Then, once again, Günter Aben broke the silence.

"Then perhaps you are the one to answer this," Aben said. "Is it also correct to say that we must not allow ourselves to be apprehended by the authorities, under *any* circumstances?"

"We *are* the authorities," Lisa Abercombie said after a moment's pause, "but not everyone in the government would agree with what we are doing."

"But what does that mean?" Günter Aben demanded.

"It means that we have to be careful," Dr. Reston Wolfe interrupted in a quiet voice. "It is possible that our activities could attract the attention of one or more of our country's law-enforcement agencies. If that happens, we have to be ready to deal with the situation immediately."

"And how are we to do that?" Dr. Morito Asai asked politely, even though cold, glittering darkness remained in his eyes.

"First of all," Wolfe said, his composure returning, "discounting state and local police agencies, there are only a couple of federal law-enforcement agencies likely to cause us any concern."

"And those are?" Asai pressed.

"The FBI, of course," Wolfe conceded with some reluctance, "but we should not come to their attention unless we are careless. If we do our job properly, any FBI investigation will only confirm that our targets have been the cause of their own demise. Mostly because we—which is to say, *your* team, Dr. Asai—" Wolfe added with a grin, "will have provided them with physical evidence that will be impossible to ignore."

"Can you keep the FBI away from us if it becomes necessary?" Asai asked.

"No, we cannot." Wolfe shook his head. "But we *can* affect the direction of their inquiries. And if we take into account the inherent advantages of our position within the government, that should be more than sufficient."

"You mentioned that there were other federal agencies we should be concerned about," Asai reminded him, pressing the issue with polite firmness.

"Yes," Wolfe nodded, "but I don't want to overstate the nature of that concern, because I don't think it's that significant."

"I don't understand."

"Realistically," Wolfe said, "the only agencies likely to cause us any trouble would be the Park Service and the Fish and Wildlife Service. Because we are based in Yellowstone, of course, we must be constantly alert to the presence of the resident park rangers and the park police. However, since their patrol activities are fairly predictable, they should not cause us any undue difficulties. Especially since they've been instructed to stay out of the Whitehorse Cabin area."

"And the Fish and Wildlife Service?" Asai asked, looking up from his notebook.

"I honestly don't see them as a significant factor either," Wolfe said confidently. "The Service has a Division of Law Enforcement that is made up of less than two hundred special agents who are scattered far apart in one- or two-man duty stations. Their investigative interests are strictly limited to wildlife violations within their respective regions. The only entity within that Division that might possibly cause us any difficulty is their Special Operations branch, and they—"

"Special Operations?" Gerd Maas interrupted in his deep, chilling voice. "What is that?"

"The Special Operations branch is made up of two five-agent teams that are exclusively covert in nature," Wolfe explained. "They have their own intelligence capabilities, and they have the authority to conduct their investigations anywhere within the United States."

"Do you know who these special agents are?" Maas demanded.

"Yes, and we will provide you with that information at the appropriate time," Wolfe said. "But here again, I would emphasize that their investigations are strictly limited to wildlife violators. So unless one of our targeted environmental groups is involved in the killing or commercialization of endangered species, which is unlikely," he added with a smile, "our paths should never cross."

"In spite of the most careful planning, things rarely happen as we expect," Dr. Morito Asai said calmly. "Assuming for the moment that one of these undercover teams *did* happen to be investigating one of our targets, would we be made aware of it?"

"Almost immediately," Wolfe nodded. "I have made the necessary arrangements to have both the location and investigative activities of these undercover teams closely monitored. If either team begins an investigation anywhere near one of our targets, or anywhere near Yellowstone for that matter, we will know about it immediately, and we will see to it that they are diverted."

"You can do that?" Asai asked.

"Yes, at any time," Wolfe said. "They are a part of the Interior Department, of which I am a senior staffer."

"But wouldn't your actions cause these undercover agents to be suspicious?" Günter Aben asked.

"No, not really," Wolfe replied. "Like the FBI, we really can't stop them from investigating a case, but we can always redirect their efforts to a higher-priority investigation. That's a recognized and proper function of the central Washington office."

"But that would make them angry, and possibly more motivated, yes?" Aben suggested.

"They probably wouldn't like it," Wolfe conceded, "but there's really nothing that they could do about it. They are federal government employees, and they must do as they're told."

Wolfe tried not to pay attention as Gerd Maas grunted in apparent amusement.

"But Doctor Asai spoke the truth; things do not always occur as we might expect," Günter Aben commented with an insolent smile on his face. "Which is why I ask again: What are we to do if we *are* confronted by one of these law-enforcement officers? Do we allow ourselves to be taken into custody, or do we take any action necessary to escape?"

Lisa Abercombie shook her head firmly. "We have spent months planning this operation to the smallest detail. We know our targeted groups intimately. We know their strengths *and* their weaknesses, and we know exactly how we're going to exploit both. Knowing that, we have gone to unprecedented lengths to provide you with everything that you could possibly need to do your job without being detected.

"And if we've forgotten anything, anything at all," Abercombie added after a moment's pause, "you need only say the word and it will be delivered to you within twenty-four hours."

"*Anything?*" Aben smiled.

"Money is not a factor," Lisa Abercombie said flatly. "There is plenty of money available for this project. More money, in fact, than any of you could possibly use in your lifetime."

That statement brought on murmuring and more nodding of heads. The beautiful woman from the Bronx certainly had their full attention now.

"There is only one restriction," she went on in a firm voice. "*You must not fail.* That is the one thing that cannot be allowed, the one thing that cannot be forgiven."

Abercombie saw Gerd Maas turn again to stare in the direction of Paul Saltmann, the American team leader, with eyes that were both deadly cold and thoughtful.

"No one should be capable of stopping us, and therefore no one will be *allowed* to stop us," Lisa Abercombie said in a voice that was even more cold and forceful. "No one at all, under *any* circumstances, will stand in our way."

She paused for effect.

"Is it clear now?"

"Yes," Günter Aben nodded happily. "*Now* I understand."

CHAPTER EIGHT

It didn't occur to Henry Lightstone, until he was just about to drive his red pickup into the private tie-down area of the Great Falls airport, that he'd forgotten to ask McNulty what Len Ruebottom looked like.

Which was unfortunate, because at least a couple dozen adult males were standing around several of the thirty-odd planes that were lashed down on the wide asphalt field.

Lightstone glanced down at his wristwatch, winced, and muttered a heartfelt curse as he reached for the binoculars in the glove compartment. Even if he managed to link up with the resident agent-pilot within the next few minutes, he was still going to be late for his rendezvous with the Chareaux brothers.

"Come on, Ruebottom," he muttered as he began to scan the groups, searching for some sign of recognition. "McNulty must have given you a description of my truck, and I'm late, so you ought to be looking over here at me right—"

Then he blinked in pure disbelief.

For Christ's sake, McNulty, Lightstone thought despondently. What the hell have you gotten me into now?

For a brief moment, Lightstone seriously considered turning his leased pickup around at the gate, driving back to his apartment and calling the San Diego Police Department to check out the chances of getting his old job back. But then he remembered all the conflicts and problems that had caused him to question his law-enforcement career in the first place. And besides, he would never go back to the PD as a junior homicide detective, with zero seniority and a lock on every shit detail that came down the pike.

Sighing heavily, he put the binoculars back into the glove compartment and slowly drove the truck over to a tan station wagon parked next to a yellow-and-white Cessna.

A tall man in his early twenties, an attractive blond woman almost certainly his wife, and two young children were standing next to the plane, staring at Lightstone's truck.

"You must be Henry Lightstone," the young man said as he walked around to the driver's side of the truck and reached in to shake hands. He was wearing a blue baseball cap and a blue windbreaker jacket, both of which bore the easily identifiable badge insignia of a special agent of the U.S. Fish and Wildlife Service.

"I beg your pardon?" Lightstone said, keeping his hand on the steering wheel as he stared straight into the young pilot's clear blue eyes.

"Uh . . ." Len Ruebottom said, blinking in confusion as he slowly brought his hand back out of the truck window. "Aren't you Henry Lightstone? McNulty said that you'd be in a red pickup and that I was supposed to fly you to Bozeman."

For the second time in as many minutes, Lightstone seriously considered the idea of driving off and leaving the young agent-pilot and his family standing there next to the plane and wondering what the hell was going on.

It really wasn't all that bad an idea, he told himself. With luck, he might be able to catch the last half of the game, during which time he was bound to come up with a reasonable explanation that just *might* satisfy both Paul McNulty and Alex Chareaux.

Yeah, Alex, I know I was supposed to be there, but you see, the guy I hired to fly me to Bozeman turned out to be a federal agent. Saw him standing there in broad daylight wearing this agent hat and jacket. Imagine that? Yeah, hell of a deal, huh?

So anyway, what I did, I decided to go back home and catch a ball game instead. I mean, no sense in bringing the cops right into the middle of the deal when it's an illegal hunt all the way and I'm trying to get my Boone and Crockett record, right? Yeah, figured you guys would understand.

And at least a couple dozen people for witnesses, Lightstone sighed. Absolutely incredible.

"Did this McNulty fellow happen to mention a guy named Lightner? Henry Allen Lightner? Probably looks a lot like me?" Lightstone asked, trying very hard to keep a pleasant tone to his voice.

"Oh . . . uh, yeah, that's right." The young pilot winced. "Lightner's the guy I'm supposed to fly—"

"To Bozeman, where he's going to drive down to Gardiner and meet up with three guys who are just the kind of fellows who would probably kill him on the spot if they even *thought* he might be a federal agent?" Lightstone suggested.

"Uh . . . I guess I figured that since you weren't actually going to meet them in Bozeman—"

"That none of them would ever think to hang around the airport, taking pictures of the wife and kids of the pilot that this guy Lightner hires to take him around to do all his illegal hunting?"

"Oh, Christ!" Len Ruebottom grimaced, unable to keep from glancing over at his family, still waiting expectantly over by the Cessna.

"And even if they *did* take a couple of pictures," Lightstone went on, "they probably wouldn't ever think to run the registration number on the plane and then maybe fly out to Great Falls to see if anybody hanging around the airport here might have seen this guy Lightner talking with anybody who looked like a Fish and Wildlife agent."

Lightstone glanced meaningfully over at the twenty or so people who were still wandering around on the asphalt tarmac.

Len Ruebottom's hand started to come up, as though he was going to rip the cap off his sandy-haired head and then quickly pull himself out of his jacket. But then he caught himself and just stood there.

"That's right. It is a little late, and you really *don't* want to make a scene," Lightstone nodded.

"But—"

"And we won't even discuss how long it would take these bastards to find out where you live, where your wife works, where the kids go to school, what kind of locks you have on your doors, names of friends, baby-sitters, little details like that."

He hadn't meant to push it that far, and McNulty had vouched for him, but Henry Lightstone suddenly decided that he wanted to see for himself just how far he could trust the young agent-pilot.

"Jesus, I really screwed up," Len Ruebottom whispered, staring at Lightstone in shock, his sunburned face visibly paled.

"Yes, you did."

"So what do I do now?"

"Is that your plane over there?" Lightstone pointed at the yellow-and-white Cessna.

Ruebottom looked over his shoulder and nodded.

"You think it's safe to take something like that up in weather like this?"

"Oh, yeah, sure, no problem," Ruebottom said, his eyes still glazed from the shock of realizing that his thoughtlessness had exposed his family to . . . what?

"Okay, then. Why don't you hand that cap and jacket over to your wife and see if you can talk her and the kids into staying home this trip so we can get going?" Lightstone suggested.

Len Ruebottom took in a deep breath, let it out, and asked, "Anything else I should have had brains enough to think about, but didn't?"

"Duty weapon, shoulder holster, badge, registration, log book, anything else in the plane that somebody could find and link us back to the Service?" Lightstone suggested.

"You think they'd break into the plane, right out in the middle of the airport?"

Lightstone closed his eyes for a moment and sighed.

"Ruebottom," he said, "listen to me very carefully. These people, the ones you're flying me down to Bozeman to meet—if they even *thought* you had something in that plane that might send them to federal prison, they'd take it apart, rivet by rivet, right out in the middle of the fucking *run*way. You *can't* underestimate a guy like Alex Chareaux. If you do, you're going to get some people killed. And if you're real lucky, it'll only be you and me."

Len Ruebottom nodded solemnly. "Can you give me a couple of minutes?"

"Yeah, sure," Lightstone said tersely.

Two minutes later, the station wagon was slowly driving away, the kids in the back solemnly waving good-bye to their father, as Len Ruebottom walked up to Lightstone.

"Sorry about that. It won't happen again."

"If I thought it would, I'd be looking for another pilot right now," Lightstone said agreeably.

"This all your gear?" Ruebottom asked, looking at the pair of duffel bags and the rifle case lying at Lightstone's feet.

"That's it."

"Okay, let's get going."

Len Ruebottom grabbed one of the duffel bags and the rifle case and started off in the direction of a nearby hangar, walking right on past the yellow-and-white Cessna.

"Hey, where the hell are you going?" Lightstone demanded.

Ruebottom stopped for a moment to look at his passenger. "To the plane," he said, a perplexed expression on his face. "We're behind schedule. I thought you wanted to get going."

"But you said this was your plane," Lightstone said, pointing at the Cessna.

"It is, but that's not the one we're going up in today." Ruebottom started walking again toward the hangar.

Muttering yet another curse, Lightstone reached down, grabbed the other duffel bag and followed the young agent-pilot.

"McNulty and Halahan worked this thing out a couple of weeks ago," Ruebottom explained as he unlocked the hangar. He grunted with exertion as he pushed one of the heavy doors all the way over to the side. "The way I heard it, McNulty figured that one of his agents—you, I guess—might need a pilot and plane on stand-by to enhance his cover. He was willing to pay all the expenses, so Halahan said fine, do it. And then, this morning McNulty calls and tells me that you're on the way and to meet you at the airport."

"Yeah, so?"

"So what I did, a couple of weeks ago, was to work out a special deal with a rich buddy of mine," Len Ruebottom explained as he shoved the door to its fully open position on its oiled but rusty rollers.

"What kind of special deal?" Lightstone asked suspiciously.

"A very special deal indeed," Ruebottom said with a smile as he flipped on the hangar lights and then gestured with his head at the glistening metal shape inside the hangar.

"*That's* the plane that you and I are going to fly to Bozeman."

Lisa Abercombie looked up as Dr. Reston Wolfe finally put down the phone.

"Well?"

"It's all arranged," he said, smiling like a man who had just put together the deal of a lifetime.

"It sounded like you were having some problems."

"Nothing that couldn't be resolved," Wolfe shrugged easily. "He and I have done business before, and he wants to continue doing business in the future. It was just a matter of rearranging some schedules."

"And offering to pay a great deal of money," Abercombie added. "You're a smooth operator. It sounds like a nice way to thank our financial backers."

Wolfe shrugged again. "It's not often that you can offer a new experience to people with nine-digit incomes. And our going out on the first excursion will mean only a small added expense." He stared straight into Abercombie's dark eyes. "A few extra dollars is hardly worth worrying about."

Lisa Abercombie blinked.

"That's very sweet of you, Reston," she said after a few

moments, her sensuous mouth widening out into a dimpled smile that put Wolfe's blood pressure up another twenty points, "but do you think it's wise for us to leave the cabin at a time like this?"

Reston Wolfe remembered once again the sensual warmth of Abercombie's hand resting on his thigh, and the indelibly erotic image of her skintight jeans stretching across her hips and buttocks and muscular thighs when she'd walked out of the dining room to take her phone call.

Savoring a sense of heart-pounding anticipation, Wolfe held up a reassuring hand and shook his head.

"No need to be concerned. It's going to take them all afternoon to go through those briefing books. And besides, I've made arrangements with Sergeant MacDonald to move up the introductory tour of the training center to seven o'clock tonight."

"Tonight?"

"The Committee wants us to be ready to go by Thursday," Wolfe told her. "That gives us only three full days to work out the initial bugs."

"Do you really think there are going to be any bugs, with people like Maas and Saltmann?" Abercombie asked.

"I don't know," Wolfe replied. "MacDonald's the expert, and I don't think he was too thrilled about the idea of letting them go out on an operation without at least a couple weeks of orientation. Says it doesn't matter how good they are as individuals, it takes time to develop teamwork."

"He's probably right," Lisa Abercombie conceded, "but we simply don't have that luxury. Not if we're going to be effective when we need to be."

"I know, and that's what I told him."

"You told him what we're doing?" Abercombie asked, feeling her heart start to pound.

"No, of course not," Wolfe smiled. "I just told him that we've been advised that some of our targets have started to move and that we need to get certain elements of the team into position by Thursday to keep an eye on things."

"I think he's anxious to see how all his simulations work

against a guy like Maas," Lisa Abercombie said, working to keep a neutral tone to her voice.

"Me, too," Wolfe agreed. "Tonight's just an orientation. Tomorrow, at nine o'clock, we get to see the real thing. A live-fire assault on a corporate office. Four-man team. And you and I have ringside seats."

"Nine o'clock tomorrow morning?"

"Right, which gives us exactly," he glanced down at his watch, "twenty-three hours to enjoy ourselves."

"But—"

"I can assure you that we won't be missed at all, just as long as we're back in time for breakfast," Wolfe smiled. "But it's up to you," he added instinctively, going with his gut-level presumption that risk-taking was the way to reach a woman like Lisa Abercombie. "Are you sure you want to do this?"

Lisa Abercombie hesitated for only a brief, tantalizing moment as she remembered once again the almost tangible sense of being *alive* that she had not only experienced, but—what was the word?—*savored* as she watched Gerd Maas face the terrifying charge of the fearsome Bengal. It had been the most intense and visceral moment of her entire life, and she knew that she would do almost anything to be able to experience that sensation once again.

The knowledge that Maas would be there with them tonight, perhaps even standing at her side, to assist her in reliving that moment of absolute dread was almost more than she could stand.

"Yes, Reston," she nodded, her dark eyes alive with anxious anticipation. "As a matter of fact, I'm absolutely sure."

CHAPTER NINE

They were number three in line for takeoff, which gave Henry Lightstone plenty of time to check his safety harness and readjust his headset.

"Nervous?" Len Ruebottom asked, speaking into his headset mike through the Lear's intercom system as he continued to monitor the gauges on the complex instrument panel.

"Yeah, I've never strapped myself inside a goddamned rocket before," Lightstone replied through his intercom microphone as he tried to ignore the tower traffic reports coming through his headset. The controller was saying something about head winds and down drafts that Lightstone really didn't want to hear.

"The Lear's actually a pretty smooth plane," Ruebottom said as he tapped at a gauge and then keyed his mike over to the external channel to acknowledge the tower's report. "Once we reach altitude, you're going to find that she gives you a real nice ride. Almost like sitting in your living room and watching a ball game."

"I'd *like* to be sitting in my living room watching a ball game," Lightstone said seriously. "Any chance you could pick up one of the games on this?" he asked, thinking that he might not vomit in the brand-new Lear jet if he could close his eyes and concentrate on something halfway interesting.

"Sure. What do you want to hear?"

"Lakers and Blazers?" Lightstone said hopefully.

Len Ruebottom checked his watch and then consulted a half-inch-thick booklet that he pulled out of a nylon pocket beside his seat. "Would you settle for a relay feed out of L.A.?"

"You can get that?"

Ruebottom laughed into his microphone. "Are you kidding? With all the money my buddy put into this radio gear, we could probably pick up a phone call in downtown Moscow. Which reminds me," he said, pointing to a part of the instrument panel that looked like a calculator key pad, "you can call out if you need to. All you've got to do is link in with a couple of codes, then punch in a phone number and talk through your mike. No sweat."

"Except that you and anybody else with a scanner gets to listen in, right?"

"Just me," the young pilot grinned. "Stu bought himself the high-priced rig. Signals come in and go out through a satellite hookup using scrambled transponders. Pretty good for privacy, unless there's a hacker out there who knows how to break matrix codes at two-second intervals."

"I think I've already met a guy like that in Special Ops," Lightstone said.

"Oh, yeah? Probably Mike Takahara, right?"

Lightstone nodded.

"I got to meet him at In-Service last year," Ruebottom said. "Real nice guy. I took him up in a Cessna a couple of times. I think I've just about got him talked into going for his license."

"Jesus, that's just what I need," Lightstone muttered to himself. He watched uneasily as the young agent-pilot released the brakes and gently advanced the throttle, winding the Lear's engines up into a high-pitched scream as they moved along the taxiway parallel to the main runway.

They were number two in the pattern for takeoff now.

Len Ruebottom responded to the traffic controller with some numbers that he read off his instrument panel, then busied himself making notes on the latest weather report.

Finally he looked over at Lightstone with obvious concern. "You really think it's going to be okay, my leaving Sue and the kids by themselves after I screwed up like that?"

"Yeah, they'll be fine," Lightstone said reassuringly, hoping he was right. "I was just giving you a bad time back there, trying to make you think about what you were doing."

"Yeah, I know, and I appreciate it," Ruebottom said in a sincere voice. "I guess I shouldn't worry about them so much, but Christ, it's bad enough with all the normal stuff going on. People shooting each other. Kids running cars into trees. Rapes, robberies, burglaries. Jesus!"

"Exactly," Lightstone nodded. "That's why I got out of police work. Too goddamned depressing. You have to shut that part of your mind off, like in a closet in the back of your head. Then you focus in on what you're supposed to be doing out there and try not to look into their eyes too often. And while you're doing that," Lightstone went on calmly, "you keep searching around for that little bit of craziness that'll make everybody laugh so they don't have to worry about crying when they go off shift." The ex-homicide investigator shrugged as he stared out through the Lear's thick windshield, remembering the two-o'clock-in-the-morning call-outs, the blood-splattered crime scenes, the dull, vacant gaze in the eyes of the victims, the rambling statements of the witnesses, and, finally, the interminable wait for the judge to sign the warrant, knowing all the while that the suspect was . . .

Ruebottom reached for the controls as the tower came on the air and the 737 ahead of them began to move forward. Lightstone consciously brushed his fingers across the release snap of his safety harness.

A sudden burst of static provided advance warning of another message from the control tower, this time letting everyone on the taxiway know that they were getting ready to start moving airplanes again. Lightstone could feel himself starting to tense up as he realized that they were nearing takeoff.

Ruebottom was making slight adjustments to the controls to counteract the jet wash as the 737 ahead of them began to roll forward, the powerful engines sending shock waves all the way down the line.

Working quickly now, Ruebottom checked both his and Lightstone's safety harnesses, adjusted his headset, scanned the instrument board for red lights, double-checked the critical gauges, and then inched the throttles forward again.

"You about ready?"

"Ready as I'll ever be," Lightstone said with a visible lack of enthusiasm.

"Try to think about something else," Ruebottom advised, trying hard not to grin.

"Okay," Lightstone agreed, willing to try just about anything at this point. "What about you and the plane? Everything in here clean, just in case somebody does start snooping around?"

"Thanks to McNulty and his no-limit credit cards, this plane is officially leased to the Ruebottom Air Transport Service, a more or less reputable outfit that doesn't dig too deep into the sordid past of its clients," Ruebottom said as he continued to monitor controls and gauges. "Far as the flight logs are concerned, they've been cooked so that it looks like I've been taking you up on an average of about once a week for the last couple of years. You pay in cash, and what you do when you land is nobody's business but your own. I'm just a fly-for-hire, who wouldn't know a set of agent's credentials from a Crackerjack badge."

"What about ID and weapons?"

"I've got an old military forty-five in a kit bag behind the seat, handy to have in case some critter starts chewing on the wings." Ruebottom gestured with his head as he scanned the instrument panel one last time, a hand poised on the throttles. "Registration papers track back to my buddy Stu, who's got too damn much money to care about having extended conversations with people he doesn't know. He'd just tell them to buzz off or talk to one of his lawyers."

"What about your wallet?"

"Wallet, map case, kit bags, pants, shirt and jacket pockets are all clean, no incriminating evidence."

"Good habit for you young married types to get into," Lightstone advised, half serious. "That way you won't have to worry about Sue finding slips of paper with all those strange phone numbers in your pockets."

"Yeah, right," Ruebottom said absentmindedly as he began to tap at individual gauges on the instrument panel.

"By the way," Lightstone said, "I want you to call a girl named Marie when we get to Bozeman and tell her I'm sorry I stood her up."

"I should tell her how you and I get to go to Yellowstone this weekend and she doesn't?"

"For Christ's sake, don't tell her I'm at Yellowstone!" Lightstone said quickly. "That was another place I promised I'd take her to someday."

At that moment, the 737 began to accelerate down the runway in a deafening roar of jet exhaust, which meant that the Lear was next in line for takeoff. Henry Lightstone thought he could actually feel his rib cage and chest muscles begin to tighten around his heart.

"Which reminds me," Ruebottom said. "You sure you don't want me to go down to Gardiner with you, give you some backup in case things go nuts?"

"No thanks." Lightstone shook his head, making a conscious effort now to control his breathing as he spoke into the headset mike. "These guys are spooky enough as it is. They'll be watching us from the minute we touch down, and you can count on there being at least one guy on you the whole time you're in the airport, so be real careful about using the phones."

Ruebottom nodded in silent understanding as he adjusted his headset mike, keyed the radio, and made one last weather check with the tower.

Moments later the Lear jet was poised on the end of the runway, looking far more like a scrappy fighter jet than a hotdogging passenger aircraft.

"Great Falls Tower, Lear November Three-Three-Five-Charley-Papa," Ruebottom spoke into his mike as he checked each quadrant of the sky. "Requesting clearance for takeoff."

"Lear Three-Three-Five-Charley-Papa, stand by."

"Come on, guys. Let's get the show on the road," Len Ruebottom muttered, anxious to be up in the air, where he felt he truly belonged. "Any last questions?" he asked, turning to look at his copilot passenger.

"No, just get us there in one piece, and hurry it up," Lightstone instructed.

"Okay. Then how about one last set of instructions? See those pedals down by your feet?"

"Yeah."

"You want to try to keep your feet away from them."

"Why?"

"Well, because if you don't, I could lose control of the plane at a very bad moment," Ruebottom explained.

Lightstone quickly brought his feet as far away from the pedals as possible, which resulted in his knees being jammed up against the copilot's set of controls.

"And while you're at it, you're going to want to keep your knees away from the controls, too," Ruebottom advised. "Makes it a whole lot easier for me to steer this thing."

"Anything else?" Lightstone muttered as he tried with reasonable success to find a neutral position for both his feet and his knees.

"Barf bags and life vest are under your seat," Ruebottom smiled. "No parachutes, so you're stuck in here for the duration. Just try to keep the backseat driving down to a minimum, and enjoy the flight."

"Yeah, well, now that you brought it up, and since we don't have an honest-to-God copilot in this thing, what am I supposed to do if something happens to you up there?"

"Well, I'll tell you," the young pilot said with a serious expression on his young face. "You see this big gauge here?" He tapped at the glass-faced dial with a gloved finger.

"Yeah, I see it."

"That gauge tells you how much gas you've got left in the fuel tanks. If I happen to go unconscious, or have a heart attack or something like that, and you can manage to keep this thing up high enough so that the wind resistance is pretty much at a minimum, then you're probably looking at, oh, maybe six hours of flying time."

"Yeah, and just what the hell good does that do me?"

"There's an instruction manual in the compartment to the right of your seat," Ruebottom said, pointing with his right hand. "It's a pretty good read. Explains everything you've ever wanted to know about how to fly a Lear jet. If you work at it, you can probably get through the whole thing in, oh, I'd say about five or six hours. Although, if I were in your position," he added thoughtfully, "I think I'd probably skip the beginning stuff and go right on ahead to chapter thirty-six."

"Lear Three-Three-Five," the control tower interrupted, "you are cleared for takeoff. Have a good flight."

Len Ruebottom acknowledged the clearance, scanned the instrument panel for any last-minute reds, and the sky for any incoming planes that the controller might have forgotten to mention, and then keyed his internal mike again.

"You say something?"

"I was asking why the hell I should read chapter thirty-six first," Lightstone muttered through a clenched jaw, gripping his seat tightly.

Len Ruebottom looked over at his passenger and smiled. "Because by the time that fuel gauge starts to read empty . . ." he said, pausing to set the brakes, throttle each of the engines up to a high-pitched shriek, make a final instrument check, and then release the brakes.

"Lear Three-Three-Five," Ruebottom keyed his mike, "we're on the roll."

As the Lear jet began to accelerate down the long runway, Ruebottom switched over to his internal mike one more time.

". . . you're probably going to want to have at least a general idea of how to land a Lear jet without putting too much of a dent in the runway."

Then he pushed the throttles to full-forward and sent the sleek-nosed jet screaming up into the gray-clouded sky.

CHAPTER TEN

Given the proximity of Bozeman to several first-class Montana ski resorts, the arrival of a Lear jet at Bozeman Airport wasn't exactly a media event. Still there were at least a dozen people in the terminal who turned to watch Len Ruebottom bring the incredibly agile aircraft in for a near-perfect touchdown landing.

Two of those people were Butch and Sonny Chareaux.

As the Lear taxied to a stop about fifty yards from the main terminal building, Butch Chareaux focused a pair of camouflaged binoculars on the jet's small windshield.

Chareaux, who was dressed in hunting clothes and looked as though he had spent every day of his life in the woods, waited patiently for the man in the copilot's seat to remove the headset so that he could see his face clearly.

After a few moments, he muttered something to his brother, who immediately walked to a nearby telephone and dialed a long-distance number.

"Yes?"

"He's here."

"What type of plane?"

"A Lear jet."

At the other end of the line, Alex Chareaux tapped his index finger on the table as he considered this new bit of information.

"What is the registration number?"

Sonny Chareaux, the largest of the Chareaux brothers at six-five and two hundred and fifty-five pounds, looked out across the terminal through the large, sound-absorbing plate glass. He saw the side door of the Lear pop open and then drop down as he noted the number painted on the base of the airplane's horizontal stabilizer.

"There's an 'N,' a dash, the numbers three, three, five, and then a 'C' and a 'P,'" he said as Alex Chareaux quickly scribbled in his notebook. "They are getting out of the plane now."

"Can you see the pilot?"

"Yes."

"Do you recognize him? Is he one of the charter pilots on your list?"

"No."

Alex Chareaux frowned.

Sometime within the next few hours, he was going to have to make a decision that might easily destroy his business and put his brothers and himself back on the run; or, if all went well, make their illegal enterprise many times more profitable.

What it amounted to was one magnificent, yet ominous, roll of the dice.

And Chareaux couldn't do anything more about it now because there wasn't enough time to make any other arrangements. All he could do was either say yes, or say no.

"Is there any sign of surveillance outside the terminal?"

"No, we have seen nothing."

"You've checked the parking lot?"

"Yes, many times."

"What about inside?"

"Only a few travelers, people with luggage and tickets, and the ones who are always here," Sonny Chareaux said. "It is not very busy today."

"What about the rental-car people? The porters? The people at the airline counters? Do you see anyone you do not recognize? Anyone who is not on your list?"

"No, they are all the same."

It was an extremely difficult decision. Alex Chareaux cursed the one who had caused him this problem: the wealthy client who always talked with so much courage on the phone, boasting of his ability to stand his ground in the face of a charging record trophy animal, and eager to spend his money freely for the privilege. And yet also the one who might freeze at the critical moment when the huge bear turned in his direction, Chareaux reminded himself.

Which was why they would need the extra set of skilled hands. Someone with the nerve, and the resources, and the underlying greed to do whatever it took. Someone they could trust. Perhaps Henry Lightner could function as that extra set of hands. But Lightner's trustworthiness had to be proven beyond a doubt.

And that, of course, was the essence of his problem.

"What about the plane? Can you see anyone else in there with them?"

"One moment. We will look again to be sure."

Impatient to set it all into motion, but yet still uneasy for reasons that he didn't clearly understand, Alex Chareaux continued to shake his head slowly and tap his finger on the tabletop.

He realized that his instincts were telling him to play it safe and call the hunt off, and he was sorely tempted to do just that because the risks on this one were significant.

But in this particular case, the payoff—and the potential for future payoffs—was even greater.

Alex Chareaux understood as well as anyone that successful conquests were almost invariably based on opportunity and risk. He had always despised the cowards who played it safe. The timid ones who could only look forward to dying peacefully in their beds once their hands became too feeble to work the remote controls of their TV sets. Alex Chareaux, the oldest of the three brothers and their natural leader, knew with absolute certainty that he would never die that way. But he had also sworn a blood oath that neither of his brothers would ever die in prison, no matter who or what stood in their way. Because to rot away slowly in a cage like a trapped animal was the worst thing that could happen to men like Alex Chareaux and his brothers.

"There are only two of them on the plane," Sonny Chareaux said, finally coming back on the line.

"Has anyone gone out to meet them?"

"No, not so far."

He needed more. Something that he could dig his fingers into, and analyze. Something that he could examine, pull apart, and finally use for the crucial decision.

"What about a rental car?"

"We think he has a reservation with Hertz. There's a packet on the wall with the name 'Lightner' on it."

"Get a photograph of the pilot," Alex Chareaux said. "Find out who he is, and do it quickly. See what you can discover from the rental agency, too."

Sonny Chareaux motioned to his brother, who immediately exchanged his binoculars for a medium-format camera with a Polaroid back and telephoto lens.

After double-checking the settings, Butch Chareaux braced himself against the window frame and waited until Len Ruebottom stepped out onto the Lear's small stairway.

The loud click of the shutter was audible fifteen feet away in the small, uncrowded airport terminal.

Still at the phone, Sonny Chareaux watched as his brother quickly pulled the undeveloped photo out of the camera, set it aside, and then brought the heavy camera up again for a second shot.

Butch was the smallest, and the youngest, of the three Chareaux brothers; he was five-nine, one-eighty-five, and twenty-nine years of age. He was also the most technically adept of the brothers, with a knack and a feel for fine machinery like cameras and video recorders. But his true love was the 7mm Winchester Model 70 rifle with the adjustable Zeiss scope that his brother Alex had given him for his thirteenth birthday. The one he'd used to kill his first human being two weeks later, and the eleven others since.

Unlike his brothers, who preferred to be in close when they killed, Butch Chareaux liked to work from a distance, using hand-cast sabot rounds—projectiles with a thick coating of plastic that isolated the solid-core slug from the constraining grip of the barrel rifling but then split away in mid-flight to give the bullet additional velocity and stability. He liked the precision and the quickness of the kills, and the fact that there would never be a land or a groove on the bullets that could be matched back to his treasured rifle. But he really didn't need to worry about that, because his preferred target was the neck—actually, the larynx and one of the carotid arteries; the shock left the victim mute and rapidly dying, while the mostly unaltered bullet continued on its ballistic path to disappear into the forest.

"It's done," Sonny Chareaux said. "We have the photograph."

"Good. Check him out then, quickly, and use the radio to contact me as soon as you know."

"But if I can find out nothing about him easily, how far should I go?" Sonny Chareaux asked. "Or perhaps I should say, what are the limits? How hard should I push?"

Alex Chareaux hesitated for a brief moment. "There are no limits on this one," he answered finally. "Do whatever you have to do. We need to know before sunset."

"I understand."

After hanging up, Sonny Chareaux walked over to his brother and waited the remaining seconds until both Polaroids were ready. He examined each of them, taking extra time with the one that showed the pilot and the man they knew as Henry Lightner coming down the ramp.

"Do we get to kill them?" Butch Chareaux asked hopefully.

"I think so," his older brother said, looking out the terminal window at the two men who were unloading duffel bags and a rifle case out of the Lear's storage compartment. "We shall see."

"So what do you think?" Len Ruebottom asked in a low voice as they walked in through the wide terminal door, causing Henry Lightstone to wince. Fortunately, of the ten or eleven people that he could see inside the Bozeman Airport terminal, none of them were within earshot.

Lightstone had given Ruebottom the rifle case and one of the duffel bags to carry in the hope that the task would be sufficiently distracting. But the young rookie agent-pilot had already forgotten one of his primary directives.

"You've seen one small airport, you've seen them all," Lightstone observed as he paused to take in the entire waiting area in one long, appraising glance.

Of those ten or eleven people, he noted, at least a couple of the men looked big, mean, sinister, or vicious enough to be Alex Chareaux's brothers. Which meant that he had to get rid of Len Ruebottom as quickly as possible.

"No, I mean . . ."

Deliberately ignoring the young pilot, Lightstone made a visible show of looking around and then finally managing to locate the large, bright-yellow Hertz sign that would have been easily visible a hundred yards away. He walked over to the counter, dropped his duffel bag, and turned to stare straight into Len Ruebottom's clear, innocent eyes.

"Really appreciate you're getting me up here on short notice, Len," he said, giving him a friendly employer-to-employee type of smile. "I'll give you a call when I need a pickup."

"Uh, yes sir," Ruebottom acknowledged, finally remembering his proper role. "Anything else I can do in the meantime?"

"Not a thing," Lightstone said firmly. "Just look after the plane, hang on to that paper, and stay near a telephone."

Then he turned to face the waiting Hertz clerk before Len Ruebottom had a chance to say anything else that just might get one or both of them killed.

"Hello," Lightstone said, smiling pleasantly at the attractive young woman. "The name's Lightner."

"Oh, yes, of course," she said, nodding in apparent recognition as though she had memorized all of the names on the displayed reservation packets. With barely a glance backward, she reached around for the one that was marked "Lightner" in big capital letters.

"First name Henry?" she asked before opening the envelope.

"That's right."

As he handed her Henry Lightner's driver's license and credit card, Lightstone turned his head just enough to see Len

Ruebottom's broad back as he walked out the wide terminal-door access to the tarmac and the waiting Lear jet. He also noted that he couldn't see either of the two men who had seemed to resemble Alex Chareaux, but he really wasn't worried about the Chareaux brothers at this point.

Not as long as Len Ruebottom got the Lear *and* his rookie-agent ass back up in the air and out of Bozeman within the next few minutes.

God save us all from the nice guys. They're the ones who get you killed every time, he told himself as he returned his attention to the attractive Hertz clerk.

"Do you know where you'll be staying?"

Lightstone sensed the presence of a man behind him, but he didn't worry, because it didn't matter now if Sonny or Butch Chareaux were standing behind him or waiting for him out by the Bronco. He could deal with the Chareaux brothers on his own just fine. The only thing that he was really interested in right now was hearing the high-pitched whine of two powerful jet engines revving up as Len Ruebottom taxied the Lear back out onto the runway for takeoff.

"Somewhere between Big Timber and Lewistown," he lied reflexively. "Depends on how far I get."

"Okay then, Mr. Lightner, I think we have everything all ready for you," the young woman said cheerfully as she handed him the contract. After he had signed it, she took the multipage form back, separated out and folded his copy, then handed him the packet along with a set of keys. "I've marked the stall where it's parked, and it's filled with gas. You want to be sure to fill it up . . . but you know all of that, don't you?"

Lightstone nodded.

"Then just watch out for those storms, and have a nice trip." She smiled one last time before looking back at her dwindling row of reservation packets with an oddly forlorn expression.

Thirty minutes later, after having made a trip to the bathroom, buying a container of coffee to go, and stowing the duffel bags and rifle in the back of the Bronco, Henry

Lightstone drove out of the airport en route to U.S. Highway 90.

In doing so, he tried very hard not to look at the sleek and shiny Lear jet that was still parked all by itself about fifty yards from the Bozeman Airport terminal building.

The eighty-mile drive from Bozeman to Gardiner wound down along the shallow Yellowstone River and through one of the more spectacular high-peak passes in the western United States. But the view was wasted on Lightstone, who was having trouble just paying attention to the road.

He kept thinking about the empty Lear jet sitting out on the Bozeman Airport tarmac with the U.S. registration number Three-Three-Five-Charley-Papa painted in nice readable block print on its side.

And a twenty-five-year-old rookie agent-pilot, with a pretty wife and two young kids, who had no business getting drawn into an undercover investigation with a freak like Alex Chareaux if he didn't know enough about covert work to do *exactly* as he was told.

"God *damn* you, McNulty," Lightstone swore to himself, over and over again.

He almost pulled off the road at Miner to find a phone and warn McNulty to get Carl or Larry or Dwight out to Bozeman to find out what the hell was going on with that plane. But he knew that if he did something like that, the word would immediately get back to Alex Chareaux.

And besides, Lightstone reminded himself, there were at least six vehicles behind him, any one of which might be driven by Sonny or Butch Chareaux. He really didn't want to have to explain a sudden phone call.

So he kept driving and tried not to think too much about all the little mistakes that a novice investigator like Len Ruebottom could have made. And it didn't help that every time he thought about Len Ruebottom and his family, he saw the ravaged face of Bobby LaGrange, his ex-partner from San Diego, bruised, beaten, and near death in that hospital bed.

Thus by the time Henry Lightstone finally pulled into the

parking lot of the Best Western Motel in Gardiner, he was seriously considering taking Alex Chareaux out into the woods with a .38 shoved into the base of his skull, and to hell with the investigation.

Lightstone drove around to the back side of the motel and pulled into the parking space in front of 101, the first ground-floor room to the right of the manager's office. Leaving the driver's-side door unlocked as a precaution, because he wasn't sure of what would be happening in the next few minutes, Lightstone walked around to the rear of the Bronco. He opened up the back door, pulled out the rifle case and his duffel bags, relocked the door, and slid the keys into his pocket.

Then he turned around and found himself staring directly into the piercing, red-streaked eyes of Alex Chareaux.

"We have a problem, Henry," Chareaux said without preamble, the cold, somber expression on his bearded face giving away nothing at all.

"Oh, yeah? What's that?" Lightstone asked, standing there with the rifle case in one hand and the duffel bags in the other as he instantly switched his mind into the full role of Henry Allen Lightner.

"We need to talk," Chareaux said, gesturing with his head to his left. "I think we should go to my room, where we can be more private." He started to turn away in the direction of the motel, but Lightstone stood firmly in place.

"What exactly is the problem, Alex?" he asked in a cold, quiet voice, having no intention of allowing himself to be trapped in a small hotel room until he knew a lot more about what was going on.

"It is better not to talk of such things in public," Chareaux said insistently.

The expression in Alex Chareaux's reddened dark eyes was completely unreadable, and Lightstone didn't like that. The image of Len Ruebottom sitting in Chareaux's room, tied upright in a chair, gagged, and most likely beaten half to death, flashed through Lightstone's mind.

"What do you mean, in *public*?" Lightstone demanded,

putting on all of the frustration and impatience of a wealthy businessman and sportsman who wasn't the least bit accustomed to being hassled. He made a deliberate show of looking around the parking lot. "For Christ's sake, Alex, we're standing in a goddamned parking lot, out in the middle of nowhere, and there's nobody around. What the hell's the matter with you?"

If Len Ruebottom was in that room, Lightstone knew that Sonny and Butch would be there, too; and that would make it three to one, with Ruebottom as a hostage. There wouldn't be any chance at all.

Chareaux just stood there, looking equally frustrated and impatient and about ready to explode.

That's it, Alex, Lightstone smiled to himself. Go ahead and get upset. Yell, scream, and throw a fit. Give me an excuse.

"Look, man," he said, deciding to see how far he could push Alex Chareaux, "I just spent a half-hour bouncing around the sky in a goddamned airplane because *you're* the one who called and said it was now or never. And now I'm here, and I'm in no mood to—"

Focused on Alex Chareaux, and standing with his back to the motel, Lightstone never heard the door to Room 102 open. Thus he became aware of their presence only when one of the camouflage-dressed individuals came up behind him and spoke.

"Alex," Dr. Reston Wolfe demanded as he stared down at the rifle case in Lightstone's hand, "would you be so kind as to explain what the hell is going on out here?"

CHAPTER ELEVEN

The mood in Room 102 was tense.

Lisa Abercombie and Dr. Morito Asai, each dressed in brand-new military combat boots and camouflage gear, had departed for a nearby restaurant a few minutes before, leaving Wolfe, Lightstone and Alex Chareaux standing around the bed in the small motel room glaring at each other.

Alex Chareaux had already spent about five minutes trying to explain that there had been a mix-up in the scheduling, but that everything was okay now because his brothers had spotted two record-sized bears. It would all work out just fine if everyone would just agree to hunt together.

For someone like Alex, it was a remarkably calm, dispassionate and even reasonable speech; but it hadn't helped because neither of his clients was willing to give in.

"This is pure bullshit," Lightstone growled, having to work now at keeping this new and very alluring woman out of his mind.

"That's one thing we agree on," Reston Wolfe nodded.

"But you are all here now, and my brothers and I are ready," Chareaux said with forced restraint, "so why should we not try to make the best of it?"

"I've got one good reason," Lightstone said. "I knew this hunt was going to be risky to begin with, but if you're going to add three more people, it's going to be goddamned *dangerous*. It'll be like a New Year's Day parade out there."

"You have a point," Chareaux admitted, "but there are ways of dealing with such risks. It is only necessary that we be careful."

"Seems to me you're asking all of us to be pretty goddamned trusting," Lightstone added. "We don't even know each other."

Lightstone wanted Chareaux to think that Henry Allen Lightner was still nervous about the possibility of getting caught on an illegal hunt, but what he was really trying to do was to stay in character. He'd already decided to go along with whatever arrangement Alex Chareaux managed to work out with the three newcomers, figuring that Chareaux was already suspicious and that his chances of getting another hunt set up in the near future were probably nil.

Lightstone knew that as far as Paul McNulty was concerned, all he had to do was to get Alex Chareaux and his brothers linked to an illegal hunt, and then maybe get a line on the taxidermist they used. The fact that there might be a couple of extra hunters along for the ride probably wouldn't matter one way or another.

But it was becoming increasingly obvious that a shared hunt wasn't acceptable to the other man in the room, whom Chareaux had so far declined to introduce.

"And I'm telling you I'm *not* willing to be that trusting," Wolfe was saying insistently.

"Then what am I to do?" Chareaux asked, bringing his arms and shoulders up in an exaggerated shrug.

"I offered you a multiyear contract, with very generous terms," Wolfe responded. "But if we're going to work together, I expect you to keep your word."

The expression in Alex Chareaux's dark eyes froze, and for a brief moment, Lightstone thought Chareaux might kill his foolishly arrogant client right there in the motel room.

But then, with a visible display of effort, Alex Chareaux brought himself under control.

"I understand your point," Chareaux said in what Lightstone thought was an incredibly calm voice. "But remember, it was *you* who asked to change the day of your hunt at the last minute. Had I been able to reach my friend here in time," he nodded in Lightstone's direction, "we could have rescheduled his hunt for another day. But now that he is here . . ."

"Okay, I think I see where all of this is heading," Wolfe said disdainfully as he turned to Lightstone. "How much is he charging you?"

"That's none of your business," Lightstone replied evenly.

"Look, I'll make it real easy. You walk away today, reschedule for some other time, and I'll cover the entire cost of your hunt."

"What?"

"I'm talking everything," Wolfe said confidently. "The mount, the delivery, the whole ball of wax. All you have to do is come back another day."

Incredible, Lightstone thought, finding it difficult to believe his ears. Ten weeks of delicate undercover work was about to go down the drain, all because some rich asshole couldn't wait another day to bag his illegal bear.

"No deal." He shook his head.

"Look—"

"No, *you* look," Lightstone said firmly. "I really don't give a shit about the money. I've got more goddamn money than I know what to do with. But what I *don't* have is time to waste on bullshit. I've been working on this deal with Alex for months now, and every time we try to get together something goes wrong."

"That's not my—" Wolfe tried to interrupt, but Lightstone ignored him.

"So now I'm finally here," he said firmly, "and I've got a pilot waiting on stand-by, and what I *want* is my goddamned bear. You and your friends want to go along on this little shebang, it's fine by me—" he shrugged "—but I want my bear."

"But we have a time factor also. You know that, Alex," Wolfe persisted, turning to Chareaux to make his argument.

"Henry," Alex Chareaux said quietly, "perhaps we can talk outside."

"Yeah, sure," Lightstone nodded. He followed Chareaux out the door, leaving Reston Wolfe alone and fuming in the motel room. Wolfe had already had to confess to Lisa Abercombie that Gerd Maas wouldn't be coming on this hunt after all, and it wasn't clear that the mercurial woman would still be waiting for him at the restaurant when he finally managed to get this latest problem resolved.

"More money than you know what to do with?" Chareaux asked with curious amusement when they were well clear of the door.

"No such thing." Lightstone said brusquely as they continued walking; he was working hard now to stay in character. "I'm doing okay, but I'm not fucking rich. The guy just got my goat."

"Yes, I understand. Listen, my friend, I apologize for allowing you to become involved in my problem," Chareaux said as they stopped beside the rented Bronco. "And I will not go back on my word in any case, you know that. But I want you also to understand that this man represents—how do you say?—very *big* business to me."

"Alex, if money's really the problem—"

"No, of course not." Chareaux shook his head. "I do not mean it in that way. I am told by your references that you always pay well, and anyway, I would not play such games with you."

"I want that bear, Alex," Lightstone said quietly, being careful now because he knew he was walking right on the edge of entrapment. "Boone and Crockett. You promised me that."

"Yes, I understand. And you will have your record trophy," Chareaux said. "But I must explain to you now that I did not tell the entire truth back there."

"Oh?"

"I said that my brothers and I have located two trophy animals, but that is not actually the case. We have located two animals, yes, but only one of record size. The other is the smaller one I told you about this morning. The woman and the Oriental man would not know the difference, I think, but neither of you would be satisfied with her."

"So now you've got one record bear promised to two trophy hunters. Sounds to me like you have yourself a real problem," Lightstone commented.

"Actually, it is far more complicated than that, because the other two wish to hunt also," Chareaux said. "But yes, you are exactly right. And it is even worse because this man has asked me to arrange a great many hunts for him in the future, and he is very careless about his money."

"In other words, he's a fat cat that you really don't want to lose, because if you play him right, you're going to skin him alive without his ever knowing it."

"You are a businessman, too. You understand these things."

"Alex, I know all about taking advantage of business opportunities," Lightstone said. "And I really sympathize, but—"

"So that is why I am willing to make you a very special offer," Chareaux interrupted. "One that will appeal to you as a businessman."

Lightstone blinked. "Oh, yeah? What's that?"

"There is another bear. It is huge, this one. So big and so aggressive that we have not yet dared to get close enough to make accurate estimates."

"You're offering me a *bigger* bear than the one I'm supposed to get today?"

"Yes."

"So what's the catch?" Lightstone asked, fully aware that Chareaux was playing Henry Allen Lightner's strings like a virtuoso.

"This one is still in the park," Chareaux explained simply. "He will not come out."

"Meaning that we'd have to go after him?" Lightstone asked, stunned; he hadn't expected this at all.

"Yes, exactly," Chareaux nodded. "Of course I don't have to explain to you that the risks involved in such a hunt would be far greater."

"You mean from other animals that might take us by surprise?"

"I mean park rangers, as well as the state wardens and the federal wildlife agents. Because even if it were the season for these bears now, which it is not, this hunt would be completely illegal. If we were caught in the park, we would have no way to explain ourselves."

Lightstone forced himself to hesitate, reminding himself that he was Henry Allen Lightner and that Lightner was still very much afraid of being nabbed by the feds.

"How far into the park would we have to go?" he asked. He was still hesitant for a number of reasons, including the unknown whereabouts of Special Agent-Pilot Len Ruebottom.

"A mile, perhaps. Maybe more, maybe less," Chareaux said. "This one is more difficult to predict because he has claimed a much larger territory than most. He also likes to move around at night, so he will not be easy to locate. We would have to take him at night."

"At night?"

"There is no other way," Chareaux said. "We would wait until very late this evening, and then go in on foot. Just you and I and Sonny. We know roughly where he is right now, so perhaps we would not have too much difficulty."

"A mile or so hike through the woods, at midnight, I assume with no lights, watching out for the park rangers, agents and wardens, to hunt down a bear that scares *you* and *Sonny*? You don't call that difficult?"

"We would use night-vision equipment, of course, and protected radios," Chareaux said, "but even so, we would be limited in our options. For example, you would have only one shot, or perhaps two at the most, because the people in the park would be alerted immediately by the noise."

"That's right," Lightstone concurred.

"One shot, unexpected, would be just an echo in the night," Chareaux went on. "But two, some time apart . . ." He left the rest unspoken.

"If I had any common sense, I'd say no, right now."

"Yes, of course you would, as I would," Chareaux nodded understandingly. "But isn't it true that we are always drawn to the things we fear? The true man who fears the sharks will continue to dive. He who fears the heights will continue to climb. Who are we to change what has always been?"

"So what all this comes down to is that you want me to give up my nice easy hunt for one that's a hell of a lot more risky, just to keep your rich buddy in there happy. Is that about it?"

"That is it exactly," Chareaux agreed. "That is why I make the offer to you. This other one—" he gestured with his head back toward the motel "—I think he is not so much interested in the challenge of the hunt as he is in impressing the woman. I have seen it many times before. It is in his eyes . . . although I think not so much in hers," he added with a smile. "For him, the risks of this special hunt would be much too great."

"I think I know why I'm willing to take the chance," Lightstone said after a moment. "But what about you? I'm paying you good money, but I'm not paying you that much."

"I value you as a customer, and you do not insult me by questioning my word." Chareaux shrugged. "Beyond that, I have caused you difficulty and I would owe you that much in any case. But even so," he added, "there is yet one more condition."

"What's that?" Lightstone asked suspiciously.

"If I have to send one of my brothers out into the park to find your bear, and have the other stay close to the ones we have already located, then I will have no one to assist me in helping my rich fool of a client to impress his woman."

"Yeah, so?"

"So in exchange for a more dangerous amusement later this evening, for which I charge you nothing because he will pay," Chareaux nodded back toward the motel again, "I would ask you to be my assistant now."

"You want me to *work* for you?"

"I think it would not be so much work as perhaps pleasure," Chareaux said. "After all, I am told that your aim is true. You are healthy and strong, the woman is sexy and beautiful, and it is clear that my foolish client has already made her angry for some reason. Who is to say that she would not be more impressed by you than by him?"

"What exactly would I have to do?" Lightstone asked, trying to convince himself that the woman had nothing to do with this.

"Carry a heavy pack. Help my brother to drive the animals. Be there with your rifle if a shot is missed and any of them are in danger. Assist me in cleaning and transporting their trophies. Be available as a distraction if the need should arise." Chareaux shrugged again. "It is not so much."

Only everything that I need to put you away, Lightstone thought, wondering if he was pushing his Henry Allen Lightner role too far.

"It is up to you," Chareaux said. "If you are agreeable, I can go ask him right now."

Lightstone hesitated for one last time, determined to make it look right, because he would never again have a chance like this with Alex Chareaux. Especially not if "transporting their trophies" meant what he thought it meant—that he would be allowed to help deliver the illegally killed animals to the Chareauxs' illegal taxidermist.

Wait until McNulty hears about this, he thought.

"I'm agreeable," he finally said. "Go ahead and ask."

CHAPTER TWELVE

Henry Lightstone watched the door to Room 102 close behind Alex Chareaux's back.

Then, for a few long moments, he just stood there, alone in the parking lot, and thought very seriously about getting back into the Bronco and simply fading away.

He figured that he had five minutes for sure, maybe fifteen at the outside. For that length of time, the fade would still be a viable option. All he had to do was to toss the rifle case and duffel bags in the back of the rented vehicle, get into the front seat, start up the engine, drive right on out of the parking lot, turn left at the intersection, and that would be it.

No more Chareaux brothers, and no more Henry Allen

Lightner. Just Marie, and whatever else he could find to amuse himself with until McNulty came up with another suitable project for the wild-card member of his respected covert team.

Just like the old times.

Hey, man, heard you did the Fade on ol' Papa-Q last night.

Yeah, that's the way it went. One minute I'm right in there, all set to do the deed, and the next minute, wham, I'm gone. Just like that. Never even saw it coming. Just up and walked away.

The gut always knows, man. You gotta listen to it. That Papa-Q's a stone freak from way back. You just let him slide for a while. We'll take him down another day.

The Fade.

That was what they called it when he was buying narcotics in back alleys from crack-crazed freaks. The sudden, unconscious decision to walk away from the deal at the last second because some gut-level instinct didn't like what it saw, or sensed, or heard.

Henry Lightstone was perfectly aware that he was working a wildlife case that had little if anything to do with dope, but that didn't matter, because he knew that Alex Chareaux and Papa-Q were kindred souls . . . amoral creatures who would think nothing of killing a man for the simple pleasure of watching him die.

The Fade. He knew that he could do it. All he had to do was to turn around and walk away. He could do that, and nobody on the Special Operations team—not Paxton, or Stoner, or Scoby, or Takahara, not even McNulty—would ever second-guess his decision, because they understood that it wasn't a question of giving in to fear.

Covert operators, or at least the good ones, knew, understood, and respected fear for what it was: an ancient early warning system that kept the Stone Age hunters alert and wary and alive in situations where most sophisticated thought processes were simply too slow. In effect, a mental trip wire that might just give that hunter a second chance to survive if he was alert, and cautious, and paid careful attention to his instincts.

But it wasn't fear alone that was making Henry Lightstone

consider the Fade. And it wasn't the unexpected appearance of Alex Chareaux's three new clients, who had certainly added a dangerous complication to his carefully worked-out game plan. It was the sudden realization that the pace of the entire operation had accelerated to the point where he no longer had any control over its direction or its timing.

When the door to Alex Chareaux's motel room finally opened fifteen minutes later, Lightstone was still standing there, trying to convince himself that he was ready to face just about anything.

Which, as it turned out, wasn't true at all. Nothing had even remotely prepared Henry Lightstone for the sudden rhythmic thunder of rotor blades as the glistening helicopter swooped down over the Best Western parking lot and then came around in a tight, tail-sweeping turn to hover in a dust-swirling position over the nearby field.

"Tell me, Henry," Chareaux said as he leaned over and patted Lightstone's shoulder, "is this not an incredible surprise?"

"What?" Lightstone rasped, trying not to move his head lest he lose what little equilibrium he had somehow managed to retain. He was trying to decide if tingling arms and legs, clammy skin, and a rapid pulse meant that he was about to faint, or about to be airsick.

"Here, you need your headset on, so we can talk," Chareaux said, reaching up and removing Lightstone's headset from the overhead clip, then helping him adjust the cord and earphones around his throbbing head.

"I said, are you not surprised by all of this?" Chareaux repeated, keying the switch for the cabin intercom on the headset cord as he spoke into the small mouthpiece speaker.

"Yeah, that's the word for it, Alex, no doubt about it," Lightstone nodded weakly.

"Here, we must use this intercom switch if we wish to talk among ourselves," Chareaux said, showing Lightstone how to go back and forth between the helicopter's cabin and pilot intercom systems.

Lightstone wanted Chareaux to take his cheerful little

surprises, and the headset that was already starting to hurt his ears, and his goddamned intercom switches, and stuff them right up there along with his "special hunt." But he couldn't say so because, he figured, it would probably start a fight.

He could blame McNulty and Scoby right off for this, Lightstone told himself, since there had been absolutely nothing in any of the team's extensive intelligence reports to suggest that the Chareaux brothers had ever used any transportation equipment more sophisticated than a four-wheel-drive Jeep.

The background report on Alex Chareaux's illegal guiding operation had been over three hundred pages long. And among other things, it had listed in great detail the methods that Chareaux and his brothers had used during the past three years to take at least twenty-three subjects on a total of eighty-seven illegal hunts.

The information had also included the date and duration of each hunt, the state and county where the hunts took place, the number of species wounded or taken, types and calibers of weapons used, the makes and models of the suspect vehicles, license-plate numbers, types of clothing worn, game tags used or altered, access routes, meeting points, contacts with game wardens, and details of previous hunts discussed over evening camp fires.

Everything that an investigating wildlife officer could possibly want, except for current photographs of Butch and Sonny Chareaux, and the name and location of the taxidermist that the Chareauxs used for mounting their clients' illegal trophies, which was why McNulty had sent Lightstone in on the Chareaux brothers in the first place.

The thing was, Lightstone told himself, if there had been as much as a single instance in which the Chareaux brothers had even *talked* about using a helicopter in one of their illegal hunts, there would have been at least a half dozen cross-indexed references to that fact in the report.

But there had been no mention of helicopters. That was one thing he'd specifically looked for in the index because he was deathly afraid of helicopters. He couldn't imagine McNulty—

or Scoby, who functioned as intelligence officer for the Special Operations Unit and had spent three months working up the information on the Chareaux brothers—being that careless.

"In case anybody back there is interested," the pilot spoke over the intercom, "we're just crossing over into Custer National Forest now."

There was something about the whole situation that nagged at the edge of Lightstone's subconscious. It just didn't read right. He had been working on the assumption that the hunt would have to take place within easy hiking distance of one of the few roads in or around Gardiner. There was no other way for five hunters to get far enough out in the woods on a Sunday afternoon to hunt successfully and then get back to Gardiner by nightfall.

Except, of course, by helicopter.

The helicopter in question was a brand-new Bell Ranger, with plenty of room for the pilot, the copilot, and five passengers with backpacks and rifle cases. According to the copilot, who seemed to know what he was talking about, the aircraft had cost somebody the better part of seven million dollars. Suddenly it dawned on Lightstone that Alex Chareaux's new clients owned the seven-million-dollar helicopter and that it was one hell of an expensive piece of equipment to be used with the likes of Alex and Sonny and Butch Chareaux.

"Are we anywhere near the battlefield?" Lisa Abercombie spoke into her headset speaker, starting to get caught up in the excitement of the hunt.

"You mean Little Bighorn?" the pilot asked, glancing back at Abercombie, who was strapped into one of the center seats just behind the copilot.

"Yes," Abercombie nodded. She turned to Reston Wolfe, who was sitting next to her. "Haven't you always wondered what Custer must have thought when he got up on that hillside and saw all of those Indians?" she asked.

"Last Stand Hill, the actual battlefield, would be, oh, about a hundred miles due east of here," the pilot informed them as he reflexively adjusted the controls to compensate for a sudden air pocket, causing the rumbling aircraft to shudder violently.

"Better hang on back there, folks. It's liable to be a little bumpy for the next couple of minutes," the copilot said cheerfully over the intercom.

Lightstone closed his eyes and gripped the armrests tightly, trying to console himself with the irrational thought that he would have chosen a confrontation with six thousand Sioux and Cheyenne warriors over a chopper ride any day.

"About how long would it take to make a quick loop over the battlefield?" Reston Wolfe asked after keying his headset speaker over to the pilot's channel.

"Oh, I'd say an extra hour, if we take her up to about six thousand feet and give her a little more throttle," the pilot answered. "No problem with the fuel, but it's liable to be a pretty bumpy ride. You sure everybody back there's up to something like that?"

Oh God, no, Lightstone whispered to himself. If he had to stay up in this helicopter another goddamned *hour*—just because one of Chareaux's clients wanted to impress some coldhearted bitch by showing her some goddamned battlefield—

"I think we are running late, so perhaps it would be better if we waited for the next trip," Alex Chareaux said, his gruff voice amplified by the aircraft's headset speakers.

Good man, Chareaux. I take back every lousy thing I ever thought about you, Lightstone nodded gratefully.

"That's fine with me," Lisa Abercombie said agreeably as she gave Alex Chareaux another appraising glance.

"Okay, next trip," the pilot assented. "That's Granite Peak over to the right, and that little spot of water straight ahead is Mystic Lake," he continued in his cheerful litany.

"Is that where we're going to be putting down?" Lisa Abercombie asked.

"Just south of there," the pilot told her.

"It's a magnificent sight," she said as she leaned forward to look over the copilot's shoulder, giving the clear impression that she was just as indifferent to the air turbulence as the two pilots were.

"Worth the price of the ride all by itself," the pilot agreed, joining Lisa Abercombie in amused laughter as the helicopter shuddered violently once again.

Henry Lightstone had no way of knowing that he was in the highly competent hands of two U.S. Army warrant officers who flew armor-plated gunships for a living. These professionals thought nothing of flying an exceptionally airworthy craft like the Bell Ranger through a measly little Rocky Mountain storm, especially when no one was shooting rockets, missiles, or bullets in their direction.

Convinced instead that the aircraft was being flown by daredevil friends of Chareaux's wealthy and obviously insane client, Lightstone simply resigned himself to the fact that he was probably going to die soon in a violent air crash. He tried to console himself with the morbidly cheerful thought that if they did crash, Alex Chareaux would die too, and Henry Allen Lightner's assignment would be concluded.

Chareaux covered the mouthpiece of his headset speaker with one hand and leaned over to talk directly against Lightstone's headset. "I am not one who enjoys flying so much, either." He gestured toward Lightstone's crumpled airsick bag.

"You don't like to fly?" Lightstone asked, reflexively covering his mike.

"No, not at all." Chareaux shook his head. "I would much rather walk for a month than fly for even an hour in an aircraft like this."

"So why the hell did you hire these guys in the first place?" Lightstone demanded weakly.

"Believe me, this was not my doing. All of this was arranged by them," Chareaux said, nodding in the direction of his three new clients.

"Wonderful," Lightstone muttered as he carefully set his head back against the vibrating bulkhead and closed his eyes, vaguely aware that something here seemed important.

"Do not worry, my friend," Chareaux said, patting Lightstone on the shoulder. "One way or another, this will all be over with very soon."

CHAPTER THIRTEEN

Paul McNulty had been waiting by the phone in his Denver office for almost a half hour when Carl Scoby finally called in to report that he, Larry Paxton, Dwight Stoner, and Mike Takahara were on the last leg of a commercial flight to Bozeman.

"Any word on Ruebottom?" Scoby asked after he'd given McNulty the flight number and expected arrival time.

"Nothing so far," McNulty said. "According to the airport manager, the Lear's still sitting there on the tarmac with the wheels blocked and the doors shut. No sign of Ruebottom anywhere in or around the terminal."

"Anybody take a look inside the plane?"

"Not yet. I just finished talking with the airport manager a few minutes ago. It looks like Len amended his flight plan to give himself an open return flight to Great Falls."

"When did he do that?"

"About twenty minutes after they landed," McNulty replied.

"I thought the plan was for him to drop Henry off and then get the hell out of there."

"It was."

"Shit," Scoby cursed. "You know what it sounds like?"

"Ruebottom's hanging around Bozeman to act as a backup for Henry?"

"Exactly."

"You think Henry would go along with that?"

"Hell, no," Scoby snorted.

"So?"

"So that means he's probably doing it on his own, which also means that he's probably sitting on his ass in some bar in Bozeman right now, drinking a beer, with no idea at all that he's giving everybody else on this detail a goddamn coronary."

"I'd like to believe that," McNulty said. "But if that's the case, why hasn't he reported in?"

"Because he's a goddamn rookie, and we should have known better than to use him on a deal like this," Scoby muttered, irritated at himself because he was the one who had talked McNulty into borrowing the rookie agent-pilot from Halahan.

"Ruebottom's a trained agent, and he's supposed to know how to take care of himself in a situation like this," McNulty argued.

"Yeah, well, he's doing a lousy job of it so far," Scoby grumbled. "What about Henry? You hear from him yet?"

"No, and I'm not expecting to for at least another four or five hours. He's supposed to be out on a hunt with Alex Chareaux right now."

"No way to contact him."

It wasn't a question. Scoby knew how Henry Lightstone operated. Completely on his own. No beepers, no transmitters, no backup. Nothing on his person or in any of his luggage or equipment that could be found by the bad guys and used to break his cover. Nothing but guts, brains, incredibly quick reflexes, and an absolute refusal to lose, which was exactly why they had recruited him in the first place.

"Not until he gets back and calls in," McNulty said.

"Any idea where they're hunting?"

"Henry figured they'd end up somewhere between Gardiner and the northern border of Yellowstone, but he also said that Chareaux was pretty vague about the details."

"So you're saying he could be anywhere within a hundred-mile radius of Gardiner."

"That's about it," McNulty said. "All we know for sure is that he rented the car in Bozeman at eleven forty-five and ended up at the Best Western in Gardiner some time before two in the afternoon."

"You sure he checked in?"

"Yeah. I called the motel and asked to speak to him, and they put me through to his room."

"Anybody answer?"

"No. I had one of the locals do a drive-by. They confirmed that his rental car is still out there in the parking lot."

"So hopefully Henry and Alex met like they were supposed to, then took off immediately on the hunt because they're getting such a late start," Scoby said.

"That's the way I figure it. Otherwise Henry would have called in."

"But either way, that still means he's a sitting duck if those bastards scooped up Ruebottom and broke him," Scoby growled. "You want us to try to pull him out?"

"I don't know how you could," McNulty said. "Tell you the truth, right now I'm more worried about Ruebottom than I am about Henry."

"What about Halahan? You going to fill him in?"

"No. Not until I've got something more to go on."

"Christ, this is just what we need—a blown investigation when every goddamn butt-protecting bureaucrat in D.C. is trying to shut Special Operations down."

"It's bad timing all the way around," McNulty agreed. "The way I see it, the only thing we can do now is to put the team in the area and play it by ear. I told the airport manager at Bozeman to stay away from the Lear until one of you guys gets there. No sense in making people suspicious if we don't have to."

"Understood. What do you want us to do when we land?"

"Find a hotel near the airport and set up a command post," McNulty said. "Bozeman's a pretty small place, so you better figure on at least five or six rental cars. Give yourselves enough variation that they don't pick up on a tail. Put everybody on a twenty-four-hour stand-by, ready to move the moment we hear something."

"What about Mike?"

"Send him over to the airport manager's office. I'll see if I can get the manager to rig him up in some kind of official-looking uniform. Airport maintenance, repairman, something like that. Anything that'll let him move around inside and outside the terminal. With any luck, he ought to be able to get in fairly close to that plane."

"Gotcha," Scoby acknowledged.

"Anything else you can think of?" McNulty asked.

"Call Len's wife?" Scoby suggested hesitantly. "See if he checked in with her?"

"I don't want to do that just yet. No sense scaring the hell out of her if we don't have to."

"Yeah, right," Scoby sighed heavily. "The big question. What do we do if we spot Ruebottom in Bozeman? Get him out, or leave him there in place?"

McNulty didn't hesitate for a moment.

"Until we know more about what happened," he said, "we have to assume that Len's being watched and that he's too hot to approach. If anybody spots him, they shouldn't go anywhere near him. If he's in a motel, don't even call his room. Just put on a loose tag, stay as far back as you can, and get ahold of me right away."

"And if we spot him with one of the Chareaux brothers?"

This time McNulty did hesitate.

"Then he's either spilled everything he knows about Henry or he's still holding out," he said finally. "And in either case, if you spot him out in the open, that means they're staking him out as bait."

"So who do we leave hanging, Len or Henry?"

"I don't know. Call me when you get into Bozeman," McNulty said and hung up.

In the cool, crisp mountain air just northeast of Yellowstone National Park, surrounded by reflecting masses of rocky outcrops and high mountain peaks, and watched over by a pair of golden eagles that soared and swooped among the rising thermal currents, things that were actually quite far away could seem very close indeed.

Like a bull elk, with a seven-point rack and a mean disposition, that had been turned and was now heading their way.

They could hear him clearly, coming fast, being driven away from the shelter of the huge trees by the stomping of heavy boots, and thrown rocks, and two carefully placed shots from a thirteen-year-old 7mm Winchester Model 70 that had seemed to echo throughout the entire valley like a Civil War artillery barrage.

Very close, or still far away, it really didn't matter, because it had already been decided that this one was hers.

"Be ready," Alex Chareaux whispered.

About fifteen feet away, Lisa Abercombie braced herself against the trunk of a forty-foot cedar, set the forearm of her eighteen-thousand-dollar .375 Rigby rifle over a low-lying branch, and tucked the hand-carved cheek piece in tight against her right cheek and shoulder. She moved her head slightly to bring the field of the adjustable scope into clear view, gently slipped her right index finger in through the trigger guard and over the trigger, thumbed the safety to the "Off" position, and then began to breathe slowly and carefully as she waited.

They could hear the crashing of the brush more distinctly now. He had to be close. Something in the range of twenty yards, Lightstone guessed as he eased the safety to the "Off" position on his twenty-eight-hundred-dollar bolt-action Mc-Millan Signature Alaskan rifle.

He had purchased the .300 Magnum rifle with some of McNulty's covert funds several months ago. He hadn't really been concerned about the money because he had believed that he was buying exactly the type of weapon that a man like Henry Allen Lightner would have purchased, to bolster both his ego and his image.

But that, of course, was long before Alex Chareaux had described to Lightstone the weapons that his three new clients had brought on their illicit hunt.

Much to Henry Lightstone's amazement, it seemed that the woman's eighteen-thousand-dollar Rigby really wasn't all that big a deal in terms of *serious* big-game hunting; because, according to Chareaux, the two men had armed themselves with a pair of matched Holland and Holland, African Hunter, side-by-side, double-barreled hunting rifles. Both weapons had been chambered for the incredibly powerful .416 Rigby big-game round, and each had been purchased for the tidy sum of one hundred and twenty-five thousand dollars.

The etching alone on the two weapons—again according to Chareaux, who seemed to know what he was talking about—had apparently cost over ten thousand dollars apiece.

Which, Lightstone realized, made his twenty-eight-hundred-dollar McMillan the equivalent of a K-mart special.

"Where will he come out?" Lisa Abercombie asked as she looked out over the telescopic sight of her rifle, talking to Reston Wolfe, who was standing just behind her and to the right.

Wolfe looked over to Chareaux for guidance.

Chareaux spoke into his packset radio, held the speaker against his ear for a few moments, then extended his hand toward a large boulder at the edge of the tree line. It was about two hundred yards out at eleven o'clock.

"To the right of that boulder, this side of those tall pines," he whispered. "Very soon now. Be ready."

From his position a few yards to the left of Chareaux, Henry Lightstone watched the bull elk burst out of the clearing, swing his wide span of antlers in their direction, and then turn to lunge away just as the concussive roar of the woman's .375 Rigby echoed through the trees.

But the magnificent animal reacted too late, and the copper-jacketed soft-point bullet slammed into the midpoint of the bull's massive rib cage, the force of the impact and the subsequent hydrostatic shock sending him staggering forward to his knees.

He started to come back up, shaking his huge antlers and bellowing with pain and rage, and Lightstone heard the oiled clack of the Rigby's silk-smooth bolt action as the woman smoothly ejected the spent casing and fed another round into the chamber.

Standing back at a distance, Lightstone found himself thoroughly impressed by the spirit and resilience of Lisa Abercombie, whom he had initially only been able to imagine as scantily clad in a bedroom. He could tell that the Rigby's sharp recoil had severely jarred her arms and shoulder. But as he watched in amazement, the seemingly unfazed woman brought her weapon back up into firing position without hesitation.

That's it, take your time, Lightstone thought to himself. Keep it tight against your shoulder. Gentle pull, nice and easy.

Lisa Abercombie had the cross hairs of the scope centered at the point where the bull's thick neck joined its shoulder and was about to squeeze the trigger once again when the sound of Chareaux's voice held her back.

"No, he is finished," he said, "but watch out for—"

At that moment, a pair of young females burst into the clearing.

Caught by surprise, Abercombie tried to bring the cross hairs back around to bear on the first of the panicked animals, but they were moving too fast and the shot went high and to the right.

Then, before she could eject and reload for a third shot, Dr. Reston Wolfe brought his Holland and Holland double-barreled rifle up to his shoulder and triggered off two quick rounds.

The first of the 410-grain bullets caught the rearmost elk in the hindquarters, sending her tumbling to the ground in a frenzy of dirt clods, kicking legs, and thrashing torso. The second round-nosed slug struck the lead elk across the side of the head, tearing off most of her right ear and sending her stumbling forward for a few steps before she managed to regain her balance.

Then, seriously injured but still on her feet, she continued to run in a staggering gait away from the direction of the terrible noise and pain.

Lightstone shook his head slowly.

When Alex Chareaux had finally gotten around to introducing his three clients to Lightstone, indicating that their names were Reston Walters, Lisa Allen and Morrey Asato, it had been impossible to miss the fact that only the older Japanese man seemed able to remember his last name well enough to respond in a reasonably timely manner.

Which really didn't matter, Lightstone thought, because even though this Reston Walters—or whoever the hell he was—had absolutely nothing to do with their investigation against the Chareaux brothers, he had already decided that he was going to track the man down some day and give him a lecture on hunting ethics if he couldn't talk McNulty into including the arrogant asshole in the indictment.

Lightstone had watched the man he knew as Walters quickly break open the double-barreled weapon and feed two heavy .416 Rigby cartridges into the side-by-side chambers, which meant that he had two live rounds ready and available that he could use to put both animals out of their misery.

But the pompously arrogant hunter simply stood there, holding the outrageously expensive rifle against his hip, the still-smoking barrels pointed skyward. He shook his head.

"Too small. Not worth bothering about," he commented with an indifferent shrug, apparently having lost all interest in his prey as he reached down to pat Lisa Abercombie on the shoulder, congratulating her on her shot.

For a few long moments, Henry Lightstone watched as the severely injured female on the ground continued to thrash around while her crippled but still mobile companion struggled to put more distance between herself and the hunting party.

Then finally, out of pure revulsion, Lightstone brought the .300 McMillan up to his shoulder with the intention of finishing off both animals, when Alex Chareaux's voice made him pause.

"No," Chareaux whispered as he came up beside Lightstone. "Not yet."

As Lightstone watched the crippled female elk stumble away, the two male hunters continued to hover around their own female companion, the Asian offering his congratulations, while the other man—the ever-pompous Walters—made a show of rubbing her almost certainly bruised shoulder. Then, after a couple of minutes, all three of them walked over to Chareaux and Lightstone, their rifles in their hands.

"We'd like to move over toward those rocks," Reston Wolfe said to Chareaux, pointing toward a large pile of boulders about a half mile east of the clearing. "That's where your brothers saw the bear last night, right?"

"Yes, in that area," Chareaux nodded. "Go on ahead. We will check the kills and then be over there with you in a moment."

Chareaux waited until the three had gone about fifty yards. Then he walked over to the tree that Lisa Abercombie had used as a brace and poked around with a stick until he had located all four of the spent casings. After picking them up and slipping them into his jacket pocket, he waited again until the three hunters had disappeared from sight before he brought the small packset radio up to his mouth.

Moments later, a shot rang out from the general area where the bull elk had first emerged, and the staggering female dropped to the ground and lay still. A second shot, moments later, ended the agonized thrashing of the other one.

Lightstone couldn't tell one rifle shot from another, but he figured that the killing slugs would probably turn out to be from an old 7mm Winchester Model 70. The one that Alex Chareaux had given to his youngest brother, Butch, many years ago.

"You disapprove," Chareaux said, slipping the packset radio back into his jacket pocket as he came up beside Lightstone. The way he spoke the words, it was a statement, not a question.

"If I had ever let a cripple run like that when I was a kid, my grandfather would have taken out his razor strop and beaten me half to death," Lightstone said, aware that he was allowing some of his own background to merge into his Henry Allen Lightner persona.

"Yes, mine also. But I must tell you that most of my clients have had no such training. That is why I must be sure that my brother is always there with his rifle."

"But you waited," Lightstone said half-accusingly.

"The animals are there to be hunted. That is why they are put on this earth." Chareaux shrugged. "And besides, one must always be a businessman first," he added as if that explained everything.

Which it probably did to a cutthroat opportunist like Henry Allen Lightner, Lightstone thought, reminding himself to stay in character.

"So what was that last one, a five- or six-hundred-yard shot?" he asked, making a deliberate effort to shift the topic of conversation.

"Perhaps," Chareaux nodded. "Butch is capable of that, certainly."

At that moment, four quickly spaced shots rang out. Both Lightstone and Chareaux turned in time to see the pair of soaring golden eagles tumble through the sky in a burst of feathers before spinning down to the ground.

"I think, perhaps, that we should catch up with our clients," Chareaux said, "before they kill everything in the valley and draw too much attention to our little game."

CHAPTER FOURTEEN

"McNulty."

"We just checked into the Baxter Holiday Inn, out at the north end of town," Carl Scoby said into the phone, moving aside as Dwight Stoner and Larry Paxton came into the room, their arms loaded with duffel bags and equipment cases.

"Everything clear?"

"So far."

"What have you got for rooms?"

"Mike and I are in two-ten, Dwight and Larry are in two-twelve. Two-fourteen's yours, and we've got two-sixteen on hold for Henry or Len. We've been paying cash for everything, like you said. Had a little trouble with the car rentals. Mike finally had to use a credit card from one of our stand-by dummy businesses."

"Which one?"

"Herpitol Imports, the one we were going to use for the Caiman hide trade."

"Anything going to come back to us on that?"

"Not as long as we pay cash when we drop the cars off," Scoby said. "Of course that assumes we turn them back in one piece," he added thoughtfully. "If not, we're going to end up putting a pretty big dent in our petty-cash account."

As the two muscular agents began to set duffel bags and equipment cases against the wall that separated the two queen-sized beds from the small bathroom, Scoby gestured to Mike Takahara, who quickly put down his soldering iron and moved forward to shut the door and pull the blinds.

"Okay, I'll get all that settled with Purchasing," McNulty said. "What about the comm link?"

"I'll let you talk to Mike," Scoby said. He held the phone out to Takahara. "He wants to know how soon you're going to have that computer hookup ready."

"All set to go, boss." Takahara spoke into the mouthpiece as he reached over and unplugged the soldering iron. "I've got the modem hard-wired into the phone in our room, using one of our handy-dandy little switch boxes as the primary link. I checked out the phone lines, and they're pretty decent. Shouldn't run into any more breakdowns like we had in New York."

"Christ, I hope not," McNulty swore, not wanting to even think about the time he had suddenly lost contact with three of his covert agents—just moments after he had received word from a reliable snitch that the buy of rhino-horn pills that they were scheduled to make from a gang of six armed Haitians had gone sour—when the lines between New York and New Jersey had overloaded and shut down.

It had taken Mike Takahara nearly two hours to restore the contact so that McNulty could finally learn that Scoby, Stoner, and Paxton had survived the incident with only four of the six Haitians sustaining injuries that were serious enough to require hospitalization.

"You can trust me on this one," Takahara chuckled. "We're cool."

"How did you rig the switch?"

"Standard codes. Figured we'd better stick to those because they're the only ones that Henry's worked with so far."

"Straight-in call?"

"Right. All you have to do is ring our room, wait for the tone, and then add the two-digit code for access. Anything else gets you a busy signal."

"Good. What about the lifeline? You manage to get that set up?"

"First thing I did when I got here," Takahara replied. "The eight-hundred number will ring once back at the office, twice at your home as an alert, and then bounce back to the switch box here. You can pick it up at your place or let it go, doesn't matter. Either way, as long as Henry remembers the number and can get to a phone, we'll have him."

"Okay, good. Listen, can you change the dial-up number for my home?"

"Uh, yeah, sure. What's the number?"

McNulty read off a new phone number with a 303 area code.

"Okay, got it," Takahara said. "What happened, you start getting some crank calls?"

"Something like that," McNulty muttered and then smoothly switched the subject. "Any problem with the phone company this time?"

"Nope, we got lucky. I managed to track down a guy at Ma Bell who shows up at some of our tech meetings every now and then," Takahara said. "Turns out he's more of a bigwig than I thought. Took time out from his afternoon tea and crumpets to drop in the connections himself. His boss is going to be calling you for an after-the-fact verification, and I owe him a couple of six-packs. Other than that, it looks like we're home free."

"Okay, we're going to keep the telephone calls in the room down to a minimum anyway," McNulty said. "We'll stay with the computer link for outside messages unless there's an emergency time factor."

"You *really* think the Chareaux brothers are that sophisticated?"

"No, not really, but we know they're dangerous, and I don't see any sense in taking chances. Which also means that you watch yourself out there at the airport if you get anywhere near that plane," McNulty emphasized.

"You got it, boss."

"Okay, let me talk to Carl."

Mike Takahara handed the phone to Carl Scoby, then returned to the task of putting away his tools and electrical equipment.

"Okay, I'm back on," Scoby said.

"I'm heading for the airport in a few minutes. Anything else you guys need out there?"

"Name of the airport manager, for a start," Scoby said, looking over at Takahara, who nodded. "Then you might start looking for a friendly magistrate in case we need a warrant."

"Hold on," McNulty said as he flipped back through two pages of his notebook.

"The manager sounds like he's older than the hills, but he's friendly and cooperative over the phone. Probably ask for him at one of the airline counters. He knows somebody's going to be coming by."

Scoby quickly wrote the name down on one of the motel note pads. He tore off the page and handed it over to Mike Takahara, who glanced at the paper and slipped it into his pocket, then pulled on a light jacket to cover his shoulder-holstered automatic, grabbed one of the small packset radios off the bed and headed out the door.

"Okay, Mike's on his way," Scoby said.

"Good. I'll call the regional office, ask them about the magistrate, see who they got to down there."

"Any word on Henry?" Scoby asked hopefully.

"No, but it's still too early," McNulty said. "We know he rented the car at Bozeman at about eleven forty-five. Assuming he left the airport right away, I figure the earliest he could have met Chareaux and been out on the road would be about one thirty. So that's what, three hours at the outside? Hell, even if they just went out in the woods for a couple of miles and started shooting right away, I don't see how they could possibly get back to the motel before dark."

"Assuming they *do* come back," Scoby muttered darkly.

"Stay positive, Carl," McNulty said, his voice calm and firm. "Henry's a survivor and his cover is tight, so let's keep our focus on Len and see what we can do there. What's the status on Dwight and Larry?"

Scoby looked over at the two agents who were in the process of reassembling their armory. Larry Paxton was fitting and securing the short barrels of a pair of Remington Model-870 pump shotguns into their dull Parkerized receivers, while Dwight Stoner was taking five-round boxes of deer slugs and double-ought buck out of one of the heavy duffel bags and tossing them onto the bed. A pair of extra-large Kevlar vests, three identical SIG-Sauer .45 automatic pistols, leather gear, and extra magazines were already laid out on the bedspread, along with three small scrambled radios and six sets of handcuffs.

"They're loading up for bear and getting ready to hit the streets right now. I'm going to have them make a sweep of the bars and lounges, see if they can get lucky."

"What about the other motels?" McNulty asked.

"The phone directory lists seven places in Bozeman," Scoby said. "We contacted every one of them, and a couple more places outside of town. Far as we can tell, nobody named Ruebottom has checked into a motel anywhere near Bozeman today."

"He might have had help," McNulty reminded. "You use his description?"

"No, I just went with the operators," Scoby said. "Asked them if they'd connect me to his room. Figured we didn't want to take a chance with the desk clerks. Knowing Chareaux, he's probably paranoid enough to have at least a couple of them working on a retainer."

"What about Sonny or Butch? You ask about them, too?"

"No. I didn't want to risk that just yet either," Scoby said. "They're still hanging around Bozeman, and anybody but Alex rings their room, everybody's gonna start getting jumpy. I didn't figure that Henry needed that kind of confusion right now."

"Yeah, you're right," McNulty agreed. "We'll stay clear of the motel lobbies for a while unless we get something specific. What about license plates?"

"We've got four knowns, but they like to switch vehicles a lot," Scoby said. "Dwight and Larry are going to check the parking lots anyway, but I figure if they're worried about the Lear, they're probably going to use something we haven't seen before."

"Makes sense," McNulty agreed again.

"So what's the plan at your end?" Scoby asked, watching as Dwight Stoner and Larry Paxton worked themselves into their shoulder holsters, their normally animated faces now somber. They were experienced field operatives and could sense that something had gone horribly wrong with the Chareaux investigation. Something that most likely involved a careless rookie agent named Len Ruebottom.

"I've got a five-o'clock flight out of Stapleton," McNulty said. "I'll pick up a car at the airport and meet you at the motel."

"You going to rendezvous with Mike when you land, and help him check out that plane?"

"No, I don't think so. Too risky. If these guys are paying attention, they're going to put a tag on Mike the moment he steps foot inside that plane. No sense in burning two of us right off the bat. Which reminds me, you better get him a room in another motel, just in case."

Scoby hesitated for a moment.

"We can probably reserve a couple of rooms at the Prime Rate," he finally said. "It's right across the Interstate. Easy to keep an eye on things."

Paul McNulty had not risen to the position of supervising a covert operations team by being insensitive to the moods of his agents.

"Something the matter?" he asked.

"I guess that's what *we're* wondering," Scoby answered carefully. "I guess we're all wondering why you've got us jumping through so many hoops to work a bunch of low-lifes like the Chareaux brothers. Comm links, message switching, motel cutouts. Christ, you've even got Mike looking over his shoulder. He must have swept this place for bugs at least three times in the past half hour."

Carl Scoby paused, as if hoping that McNulty would break in and offer some sort of explanation, but he didn't.

"Look, Paul," Scoby went on, "we all know that the Chareauxs are dangerous and that this deal with Len Ruebottom is rough, but those guys aren't exactly the KGB either."

"No, they're not," McNulty finally said in a quiet voice. "But I've been picking up some quiet rumblings from the Washington office the last couple of days."

"About what? Our investigation?"

"No, I don't think so," McNulty said. "It's something else. Nothing I can really put my finger on, but there's a bunch of people who are getting awful curious all of a sudden about what kind of cases we're working. Law Enforcement in general, and Special Ops in particular."

"You mean people in the Service?"

"Them, *and* Interior, and maybe even higher up," McNulty replied evenly. "The last guy I talked with was one of the PR types. He got a little more specific. He wanted to know if we were working anything interesting in Idaho, Montana, Colorado, or Wyoming. Looking for some background stuff, so that he could brief the local senators, was the way he put it."

"You're shitting me."

"Then I got a call from one of my old Marine buddies who happens to be one of the top headhunters for the J. Edgar team. He wanted to know if I was bucking for some kind of political appointment. Figured it had to be one hell of a deal to justify a priority screening."

"Somebody's running a background on you?"

"On the two Special Ops teams," McNulty said. "All ten of us," he added pointedly. "And apparently a bunch of other people, too. Law-enforcement types from the other Interior agencies. Park police and park rangers especially. My friend wouldn't say, but I got the impression that it's a pretty big list."

"So it's just some sort of overall departmental sweep?"

"Maybe," McNulty said. "Let's put it this way, you ever been to Terry Grosz's place?"

"You mean his rib joint? Yeah, sure. Why?"

"I'm sitting in Terry's office right now."

"Oh, yeah? I didn't know they were open on Sundays."

"They aren't," McNulty said. "I talked Terry into lending me a key. And while I was at it, I made arrangements for Martha to stay with them for a while, until I get back. That's why I had Mike switch the alert phone to Terry's house."

"You moved Martha out of your house?" Carl Scoby blinked in surprise.

"We had an interesting caller yesterday while I was at the office," McNulty went on calmly. "Guy in his mid-thirties coming around asking for donations, some kind of environmental fund."

"Your typical yuppie activist," Scoby chuckled sympathetically. "We get our share of those, too."

"Yeah, well, according to Martha, this one looked a whole lot more like the lead man on a SWAT team."

Carl Scoby felt a cold chill run down the back of his neck.

McNulty didn't have to explain the significance of his statement. Everyone on the team knew that Martha McNulty's older brother had recently retired as commander of the Los Angeles Police Department's Special Weapons and Tactics Unit. The McNulty household had been a social gathering point for many of LAPD's finest when Paul McNulty was senior resident agent of the Fish and Wildlife Service's Long Beach office.

And having served more meals to more special agents, game wardens, cops, narcs, and SWAT team members than she cared to think about, Martha McNulty often claimed that she could walk into a room and pick out the covert operators almost immediately. Something about the set of their shoulders, and their eyes, and the way they moved.

"That doesn't necessarily mean anything," Scoby suggested cautiously.

"No, it doesn't," McNulty agreed. "But Martha remembered that the guy had personal checks from a couple of our neighbors on his clipboard, so this morning I went around and talked to the people in our cul-de-sac. Seems that he made his pitch to three houses before us, but nobody after us."

"Okay, but—"

"And before I forget," McNulty interrupted, "tell Larry that I made similar arrangements for Dasha and the kids. They're getting on a plane for Jamaica tomorrow morning. Going to stay with the grandparents for a couple of weeks. I told her it was a surprise from Larry, to make up for him being gone all the time."

"What the hell's *that* all about?"

"Same guy showed up at Dasha's place Saturday afternoon. Same description and same pattern. Three houses before, none after."

"Jesus," Scoby whispered after a long moment. "What the hell did we trip over?"

"I don't know," McNulty said. "Maybe nothing. *Hopefully* nothing. For all I know, this may be nothing more than a routine sweep. Update on our security clearances. Something like that."

"You think the Chareauxs might be involved in all this?"

"First thing I thought of, but I don't see how," McNulty answered. "If they're looking at us as a team, it's got to be one of two things. It's either the specific individuals that we're targeting, or the fact that we're a covert team, and therefore represent a potential threat."

"To somebody with a guilty conscience?"

"Presumably."

"And since everything's pretty much shut down right now *except* for the Chareaux operation—"

"That kinda narrows it down, doesn't it," McNulty muttered sarcastically.

"You check in with John?" Scoby asked, referring to John Marsh, chief of the Fish and Wildlife Service's Law Enforcement Division.

"First thing I did," McNulty said. "As far as he knows, there's nothing going on. They've been getting a lot of questions from the Hill about field operations in general during the last couple of weeks, but he figures it's probably just some posturing over the budget."

"What about Internal Affairs?"

"He doesn't think so," McNulty told him. "Unless the chief himself is a primary suspect, the IA boys have to check in with him first before they start any kind of serious investigation of anybody in the division. Outside of the Haitian counsel flap, which is just about wrapped up anyway, he hasn't heard a word about any of us for the last couple of months. Far as he knows, we're all clean, and he mentioned that he'd like us to stay that way for a while."

"So why the FBI probe?"

"The only thing he can figure is that maybe it's a couple of high-level game-players with nothing better to do than rummage around the department, looking for some dirty laundry before they make a run on somebody else's turf."

"That's happened before."

"Yeah, no shit," McNulty muttered. "And with any luck, that's *all* this is. But I want to be damn sure before I stop looking over my shoulder."

"Okay, so how do you want us to . . . hold it," Scoby whispered, the tone of his voice suddenly taking on a tense urgency as everyone in the motel room heard the distinctive sound of a key being forced into the outer door lock of room two-ten.

CHAPTER FIFTEEN

Alex Chareaux had been right after all, Henry Lightstone decided. The bear *was* a monster.

As best as he could judge from his vantage point, it was bigger than any grizzly he had ever seen, including the stuffed mounts that had been prominently displayed behind glass in the lobby of the Anchorage Hilton.

Lightstone was hopeful that the bear wouldn't be all that active for the next half hour or so. Not with a tranquilizer-dart dose of sodium secobarbital still swimming through its bloodstream.

But then, too, Lightstone reminded himself, all of that just might change if somebody with more guts than brains decided to do something *really* stupid.

Like ricocheting a navel orange-size rock off a huge male grizzly bear's thick skull.

After bracing himself against the protective bulk of a fifty-foot Douglas fir and checking with his thumb to make absolutely certain the safety of his rifle was in the forward "off" position, Lightstone used his right hand to remove the small packset radio from his jacket pocket.

Then he looked over at Butch Chareaux, who was standing about thirty yards back and to his right, his old weatherbeaten 7mm Winchester rifle held up in the ready position. Lightstone waited until Chareaux waved his hand to indicate that he was all set before he keyed the radio mike.

"Okay," he whispered. "I've got him in sight."

"Describe your position," Alex Chareaux demanded, his voice sounding clear and very close through the expensive digital radio.

Lightstone looked out around the big Douglas fir, made an estimate of the distance, and decided that he was much too close by at least a factor of three.

"I'm about twenty yards away from the bear right now," he said quietly into the radio's external microphone. "I figure that puts me just about due south of your position, maybe a hundred and fifty yards at the outside. There're a couple of pretty steep gullies with a lot of rocks and trees between us, but the way he's positioned right now, we ought to be able to keep him running straight in your direction."

"What is he doing now?"

"Sitting on his ass, rocking his head back and forth like it weighs a couple hundred pounds, making some kind of weird grunting noises. Acts like he's got one hell of a hangover," Lightstone said uneasily.

"The drugs should start to wear off soon now," Chareaux acknowledged. "Does he know that you and Butch are there?"

"I think so, but it's kinda hard to tell," Lightstone said, ready to drop the radio and bring the heavy-barreled .300 McMillan up to his shoulder the moment the huge bear made the slightest move in his direction.

"He will still be confused by the drugs for a while, so he should not be too difficult to move," Chareaux said. "You know what to do then, do you not?"

"Pretty much. I just hope to hell somebody gave a copy of the script to the bear, too."

"It is just as I promised you, Henry—" Chareaux said reassuringly "—an adventure unlike anything that you've ever had before."

"Okay, Alex, just tell me when," Lightstone said.

Alex Chareaux looked around to confirm that his three hunters were in position, with Reston Wolfe in the center, braced against a fallen oak; Lisa Abercombie about fifteen yards to Wolfe's left; and Dr. Morito Asai an equal distance to his right. All three were facing the area where Chareaux had predicted the bear would most likely appear.

"We're ready here," Chareaux whispered into his radio. "Do it now."

Taking a deep, steadying breath, Henry Lightstone propped the beautifully finished McMillan up against the tree with his left hand and then slowly knelt down and picked up a pair of rocks that were sitting by his boots, each of which was about the size of a large navel orange.

Then, after slipping one of the rocks into his jacket pocket and holding the other in his gloved hand, he slowly stood up and looked over at Butch Chareaux, who gave him a thumbs-up sign.

Okay, McNulty, Lightstone thought to himself, I hope to hell you and Scoby and that maniac Stoner are going to appreciate this.

After picking up his rifle and holding it tightly in his left hand, Lightstone took in one last deep breath and stepped away from the tree, nervously aware that the bear was staring groggily in his direction.

Sliding his boots forward in slow, easy steps, Lightstone moved closer to the huge animal, until his right foot crunched down on a small twig.

The sound seemed to focus the bear's attention, resulting in a low, guttural *"Woof!"* as it slowly brought its huge furry body around to a position where it could watch the approaching upright figure without having to lift its head.

Lightstone froze. Now that he was out in the open and fully exposed to a sudden charge, the huge grizzly looked a least twice as big as it had from behind the protective bulk of the fifty-foot Douglas fir. It seemed to be increasingly aware of its surroundings, as though the sound of the snapping twig had activated some sort of survival mechanism that was helping it to counteract the dwindling effects of the secobarbital.

For a long moment, Henry Lightstone and the bear remained in their respective positions, each staring silently at the other.

Then, in an act of pure madness, Lightstone lunged forward in a headlong charge toward the squatting bear, yelling as loud as he could as he heaved the rock at the large cluster of pinecones hanging just above the bear's head.

Lightstone had previously decided to aim for the

pinecones—instead of for the bear's head as Butch Chareaux had advised—because he hoped that the noise of the falling cones might confuse and scare the huge animal, rather than making it madder than hell.

But Lightstone hadn't counted on the grizzly suddenly bringing its head up in an instinctive response to the sound of his voice. Thus, instead of sending a shower of pinecones tumbling down over the bear's broad head, the orange-sized rock caught the unsuspecting grizzly right square in the center of its much-too-sensitive nose.

Still running forward and now less than a dozen yards away, Lightstone had already started to pull the second rock out of his jacket pocket when the huge bear roared in pain and fury, and then suddenly rose up on its oddly short and stubby legs to its full, terrifying height of over nine feet, with its four-inch claws fully extended and savage mouth wide open.

Lightstone took less than a half second to realize that he had made a horrible and possibly fatal mistake before his survival instincts took over.

Screaming as loudly as he could once again, he heaved the second rock at the still-dangling clump of pinecones next to the grizzly's head and then frantically swung the heavy barrel of the McMillan around as the impact of the rock sent pinecones spinning away from the tree in all directions.

One of the sharp-edged cones caught the huge bear across the eye. The big creature slashed awkwardly at it with a massive paw. The rapid-acting barbiturate was clearly still affecting the grizzly's motor reactions and coordination; but from Henry Lightstone's stunned perspective, the animal's incredible strength seemed untouched.

Suddenly the huge bear turned its attention back to the puny creature that was now less than a dozen feet away. Furiously intent on ripping this new adversary to bloody shreds with its incredibly powerful claws, the bear lurched forward on unsteady legs, claws outreached and teeth bared. The sticklike object in the human's hand suddenly exploded with a horrendously *loud* noise as a high-velocity slug streaked past the bear's right ear.

Lightstone hadn't had time to bring the rifle up to his shoulder, and the recoil of the detonated .300 Magnum round almost tore the powerful weapon out of his hands. But more important, the shock effect of the concussive explosion so close to the bear's face gave Lightstone the opportunity to do the one thing that he figured just might save his life.

Which was to run like hell.

Lightstone made a desperate lunge for the nearby trees, but the only thing that truly saved him in those first few seconds was the fact that the bear had turned its head away from the muzzle blast and the eye-stinging spray of burning gunpowder.

Thus by the time the grizzly blinked its eyes clear and realized what had happened, Lightstone had already disappeared into the surrounding woods in a fully panicked sprint.

Running faster than he had ever run in his life, Lightstone managed to put about twenty yards between himself and the clearing at his back when he heard the unmistakable sounds of the bear tearing its way through the brush and trees in hot pursuit.

Lightstone hadn't thought that he could run any faster, but the fearsome roars and grunts of the infuriated bear, the crash of dried brush being trampled and uprooted, and the splintering sounds of tree limbs being ripped from their trunks provided the incentive his shaky legs needed.

The next thirty seconds of Henry Lightstone's life flew by in a blur of slippery pine needles, thorny vines, entangling branches, and torn clothing as he scrambled up the rocky slope of the gully and over what seemed to be hundreds of exposed and interwoven tree roots.

Somewhere in the middle of those seemingly endless thirty seconds, Lightstone managed to work the bolt action of the McMillan, driving and locking another .300 Magnum round into the chamber of the powerful rifle, whose beautifully finished stock was now gouged and scratched and muddy from numerous impacts against rocks and trees and anything else that had stood in Lightstone's frenzied path. But he'd held on to the rifle as a last-ditch desperation option even though he wasn't at all sure that with one shot he could kill an animal the size of the enraged grizzly.

The next slope was steeper, and covered with rocks and slippery mats of long pine needles. He lost ground as his boots dug for traction. But the trees up ahead were closer together, and that gave Lightstone something in the neighborhood of a two-second advantage as he zigzagged between the thick trunks like a pro halfback and then flung himself through a tangle of brush and smaller trees that suddenly opened into another clearing.

The sound of the bear as it came ripping and roaring through the brush at his back, and the volley of rifle shots that seemed to come from everywhere at once, echoed in Henry Lightstone's ears as he felt the claws reaching and then tearing into the back of his jacket.

He started to come around to his left with the rifle, determined to jam the heavy barrel into the raging creature's mouth and pull the trigger if it was the last thing he did in his life.

But then one of the incoming .416 Rigby slugs tore the rifle out of his hand and another spun him around in the opposite direction, mercifully silencing the bellowing screams of the fearsome beast as Lightstone tumbled down into a warm and liquid darkness.

CHAPTER SIXTEEN

The first of the three men who pushed the door of Room 210 open and lunged in yelling, "Surprise, you son of a bitch!" was incredibly fortunate that Special Agent Dwight Stoner happened to be standing closer to the doorway than to the bed.

The result being that he caught Stoner's thick-knuckled fist in his eye instead of the butt of a 12-gauge pump shotgun. Fortunate or not, the impact still sent him headfirst over the side of the second-floor railing.

The second and third members of the intoxicated raiding party—the ones holding the .44 Ruger rifle, the three bottles of inexpensive champagne, *and* the video camera for filming their presumably "otherwise occupied" newlywed friends—were even more fortunate.

Instead of following their friend over the railing, they simply found themselves sprawled out on the second-story walkway next to the three shattered magnums of champagne. Twin SIG-Sauer 45-caliber automatic pistols were aimed at their heads, while an incredibly large, snarling, and absolutely terrifying man pinned them to the rough concrete walkway, his muscular hands pressing the stock of the .44 Ruger rifle across their exposed throats.

Paxton tried to explain to the stunned, shaken, and still-trembling celebrants that ex-tackles from the Oakland Raiders sometimes just couldn't control themselves. Then he and Scoby helped the men down to their car so they could check on the condition of their decidedly less fortunate companion.

Fifteen minutes later, Scoby remembered what he had been doing before the unexpected assault on their motel room. Shaking his head, he went back up the stairs and retrieved the phone off the floor.

"Sorry about that," he said as he sat down into the chair again with a loud sigh.

"Jesus H. Christ, what the hell's going *on* out there?" Paul McNulty demanded.

"Well, as best as we can tell, it seems that we were the unintended target of a little honeymoon surprise."

"*What?*"

"Three men, mid-twenties, drunk on their collective asses," Scoby explained. "Armed with a video camera, three bottles of champagne, and a .44 Ruger autoloading rifle, the last two of which were supposed to be gifts. At least that's what they claim. Or rather, that's what two of them claim," he corrected after a moment's thought. "The third one isn't up to talking just yet. Last time I looked, the police and the paramedics were still extracting him out of the front windshield of his car."

There was dead silence on the other end of the line.

It took McNulty a few moments.

"You mean they came in on you guys because they thought—" He couldn't bring himself to finish the sentence. "They went to the wrong room?"

"Oh, no, right room. Just the wrong motel," Scoby said. "Apparently they were so busy negotiating with the desk clerk for the extra key that they didn't happen to notice the sign that said Holiday Inn."

"So what happened?" McNulty forced himself to ask. He hadn't heard any shots, but the crash of broken glass, the sound of Stoner's fist colliding with tissue and bone, and the agonized gasps as the ex-Raider's scarred knees slammed down hard into a pair of flabby stomachs had been unmistakable.

"It seems that the Lord, in His infinite wisdom, continues to watch out for all of the drunk assholes of the world," Scoby said with an exasperated sigh. "Stoner caught the first guy square on the button, put him back over the walkway railing. Then he gang-tackled the other two before we could shoot them," he added in a tone that suggested some undefined level of disappointment. "Understandably, they surrendered on the spot. Also pissed their pants."

"Was anybody hurt?"

"No friendly casualties, other than Stoner's knuckles, but he says they don't bleed much anymore anyway. No big deal. Nothing too serious on the other side."

There was another long pause as McNulty considered some of the ramifications of Scoby's summary report.

"The guy who went over the railing. I take it he's okay?" he finally asked in a hopeful voice.

"Well, no, not exactly," Scoby hedged. "His nose is definitely not okay, and his car doesn't look much better.

Couple of pretty serious dents in the hood and roof, and the windshield's all over the parking lot. He's probably going to have a hard time explaining things to his insurance company, but other than that, he seems to have survived the incident fairly well. Apparently there's a lot to be said for being unconscious when you land face-first on the roof of your car. Anyway, the cops and the paramedics were pretty impressed."

"Who called them?"

"The desk clerk. She claims that she had second thoughts about accepting a two-hundred-dollar bribe, but I think the rifle was the kicker. Probably worried that she was setting somebody up for a bullet."

"Nice of her to be concerned," McNulty muttered sarcastically. "Everything okay with the locals?"

"Yeah, I think so. We've got three uniforms, the field supervisor, and the watch commander out here, which I think is probably the entire shift, but everybody's being cooperative. Larry and Dwight are out there right now giving them enough of a story to keep the paperwork straight."

"Are they going to take them in?"

"Yeah, looks like it," Scoby said. "Apparently no one in the group was sober enough to have driven here legally, so they're all gonna get put on ice for about twenty-four hours. Drunk driving, disturbing the peace, littering the parking lot. Couple down below got a little shook up when they looked out their window and saw the guy land on his car, but outside of that, everything seems to be settling down."

McNulty was silent for a few moments.

"Listen," he finally said, "are you absolutely certain that this thing wasn't a probe?"

"Paul, to tell you the honest-to-God truth, I think the whole thing's too fucking absurd to be anything *but* the truth," Scoby said. "We're going to check out their hotel just to make sure. You think we ought to move the command post?"

McNulty hesitated. "Yes, I do, but that means shutting down the communications system, right?"

"Afraid so, unless we wait for Mike. He should be back pretty soon, though. Anyway, if we left right now, Mike wouldn't know how to find us unless we contacted the airport."

"You guys have been made, and we don't know if Alex Chareaux has connected with the locals," McNulty said. "What about the radios?"

"Mike's got a packset with him for emergency use, but it's a one-way deal. It's not likely he's going to be in any position to leave it on."

"Which means that if he *does* find something in that plane, we're not going to know about it until he tries to call in—or goes back to the motel, and finds out you've moved."

"That's about it," Scoby acknowledged. "I'll try to get us checked in over at the Prime Rate. That's the place right across the freeway, so we shouldn't have any problem picking up a radio call when he tries to find us. Trouble is, where does that leave Henry?"

"He's still got the lifeline," McNulty said. "I had Mike reroute the link to Terry's house before he went out to the airport. I'll give Terry a call before I leave, make sure he knows that you're relocating."

"Yeah, that's fine, but maybe you ought to work it out so that Martha's the one who answers the phone. Far as I know, I don't think that Henry and Terry have ever met."

There was a short pause on the other end of the line.

"Shit," McNulty muttered.

"What's the matter?"

"Martha left about a half hour ago. She was going to drop off the dogs at the kennel, run some errands and do some shopping. Last I heard, she wasn't planning on getting up to Terry's until nine or ten this evening."

"Can you get ahold of her?"

"Not unless I put out an APB on her car."

"Christ, if Henry hears a strange voice on the other end of that lifeline, he's just going to hang up."

Carl Scoby could almost hear McNulty's mind churning.

"I'm getting too goddamned old for this kind of shit," the team leader finally muttered.

"You and me both," Scoby said in heartfelt agreement.

"Okay," McNulty sighed, "here's what we'll do. We've still got a fair amount of time before Henry should be coming back from that hunt, so let's make good use of it. You turn Dwight and Larry loose, see if they can get a lead on Ruebottom. I'll make sure Terry knows where to contact us in case somebody calls him and then hangs up. In the meantime, it shouldn't take Mike long to find out what's going on with that Lear jet, so if we're even halfway lucky, he'll find you guys and get back in time to reconnect the communications system before Henry tries to report in."

"You do realize that this is beginning to sound like New York all over again," Carl Scoby commented dryly.

"Yeah, tell me about it. That's why I'm heading down there. I'll be damned if I'm going to spend another night sitting around on my ass by a phone, waiting to find out if I still have a team."

"Sounds good to me," Scoby said gratefully, more than willing to hand the supervision of *this* detail over to McNulty. "Anything else you want done before you get here?"

"Just make sure everybody down there stays alert," Mc-Nulty emphasized. "We don't need any more goddamned incidents drawing attention to what we're doing. And keep in mind that until Henry gets back from the hunt and starts calling around trying to find his pilot, there's no reason why somebody should be looking real hard for a guy named Len Ruebottom."

"Maybe we're trying to hook him up for another charter?"

"No, I think we'd be pushing our luck trying something like that. Henry's got Chareaux convinced that he's a big enough player to have a plane of his own on stand-by twenty-four hours a day. But even so, we took a hell of a chance using the Lear. A plane like that is way out of Henry Lightner's league."

"So now Chareaux has to figure that Henry's got himself some kind of Sugar Daddy hanging around in the background, which is bound to make him a little uneasy, because we set up Lightner as an independent operator," Scoby said.

"That's right. But to a guy like Chareaux, the smell of

serious money is like blood in the water for a shark. So he starts sniffing around . . ."

". . . and comes across a rookie agent named Len Ruebottom thrashing about on the surface like a goddamned cripple," Scoby finished dourly.

"Exactly."

"You really think they made him?" Scoby asked. Stoner and Paxton had come back into the room and were now sitting on the bed, staring at him.

"Yeah, I'm starting to think it's a strong possibility."

"So where does that leave Henry?"

"I don't know. That's the problem."

"There's always the chance that they made Ruebottom as an agent, but then came to the conclusion that he's working on Henry instead of on them," Scoby suggested. "Be a hell of a cover, when you stop to think about it."

"That's a possibility, too," McNulty acknowledged. "Henry told Alex that he's been hunting illegally since he was a kid and that he's got one hell of a trophy collection hidden away somewhere."

"Christ, with clients like that, the Chareauxs ought to *expect* the feds to be snooping around," Scoby said.

"Sure, hazards of the game. But would they be crazy enough to take Lightner out on a hunt if they knew he had a federal wildlife agent right on his ass?"

"Any halfway sane crook would have been long gone by now," Scoby agreed, "but I wouldn't put the Chareaux brothers in that category."

"No, I wouldn't either," McNulty agreed. "Especially not Alex. And that's exactly what's bothering me right now. I'd like to believe that everything's on track and that Len Ruebottom's just sitting around in a bar somewhere in Bozeman wondering if he's going to get his butt chewed for not doing as he was told. And I'd also like to believe that Henry's going to show up sometime in the next three or four hours with all the evidence we need to put these coon-ass bastards away for good."

"But you don't think so, do you?"

"No, I don't."

"So how long do you figure we've got?"

"We'll let it run until ten o'clock. That's about," McNulty checked his watch, "five and a half hours from now."

"Ten P.M., check," Scoby said as he marked the time down in his case notebook. "And after that?"

"If we don't hear from Len or Henry by ten o'clock," McNulty said, his voice taking on a cold chill, "the five of us are going to drive down to Gardiner and have a nice heart-to-heart talk with Alex Chareaux. And in the meantime, let's just hope that Mike's gotten something useful out of that goddamn plane."

CHAPTER SEVENTEEN

"It's almost twenty to eight. We're going to be late," Butch Chareaux whispered to his brother, who nodded his head solemnly.

"Yes, I know," Alex Chareaux said as he continued to watch the bizarre ritual being carried out before his disbelieving eyes with a mixture of disgust and helpless frustration. "But they are the clients. There is nothing that we can do."

"But Lightner—" Butch Chareaux started to protest, but his brother waved him off.

"Lightner is no longer a problem," Alex Chareaux said firmly. "It is simply a matter of timing now. Before this night is gone, one way or the other, it will all be resolved."

Timing.

From the moment that Reston Wolfe had called to demand a change in their scheduled hunt, time had been a key factor in Alex Chareaux's planning, and a crucial element in provid-

ing a suitable demonstration for Wolfe and his incredibly
wealthy new clients.

But now time had become the enemy because it had taken
them much longer than Chareaux had anticipated to "find" the
smaller female grizzly and set the scene so that Dr. Morito Asai
could have his kill. Mostly because he and his brothers had
overestimated the bear's weight when they had switched over
from the maintenance doses of phenobarbital to the controlling
dose of the far more powerful but shorter-acting secobarbital.

As a result, it had been necessary for Butch Chareaux to
spend almost half an hour poking and prodding the nearly
unconscious bear—first with the barrel of his Model 70
Winchester and finally with an electric cattle prod—before he
was able to get her out of the hidden cage. And even then it
had taken another five minutes of increasingly powerful jolts
from the prod before Butch Chareaux was finally able to force
the terrified young bear up onto her weak and trembling legs,
and then drive her through the forest into the fatal path of Dr.
Morito Asai's one-hundred-and-twenty-five-thousand-dollar
double-barreled rifle.

But having learned their lesson from the previous shooting
incident involving their supposed new partner, Butch
Chareaux was careful to stay *behind* the frantically stumbling
bear and to duck down at the proper moment. And Alex
Chareaux had been equally careful to place his trigger-happy
clients in positions that gave them a clear field of fire with
their expensive, high-powered weapons.

So as a result, the second grizzly kill had been quick and
easy and relatively uneventful.

Which meant that they still should have had plenty of time
to load the bull elk, the eagles, the two bears, Lightner, *and*
their hunters into the two camouflaged pickup trucks, drive
out onto the paved road, and get to the small town of Fishtail and the previously designated phone booth by eight
o'clock that evening. Exactly as the three brothers had
planned it all out in their Bozeman motel room after having
received the unexpected call from Dr. Reston Wolfe less than
ten hours ago.

But it wasn't working out that way.

And it could all be traced back to Reston Wolfe's damnable arrogance, Alex Chareaux decided.

Chareaux was irritated because Wolfe, in his predictably insolent and patronizing manner, had offered him and his brothers the possibility of riches beyond their wildest dreams. But in doing so, he had placed them in a position of having to face the necessity—and the inherent dangers—of taking on a partner like Henry Allen Lightner.

So in what little time that remained before Henry Allen Lightner would be landing at Bozeman Airport, Chareaux and his brothers had been forced to come up with a makeshift plan that just *might* enable them, within the space of eight short hours, to determine the true nature of their proposed new partner. But in setting up the quick demonstration hunt for Wolfe, and in laying out their carefully orchestrated timetable to reveal any flaws in the supposed background of Lightner, Alex Chareaux had failed to anticipate yet another critical factor that would bring his entire operation to a stumbling halt.

In this case, it was the ancient cultural traditions of Dr. Morito Asai.

"No, must take the gallbladders first. Very important," Asai had argued insistently when Butch Chareaux started to back the winch-mounted pickup truck up against the huge carcass of the male grizzly.

And then, before Alex or Butch Chareaux could do anything to stop him, Dr. Morito Asai had proceeded to sit himself down in front of the slain bear and cut into its belly with an incredibly sharp knife that looked like a miniature version of the samurai's traditional *katana* sword.

"What is he *doing*?" Butch Chareaux had demanded in a choked and disbelieving voice, but his brother had simply pulled him aside and told him to shut up, because their new clients had agreed to spend fifty thousand dollars a week on their illegal hunts, with a minimum guarantee of fifty weeks. And if earning two and a half million dollars meant that they would be forced to stand by while their insane clients cut open the stomachs of their bears and removed their gallbladders, then that was the way it would have to be.

"But the smell," Butch Chareaux had groaned, watching in dismay as the diminutive hunter reached into the grizzly's abdominal cavity with his bare arms and removed a bloody organ about the size of an Idaho potato. With the tip of the sharp blade, Asai cut a small slit in the gallbladder.

Working slowly and carefully so as not to spill the precious fluid, Asai poured a bit of the dark bile over a small, cup-sized bowl of rice. Then, after quickly placing the gallbladder in a self-sealing plastic bag, he proceeded to eat the soaked rice with a pair of chopsticks that he produced from the inner pocket of his hunting jacket.

Polite as always, Asai had offered to share this delicacy with his companions, but Reston Wolfe and Lisa Abercombie hurriedly declined, and the two Chareaux brothers simply pretended that they didn't understand.

Instead, they had continued to load their clients' expensive hunting gear back into the short-bed pickup with the camper shell. They used the sleeping bags and Henry Lightstone's limp body to cushion the two incredibly expensive Holland and Holland rifles until the weapons could be broken down, cleaned, and returned to the twenty-two-hundred-dollar mahogany cases that had been left in the helicopter.

Then, muttering to himself in words that he had first learned at the knee of his Cajun grandfather, Butch Chareaux helped his brother winch the larger bear into the back of the larger pickup truck. Dragging the half-ton animal up next to the carcass of the bull elk, he grunted as the smell of blood and severed intestines began to fill the air.

They stood then in the twilight next to the camper shell, waiting for Dr. Asai to complete his ritual with the second bear.

"If we miss Sonny's call, what will we do with Henry?" Butch Chareaux asked as they watched Asai set the fresh bowl of rice down next to the smaller bear.

"If we miss the eight-o'clock call, Sonny knows to call again at ten. We will know then." Alex Chareaux shrugged with feigned indifference, not wanting Butch to know how badly he wanted to hear from their brother. How badly he wanted to *know*, one way or the other, before it was too late.

"But we have to be at Jacall's by ten. Do we take him there with us?"

"If necessary, we will take him to Jacall's and dispose of him there," Alex Chareaux told him, relieved to see that Dr. Asai was finally finished with the second bear.

"But the risk?"

"There are always risks, my brother." Alex Chareaux shrugged once more as he began walking toward the already overloaded pickup. "Come. If we hurry, perhaps we can still get to Fishtail by ten."

CHAPTER EIGHTEEN

Command Sergeant Major Clarence MacDonald had spent the better part of his thirty-two years in the United States Army helping to train Green Beret teams to reconnoiter, stalk, and kill their enemies with weapons that ranged from bare hands, rocks, wire, knives, and silenced firearms to far more sophisticated laser-guided rockets and miniaturized nuclear ordnance.

The men who graduated from his courses were considered to be some of the most skillful, creative, and deadly soldiers that the world had ever known, and they had been demonstrating the effectiveness of their training in remote battlefields throughout the world for the past two decades.

But aside from the British Army's Special Air Service Squadrons in general, and perhaps three or four Special Forces teams that he could remember specifically, MacDonald was convinced that he had never addressed a group of individuals whose expertise in weaponry, tactics, communications, reconnaissance, intelligence gathering, logistics, demolitions, guerrilla warfare, and hand-to-hand combat had come even close to that of the ICER assault group that sat before him in this underground conference room.

And for perhaps the first time in as far back as he could remember, MacDonald was standing before a man whose lethal skills in one-on-one combat situations were rumored to match, or possibly to even exceed, his own. As MacDonald gazed calmly into the pale eyes of Assault Group Leader Gerd Maas, however, he felt only professional curiosity, and even pleasant anticipation. In truth, he was looking forward to finding out for himself if the eye-opening reports and evaluations on Gerd Maas had any basis in reality.

At precisely 1930 hours, MacDonald stepped up to the raised podium that faced twenty-four padded theater chairs arranged on an upwardly sloping six-by-four grid. He stared out across the brightly lit room at the members of the assault group, all of whom were dressed in mountain-camouflaged military fatigues.

MacDonald noted immediately that one member of the Japanese contingent, Dr. Morito Asai, was missing.

"Gentlemen, *and* ladies," he added in deference to the three woman who comprised one quarter of the ICER assault group, "it is my pleasure to welcome you to the Whitehorse Cabin Training Center. Allow me to introduce myself. My name is Clarence MacDonald, and as some of you are aware, I am privileged to hold the rank of command sergeant major in the United States Army."

MacDonald scanned the eleven alert faces.

"Some of you I know from previous training sessions. The rest of you are familiar to me only by the information in your personnel files. But I want to begin this session by making certain that one thing is absolutely clear. I am not here as your training sergeant, but rather, as your host."

MacDonald paused for effect.

"It is clear that the United States Government has gone to

a great deal of effort to recruit and equip a top-notch counterterrorist team. Why this team has been established, and who your targets will be, has not been revealed to me. And I would emphasize the fact that such information is not of any concern or interest to the Whitehorse Cabin training staff.

"According to your records," MacDonald went on, "each one of you possesses an incredible amount of training and practical experience, both as a field operative and as an instructor. It is also apparent that you are well versed in general field operations, and that you each make the effort to maintain a high level of proficiency in your own area of expertise. Therefore, in my view," MacDonald said in his quiet but firm voice, "it would be a waste of time to provide a training course for you in the classical sense. Instead, we intend to make ourselves available to do three specific things.

"First of all," MacDonald raised a single callused finger, "we will provide you with the resources necessary for each of you to maintain and enhance your own personal skills.

"Second"—he raised a second finger—"we will provide a series of simulated exercises that will enhance your ability to function as a team against a wide range of tactical situations.

"And finally," MacDonald said as he brought up the third finger, "we will provide individualized instruction with respect to specific weapons, techniques or tactics to meet the individual needs of you and your team leaders."

MacDonald paused momentarily to note that Gerd Maas was staring at him expressionlessly.

"To my far right is Master Gunnery Sergeant Gary Brickard. Sergeant Brickard will be your range master. He is also in charge of this facility in my absence. His special area of expertise is simulated combat situations, utilizing multimedia displays and robotics."

MacDonald scanned the eleven faces of his audience once more, noting that even Maas seemed to be intrigued by the idea of robotics.

"Sergeant Brickard and I have a great deal of experience in using live-fire exercises to teach rapid-strike entries and small-squad tactics. Our goal will be to provide all of you with appropriate simulations that force you to extend your capabilities to their maximum effectiveness while working in conjunction with other members of your team.

"In effect, we intend to keep your skills honed to a state of readiness that will allow you to respond to a tactical situation at a moment's notice."

MacDonald paused to look around the room once more. "Before I go on, are there any questions?"

Much to MacDonald's surprise, Gerd Maas raised his hand.

"Yes, Mr. Maas?"

"Sergeant MacDonald," Maas said in his typical cold, gruff voice, "I am most impressed by the quality of this facility and the thoughtfulness of your planning. However, I was told this morning that we must accelerate our preparations. Therefore, I must know how soon you and your staff can be available to us."

"Starting tomorrow morning, Sergeant Brickard and I, along with the rest of the staff, will be at your disposal in these facilities from oh-seven hundred to twenty-one hundred hours, seven days a week. Meals are normally scheduled at oh-six hundred, twelve hundred, and eighteen hundred hours. At your request, with appropriate notice, we can be available at any other time of the day or night."

"And what do you consider appropriate notice?" Maas asked.

"Twenty minutes to shower and shave would be appreciated," MacDonald said matter-of-factly. "However, a knock on any one of our doors would be sufficient."

"One more question," Gerd Maas said. "Perhaps you could comment on the security of these facilities?"

"I was about to get to that," MacDonald nodded as he stepped back behind the podium.

"It is obvious that the United States Government has placed a very high value on your readiness quotient. I say that because over the past eight months, my staff and I have been allowed to spend approximately eighty-seven million dollars to create what I can honestly tell you is one of the finest covert training facilities I have ever seen."

With motions that suggested an intimate knowledge of his equipment, MacDonald moved his callused right hand across the podium's control panel, causing the room to gradually darken. A sixteen-by-twenty-foot back-lit screen behind the podium lit up with a colorful graphics display.

"As you can see from the first slide," MacDonald said, "the training facilities are located a hundred yards east of the main cabin and are connected to that cabin by three underground tunnels, two of which are reserved for utilities and supply transport. The third tunnel will be your access route to and from the facilities."

MacDonald used a small hand-held transmitter to advance to the next slide.

"The facility is constructed around a two-story, twelve-inch, steel box-beam frame. The walls are eight inches thick, constructed of precast tilt-up slabs of hardened and reinforced concrete that are welded to the frame. The floors are similarly constructed, but are twelve inches thick and have much more extensive reinforcement. The lower level has sixteen feet of clearance from floor to ceiling, and the upper level has thirty-two. The top ceiling is made up of thirty-six inches of reinforced concrete and six inches of armor plating. The entire facility is buried beneath twelve feet of soil.

"In effect," MacDonald smiled, "we have provided you with a facility that is virtually impervious to anything short of a nuclear strike. Presumably, such precautions will not be necessary."

There was an appreciative murmur of approval and amusement from the ICER team.

The next slide had apparently been taken from the air.

"As you can see, we have constructed extensive outdoor recreational facilities above the complex. These facilities consist of four tennis courts, four sand volleyball courts, eight racquetball courts, two basketball courts, a hundred-meter pool, a clubhouse, and locker-room facilities that include showers, rest rooms, and a weight room. You will, of course, have full use of these facilities at any time.

"More important, however, aside from the connecting

tunnels, the only way in or out of the Training Center is either through the access tunnel to the helipad, or the alarmed fire-escape tunnel that exits through a separate and secured underground corridor connecting the clubhouse and locker room. The escape corridors and stairwells are external to the primary building structure, and the outer blast doors are designed to withstand the impact of a HEAT-tank round. They are also coded to your fingerprints, and open only from the inside.

"Getting back to the underground portion of the Center," MacDonald said as he advanced to the next slide, "the entire training facility is based around two hexagonal conference rooms with fifty-foot side-wall dimensions that are built on top of each other. We, of course, are now in the upper conference room."

The next slide showed a blowup of the lower floor, with subdivided rectangles of varying lengths radiating out from all six sides of the two central six-sided rooms.

"Here, on the lower floor," MacDonald went on, using a light beam as a pointer, "we have the command-and-control room, armory, machine shop, ammo bunkers, mechanical room, secured tunnel access to the main cabin, instructors' quarters, student quarters, medical facilities, multimedia room, emergency food and supply storage, rest-room and shower facilities, gym and dojo.

"By the way," MacDonald said, diverting from his planned lecture for a moment, "you will be moving this evening from your rooms in the main cabin to the underground student quarters. Your new rooms will be comparable in terms of creature comforts and, of course, more secure. As you surely know, your presence here at the Center is a closely guarded secret. Should you want to wander about in the local wilderness or avail yourselves of the recreational facilities up on top, you will be provided with appropriate Park Service clothing.

"Now then," MacDonald said, returning to his lecture as he advanced the projector once again, "as you can see, on the upper floor we have three Hogan's Alleys with extensive robotics, one commercially oriented, one residential, and one designed to simulate an assault on a small mountain cabin.

"In addition," MacDonald went on, using his light pointer, "we also have two fixed-wing and two helicopter simulators, a chemical-weapons compound, a fifty-yard pistol range, a hundred-yard small-arms range with multiple weather and lighting conditions, and a five-hundred-yard-long gun range with variable cross-wind capability.

"And if that isn't sufficient, ladies and gentlemen," MacDonald said as he turned off the projector and brought the room lights back up, "we will be happy to take you outdoors into several thousand acres of our nation's finest wilderness and see what we can do to make your lives both miserable and interesting."

Standing ramrod straight, MacDonald looked around the room one last time. "That completes my introductory presentation. Are there any questions?"

Gerd Maas raised his hand.

"You described the physical security of this facility in great detail, but you did not indicate the presence of any other security personnel."

"Yes, that's correct," MacDonald nodded. "In view of your 'need-to-know' security requirements, it was decided that we should try to keep the number of personnel at the Center to a minimum."

"I would not argue with that decision," Maas said. "However—"

"As you may recall from the slides," MacDonald interrupted, "the instructors' quarters are adjacent to the secured tunnel access. My staff and I have agreed to take responsibility for security. Quite frankly, Mr. Maas—" the burly command sergeant major smiled "—if the six of us and the twelve members of the ICER assault group cannot deal with any security problem that might arise at Whitehorse Cabin, I think we have no business being here in the first place."

Maas nodded his head in apparent agreement.

"Any other questions?"

The tall, blond-haired man sitting next to Maas raised his hand.

MacDonald immediately recognized the man as Günter Aben, the one who had been described in the files as a born killing machine. Barely controllable. Tends to be malicious under stress. Known to be adverse to discipline. Extreme caution advised.

Clarence MacDonald had been looking forward to working with Günter Aben ever since he had read his file.

"Yes, Mr. Aben?"

"Only one question, Sergeant Major. Would it be possible to see a demonstration of your robotics this evening?"

MacDonald smiled in spite of himself.

"We can do better than that. If you and the other members of your group will follow Sergeant Brickard down to the armory"—he looked at his watch—"in about forty-five minutes, we will formally introduce you to a few of the more devious and persistent members of our training staff."

CHAPTER NINETEEN

Eight?

Awareness came slowly, as if the distant pinpoint of light he had been watching for quite some time was now trying to lure him up and away from the all-encompassing darkness.

He did not understand why the number eight was suddenly so important.

There was a sense—almost a suggestion coming from somewhere in the darkness—that it was the light itself that he had been trying to avoid all this time; but he couldn't accept that, because it looked so warm and comforting and inviting, drifting up there above him like that.

As if it wanted to help.

Or to warn him of some incomprehensible danger, of some creature that was at his heels and would overtake him at any moment if he wasn't careful. Which made no sense at all, because it hadn't moved and they hadn't spelled it right and he felt perfectly warm and safe and comfortable right where he was.

He closed his eyes to make it all go away. But then he discovered that his eyes *wouldn't* close, so he continued to watch the glowing pinpoint as it began to grow—both in size and in intensity—until it seemed to take on dimension . . . and extension . . . and tone.

What?

Henry Lightstone said the word silently, not wanting to move any part of his body any more than he had to, because every one of those terribly sensitive parts seemed to be directly connected to that glowing pinpoint of light that he understood now was the very thing he'd been trying to hide from.

He was becoming aware that the glowing pinpoint of light was nothing more and nothing less than pure, undiluted pain.

"Can you hear me?" the voice repeated.

"Yes," Lightstone whispered, managing to make the word audible, but just barely.

"Can you open your eyes?"

No.

He might have whispered the word, or maybe he just thought he said it. He really couldn't tell. He thought he could feel the warmth of a person's breath against some part of his body, but nothing felt connected.

"Why not?"

Hurts. Leave me alone.

"What hurts?"

Lightstone tried to make some sense out of it all. It seemed like the soft and gentle voice—a woman's voice—was responding to his answers, which meant that he must be making sound.

And the other thing she said. Or asked. Something about hurt. Or what hurts.

Right. What hurts? A question.

Easy answer.

Everything.

Somewhere in the back of his mind an urgent voice was trying to warn him that the tiny point of light had managed to come in much closer while he had been trying to listen to the voice. But he couldn't tell if that was true or not, because he could see that it wasn't a pinpoint of light anymore; rather, it was a slowly rotating disk, with edges that looked like they were very sharp and ragged.

Like an etching tool.

That's how they did it, he realized. They'd used an etching tool to warn him. Hell of an idea, he smiled to himself, having no idea of what he was talking about—or thinking about, for that matter—but for some strange reason, still confident that it all made some sort of sense.

"Listen," the other voice, the voice that was much more feminine and caring, whispered, "I'm going to try to move your arm."

No, don't do that.

The rotating disk advanced cautiously, looking for all the world like a curious puppy trying to get in closer to get a better look.

Goddamned dog, he thought. Should have warned me sooner. Wouldn't have had to go through all this.

But of course it wasn't a dog. That was exactly the point, he reminded himself. Which didn't explain why they were making such a big deal over the number eight, or the word. Why eight?

"What?"

Why eight? he thought louder, really wanting to know, because it seemed to mean something. Something important.

"I don't know. Something about a phone call. I think they missed it," the voice explained.

Oh.

"Listen, we're going to have to move you over to the other

truck so we can go home. We're going to try very hard not to hurt you, but we need you to help us if you can."

Much closer now. So close that he could see every single glistening edge of the rotating blades that were starting to pick up speed now.

"No . . ." he whispered as loudly as he could, trying to make himself heard. But now the only sound that came out of his mouth was a raspy groan.

"Okay, hold on, here we go . . ."

Then the whirling disk lunged forward.

And he screamed.

CHAPTER TWENTY

Carl Scoby was still on the phone taking notes when he heard footsteps and then a knock on the door of his newly acquired Prime Rate motel room.

"Hold it a second. I've got company."

Rising slowly from the chair, a loaded and ready to fire .45 SIG-Sauer automatic in his hand, Scoby—deputy supervisor of Paul McNulty's Special Operations team and the covert agent who invariably looked an awful lot like a cop—walked cautiously to the door and looked through the peephole.

Then, smiling in visible relief, he slipped the SIG-Sauer back into his shoulder holster. He quickly unlatched the chain bolt and opened the door.

"Thank God *you're* here," Scoby said, stepping aside as Paul McNulty walked into the room carrying a suitcase and a field duffel bag. As McNulty set the suitcase and bag next to the far bed, Carl Scoby closed and relocked the door behind him.

"What's going on?" McNulty asked, alerted by the stress in

his partner's voice. McNulty had worked with Carl Scoby for over twelve years and had long considered him the most unflappable member of his covert team.

"I'm not sure," Scoby replied honestly, "but whatever it is, I don't like it. Hold on a second."

Scoby walked over to the small motel table, sat down and picked up the phone.

"It's McNulty. He just walked in. Yeah, I think you should. Maybe it'll make some sense to him."

"Who is it?" McNulty asked as he came over and sat down across from Scoby.

"Larry. He and Stoner spotted Sonny Chareaux in Bozeman a little over an hour ago. They've been tracking him all over the city ever since. Just a second. Let me see if I can figure out how to switch this thing over to the speakerphone," Scoby said as he picked up the complex-looking telephone receiver.

"When did Mike get back?" McNulty asked, noticing that the motel phone had been replaced with one of Mike Takahara's outwardly crude but highly sophisticated communications rigs.

"He hasn't. That's another part of the problem."

McNulty blinked in surprise.

"'You mean he's *still* out at the airport with that goddamn plane?"

"We *think* he's still out there," Scoby corrected, gesturing with his head at the silent packset radio lying on the table. "But he hasn't responded to any of our radio calls, and we can't get anybody to answer at the airport manager's office."

"Christ! How long has he been out there?"

Scoby looked at his watch. "A little over four hours."

"It shouldn't have taken him that long," McNulty said, shaking his head. "All he had to do was to borrow a maintenance uniform, walk out to the tarmac, look around a little bit, and then pop the door on the plane."

"Yeah, I know," Scoby nodded. "I was getting ready to have Stoner and Paxton cruise by, see if they could find out what he's doing. But then they called in saying that they'd spotted Sonny. I'll let Larry tell you about that." Scoby pushed the small recessed button marked "SP" and then set the com-rig back down on the table so that the speaker faced both him and McNulty. "Larry, can you hear me?"

"Loud and clear," Larry Paxton acknowledged, his normally bass voice sounding even more deep and gravelly over the open speakerphone.

"Larry, I've got Paul sitting here next to me. You want to walk him through the situation with Sonny?"

"Yeah, no problem. Tell you the truth, Boss, we're not real sure *what* we have out here, other than one hell of a confused mess," Larry Paxton said. "What happened is that Stoner and I were out cruising Bozeman when we spotted Sonny at a gas station on Kagy Boulevard, parked next to an outside phone booth."

"How do you spell that?" McNulty asked as he set his ever-present notebook out on the table.

"K-a-g-y. It's one of the main cross streets at the south end of town."

"Any sign of Alex or Butch?"

"No, we didn't see either of them."

"Don't those three usually stick together on a hunt?" McNulty looked up at Scoby.

"As far as we know, that's the way they've always worked," Carl Scoby nodded.

"Larry, about what time did you spot Sonny?" McNulty asked, turning back to face the speakerphone.

"A little over two hours ago." Paxton paused to check his diary. "Make that nineteen thirty-nine hours exactly."

"What's he driving?"

"At the time, he was driving an old Chevy pickup. Red, short bed, no cover on the back. Montana plates. I gave Carl the description and the license number. But listen, before you start taking too many notes, you need to know that things have changed one hell of a lot since then."

"Okay, I'll hold off with the questions until you're finished," McNulty acknowledged. "Go ahead."

"Anyway, when we spotted him, it looked like he was waiting for a call, so we camped out across the street and staked him out. For about twenty minutes, he just sat there. Then, at exactly nineteen fifty-nine hours, he got out of the truck, went into the phone booth, and tried to make a phone call."

"You said *tried*?"

"Yeah. It looked like the phone was out of order. One thing for sure, it wasn't giving Sonny his money back. He must have put three or four quarters in the damn thing before he finally figured out it wasn't going to work."

"Brilliant," McNulty chuckled.

"Yeah, no shit. So while we're sitting there watching," Paxton went on, "and after he finishes pounding on the thing, all of a sudden he rips the handset right off the goddamn box. Then he runs back to his truck, takes off down the street and starts driving around like a fucking maniac, looking for another telephone booth."

"Got to be a check-in call," McNulty interpreted. "Sonny was supposed to check in with somebody—presumably Alex—at exactly eight o'clock."

"That's the way we read it," Paxton agreed. "So after about ten minutes, while we're trying to keep up with him without being spotted, he finally finds another phone booth at another gas station. Only trouble is, there's already somebody in this one."

McNulty looked over at Carl Scoby with a smile.

"Just wait, it gets better . . . or worse, depending on your point of view," Scoby said cryptically.

"Yeah, ain't that the truth?" Larry Paxton agreed. "So anyway, while Stoner and I are getting ourselves settled in across the street, Sonny jumps out of his truck, runs over to the phone booth, pounds on the door, and then yanks the poor son of a bitch right out of the booth when he doesn't move fast enough. They get in a hassle right off, but we figure Chareaux probably outweighed the guy by a good thirty pounds, which doesn't even begin to count his shit-ass disposition. So it doesn't take too long until the guy's laid out on the ground and Sonny's in the phone booth, only it just isn't his day, because he must have used up all his quarters at the other phone."

"Incredible," McNulty shook his head.

"Yeah," Paxton agreed. "Anyway, the next thing we know, Sonny's back on top of this guy and going through his pockets, and this time they *really* get into a hassle, except that Sonny must have been absolutely freaked about making that phone call, because he pulled out that fucking stainless-steel .357 Ruger pistol of his and stuck it right in the guy's face. Which pretty much stopped the fight, but it didn't do Sonny any good, because the guy didn't have any more quarters either."

"So now we've got him on reckless driving, assault, carrying a concealed weapon, and attempted armed robbery, all on account of a simple check-in call," Scoby summarized.

"Right," Larry Paxton's voice echoed out through the small speaker, "which brings us right up to the point where the cop shows up."

"Oh, for Christ's sake," McNulty swore.

"Carl's been claiming that Stoner and I probably just went out to a bar, had a couple of beers, and then made up all this shit," Paxton chuckled, "but I told him no way. Neither one of us has got that kind of imagination."

"Did they take him in?" McNulty asked, thinking that if Sonny Chareaux was now in custody, there just might be a way to find out if he knew anything about Len Ruebottom. Especially if the guy in the phone booth was willing to press charges.

"No, not exactly."

"What do you mean, *not exactly*? What the hell happened?"

"Well, when Sonny looked up and saw those red and blue lights, he did just about what you'd expect a good ol' coon-ass swamp boy from Terrebonne Parish to do, which was to crank off six rounds right through the cop's windshield."

"He *shot* at the cop?"

"That's right. And then, while the cop is trying to figure how he can hide under the seat and drive and scream into his radio mike all at the same time, Sonny takes off for the hills."

"On foot?"

"Oh, yeah. Left his truck sitting at the gas station with empty .357 casings scattered all over the place."

"Any idea where he is now?" McNulty asked hopefully.

"We got lucky," Paxton said. "We were checking out the bars and spotted him in a place called the Cat's Paw. He's sitting in the back, about six feet away from the public phone. And from the look on his face, he's planning to rip the head off of anybody who tries to get near the thing. I'm right across the street from there now. Stoner's inside, keeping an eye on him."

"Has he made any calls yet?"

"No, we don't think so," Paxton said. "He went to the phone once, but we think he was just making sure he was going to get a dial tone this time. Probably . . . uh, hold it a second."

There was a long pause. Then Paxton was back on the phone.

"That was Stoner," he said. "Sonny's still sitting in the back of the bar, only now he's got a pile of quarters, a set of car keys, and a piece of paper laying out on the table. He also said that Sonny keeps looking at his watch about every thirty seconds, like he's afraid he's gonna forget what time it is."

McNulty looked down at his stainless-steel Rolex watch.

"It's ten minutes to ten," he said. "Sonny was supposed to check in at eight o'clock, but he screwed up, so now he's waiting until ten o'clock to try again."

"That makes sense," Scoby said. "If he's trying to call Alex while they're on a hunt, you can pretty well figure that they've got alternate check-in times and phone numbers all worked out."

"Yeah, Stoner said he'll get the phone numbers for us if we want."

"How the hell's he going to do that?" McNulty demanded.

"Take a guess."

McNulty hesitated. "You really think he can do it?"

"Sonny Chareaux's a big, mean boy," Paxton chuckled, "but I'll put my money on Stoner any day."

"I think he'd better hold off until we have a better idea of what's going on," Carl Scoby advised. "We could really screw things up for Henry if Alex starts thinking that there's something strange going on in Bozeman."

"Yeah, I agree," McNulty nodded. "Larry, what about those keys? You think he's going to go back for his truck?"

"No, I don't," Paxton said. "I don't think those *are* his truck keys. We listened in on the local police advisory, which reported he'd left his keys in the truck."

"How far away from the Cat's Paw is his truck?" McNulty asked.

"Other end of town. Long way to hike."

"So he probably has another vehicle stashed somewhere," McNulty calculated, looking at the map of Bozeman that Scoby had spread out across the table.

"It's probably one of those in the lot next to the bar, but that's one hell of a big parking lot. Must be at least thirty or forty vehicles in there right now. And about half of them are pickups."

"You know what I'm thinking, don't you?"

"If Alex had everybody holed up in a motel anywhere near Bozeman, then this idiot wouldn't be running around trying to find a phone?" Larry Paxton suggested.

"That's right," McNulty nodded. "So I figure they're either camped out in the woods or sleeping in their cars."

"Which is also consistent with their standard operating procedure," Scoby added.

"That part is, but what about this business of them splitting up? Presumably Henry's out on a hunt right now with Alex and Butch, but why would Alex leave Sonny in Bozeman?"

"To follow Henry into Gardiner, make sure he didn't have any backup. Those guys are sure as hell paranoid enough to do that," Scoby said.

"But Henry didn't *have* a backup, unless Ruebottom decided to tag along, so there wouldn't have been anything for Sonny Chareaux to *see*, right?" McNulty asked.

"No way Henry'd let Ruebottom do something like that," Larry Paxton's deep voice echoed in the room. "No fucking way. He gets pissed off every time Stoner and I try to give him some cover on a buy."

"We keep coming back to that point," McNulty said. "The thing is, maybe Ruebottom did it anyway, and stayed far enough back that Henry never saw him. That would explain why you guys can't find him around here. Ruebottom's supposed to be a sharp pilot. Far as any of us know, he could have aced the surveillance course at Glynco. Maybe he's sitting in Gardiner right now drinking a beer and waiting for Henry to show up at the motel so he can get out ahead of him and meet him back at the airport."

"He's doing something like that, next In-Service I'm gonna take his fucking head off," Larry Paxton growled.

"Yeah, but even if that *is* what happened, that was what, six, seven hours ago?" Scoby protested. "Hell, even if Rue-bottom *did* follow Henry into Gardiner on his own, and Sonny was right on *his* ass all the way, all Sonny had to do was drive over to the Best Western and tell Alex all about it right there. End of story."

"So then why the hell is Sonny Chareaux acting like he's panicked out of his mind over a routine check-in call?" McNulty demanded.

"According to the wardens in Louisiana, Sonny's supposed to be the least emotional of the three brothers," Carl Scoby reminded. "Far as they know, the only thing he's afraid of is Alex, which, I suppose, *could* explain the situation. But still . . . oh, shit," Scoby suddenly whispered.

"What's the matter?" McNulty demanded.

"What if it isn't routine?"

"I don't follow."

"We've been assuming all along that it has to be a routine check-in because of the timing. But what if it's not? What if Sonny snapped up Ruebottom at the airport, had him stashed away somewhere, and seven hours later finally managed to break him down? So now he knows for sure that Henry's an agent and he's trying to warn Alex before it's too late?"

McNulty continued to stare at his assistant team leader while the room went deathly silent.

"But since Alex and Butch are out in the field with Henry, the only way Sonny can warn Alex is to wait for one of their prearranged check-in calls when the hunt's over," Scoby went on. "Eight o'clock at a certain number. And if he misses that one, go to the next number at ten."

McNulty looked down at his watch again. Twenty-one fifty-two hours. Eight minutes until ten o'clock.

"If that's the situation, we can't let him make that call," Scoby said.

"Yeah, but if it really *is* just a check-in, and Sonny doesn't want to get Alex pissed off, and Ruebottom's sitting on his ass drinking beer in Gardiner, then we don't dare get in his way," Larry Paxton's deep, raspy voice interrupted. "If we screw around with Sonny now, Alex is gonna get suspicious and we're gonna blow Henry right out of the water."

"But, Christ, Larry, who the hell's gonna open up on a patrol unit over a goddamn routine check-in?" Carl Scoby objected.

"Nobody with any brains, but this is Sonny Chareaux we're talking about," Paxton countered. "Far as I'm concerned, the man never did start out with a full deck."

McNulty turned around to face the speakerphone again and spoke quickly. "Larry, who's closer to the airport, you or us?"

"Uh, you are, but not by much."

"You think you and Stoner can delay him from making that call without making him suspicious?"

"We could stop him," Paxton said in his low Southern drawl, "but I don't know about *delaying* him. Way he was acting back at that gas station, I figure anybody who tries to keep him away from that phone around ten o'clock is probably going to start a riot."

"I've *got* to know more about Len Ruebottom and that plane," McNulty said, forcing himself to stay calm. "If Carl's right . . ." He looked over at Scoby. "You got a car?"

"Yeah, sure."

"Get out to the airport, *right now*. Take one of the scrambled radios with you. Soon as you find Mike, and find out what the hell's going on with that plane, get on the air and—"

At that moment, the scrambled packset radio on the table gave out a weak squawk.

Carl Scoby grabbed up the radio and quickly moved over to

the window. "Sierra Oscar Two, repeat that last transmission."

"Sierra Oscar Two, this is Sierra Oscar Five," Mike Takahara said, his voice sounding hollow and distant over the small packet speaker. "Where the hell *are* you guys?"

"We had to move. We're over at the Prime Rate."

"Okay, I'll be there in about five or ten—"

"No, no time," Scoby interrupted. "Listen, Paxton and Stoner located Sonny Chareaux in Bozeman."

"Where?"

"In a bar called the Cat's Paw. Right now he's sitting next to a telephone and looking real anxious. We think he's waiting for twenty-two hundred hours to check in with Alex."

"Shit, don't let him do that!"

McNulty came over to the window and took the radio from Scoby. "Mike, this is Paul. What's the matter?"

"They've got Ruebottom for sure, and they're fucking serious," Takahara said. "They wired the damn plane. Took me four hours but I finally got in."

"What?"

"Never mind, it's a long story. I'll fill you in later," Takahara said quickly. "What you need to know right now is that there's blood all over the inside of that plane, and the cabin's torn to shit."

"How much blood?" McNulty demanded.

"Not that much," Takahara said. "Looked like nose and mouth stuff to me. Not enough in any one spot to indicate a serious knife wound or a gunshot. What I think happened is that Len and Sonny got into one hell of a fight inside that plane, and Sonny won."

"Anybody see him leave with Ruebottom?"

"No, but there was an empty bag for a ten-by-twenty painter's tarp and a mostly used roll of duct tape in the cabin. It would have been easy to wrap him up and haul him out of there like a piece of baggage."

"What about the bomb? How did he rig it?"

"First guy who opens the passenger door pulls a nylon cord that shuts a switch and touches off fifteen sticks of engineering-grade dynamite. That should have been plenty, but I guess Sonny wanted to be sure, because he stuck about a dozen five-gallon cans of aviation gas all around the cabin as an accelerator."

"Christ!"

"Yeah, he was probably trying to make it look like some kind of accident. But one way or another, he wasn't planning on leaving us much in the way of evidence."

Paul McNulty looked down at his watch. Twenty-one fifty-six hours. Four minutes until ten. He turned to face the speakerphone.

"Larry—"

"Never mind, I heard it,' Paxton said, standing in the phone booth, the phone against one ear and a small, scrambled packset radio against the other. "What do we do?"

"Try to maintain your covers as long as you can," McNulty ordered. "But whatever you guys do, don't let that bastard make that call!"

Something about a phone call. I think they missed it.

The words had been echoing in the back of Henry Lightstone's mind for the past half hour while he drifted in and out of consciousness. He felt disoriented by the darkness, confused by the intermittent bouncing, and savagely torn by the pain.

It was the terrible odor that hit him first. A feral stench born of matted hair, gamey urine, and perforated intestines, a stench that threatened to completely overwhelm his senses. He moved one of his hands and discovered something that he finally identified as an antler.

It took him a few moments before he remembered being chased by the huge grizzly. Then he remembered the bear's powerful claws slashing through the back of his shirt, and the gunfire.

But he couldn't understand where the antlers had come from until he was able to move his hand another six inches and felt the large, stiff feathers of an eagle. Finally the fragments of his memory began to pull together again.

The eagles, the bull elk, the wounded does, the bear. It was all coming back to him now. The terrifying helicopter, the double-barreled rifles, and the men who wouldn't take the time to kill their own cripples.

Bastards, he thought.

It took a few more agonizing movements before Lightstone was able to figure out that he was lying in the back of a pickup truck and that someone—presumably Alex and Butch Chareaux—had shoved him in between the bodies of the two bears.

Like one more carcass to be disposed of after the hunt was over, he thought, finding the idea amusing for some incomprehensible reason as his mind started to drift again, reaching out for the darkness and the soothing, painless sanctuary of unconsciousness.

A screen door slammed, and he heard voices.

"Alex, Butch," someone said cheerfully. "It is good to see you both. I was worried—"

"Has Sonny called yet?" Alex Chareaux demanded.

"Sonny? No, I have not heard from him at all today."

"He should be calling here very soon," Chareaux said insistently. "At ten o'clock. It is important that I speak to him."

"It is almost ten now. Come inside. Join me in a glass of wine, and we will wait for his call. Ah," the man said, slapping his hand on the tarpaulin-covered edge of the truck bed, "I see that you *do* have some work for me after all."

"Two grizzlies, a bull elk, and a pair of eagles," Alex Chareaux said, the tension in his voice seeming to ease now that he knew he hadn't missed his brother's call. "They will make nice trophies."

"I can only assume, of course, that you have all the necessary papers?"

"But of course," Alex Chareaux chuckled. "These are for the clients I told you about. The very wealthy ones with the many wealthy friends. So the mounts, they must be superb. They expect nothing less, and they will pay twice your normal rate for your best work."

Taxidermy, Lightstone realized.

"In that case, we will open a special bottle tonight, and we will not look so closely at your papers," the man declared grandly. "Come in now, we will talk. You can put the truck in the warehouse. We will unload it later."

"Back the truck into the warehouse," Alex Chareaux instructed, "and use his hoist to put the carcasses in the cooler. I want to be in the house when Sonny calls."

"What about Lightner?" Butch Chareaux asked.

"Is he awake?"

"I will see," Butch Chareaux untied the rope at the corner of the truck bed next to the driver's side door, pulled back the edge of the tarp, and looked in. He reached in, fumbled around for a few seconds, then turned to his brother and shook his head as he replaced the tarp corner and retied the rope.

"He is alive, but his pulse is weak and he is very cold. I think that, very soon, we will not have to worry about him anymore."

"Then just leave him in the truck," Alex Chareaux ordered, shrugging indifferently. "Once Sonny calls and tells us about the pilot, we will know for sure what to do. If Lightner is already dead by then, we will bury him in the woods."

Silence.

"Something is wrong?"

"I was thinking that maybe we are worried about the wrong people," Butch Chareaux said quietly. "Maybe we should be more concerned about our new clients."

"Why do you say that?"

"I watched Lightner with the bear today," Butch Chareaux shrugged. "He did not act as I had expected."

"Yes?"

"When things went wrong, he faced the bear with courage. He had the opportunity to turn and run, but instead, he went forward and drew its charge to you and the others."

"Perhaps all the more reason to think that he is not the man he claims to be," Alex Chareaux suggested.

"It was strange," Butch Chareaux continued, a distant look in his cold eyes. "But when he stood there out in the open, facing the bear, he reminded me of the time when you were sixteen and you stood up to Beebee Fontaine and killed him with your knife when he caught us stealing his 'gators. Perhaps Henry is just a crazy person like many other people we know. Like us, even?"

"And the others?" Alex Chareaux asked.

"You saw how they reacted when they realized that one of their bullets hit Lightner. They wanted to get away. It was only the lure of the second bear that kept them there. Of the three," Butch Chareaux snorted contemptuously, "I think the woman was more of a man."

"So you think it is too much a risk to take their money?"

"They can make us rich, but I think they would turn on us instantly if they thought it necessary in order to save themselves," Butch Chareaux nodded. "Of this Henry Lightner, I am not so sure."

Alex Chareaux began to say something when a phone started to ring in the nearby house.

"That must be Sonny," he said. "Take the truck into the warehouse and then come in. I think we will soon know exactly how to deal with our new partner."

CHAPTER TWENTY-ONE

Thoroughly distracted by the realization that the lives of Len Ruebottom and Henry Lightstone were hanging in the balance, Larry Paxton stepped out of the phone booth, looked to his right at the Cat's Paw parking lot, and started to run across the street between two parked cars.

He never saw the white car to his left that made a quick turn and began to accelerate toward him.

The sudden sound of screeching brakes was the only warning that Paxton had before the bumper of the Ford Taurus caught his left leg and sent him tumbling up and over the front of the hood. The hood ornament tore through his jacket and the small packset radio, gouging against his ribs before it snapped off.

As Paxton continued on in his tumbling path into the vehicle's windshield, the smoking tires finally got a grip on the asphalt and brought the vehicle to a sudden stop that sent the stunned agent rolling backward off the front of the hood and onto the hard, cold asphalt.

"Jesus fucking Christ! What the hell's the *matter* with you?" a high-pitched voice demanded as the driver's door of the Bozeman Police Department patrol car was thrown open.

Larry Paxton had managed to get up on his hands and knees and was starting to use the bumper and hood of the damaged vehicle to work himself into a standing position when the thoroughly unnerved police officer finally got around to him.

"Sir, are you okay?" The wide-eyed face that stared down at him under the mildly illuminating glow of the nearby street light was that of a shaken, anxious young officer.

"Yeah, I'm fine. No problem," Paxton said heavily as he straightened upright, his legs wobbly and his vision fuzzy. He tried to blink his eyes clear to read the numbers on his watch, but its supposedly shatterproof face had been crushed by the Ford Taurus's hood.

"Christ, buddy, you've got to watch out where you're going. You could get yourself killed like that," the officer went on in a barely controlled voice.

"Yeah, I know. My fault all the way." Paxton nodded groggily, wondering if he had a concussion. "Had my head up my ass, didn't see you coming. Say, do you know what time it is?"

"Uh, it's nine fifty-eight," the officer said as he glanced quickly at his watch. "Listen, why don't you sit down there by the curb while I get you some help?"

"No, really, that's okay," Paxton smiled weakly, thinking he really ought to lie down. "See, I'm running kinda late, and it looks like your police car's okay, so if you don't mind, I'll just—" Then he blinked and turned away as the young officer turned on his flashlight.

"Oh, Christ."

"What's the matter?"

"You're bleeding. Deep cut over your right eye." Paxton felt his arm being taken in the firm grasp of the muscular and now very concerned officer. "Listen, you sit down over here while I call this in, get my supervisor out here. Then I'll get my first-aid kit and try to patch you up until the medics can transport you to a hospital."

"No, man, I'm telling you, I've *gotta* go," Paxton said as he twisted his arm out of the officer's grasp.

"Hey, look, buddy, calm down. You're hurt, and you need medical attention, and I've got to write this up," the young officer said insistently as he got Paxton back into his grasp. "You just— Hey, what's this?"

In trying to regain his grip on Paxton's arm, the patrol officer's hand had brushed against the grip of Paxton's shoulder-holstered SIG-Sauer.

Oh, *shit*! Paxton thought, realizing that there wasn't enough time to go through the lengthy procedure of positively identifying himself as a federal agent. Especially since his badge and credentials were locked in the trunk of the car across the street.

Responding to his academy training, the young officer instinctively shoved Paxton around to face the patrol car while he reached down for his holstered 9mm Glock automatic, which left Paxton with only one reasonable option.

Dropping his head and bracing himself against the hood of the patrol car, Paxton slammed the heel of his hiking boot into the officer's lower abdomen, trying as best as he could not to catch him square in the groin. Then, as the navy-blue-uniformed officer grunted and dropped to the ground, Paxton spun around, wrist-locked and arm-barred him down to the pavement, fumbled for the snap of his handcuff pouch and quickly secured his arms behind his back.

Then, feeling his sorely bruised ribs and every one of his

thirty-six years, Paxton started to pull himself back up to his feet.

"You goddamned bastard," the young officer snarled as he tried to get at Paxton with his free leg. The well-aimed and solidly driven kick narrowly missed Paxton's groin, catching him in the thigh instead as it knocked him back down to the asphalt.

"Nice going, man. Hell of a shot," Paxton gasped as he dragged the still-struggling and cursing officer over to the sidewalk and held him down against the concrete for a moment with his aching body.

"Listen to me, buddy. You don't want to do this. You're making a real bad mistake," the officer tried, but Paxton was in too much of a hurry to listen.

"It's okay," he said, speaking as quietly as he could between deep breaths as he looked around quickly to make sure that nobody was watching. "Take my word for it, I'm on your side. No time to explain right now. Make it up to you later."

Then, after looking *both* ways this time, he took off at an unsteady gait across the street toward the Cat's Paw.

Paxton saw Stoner look up at him when he came in through the door. Sonny Chareaux was standing with his back to the bar, feeding three more quarters into the telephone. He held up a piece of paper in his right hand and began to dial.

Larry Paxton, with a convenient glazed look in his eyes, staggered over in the direction of the Cat's Paw's single telephone. As he approached Sonny Chareaux's back, he deliberately bumped into the small table, knocking the set of keys to the floor and causing the Louisiana poacher to turn around and look. Paxton, muscular but still much smaller than Chareaux, lurched forward, knocking Chareaux sideways. As Paxton threw out his left arm to catch himself on the telephone box, the fingers of his left hand closed down over the handset receiver.

"CAN AH USE THE PHONE WHEN YOU IS DONE?" Paxton yelled in a loud, slurred voice, blinking his eyes as he smiled up at the hulking Cajun, who had already recovered his balance.

"What?" Sonny Chareaux rasped, still clutching the handset.

"WHAT AH SAID IS, CAN AH USE—?" Paxton started to repeat himself in a loud, mumbled version of a South Carolina dialect before he found himself being flung backward into the table.

"HEY, MAN!" Paxton started to protest, gasping in pain as his ribs seemed to grate against the hard surface of the table.

But the severely injured agent was wasting his breath. Sonny Chareaux had already brought the handset back up to his ear, and his eyes were widening in rage as he recognized the dial tone.

Chareaux screamed out something unintelligible— something that Paxton figured was a Cajun-French curse on his ancestry.

Turning back to the phone box, Chareaux was in the process of hurriedly fumbling for more quarters when Paxton lurched forward again, wedged himself between Chareaux and the phone, screamed out, "IT'S MAH TURN!" and then used his leverage and the full force of his right leg to send Chareaux tumbling backward into and over his table.

Working quickly now because his ribs were really hurting and he knew he wasn't going to have much time, Paxton pulled a handful of Kleenex out of his back pocket, tore off a piece about three inches wide, and then began fumbling around in his pocket for a coin so that he could stuff the Kleenex into the slot of the phone.

Behind his back, he heard the sounds of people yelling and tables and chairs being flung aside as Sonny Chareaux screamed out his rage.

Paxton had just finished jamming the last of the blue tissue into the narrow slot when Sonny Chareaux's savage roar warned him in time to duck away from the fist that slammed into the wall right next to his ear. But he couldn't avoid the second fist that seemed to explode into his already damaged rib cage, turning his knees into jelly, or the third that caught him right in the side of the head and sent him sprawling to the floor.

Paxton was still down, clutching at his ribs, shaking his

bleeding head, and Sonny Chareaux was working feverishly at the phone, when ex-Raider-tackle Dwight Stoner slammed into Chareaux's upper back with a bone-crushing forearm shot that sent Chareaux *and* the telephone through the two-by-four-studded wall and into the bar's storage room.

Nearly trampled by the crowd of half-drunken spectators drawn by the irresistible sounds of breaking glass, splintering wood, grunting, screaming and cursing, Paxton crawled under Chareaux's table and waited. As the fighters and spectators worked themselves farther into the nearly demolished storage room, Paxton reached for Chareaux's keys, and the piece of paper that had also fallen to the floor.

Getting to his feet was more difficult than Paxton had expected, but the sounds of distant police sirens offered encouragement. Within a minute, he was out the back door and walking unsteadily to the car that he and Stoner had rented. He unlocked the door, pulled himself into the front passenger seat, quickly shut the door, and then spent another thirty seconds trying to reach under the seat for the portable telephone that Mike Takahara had talked them into carrying as a backup.

He didn't know how badly he was hurt, but nothing was going to stop him, Paxton told himself for perhaps the fifth time. Not until he found a certain Chevy pickup truck. Paxton smiled, because he thought he might know where Sonny Chareaux was keeping Len Ruebottom. He paused to listen to Dwight Stoner's distinctive roar, followed by the glass-shattering crash of a large body being thrown through a window.

"Go to it, Stoner, my man," he whispered to himself. "Take that coon-ass son of a bitch apart at the seams."

Finally, his rib cage about ready to burst, the tips of Paxton's long fingers located the cold, plastic case. *Good old Snoopy*, he thought as he slowly extended his hand another half inch and managed to retrieve the heavy, battery-operated remote phone without fainting in the process. *One of your crazy-ass ideas actually came in handy.*

Lying semiprone on the seat, his head braced against the

driver's armrest, and holding the face of the radio up at window level so the numbered buttons were faintly illuminated by the nearby streetlights, Paxton carefully punched in the phone number for the Prime Rate motel.

"Operator," the soft, youthful voice spoke in Paxton's ear.

"Room one-three-seven," he said, working hard to enunciate the numbers clearly. He didn't know what time it was, but it had to be well after ten, which meant that Henry and Len Ruebottom were probably running out of time. He had to get word to McNulty.

"Thank you."

Paxton listened to the busy signal ring eight times before it occurred to him that Mike Takahara probably hadn't gotten back from the airport yet. Which meant that all of his fancy message-switching gadgets—the ones that would have alerted McNulty that someone else was trying to call in—were still sitting in their cases, waiting to be reconnected to the Prime Rate motel phone lines.

He let the busy signal ring four more times before he realized that the motel operator wasn't going to come back on the line, so he broke the connection and redialed the number.

"Operator."

"This is Larry Paxton," he said carefully and slowly, trying very hard to erase every trace of his black, South Carolina upbringing. "I'm a guest at your motel. Room one-three-eight. I need you to break into a call at room one-three-seven. The room is in the name of Paul McNulty, and it is an emergency."

"I'm sorry, sir, but I'm not allowed to do that without permission of the manager."

"Then would you please go get his permission?" Paxton asked in a voice that, in his thoroughly biased view, was far more polite and controlled than the young operator had any right to expect.

"I'm sorry, sir, but he's not in his office right now. If you could call back in a half hour—"

Paxton broke the connection with a flood of profanity. He was rapidly running out of time.

Which meant there was only one reasonable option left.

Okay, McNulty, he thought to himself, you're always telling us to be adaptable, think fast on our feet, make decisions on our own. Hope the hell you're right.

Working slowly in the streetlight-illuminated darkness because he didn't dare turn on the overhead interior light, Paxton took another half minute to decipher Sonny Chareaux's scrawled handwriting and then punch the correct sequence of numbers into the portable phone. It rang twice before an unfamiliar voice answered.

"Hello?"

"This Alex?" Paxton asked in his slow, South Carolina drawl.

"What?"

"Ah said, is this Alex?" Paxton repeated.

There was a long pause, and then a voice replied cautiously, "There is no one here by that name."

"Well, shit. Ah *know* this is the number Sonny told me to call, and Ah—"

"You said Sonny? Wait just a minute—"

"Hey, man, *you* wait just a minute! Who the hell is this?" Paxton demanded.

"This is Jacall. Please wait just one minute."

Paxton thought he heard a muffled voice yelling something in the background.

"Listen, man, Ah ain't waiting for *nobody*, and Ah ain't in the *mood* to play no fucking games. All Ah'm doing is what Sonny asked me to do. You just tell this Alex, whoever and wherever the fuck he is, that Sonny says everything's cool with the pilot, whatever the hell *that* means."

"No, wait! Don't hang up!" the voice said frantically. "What about Sonny? Where is he?"

"Probably in some *po-lice* car, heading to jail, seeing as how he just got himself in one hellacious bar fight. And *Ah'm* getting the hell out of here before *Ah* end up in the same place," Paxton said and then quickly disconnected before Alex could come on the line.

"Okay, Henry, I hope that buys you something," Paxton

whispered as he slowly pulled himself up to a sitting position and looked again at Chareaux's keys. One of the keys belonged to a Chevy, and the key ring bore the emblem of a camper supply house. He reached for the door handle and got out.

There were at least seven or eight pickups with full-sized camper rigs in the parking lot, and as it turned out, four of them were Chevys. So it took Larry Paxton almost five more minutes to discover that one of the keys Sonny Chareaux had lost in the Cat's Paw bar fit perfectly into the back-door lock of the third camper.

Barely conscious now, but still on his feet, Paxton was just about to open the camper door—to see for himself whether or not he had guessed right—when he felt the cold, hard muzzle of a 9mm Glock pistol press hard against the back of his neck.

"Sir, without turning around, and without moving a single muscle in your entire body," the young patrol officer said as he stepped in with his left foot and wrist-locked the agent's left arm behind his back, "I want you to explain to me *exactly* why you and I might be on the same side."

CHAPTER TWENTY-TWO

"Are you certain?"

"Whoever it was, he just hung up," Roberto Jacall said as he replaced the handset into its receiver. He brought his hands up in an open-palmed shrug and then looked at Alex Chareaux with an expression that clearly said "Who knows?"

"Do you get many calls like that here? People who don't identify themselves, then just hang up?"

"No, not so many like that," Jacall shrugged again.

"And you are *certain* it wasn't Sonny?" Chareaux repeated, wanting to be sure.

"Alex, there was no voice. Nobody spoke. They just hung up."

Alex Chareaux stared at his taxidermist friend for a long moment before turning away and staring out the window at the open and illuminated door of the warehouse, where his other brother was parking their truck.

"I don't like this. I think I have made a mistake," he finally said, still staring out the window at the warehouse door as Butch Chareaux got out of the truck, shut off the warehouse lights, and started walking back toward the house. "I took on a man as a partner. A man I believed I could trust."

"Yes, so?"

"I think now that the man is an undercover agent for the government."

Roberto Jacall froze, stunned, as if he had never imagined that something might go wrong. "Are you sure?" he whispered.

"No." Chareaux shook his head slowly. "If I knew that for certain, I would have killed him long before now."

"But how—"

"Sonny was told to take this man's pilot aside, ask him questions, and then call me, tell me everything he found out. We arranged two times and places. Eight o'clock at a phone booth in Fishtail, or if he was delayed for some reason, ten o'clock here."

"Then something is terribly wrong," Roberto Jacall said.

"I know."

"This agent man, can you find him?"

Alex Chareaux almost smiled. "Yes, my friend, we can find him very easily. He is in the back of the truck right now. Unconscious certainly, and perhaps already dead."

"No, my brother, he is not dead," Butch Chareaux laughed as he came into the living room, "but I think he will be soon."

Unable to speak, Roberto Jacall simply shook his head.

"We have always trusted each other to do what is necessary,"

Alex Chareaux said. "We will continue to solve our problems together." He turned to his brother.

"Lightner," he whispered. "Kill him now."

Henry Lightstone was lying in the pitch-dark truck bed, fighting a sudden surge of nausea, when he heard the sound of footsteps coming back to the warehouse. Footsteps and then a cheerful whistling as the single individual continued on past the truck and into the warehouse.

Butch Chareaux, Lightstone thought, recognizing the tune that the younger Chareaux brother had frequently whistled during the hunt.

Usually after he had killed something.

Moments later, a light in the far corner of the warehouse came on, sending a faint beam through a tear in the canvas tarp.

Then, as Lightstone continued to listen, feeling weak and nauseous, and knowing that he was almost completely defenseless against a killer like Butch Chareaux, the footsteps returned to the truck.

Continuing to whistle cheerfully, Butch Chareaux drew a long-bladed hunting knife from his belt and quickly cut through the ropes that held the tightly stretched canvas over the truck bed. He pulled the tarp aside and climbed up into the bed. Then he plunged the knife into the rigored haunch of the larger bear—where it would be accessible when he needed it—and worked his way across the carcass until he was kneeling over the sprawled and bloody form of Henry Allen Lightner.

"Henry, can you hear me?"

Lightstone blinked his eyes slowly and tried to whisper something. He could see the knife sticking out of the bear's haunch, but it was down near the tailgate of the truck. Too far away.

"What did you say?" Butch Chareaux asked, the amusement evident in his voice.

"Yeah, hear you," Lightstone rasped weakly.

"Ah, that is good. Here, I will get you out," Chareaux said

as he started to pull up on Lightstone's right arm, and then heard him gasp in pain as something seemed to hold him back.

"No, wait. Elk horn, caught on my shirt," Lightstone mumbled, and then his eyes widened in agony and he grabbed the right side of Chareaux's shirt collar in a reflex action as the muscular Cajun reached around his extended arm and tried to work him loose from the horn.

"That's right, Henry, grab my shirt. Help me pull you out." Chareaux smiled as he pulled some more.

But then his eyes widened in shock as Lightstone suddenly thrust his left hand across and underneath his right arm, grabbed the opposite side of Chareaux's shirt collar and pulled him down in a cross-armed choke hold that jammed the edges of his hands into Chareaux's carotid arteries.

"You bastard!" Butch Chareaux snarled as he tried to strike at Lightstone with his strong, callused hands. But the bear carcasses protected Lightstone's head, making the otherwise lethal blows ineffective; Chareaux tried to push himself up and away instead. But he couldn't do that either, because Lightstone had his elbows jammed under the bears' rib cages, and the elk horn still held him in place. His wrists were twisting tighter and tighter . . .

It was at that moment that Chareaux felt himself start to black out, and he reached desperately behind him for the knife, but it was too late.

Lightstone waited until Butch Chareaux's body went completely limp, then held his wrists locked in position for another ten seconds—just to be absolutely sure—before he finally released the hold and started to use his hands and feet to shove and push himself clear.

Halfway through the process, Lightstone had to turn his head quickly to vomit between the two bear carcasses. But less than a minute later, he was using what little strength he had left to drag the unconscious body of Butch Chareaux off the opened bed of the truck.

Then, after resecuring the gate and bringing Chareaux up to a kneeling position in front of the truck bumper—where

Lightstone assumed he'd be hidden from view—he started working to restore the muscular Cajun's breathing.

Lightstone knew he'd held the choke hold longer than necessary, and he thought he'd lost him, but then Chareaux started to twitch and gasp and move his hands in trembling, spasmodic motions, which made Henry Lightstone smile.

"Thata boy, Butch," Lightstone whispered weakly, wobbling on trembling legs as he held the Cajun's head up for a couple more seconds. "I knew you were too goddamn tough to die yet."

Then, with every ounce of energy he had left, Lightstone slammed Butch Chareaux's face square into the back bumper of the truck.

A few moments later, Lightstone was able to bring his own head up off the truck bumper long enough to confirm that Chareaux was still breathing through his bloodied lips and nose.

After looking around at the stacks of hides and rows of tanning vats that covered a good half of the huge semidarkened warehouse floor, Lightstone staggered over to the near-corner area that seemed to serve as an open office, pulled the wall phone off the hook, and quickly began dialing a long-memorized number.

Three rings later, a deep, unfamiliar voice answered Mike Takahara's carefully routed but temporarily disabled lifeline, and Lightstone immediately hung up the phone before barbecue restaurant-owner Terry Grosz had a chance to say anything.

"Shit," he muttered to himself, still holding the phone and wondering how the hell he could use it to stay alive and alert McNulty without blowing his cover.

Then he looked out the open roll-up door of the warehouse and saw the side door of the house burst open as Alex Chareaux lunged out onto the porch.

Roberto Jacall was in shock.

All his life, from the day he had skinned his first squirrel and then tried to stuff it with grass and leaves, he had dreamed of having his own taxidermy shop, where he could create beautiful mounts of rare and wonderful animals that had been hunted and killed all over the world.

Thanks to Alex Chareaux and his incredibly wealthy clients, Roberto Jacall had realized his dream. Each year, he and his most trusted assistants labored long hours in his hidden tannery to prepare hundreds of meticulously crafted mounts of rare, endangered and threatened species. Other, less-trusted workers tanned and prepared the hundreds of legal skins that provided him with a legitimate source of declarable income.

And accordingly, each year, he and his assistants buried hundreds of thousands of dollars deep in the forest—in tightly sealed and carefully documented canisters—where no IRS agent or bank auditor would ever be able to find them.

But now, because of that very same man, Roberto Jacall was facing the ruin of his cherished business . . . and possibly worse, he realized as he stared out into the darkness.

Jacall knew that at any moment now, Butch Chareaux would return to the house and tell his brother that the suspected government agent was dead. And Roberto Jacall also knew that when that moment came, he would be a hunted man.

"Alex," he said softly, terrified of enraging his volatile partner, "are you absolutely certain that there is no way for you to contact Sonny?"

"If there were any way I could, I would have already."

"But to kill a government agent," Jacall whispered. "They will never stop looking for us."

"That is not such a bad thing." Chareaux shrugged. "There are game wardens in Terrebonne who will never stop looking for us either. But they haven't found us yet. We will bury this man deep in the woods, so they will never know for sure."

"But just one phone call could make all of that unnecessary," Jacall pleaded. "One simple phone call."

"Jacall, listen to me," Alex Chareaux said with barely controlled patience. "We have been standing here by this phone for . . ."

Then he looked more closely at the living-room phone and blinked in confusion.

"What is this?" he demanded, pointing at the flashing light on one of the phone buttons.

"Oh, that is the warehouse extension." Jacall shrugged. "Your brother must be making a call."

"*What?*"

As Alex Chareaux lunged toward the side door, the phone in the living room suddenly began ringing, but he paid no attention to it.

Chareaux was on the porch, a long folding knife in his hand, when Jacall yelled out, "Alex, it is all right. He must be calling us here. Or maybe it's Sonny."

As Alex Chareaux hesitated, Jacall reached for the phone.

"Hello?" he said hesitantly.

"This Alex?"

"What?"

"Ah said, is this Alex?"

For a long moment, Roberto Jacall hesitated, uncertain of what he should say or do, because he knew immediately that this was not the voice of Sonny Chareaux either.

"There is no one here by that name," he finally said.

"Well, shit. Ah *know* this is the number Sonny told me to call, and Ah—"

Like a drowning man suddenly thrown a life ring, Jacall lunged at the mention of Sonny Chareaux's name.

"You said Sonny?" he whispered, his voice almost cracking in disbelief. "Wait just a minute—"

"Hey, man, *you* wait just a minute!" the voice snarled. "Who the hell is this?"

"This is Jacall," the taxidermist stammered, struggling desperately to find some way to keep this man on the line. "Please wait just one minute."

Jacall placed his hand over the phone and yelled out in the direction of the side door, "Alex, come back. Quick! It's about Sonny!"

"Listen, man, Ah ain't waiting for *nobody,* and Ah ain't in the *mood* to play no fucking games," the voice at the other end of the line snarled. "All Ah'm doing is what Sonny asked me to do. You just tell this Alex, whoever and wherever the fuck he is, that Sonny says everything's cool with the pilot, whatever the hell *that* means."

"No, wait! Don't hang up!" Jacall said frantically. "What about Sonny? Where is he?"

"Probably in some *po-lice* car, heading to jail, seeing as how he just got himself in one hellacious bar fight. And *Ah'm* getting the hell out of here before *Ah* end up in the same place."

Click!

Jacall was still staring at the telephone in his hand when Alex Chareaux came bursting into the living room.

"What about Sonny?" he demanded.

"A man just called," Jacall said quickly, frightened by the look in Chareaux's reddened eyes. "He said Sonny got in a fight, in a bar, and the police have taken him to jail."

"Sonny is in *jail*?"

"Yes," Jacall nodded his head frantically, "but this man, he said that Sonny gave him this number and asked him to call you and tell you that the pilot is cool."

"What!" Chareaux exclaimed, blinking in confusion. "What do you mean by *cool*?"

"That's the word he used." Jacall shook his head. "Maybe the pilot is okay, so that means that the man in the truck might not be a government agent after all."

"Not an agent?"

"Alex, if this is true, you must stop Butch before—"

But Alex Chareaux was already out of the living room and running for the door.

"Butch, wait!" Chareaux yelled out in the darkness, and then kept on running until he was at the doorway of the dimly lit warehouse, looking around with the long folding knife still in his hand.

"Over here," a voice whispered weakly on the opposite side of the truck, and Chareaux moved quickly, coming around the back of the truck, the knife blade exposed and ready, only to see Henry Allen Lightner sitting on the floor of the warehouse, leaning back against a steel I-beam pillar that was about three feet away from the back of the truck.

To Chareaux's absolute amazement, Lightner was holding his blood-soaked shirt against the bloodied and swollen face of Butch Chareaux, who was sprawled out on the floor with his head in Lightner's lap.

"What happened?" Alex Chareaux demanded, dropping down to his knees and staring first at his unconscious brother and then at the equally blood-streaked face of Henry Lightner.

"He was trying to help me out of the truck," Lightstone explained in a weak whisper, "but he slipped in the blood, and I think his foot caught under the bear—" Lightstone pointed over at the bear carcass that was hanging half out of the truck. "He couldn't catch himself and he fell and hit his head on this post. Sounded like he hit it hard. Like a goddamn melon," he added, laying his own aching head back against the solid pillar.

"Is he alive?" Chareaux asked as he felt for a pulse, still disoriented by the sight of his brother sprawled out on the floor.

"Yeah, he's breathing, but I think . . ." Lightstone paused to catch his breath. "I think he's hurt pretty bad. Need to get him some help. Tried to call you guys, phone over there," he mumbled, making a weak gesture in the general direction of the wall phone, "but I couldn't figure . . . how to call the house. Kept getting a busy signal. Thought you'd never get here."

"We have to get him to a doctor," Chareaux said, his mind racing as he tried to keep all of the confusing pieces together.

"No, it's okay," Lightstone mumbled softly, looking as though he was about ready to slip back into unconsciousness at any moment. "Already . . ."

"What? What did you say?" Chareaux demanded, bending down closer to try to hear what Lightner was saying.

"I said I already . . ." Lightstone tried again, but his words were drowned out by the sounds of the paramedic truck that came roaring into the driveway and headed directly toward the open warehouse door with all lights and sirens blazing, closely followed by a fire rescue truck and two sheriffs' patrol cars.

". . . called them for you," Henry Lightstone finished, smiling weakly up at the stunned and shocked face of Alex Chareaux.

CHAPTER TWENTY-THREE

MONDAY, JUNE 3RD

At precisely ten thirty-five hours on the following morning, in the armor-plated control room that overlooked the Whitehorse Training Center's expansive underground LIFET (Live Fire, Evasive Target) Range, Dr. Reston Wolfe was standing next to Lisa Abercombie and Command Sergeant Major Clarence MacDonald when an aide quietly entered and tapped him on the shoulder.

"Yes?" Wolfe said absentmindedly, keeping his eyes focused on the bank of color monitors mounted on the far wall.

"Phone call, sir."

"Who is it?"

Wolfe wasn't the least bit interested in taking a phone call just then. He had been watching live-fire exercises by integrated German, Japanese, and American ICER teams through the bulletproof observation windows and the banks of color monitors since eight o'clock that morning, and was far from tired of it. Each of the increasingly complex exercises had been fun to watch from the safety of the protected booth (a considerable improvement over the tiny tree platform on Tom Frank's West Texas hunting ranch, he reminded himself.) It was the follow-up to yesterday's highly successful late-afternoon hunt.

"It's your message service, sir."

Wolfe continued to ignore the young aide, thinking instead about the growing heat from Abercombie's body as she stood close to him, lost in the drama being displayed on the screens before them.

"Ah, sir . . ."

Both Wolfe and Abercombie were now focusing their attention on the oversized monitor in the far corner of the control room that was showing—in slow motion and from the robotic target's point of view—Gerd Maas, in night-vision assault gear, diving into a darkened room, twisting away to avoid the small, high-velocity, paint-pellet rounds and then "killing" the humanoid target with a single shot to the forehead.

"Tell them that I will take my messages when the exercise is completed," Wolfe said firmly as he shifted his gaze over to the adjacent monitor, which was replaying the humanoid robot's futile efforts to track its target—the white-bearded Maas—at its programmed but clearly limited "human reaction" speeds before its finely tuned servo motors went dead in response to the kill shot.

Caught up in the simulated drama on the color monitor, Lisa Abercombie brushed her arm up against Wolfe and briefly squeezed his wrist.

"I tried to tell them that, sir," the aide said in a quiet, differential tone, "but apparently one of the people who called in was very insistent. He wants to talk to you immediately."

"*After* we're finished here," Wolfe said emphatically, determined not to leave Lisa Abercombie's side.

Not now.

Not when she was clearly starting to comprehend the nature of the ICER team that *he* had put together.

"I'm supposed to tell you that the caller's name is Alex and that the message appears to be very important, sir," the aide said, standing his ground.

Wolfe blinked and turned to look at his nervous but still determined young assistant.

"When did he call?"

"At quarter after ten this morning."

"Do you know what the message is about?"

"No sir, I don't. All I know is that the call is from Alex and that it's *very* important."

Wolfe turned to Lisa Abercombie. "I have to go," he whispered. "I'll be back in a few minutes." He quickly followed the aide out the door, oblivious of the fact that Abercombie—her dark eyes still glued to the monitors—had barely noticed his departure.

Hurrying into one of the small offices adjacent to the much larger command-and-observation center, Wolfe closed the door behind him and immediately reached for the phone.

"This is Wolfe," he spoke into the mouthpiece. "I understand you have something for me?"

Then Reston Wolfe stood in absolute silence, the color draining out of his face, as the duty operator carefully repeated Alex Chareaux's message, word for threatening word.

At precisely twelve thirty that afternoon, Executive Director Reston Wolfe and Special Executive Assistant Lisa Abercombie ran to the helicopter that was waiting to transport them immediately from Whitehorse Cabin to the Bozeman Airport, where—at that very moment—a private jet was being fueled for a nonstop flight to Washington National Airport.

Command Sergeant Major Clarence MacDonald and Master Gunnery Sergeant Gary Brickard stood at the edge of the heliport, watching through the rain.

To MacDonald's left, a ground controller held a pair of red signaling lights in his outstretched hands as he talked through his helmet microphone to the pilot of the jet Ranger.

"Flight Yankee Four, this is Whiskey-Charlie One. All priority passengers are now on board."

"Roger, Whiskey-Charlie One," the pilot responded as the cabin door of the Bell Ranger was pulled shut and the speed of the sweeping rotor blades began to increase. "We've got a couple of extra seats. Anybody else out there want a ride into town?"

The controller looked at MacDonald and Brickard, who were monitoring the radio traffic with hand-held radios. Both men shook their heads.

"Whiskey-Charlie One to Yankee Four, that's a negative," the ground controller responded. "Lousy day to fly."

"Roger that," the combat-qualified pilot acknowledged. "Flight Yankee Four requesting clearance for takeoff according to flight plan. Directional heading zero-niner-zero. Climbing immediately to fifteen thousand feet. Final heading three-three-zero."

The ground controller switched frequencies on his short-range helmet radio to consult with his counterpart, who was manning Whitehorse Cabin's concealed radar system, and then switched back over to the pilot of the Bell Ranger. The controller was acting as the go-between in order to minimize control-tower radio transmissions—much more powerful and therefore more easily detected and monitored by other planes or stations.

"Whiskey-Charlie One to Yankee Four, be advised that there is negative traffic in the immediate area. Just you and the ducks. You are clear for takeoff, zero-niner-zero, fifteen thousand, final heading three-three-zero. Repeat, you are clear for takeoff."

Then, after receiving a thumb's-up from the pilot, the controller used his signaling lights to send the powerful aircraft rotating up and outward into the dark, cloud-filled sky.

"Any idea of what that's all about?" Brickard asked as the two veteran soldiers secured their radios and began walking back to the main cabin, completely unmindful of the lightly falling rain.

MacDonald shook his head. "They've been using a scrambled T1 line to communicate with the outside, but I got the distinct impression that our executive director received some bad news this morning."

"Yeah, I thought he looked a little pale," Brickard observed. "Think maybe the rabbit died?"

"Tell you the truth, I don't think a rabbit would last five seconds with those two," MacDonald grunted. "You see the artillery they came back with last night?"

"Yeah, they dropped it all off with Thomas. Told him they wanted everything cleaned and ready for tomorrow." Brickard chuckled. "Way I heard it, John was just about ready to tell them to blow it out their ass when he saw the make on the double barrel. Guess he'd never held a rifle before that cost more than his house."

"A three-seven-five Rigby and a four-sixteen Holland and Holland." MacDonald shook his head. "That's a lot of fire-power for a couple of desk jockeys."

"Yeah, especially when they come back at twenty-three hundred hours with blood and hair all over their brand-new cammies."

"No shit?"

"Dumped everything in the laundry," Brickard nodded. "Same instructions. Wanted everything ready for tomorrow."

"Gonna turn old John-boy into a pretty good butler at this rate," MacDonald commented. "He run a wash this morning?"

"Yep, sure did. Everything washed, folded, and stacked on their beds, just like they were a couple of brigadiers. Only thing is, John kinda made a mistake and washed a couple of brand-new sets instead. Hell of a job though. Can hardly tell they just come off the shelf." Brickard smiled.

"What did he do with the dirty ones?"

"I told him to wrap 'em up in brown paper bags and put 'em in the freezer, hair and all."

"Think it's going to tell us anything?"

"I don't know," Brickard shrugged. "But I've got a buddy who works in the Army Crime Lab in Georgia. Thought I might give him a call, see what he can figure out with all those fancy microscopes and shit."

"Might turn out to be useful," MacDonald nodded. "Sure as hell can't hurt."

"You really think they're doing something illegal?"

"Gunny, I've got some serious doubts about this entire operation, but what do I know?" MacDonald snorted. "Hell, I'm still trying to figure out who the bad guys are in this deal."

"I sure as hell wouldn't want to take these ICER characters on in a fair fight," Brickard said. "You see the latest computer scores?"

"No, how'd it go?"

"For the most part, pretty much the way we expected. Osan, Saltmann, and Aben were way up there with two-point-seven, two-point-eight, and three-point-one. Everyone else is in a pretty tight group from one-point-eight to two-point-six."

"Two-seven for Osan? That's a hell of an improvement," MacDonald commented.

"Yeah, she's quiet, but she learns quick," Brickard agreed. "Which reminds me, I think Kobayashi's in love. Osan tagged him this morning with a reverse back fist coming out of a spin kick. Nearly took his head off. Never saw him smile like that."

"She took Kobayashi?" MacDonald blinked.

"Oh, hell, no," Brickard laughed. "He extended her out with an arm bar, caught her in the solar plexus with an elbow, locked her into a *morote* shoulder throw, and had her choked out before she hit the floor."

"Sounds like true love to me," MacDonald smiled with relief.

"Yeah, you should have seen it," Brickard grinned. "He brought her back around, took off his belt and gave it to her, 'cause I guess nobody's tagged him like that in about fifteen fucking years, which sent her running off the mat with tears in her eyes. So our number-one *Sensei* evens it all out by stomping the living shit out of Aben, maybe fifteen out of fifteen, until the goddamned arrogant Kraut finally gives up and staggers back to the simulators, where he can play Cowboys and Indians with his buddy Maas."

"Speaking of Maas," MacDonald said, "I'm glad to hear he's mortal after all."

"Yeah, who said that?"

"You did. You said everybody else fell into the range of one-eight to two-six."

"Everybody except Maas." Brickard shook his head. "He pulled a clean three-five."

"Three-*five*?"

"It's all on tape, and you're going to want to see it," Brickard nodded. "He and Aben went in as a tag team and tore the goddamn course apart."

"*Both* of them logged a three-five?"

"Nah, not really. Our buddy Günter can probably get it up to a three-two, or maybe even a three-three when he's dead-on, but mostly he's pretty inconsistent. Loses his temper and goes ape-shit every time he takes a little paint. That's when they really pick him off."

"And Maas?"

"Cold as a goddamn ice cube," Brickard said. "Con him with a fast shuffle and he goes back in with that look in his eye. Took him three tries with R-twelve, but now he's got that one knocked, too. Three more simulators and he's got the place maxed."

"Three and a half times normal human reaction." MacDonald shook his head. "Where in hell did they find a guy like that?"

"Beats the shit outta me," Brickard shrugged. "I'm about ready to have him X-rayed for wires and chips as it is. Hard to figure a guy like that as being human."

"We could always ratchet the simulators up a couple more notches," MacDonald said contemplatively, "but what's the point? Anything over a three-six just isn't realistic. You're never going to run up against anybody in a field situation with that kind of reaction time."

"Actually, Maas came up to me after the exercises with an interesting request."

"Yeah, what's that?"

"He wanted to know if we could set up an exercise that's a little more competitive. I think that was the word he used."

"More *competitive*?"

"Yeah. He wants us to put a couple of live rounds in the

simulators, random feed, random mags, and then let him run the course on his own."

"*What?*"

"Said if we were willing to do that, he thinks he can make a four-oh. Added stimulation. Heightened awareness. Shit like that."

"Christ!" MacDonald whispered.

"Yeah, that's roughly what I said," Brickard nodded. "And I'll tell you what. The more I think about it, the more I'm about half tempted to let him try it."

"Any particular reason?" MacDonald asked after a moment.

"Just one," Brickard said as he reached for the back door to the main cabin. "I'm starting to think we ought to let the robots put this guy down while he's still on our side."

CHAPTER TWENTY-FOUR

WEDNESDAY, JUNE 5TH

Walter Crane, chief investigator for the firm of Little, Warren, Nobles and Kole, waited until Albert Bloom, Lisa Abercombie, Dr. Reston Wolfe, and the other five members of the ICER Committee were seated around the teak-and-rosewood table in the quiet, luxurious, and tightly secured conference room.

Then he picked up the crisp manila file folder containing his summary notes, glanced through the first page briefly, and discreetly cleared his throat.

"This is an interesting case," he began, showing the lack of discernible emotion that most of his audiences seemed to find comforting.

"If I were to summarize all of the facts in one brief statement, I would say that our clients apparently stumbled into a federal undercover investigation being conducted by a team of special agents from the U.S. Fish and Wildlife Service's Division of Law Enforcement.

"The team, which seems to be comprised of six special agents operating under the code designation 'Bravo,' is a part of the Special Operations Branch based out of the central Washington, D.C., office.

"I should note here," Crane said, pausing to look up at his audience, "that the Special Operations Branch is authorized to conduct undercover operations throughout the United States. There is no question of illegal or improper jurisdiction on the part of these agents. Or," he added significantly, "at least none that we are aware of at the moment."

"At any rate," he went on when there were no comments from anyone around the table, "the essence of the case is that on or about June the second of this year—which is to say, last Sunday afternoon—three brothers, named Alex, Butch, and Sonny Chareaux, took a Mr. Henry Allen Lightner, and of course our clients," Crane added without the slightest suggestion of sarcasm in his voice, "out on a guided hunt that turned out to be illegal."

"In what sense?" one of the ICER Committee members asked.

"Illegal in the sense that several protected, threatened or endangered animals—specifically, two grizzly bears, at least four elk, three whitetail deer, one peregrine falcon, one red-tailed hawk, and two golden eagles—were illegally killed, transported, and or possessed within or near the boundaries of Yellowstone National Park," Crane explained.

"But can they prove that all of these animals were taken by our clients?" the same man asked.

"That may be the relevant question," Crane nodded. "Right now I can tell you that some of these animals were subsequently found in the possession of Alex and Butch Chareaux at a local Montana taxidermist shop owned and operated by a Mr. Roberto Jacall. We also know that federal agents and state wardens spent several hours in the supposed hunting area taking photographs and collecting evidence. We are still waiting to receive copies of these crime-scene reports. Also, as far as we are aware, none of the individuals involved in the hunt had any hunting licenses, tags or permits that might have allowed them to take or possess these animals legally."

"But this *is* a federal case, and not state?" Albert Bloom interrupted, his normally tanned face looking pale.

"It is predominantly a federal case, although I would expect the state of Montana to be involved at some level, if for no other reason than a desire for mutual cooperation among federal and state agencies," Crane explained. "The initial arrests were made by Montana State Fish and Game officers, based upon the observations of two Stillwater County sheriff's deputies who responded to Mr. Lightner's nine-one-one call. The case was then transferred in fairly quick order to the local federal agent, who appears to have gotten into immediate contact with members of the Bravo Team."

"Which suggests that these federal undercover agents were almost certainly involved in all of this from the start," Bloom said, favoring Reston Wolfe with an ominous glare.

"Yes, it does," Crane nodded, "although I would caution all of you to keep in mind that it is still early in the process and that not all of the facts are in a format to be discoverable."

"What exactly does that mean?" another of the ICER Committee members demanded.

"While the case *has* been filed with the U.S. Attorney," Crane explained, "not all of the follow-up reports have been completed. At least two of the agents involved in the investigation are recovering from rather severe injuries and have not yet been able to put together all of their supplemental reports.

"But I should warn you," Crane added, "that while the investigative efforts of these agents have been summarized in detail by their supervisor—and there is no reason to think that any new information will be revealed in their final reports— there is *always* the possibility that additional charges could be filed as a result of these reports."

"When will we know about that?" the Committee member asked.

"That's difficult to tell," Crane shrugged. "Considering the nature of the injuries sustained by these officers, I would expect the judge to be very lenient in approving requests for continuances.

"One interesting aspect of this case, however," Crane went on, "is the readily apparent fact that there would have been *no* seizure of evidence, and certainly no arrests, at either the state *or* the federal level," he emphasized, "had it not been for a series of accidental events.

"These being," Crane raised three fingers in succession, "the very severe wounds sustained by Mr. Henry Allen Lightner during the hunt itself. The subsequent accident in which Mr. Butch Chareaux was seriously injured during the process of unloading the carcasses at Mr. Jacall's taxidermy establishment. And the fact that one of the responding deputies—whose brother happens to be a Montana State Fish and Game officer, and is therefore somewhat familiar with hunting regulations—found himself in a position to notice the carcasses in the back of Mr. Chareaux's truck."

"Incredible!" Albert Bloom shook his head.

"An unfortunate series of events at best," the chief investigator nodded.

"What charges have been brought so far?" another ICER Committee member asked.

Crane turned to the seventh typed page of his summary notes.

"So far," he said, "Alex, Butch, and Sonny Chareaux have been charged with a total of seventeen felony and five misdemeanor counts. These include assault on a federal officer, resisting arrest, and violations of the Endangered Species Act, the Migratory Bird Treaty Act, the Lacey Act, and the Airborne Hunting Act.

"In addition," Crane said after pausing for effect, "there are indications that other charges, such as kidnapping and the placing of an explosive device on a passenger airplane, may also be filed against one or more of these individuals at a later date."

"Jesus *Christ*!" some member of the committee whispered under his breath.

"Based upon our initial contacts with the U.S. Attorney's office, I think we can expect the court to set a bail of at least five hundred thousand dollars for each until a decision has been reached on the additional charges."

"Money is not the issue here," Albert Bloom said calmly. "What about the other charges?"

"Roberto Jacall and Henry Allen Lightner," Crane went on, "have been charged with two felony and one misdemeanor counts each, which include possession of untagged hunting trophies and unauthorized possession of a weapon in a national park.

"Mr. Jacall is likely to be charged with additional counts, depending on the lab analysis of hides and furs collected at what appears to be a hidden and illegal taxidermy operation located on his property. Bail is expected to be set at approximately one hundred thousand dollars.

"Mr. Lightner is currently hospitalized in federal custody. He may or may not be charged with the hunting and possession violations, depending upon the lab analysis of the bullets removed from the seized carcasses, footprints at the scenes, and the blood and hair on his clothing. His bail is expected to be set at approximately fifty thousand dollars.

"I should note here that based on our extensive interviews with Dr. Wolfe and Miss Abercombie, there seems to be some question as to the extent of Mr. Lightner's actual involvement in the hunt. Apparently he was scheduled to hunt that day, but then agreed to allow our clients to take his place at the last moment as a result of some financial arrangements.

"While Mr. Lightner certainly did take an active part in the hunt, it is not clear whether he actually shot at or killed any of these animals. Nor is it clear that he could be charged with transportation or possession, since he was apparently unconscious at the time.

"In essence," Crane explained, "it is our considered opinion that of all the subjects involved in this case, Mr. Lightner is the least vulnerable in terms of substantive charges, and therefore, the one most likely to consider a plea agreement with the U.S. Attorney's office."

"You mean testifying for the prosecution in exchange for a lesser sentence?" an ICER member asked.

"Or possibly he will face no prosecution at all," Crane nodded. "One thing we need to keep in mind about Mr. Lightner is that the majority of his injuries were apparently caused by misdirected gunfire . . . that is to say, bullets fired by our clients."

Albert Bloom closed his eyes and shook his head slowly in disbelief.

"And that, ladies and gentlemen," Crane said quietly, "is the sum of all charges filed in this case to date. Are there any questions?"

"That's *all*?" Albert Bloom blinked.

"Yes, sir," Crane nodded. "As best we are able to tell so far, and—" he gestured toward the thick pile of documents that he and his highly paid team of private investigators had managed to collect during the previous twelve hours—"I would emphasize that we have only *begun* to sort things out. The focus of the federal investigation seems to have been on Alex Chareaux and his brothers. At this point, there is no indication that Dr. Wolfe or Miss Abercombie were ever targets of this undercover operation.

"In fact," Crane said as he carefully replaced his summary notes in the crisp manila file folder, "as far as we can tell, there is no indication that the federal officials are even *aware* that Mr. Wolfe and Miss Abercombie were ever involved in that hunt.

"But then, of course," he added, "so far, none of the individuals in custody have chosen to cooperate with the investigators by making a statement. Obviously, that could change at any time."

"What are we doing about that?" Bloom asked.

"As you know, we are currently representing the Chareaux brothers as their legal counsel; and we have, of course, advised them in the strongest possible terms to make no statements whatsoever. And as you directed, we have also offered our services to Mr. Jacall and to Mr. Lightner, making it clear that all costs will be borne by the Chareaux family . . . the very least that they could do under the circumstances."

"And their response?"

"It is our understanding that Mr. Jacall will accept our offer and sign the necessary papers this afternoon. We have been unable to reach Mr. Lightner in the hospital; however, we *have* been in contact with his family attorney, and the initial indications are that he will accept Mr. Chareaux's offer on behalf of his client," Crane said with an absolutely straight face. "Apparently this attorney has some limited experience with criminal law and is thus very impressed with the number and quality of the resources—trial attorneys *and* support staff—that we are willing to put to work in his client's defense. And it seems that he is perfectly willing to accept an appropriate retainer to act as co-counsel in this matter. I have been instructed, by the way, to tell you that Mr. Kole considers the terms of your contract to be exceptionally generous. As we discussed previously, the contingency provisions should cover any unexpected situation. And in any case, Mr. Kole feels that the bonus clause will certainly compensate us for any foreseeable overage costs at our end."

"Keeping in mind that the bonus clause applies only when and if you win," Bloom reminded.

"Yes, of course," Walter Crane nodded, actually smiling as he did so.

"Are there any other questions that I can answer for anyone at this time?" Crane asked politely.

"No, Walter. Thank you for coming," Albert Bloom said, getting up and shaking the chief investigator's hand as he led him over to the door.

After closing the door, Bloom walked back to his chair, sat down, and then stared down the full length of the teak-and-rosewood table at the two people whose inconceivable stupidity had triggered this multimillion-dollar coverup.

"Do either of you have a sense, any sense at all, of the *damage* that you may have caused with this, this . . . *hunt?*" he asked, his voice nearly choked with rage.

Lisa Abercombie knew Bloom well enough to keep her mouth tightly shut. But Reston Wolfe still viewed himself as a high-level government bureaucrat, one who would therefore have some degree of leverage over a mere captain of industry.

"I think you're overreacting, Mr. Bloom," Wolfe started in. "There was no reason at all for any of us to think that—"

But Albert Bloom cut him off in mid-sentence.

"No, don't you see, Mr. Wolfe, that is *exactly* the point," Bloom said emphatically. "There was every reason why you *should* have been thinking. Every reason in the goddamn world."

"But—"

"You repeatedly assured me that there were no federal investigations of any sort being run near the Whitehorse Cabin Training Center and that you had everything under control," Bloom rasped. "But there *were* investigations being conducted, and you *didn't* have everything under control, because you stepped right into the middle of a major covert investigation like it was a pile of horse shit lying there *right in front of your goddamn eyes!*"

Bloom paused as if determined to maintain some semblance of self-control.

"You may think that this is all just a sort of game, Mr. Wolfe," he said in a soft, menacing voice that barely carried across to the other end of the table. "But I want you to understand, very clearly, as clear as I can possibly make it, that Operation Counter Wrench is *not* a game. And it is *not* one of your infantile government projects where you can simply step back and blame one of your subordinates when something goes wrong."

"But—"

"Operation Counter Wrench, Mr. Wolfe," Bloom went on forcefully, ignoring his executive director's feeble protests, "is the most important and crucial project that you will ever be involved with in your life. And if you have caused it to falter—or, God forbid, to fail—because *you* couldn't resist the opportunity to go out in the woods and kill things with a goddamn *gun* . . ."

Bloom's face was red, his hands were extended out like claws, and he seemed to be temporarily incapable of doing anything other than shaking his head slowly in pure, incredulous disbelief.

"Mr. Bloom," Wolfe said after a few moments, using every bit of willpower he possessed to maintain what remained of his dignity, "I was assured by people high up in the Interior Department that there were no such investigations being conducted anywhere near Yellowstone National Park."

Wolfe paused, sighed deeply, then went on.

"I have no justifiable excuse for my behavior in this matter; however, I do believe that we may be able to take advantage of a procedural loophole to derail this investigation completely."

The word "derail" seemed to get Albert Bloom's attention. He blinked and then stared at Wolfe.

"Yes, go on," he growled.

"All major covert investigations conducted by our Fish and Wildlife Service officers must be approved at a higher level," Wolfe explained. "We insist on that to make certain that overzealous agents don't cause Interior undue embarrassment by conducting investigations that are, shall we say, politically inconvenient."

"You think that you can block this investigation on the basis that it might *embarrass* you?" Bloom whispered incredulously, finding it difficult to comprehend the arrogance and the stupidity of the man sitting before him.

"Oh no, of course not," Wolfe smiled. "What I'm talking about is a procedural issue. Or more to the point, a failure of procedure."

"Yes, go on," Bloom said, motioning with one hand impatiently.

"As best we can tell," Wolfe said with growing confidence, "this investigation was not approved at a higher level. At least there are no approval forms on record, which would suggest that the agents conducted the investigation on their own. Basically, a failure to follow proper administrative procedures.

It happens occasionally. Not necessarily the fault of the agents, of course." Wolfe smiled. "As we all know, they are a very dedicated group of men and women. But occasionally their dedication and their enthusiasm will carry them a little too far. And when that happens, the courts have no option but to drop the case."

Albert Bloom still wasn't smiling, but his face was more composed now, and he was starting to nod slowly in understanding.

"It's a shame," Wolfe went on, "especially when career criminals like the Chareaux brothers occasionally get off. But I believe the public understands that our system of justice is far too precious to be undermined by failures of procedure, well intentioned as they may be."

"Do you seriously believe that you can, as you put it, *derail* this investigation without attracting any suspicion to yourself or anyone else associated with ICER?" Bloom asked skeptically.

"Yes, I do," Wolfe said calmly. "In fact, I'm absolutely certain of it."

"Well, I'm not," Bloom responded, but the anger in his voice had clearly receded.

"Albert," Lisa Abercombie finally said in an uncharacteristically subdued voice, sensing her opportunity, "Reston and I realize that we have made a horrible and unforgivable mistake, but we are absolutely certain that we can recover."

"How, by invoking 'failure of procedures'?" Bloom demanded.

"That, and by making absolutely sure that no one can connect us to that hunt," Abercombie nodded.

"And how do you intend to do *that*?"

"Only three people can testify that they actually saw us hunting illegally," she said. "Alex Chareaux, his brother Butch, and this man Lightner. You have already made arrangements for their defense. We will simply add whatever incentives are necessary to insure their silence in the future."

"Will that work?"

"I'm convinced it will," Abercombie nodded. "We understand that the Chareaux brothers have had some previous difficulties with the law in Louisiana. Something about two game wardens being tortured and killed. Under the circumstances, they might even be agreeable to a complete relocation out of the country. As a matter of fact, South Africa strikes me as the perfect solution. A place where they could hunt and guide to their heart's content.

"And in the meantime," she went on, encouraged by Albert Bloom's grudging nod, "we will see to it that every one of the items that could possibly link Reston and me to that scene— vehicles, guns, everything—are immediately destroyed."

"Now wait a minute!" Wolfe started to protest. "I spent a hundred and twenty-five thousand dollars on that rifle, and I'll be damned—"

"You will destroy it, *immediately*," Bloom snarled. "The rifle, and the paperwork or photographs or anything else that would indicate that you ever *possessed* such a weapon."

Then he shifted his gaze back to Lisa Abercombie.

"And what about this man Lightner?"

"Don't worry about that either," Lisa Abercombie said, her voice as cold and determined as always. "I will see to it personally that Mr. Lightner is taken care of."

"Are you still mad at me?" Lisa Abercombie whispered as she used her trembling arms to push herself away from Albert Bloom's amazingly hairy and muscular chest.

It was late, and they had argued some more over dinner, but Lisa Abercombie was patient because she knew that once they were back in Bloom's penthouse suite, she would have the advantage.

They had deliberately left the window open, and the hot, humid Washington, D.C., air had immediately filled the darkened and luxurious master bedroom, providing a continuous source of sweat that allowed their well-toned bodies to slide smoothly against each other.

Albert Bloom slowly slid his fingers up along Abercombie's sweaty torso until her slick and swollen breasts were resting in the palms of his hands.

"No, I'm not mad, I'm worried about you," he finally said in a soft whisper. "I know that you like to take risks, and I love you *because* of that, but you must never let it get out of control." Then he slid his thumbs across her hard nipples.

Lisa Abercombie moaned softly and brought her lips down against his ear.

"You know," she whispered in a silky-smooth voice, "that I *never* allow things to get out of control."

CHAPTER TWENTY-FIVE

THURSDAY, JUNE 6TH

Supervisory Special Agent Paul McNulty looked at the five members of his Special Operations Bravo Team—two were lying in rented hospital beds, and one looked like a monstrous reject from a low-budged horror film—and raised his nearly empty beer bottle in salute.

"To the Chareauxs," he said, smiling contentedly. "May they rot in the can for a hundred years."

"Right on!"

"Hear, hear."

"Fuckin'-A."

"You betcha!"

"Banzai!"

McNulty's five covert agents responded from their chairs and beds by raising and then rapidly emptying their own beer bottles. Six more bottles were then lobbed into the general direction of the large plastic trash can that had been set in the far corner of the room, the corner walls showing the effects of several failed bank shots.

In the meantime, Dwight Stoner, their resident mummy, obligingly began to pull the caps off of another six-pack.

"Okay, boys," Marie Pascalaura said as she cautiously opened the door and then came into the room, looking thoroughly professional and absolutely beautiful with her darkly tanned facial features, her patient smile, and her long, dark hair flowing over her crisply white—albeit snug—nurse's uniform. "How's everyone doing in here? Is my house going to survive your visit?"

"Oh-oh, Henry. Watch yourself, it's the nurse," Mike Takahara observed, his face red from the two beers he had slowly but determinedly consumed. "She's probably tougher here than at the hospital."

"Yeah, man, better watch out for your *ass*," Larry Paxton advised. "That lady packs a mean needle."

"Oh, I don't know, *I* think she's pretty nice," Stoner said as he started handing out the open bottles, holding three in each thickly bandaged hand.

"I can see it coming, Henry," Carl Scoby warned as he accepted another beer from Stoner. "The monster falls in love with the hero's girl, the girl falls in love with the monster, and they run off into the sunset with each other."

"That's right. Happens in all the best movies," Mike Takahara confirmed.

"Hero, mah ass," Paxton grumbled. "Since when does a hero have to call nine-one-one to get his butt out of trouble?"

"That's a good point, Henry," Carl Scoby nodded. "Here we hire you as our ace crazy man, wild-card agent *extraordinaire*, and the first chance you get to show your stuff, you take the easy way out."

"Yeah, and then when he's conscious again, all he wants to know is who won some fucking ball game," Larry Paxton added.

"Hell of a disappointment, Henry," Scoby commented solemnly.

"Yeah, especially since *Ah* had to go out and *save* my partner's ass," Paxton complained. "And nobody never told me Ah could call nine-one-one to do it, either."

"Paxton, you couldn't save shit in a bucket," Dwight Stoner growled through his swollen and split lips as he made a threatening motion to smack Paxton with a handful of beer bottles. "All you did was walk in, start a bar fight, and then haul ass out the door. Left me there to fight three hundred goddamn drunken redneck cowboys and a flipped-out coon-ass all by myself."

"There were only two hundred drunk cowboys, a couple of Indians, and the coon-ass," Paxton corrected, then drained about half the bottle in one long gulp. "I counted to make sure before I went out to get the cavalry."

"Who immediately proceeded to run you over and throw your ass in jail," Scoby reminded.

"Yeah, well, they don't 'xactly make cavalry rescues like they used to," Paxton conceded.

"Did I come in at a bad time?" Marie looked over at Paul McNulty, who seemed to be the only halfway sober member of the group.

"No such thing with these fellows, my dear," McNulty said, shaking his head and smiling. "You are always a breath of fresh air, and we're certainly grateful for your help. I just hope we're not making too much noise."

"As long as they keep on hitting the walls and not the windows, I think the neighborhood will survive," she said as she walked over to Henry Lightstone's partially raised hospital bed and began to appraise her patient's condition.

"So how you doing, sport?" she asked as she reached down and peeled up Lightstone's eyelids, one by one, to check the dilation of his pupils.

"I think I need more medical attention," Lightstone replied with a cheerful leer.

"Yeah, I *bet* you do," Marie nodded skeptically.

"Shit, he's *fine*," Larry Paxton complained from the adjoining bed. "*Ah'm* the one who needs medical attention. And besides, how come *he* gets the girl?"

"'Cause he's the hero," Carl Scoby explained. "It always happens that way."

"Personally, I think this is starting to sound like an ethnic solution," Mike Takahara said.

"See! There, what'd I tell you?" Larry Paxton nodded. "And that's exactly what it is, too. Ah'm being prejudiced against."

"So I think *I* should get the girl," Takahara finished.

"Mah *ass*!"

"I don't suppose there's any point in asking anybody how many beers these two have had so far," Marie said, looking around the room.

"Uh, three?" Lightstone guessed, mistakenly holding up five fingers.

"Yeah, that's right, 'cause Ah think he drank one of mine," Paxton agreed.

"Uh-huh," Marie nodded, having confirmed her suspicions. "As I recall, gentlemen, the deal we agreed upon was very simple. No painkillers in the morning and the afternoon, and you could have three beers apiece. So what we've got here is a choice. You can either skip on that last six-pack, or you can wait until about six o'clock this evening for your next pain pills. Take your pick."

"Hell, Ah don't need no pain pills." Paxton shook his head bravely. "Ah'm tough."

"And if he's tough, then I'm tough," Lightstone nodded in agreement.

"You're both a couple of wimps," Dwight Stoner smiled as he drained his beer bottle in one gulp and reached for another.

"Okay, guys, you asked for it," Marie Pascalaura said agreeably as she checked her watch. "You are hereby advised that serious drugs will not be available until six o'clock this evening. Any complaints, bitches, moaning, groaning, or whining will be referred to Special Agent Dwight Stoner for arbitration."

"Shit, if it's up to me, they ain't gonna get nothin', period," Stoner growled. "Couple of candy asses, that's all they are. Wanna work in this outfit, they gotta learn to play with *pain*."

"And on that cheerful note, I think I'm going to go to work," Marie Pascalaura smiled, walking back out the door with a deliberate roll of her muscular hips that left the agent team whistling and cheering in her wake.

"God, I love the medical profession," Henry Lightstone sighed.

"Yeah, well as long as you and me are roommates, and you ain't gonna share," Paxton muttered, "you can just forget about—"

There was a knock at the door, and a familiar face looked in.

"Hey, Counselor!" Henry Lightstone exclaimed, raising his beer bottle in salute. "Come on in."

"Am I interrupting anything?" Deputy U.S. Attorney Jameson Wheeler asked cautiously.

"Nah, just some general bullshit." Lightstone grinned. "Come on in and have a beer."

"Don't mind if I do," the tall and lanky government lawyer said as he entered, shut the door, and then walked over and handed McNulty a note. "But first, the mail run. Office wants you to call in right away. Sounds like they think it's important," he advised.

McNulty looked at the number, nodded, and then quickly disappeared out the door as Wheeler accepted a beer from Stoner and took McNulty's chair.

"So how's Mr. Henry Allen Lightner's highly reputable 'family attorney' doing these days?" Carl Scoby inquired after Wheeler had taken his first grateful sip of the cold brew.

"Well, to tell you the truth, pretty damned good," the Deputy U.S. Attorney nodded. "Fact is, I think I've just received the first official bribe of my entire legal career."

"No kidding?" Carl Scoby laughed. "They make it worth-while?"

Jameson Wheeler pulled a folded check out of his breast pocket and handed it over to Scoby. "I don't know, maybe I'm not reading it right. What do you think?"

"Holy shit!" Scoby whispered and then passed the check around until it got to Lightstone, who glanced at it briefly, blinked, looked again, and then stared up at Wheeler.

"Somebody's offering you two hundred and fifty thousand

dollars?" he said, blinking in astonishment. "What the hell for?"

"Basically, to be your attorney, more or less."

"Oh, yeah?" Lightstone laughed. "Well, if you don't mind my asking, Counselor, just what in hell are you planning on doing for me that's going to be worth a quarter-of-a-million-dollar fee?"

"Looks like you ain't gonna need Marie no more," Larry Paxton guessed. "Can I have her?"

"Of course you have to understand," Jameson Wheeler said, "that this is what we in the legal profession would call a 'retainer.' Just a little pocket change to keep a legal-beagle like myself hanging around on stand-by and twiddling his thumbs for the next few weeks."

"That mean you wouldn't get to keep the money unless you actually did the work?" Mike Takahara asked.

"Oh, good Lord, no," Wheeler laughed, shaking his head in mock dismay. "I'm always amazed that you law-enforcement types have so little understanding of our legal system. What kind of professionals do you think we are?"

"Gimme another beer before I say something I might regret later on," Paxton mumbled to Stoner.

"As a member in good standing of the District of Columbia and the Idaho State bars," Jameson Wheeler went on, still smiling, because he and Paxton had known and worked with each other for the past sixteen years, "I would certainly be allowed to keep my retainer whether I worked my butt off on behalf of my client or did nothing much at all. In fact, as I understand the situation, in the unlikely event that I might actually *do* something halfway significant in this particular case—say, for example, pass gas at an appropriate moment when the opening counsel is trying to make a point to the jury—I can expect to receive another check of similar if not greater value."

"I take it all back, Henry," Paxton said comtemplatively as he sipped at the cold beer. "You better stick with Marie. At least she ain't gonna run off with your wallet afterward."

"Which brings us to the basic question," Lightstone said. "Who the hell's offering to pay the freight on this deal?"

"Alex Chareaux, if you care to believe that," Wheeler shrugged.

"What?" Lightstone blinked in disbelief.

"Hey," Jameson Wheeler smiled as he brought his thin shoulders up in an exaggerated shrug, "all I know is that you and Roberto Jacall are being offered the use of one of the top legal firms in Washington, D.C., at no cost to yourselves, and I'm being offered a quarter of a million dollars to step aside and keep my mouth shut. And if that makes any sense to any of you here—" he raised his beer bottle in salute, "—then you're way ahead of me on beer."

"Sure as hell don't make any sense to me," Stoner said.

"Quite frankly," Wheeler confessed, "it's almost enough to make me wonder what I've been doing with my career all these years."

"Well, I should fucking well hope so," Paxton muttered.

"Uh, I'm not sure I'm following all this," Lightstone said, his eyebrows furrowed in confusion beneath the tape and bandages. "You mean that these people, whoever they are, don't even want you to be my attorney of record?"

"Absolutely not. Co-counsel at best, and even that in name only," Wheeler said emphatically. "As I understand it, there would be twelve trial attorneys from the firm, who would actually handle the case."

"Twelve fucking attorneys, for *me*?"

"For you and Alex, Butch and Sonny and Jacall," the Deputy U.S. Attorney nodded. "Package deal. I understand it works out so much easier that way."

"And Alex Chareaux is offering to pay the bill?" Lightstone laughed. "Come on, Jameson, you're trying to tell us that Alex Chareaux and his brothers have been making money like this from taking people out on illegal *guiding* trips?"

"Not unless they've been dealing cocaine in kilo lots on the side," Carl Scoby commented.

"That's exactly right, and, no, I'm not trying to tell you that," Jameson Wheeler said. "But what I *am* telling you, my friends, is that the firm of Little, Warren, Nobles and Kole does not come cheap. If for no other reason than the fact that they have a high overhead. The fact is, the senior partners can count on raking in a seven-figure income, clear, and a straight partnership is supposed to be good for at least a mid six. So you add up the cost of twelve criminal lawyers of that caliber over a period of several weeks, if not months, and figure out where that puts you."

"Never-never land," Lightstone grunted.

"And that doesn't even begin to count the support troops," Wheeler added. "Just as an example, I don't know what they pay Walter Crane, their chief investigator, but it has to be a bunch because I'd say he's probably more aggressive than the five of you put together."

"Sounds like a real nice guy," Stoner commented.

"To give you an idea of how nice a guy he is," Jameson Wheeler smiled, "I can tell you that if Walter Crane focused his team of investigators on Henry's cover, which I happen to know is pretty decent because I helped build it, I don't think it would take more than two days—maybe a week at the outside—to figure out two things: one, that Mr. Henry Allen Lightner does not exist; and two, that yours truly has been working as a poor but honest government lawyer in Denver for the past twenty years."

"Two days?" Scoby blinked.

"At best," the Deputy U.S. Attorney said. "I'm telling you, the man is good."

"So what does that do for our case?" Scoby asked.

"A very good question," Jameson Wheeler nodded, impressed by the realization that all five of McNulty's agents, who had been about half drunk and cheerfully celebrating when he'd walked in, were now stone-cold sober and listening carefully.

"First of all, it certainly forces us to move quickly in terms of Henry's cover if Paul wants to keep him working in the area. Fortunately," the Deputy U.S. Attorney added, "we don't have to expose Henry as an agent to prosecute the Chareauxs because, as much as I hate to admit it, managing to get himself shot like that and then making that nine-one-one call were strokes of pure genius."

"His fellow agents would prefer to think of it as dumbshit blind luck, but don't mind us," Larry Paxton smiled.

"Understandably," Wheeler chuckled. "Anyway, we obviously can't let Henry Allen Lightner go on trial, nor can I possibly put myself in a position to establish any sort of co-counsel relationship with the Little, Warren, Nobles and Kole team. As it is, I think we are dangling on the very precarious edge of confidentiality with respect to the client-attorney relationship. Judge Wu is pretty open-minded for a circuit-court judge, and he wasn't the least bit pleased when Paul told him about the probes on your team, but I can't see him allowing us to carry out this little game much further."

"So how do you figure it?" Scoby asked.

"Henry Allen Lightner completely disassociates himself from the Chareauxs and their attorneys and then offers to plead guilty to knowingly taking part in an illegal hunt, because there isn't any evidence to tie him into any other part of the case," Jameson Wheeler said offhandedly. "The U.S. Attorney and I agree to probation, with no requirement to assist the prosecution, and Henry Lightner simply disappears. Another satisfied customer of our criminal justice system."

"You think it'll work?"

"I don't see why—"

At that moment, Paul McNulty shoved the door open and entered the room, the furious expression on his face causing even Stoner to back away.

"They want to talk with you," McNulty growled at Wheeler.

"Me?"

"Yeah, you," McNulty nodded. "Right now."

McNulty waited until the puzzled Deputy U.S. Attorney had left the room, then looked over at his team.

"They want to drop the case," he said.

"*What?*" five agents yelled in unison, causing Paxton to

wince in pain and Lightstone to grab at his head as McNulty held up his hand for silence.

"Who's 'they'?" Carl Scoby demanded.

"The Department of Interior, for one."

"Any particular reason?"

"Pretty much the classic reasons," McNulty shrugged. "Failure to follow proper procedures. Concern that Special Ops is running amok. Perception that severely limited resources have been devoted to a relatively minor case. Clear need for better oversight. It goes on, but I think you get the drift."

"You mean that somebody in the Department of Interior actually cares about the Chareaux brothers?" Lightstone asked.

"Apparently," McNulty nodded.

"Who do those bastards *know*?" Larry Paxton muttered.

"What about those three characters you guys took out on the hunt?" Mike Takahara suggested. "Any way they might be a reason?"

"I can't see how or why," Henry Lightstone shrugged. "They aren't even charged with anything. Why the hell would *they* care?"

"I don't know," Takahara admitted, "but *somebody* cares."

"That's right," McNulty added, tight-jawed. "Somebody cares a lot. The Department now thinks that two Special Ops teams may be one too many. So it's going to dismantle one team. Guess which one."

"Bravo team," Carl Scoby whispered.

"Can they do that?" Henry Lightstone asked.

"Oh, yeah, they sure as hell can," McNulty nodded. "It's called 'priority management.'"

"Can we fight it?" Lightstone asked.

"Sure we can," McNulty told him. "We can pull all of our stats together, document our cases, write it all up in one big, summary report. And then demand a hearing."

"So when do we start?" Lightstone demanded.

"Right after we get reassigned to the New York office," McNulty replied evenly.

"Oh, God, no," Carl Scoby and Larry Paxton whispered in unison.

"Either that," McNulty shrugged, "or we can go along with the program . . ."

"Yeah?" Lightstone said suspiciously.

". . . and receive immediate and permanent transfers to the duty stations of our choice."

"*What?*"

"For example," McNulty went on, ignoring Lightstone's exclamation, "they've offered me the Region Seven SAC job in Anchorage, where Martha and I had hoped to retire in a couple of years. Carl would get the training coordinator's position that just opened up at Marana. Larry drops into a newly created agent-pilot slot in Miami. Dwight would get—"

"Goddamnit, we're being split up and bought off!" Lightstone exploded just as Jameson Wheeler came back into the room, closed the door, and looked at McNulty with a grim expression.

"What'd they offer you?" McNulty asked.

"Chief of the Lands and Natural Resources Division if I decide to be cooperative," the Deputy U.S. Attorney replied evenly.

"And if you don't?"

"Newark office, working toxic-waste dump sites."

Larry Paxton muttered something unintelligible.

"See, the thing is, Henry," Carl Scoby said in a voice tightened with barely controlled rage, "what we're being offered is the carrot or the stick. New York and Newark are the sticks. And they are big mothers, let me tell you."

"So fuck 'em," Lightstone said. "How bad can New York be?"

"Henry," Deputy U.S. Attorney Jameson Wheeler said softly, "before you fellows take a vote on this, which I have no doubt you will, why don't you let me tell you a few things about the New York office?"

CHAPTER TWENTY-SIX

FRIDAY, JUNE 7TH

The crew of the Bell Ranger dropped Dr. Reston Wolfe off at the Whitehorse Cabin heliport and prepared to wait on stand-by. The executive director of ICER hunched way down for several awkward steps until he was clear of the sweeping rotor blades and well beyond the more distant yellow-painted warning stripes. He then hurried on past the stone-faced ground controller with a briefcase clutched tightly in his small, bureaucratic fist.

Three minutes later, Wolfe walked through the private entrance to Lisa Abercombie's underground office, closed the door, and set his briefcase down on her desk. Abercombie ignored him as she continued to read through a stack of faxed press clippings.

Undaunted, Wolfe opened the briefcase, removed a handful of thick file folders, and tossed them onto the desk top.

"It's a done deal," he said proudly.

"Meaning?" Lisa Abercombie asked as she finally looked up.

"Bravo Team no longer exists," Wolfe said. "At five o'clock Eastern Standard Time, which was—" he glanced down at his watch "—exactly one hour and twelve minutes ago, the team was officially disbanded and all assigned special agents were officially transferred to new duty stations of their choice."

"You're certain of that?"

"It's all right there in the files." Wolfe gestured to the stack of personnel folders. "Six voluntary requests for transfer with accompanying approvals and personnel actions, all signed, sealed, and delivered."

"Wonderful," Abercombie nodded.

"And, coincidentally," Wolfe went on, "you might be happy to learn that the case against the Chareaux brothers has been dropped."

"Oh, really? On what basis?"

"Failure to follow official policies and procedures. Covert operations require law-enforcement agents of the Fish and Wildlife Service to obtain prior written approval before conducting undercover investigations against individuals with sensitive backgrounds."

"You identified the Chareaux brothers as having *sensitive* backgrounds? Are you out of your goddamned mind?" Lisa Abercombie demanded, her eyes suddenly widening with fear.

"What Paul McNulty and his covert team simply didn't realize when they began their little probe," Wolfe went on confidently, "was that the Chareaux brothers have been working as confidential informants for an extremely sensitive government operation, the details of which cannot be revealed at this time without putting other agents and informants at risk."

"You have that documented?" Abercombie asked uneasily.

Wolfe nodded.

"So what did you threaten them with?" Abercombie asked.

"Immediate transfers to New York, with occasional forays into Newark."

"You really think that's going to be enough of a threat to keep them quiet?"

"As I understand it," Wolfe smiled, "a typical New York import-export case can take several years to resolve, rummaging through filthy warehouses, sifting through hundreds of thousands of records. And, of course, it's virtually impossible to find a decent place to live anywhere near the office on a special agent's salary."

Lisa Abercombie was quiet for a long moment.

"Nice," she finally said. "In fact, very nice." She nodded in grudging approval.

"I thought you'd like it," Wolfe smiled, clearly pleased with his clever bureaucratic maneuvers.

"But we have another problem that you may not know about yet," Abercombie said. "Have you seen the papers?"

"Not today. Why?"

"Read these," she said as she tossed the faxed news clippings across the desk.

Wolfe scanned the clippings, then went back and read the first two articles more thoroughly.

"They did it," he whispered.

"They certainly did," Lisa Abercombie concurred. "And what's more, they did it perfectly. I don't think we could have asked the team for a better demonstration."

"How did you manage to set it up?" Wolfe asked.

"That's the beauty of it," Abercombie smiled, her dark eyes flashing with unconcealed amusement. "The stupid bastards set it up themselves. Five known militant activists from three of the top environmental groups deciding to get together for an informal meeting at a remote location on Long Island. It was perfect."

"Any idea why they called the meeting?"

"Probably to discuss strategies, or maybe just to exchange tofu recipes," Abercombie shrugged. "It doesn't matter now, though. One of them was well known for making violent threats against specific industrial targets. Apparently he liked to spout off to the press about how the environmentalists ought to declare war on the industrial world. I mean, what more could we ask for?"

"That quote I read." Wolfe flipped through to the second clipping. "Ah, yes, here it is: 'He was always talking about using bombs as a last resort, but we never took him seriously because nobody ever thought he'd really be stupid enough to do it.'" Wolfe shook his head in admiration. "God, that's beautiful!"

"We were able to get some preliminary reports from the Justice Department," Abercombie smiled. "Apparently they found enough evidence in the basement—including some buried explosives and a couple of crude timing devices—to tentatively conclude that the victims were probably examining a completed bomb when something set it off."

"What if they try to track all of that stuff back to a source?" Wolfe asked.

Abercombie smiled. "It seems that our tough-talking victim really did have a thing for explosives. What little he did have—just a few sticks of dynamite and the timers—was carefully stored away at a warehouse in Connecticut. So all Maas and Asai had to do was relocate his pathetic little armory to the basement of the Long Island meeting site and then see to it that the Radio Shack receipts and the sketches in his handwriting would survive the blast."

"Sounds perfect," Wolfe murmured.

"That's what I thought," Lisa Abercombie said with a curious edge to her voice. "Until I discovered the problem." She opened her desk drawer and removed another set of clippings, which she tossed over to Wolfe.

"A Bozeman newspaper?" he asked with a quizzical expression as he glanced at the first header.

"Would you believe that one of the victims who was killed in the explosion just happened to live in Bozeman, Montana?" Abercombie asked as the executive director of ICER started to scan through the small type.

"Oh, for Christ's sake," Wolfe winced. "Didn't anybody *know* that?"

"No." Abercombie shook her head. "Other than our mad bomber, who was also the primary coordinator for the meeting, we had no idea of who the other representatives might be. It was simply an unexpected opportunity, and we took advantage of it."

Wolfe sat for a moment in contemplative silence.

"These are just local papers," he said finally. "They run an article one day and by the next day, it's forgotten."

"Yes, that probably would have been the case *if* the local NBC affiliate hadn't stopped by the victim's home to interview his parents," Abercombie nodded. "Do you know what those people gave him?"

"No, what?" Wolfe asked uneasily.

"A homemade video tape showing what a wonderful person their son was because he had always spent his summers

working as an outdoor naturalist at—you'll never guess—
Yellowstone National Park. Naturally, Brokaw picked it up
immediately for his Nightly News show."

"Christ Almighty!" Wolfe whispered.

"Do you know what that *means*?" Lisa Abercombie asked in
a quiet, chilling voice. "It's a link. Something that we can't
afford right now."

"But I don't see how *anyone* could make the connection
between a Bozeman naturalist who died in an accident on Long
Island and three illegal hunting guides at Yellowstone, one of
whom happened to be arrested in Bozeman," Wolfe said. "The
two incidents seem completely unrelated."

"The only problem is that they are *not* separate and they are
not unrelated," Abercombie reminded. "Dr. Morito Asai was
involved in both. So were you and I, to a lesser degree. And
keep in mind," she added, "that if we start talking investigations, we're talking the FBI."

"But no one can link us to Asai or Bozeman—" Wolfe
started to protest.

"Except for Alex and Butch Chareaux, and the covert agents
who were investigating them," Abercombie responded quietly.

"How could the FBI possibly make that connection?"

"Perhaps because *we* directed *them* to investigate the activities of a certain Fish and Wildlife Service Special Operations
team. A team that was coincidentally dismantled after investigating the Chareaux brothers, who were arrested in the
Yellowstone National Park area." Abercombie's voice was
tinged with sarcasm.

Wolfe shook his head slowly. "I think you're reaching," he
said, trying to remain calm. But he was tapping his fingers
nervously on his leg and he could feel his heart starting to
pound.

"The committee and I would like nothing better than to
believe that," Abercombie said.

"But we bought them all off," Wolfe protested. "It's all
history. The Chareauxs are going to be relocated to South

Africa, and all the agents got their dream duty stations. Why would they even *care* about this case any longer?"

"Because they lost, and people like that don't like to lose."

"But they lost against each other," Wolfe said, desperate to find some handle on the situation because he was starting to sense where all of this was heading. "I mean, at the very worst, why would they be interested in *us?*"

"Precisely," Lisa Abercombie nodded as she reached into her desk drawer, brought out three more file folders and tossed them on top of the six that Wolfe had brought with him from Washington, D.C. "Which is why we are going to make certain that they are *completely* focused on each other before we take another step with Operation Counter Wrench."

Then, as Wolfe stared at the pile of manila folders with growing dread, Abercombie reached over and pressed a button on her intercom.

"Tracy," she said in a cold voice, "would you please have Mr. Maas report to my office, *immediately.*"

HUNTED . . .

CHAPTER TWENTY-SEVEN

SUNDAY, SEPTEMBER 12TH

The Kenai Peninsula, a huge expanse of wilderness extending out from the south-central edge of Alaska, is a land of extremes. High mountain ranges, huge pondering glaciers, hundreds of lakes, and an unimaginable diversity of plants and animals make the Kenai a place where legends are born. It is a place where sun-drenched summers and crisp autumn winds can suddenly give way to a winter storm of incredible proportions; where ice and soil fight an age-old battle measured in inches, while the land itself is described in millions of acres.

But more important, it is a place where predator and prey meet, where the strong and aggressive triumph, and the weak perish.

It has always been that way, even on the two-million-acre Kenai National Wildlife Refuge, a huge area of wilderness set aside as a sanctuary from man—the most prolific and dangerous predator the earth has ever known.

It was approaching mid-September, still early in terms of the winter calendar, but the mother Kodiak bear could sense the changes in the valley formed by the joining of Benjamin Creek and the Killey River. Changes that would spell certain doom for her two late-born cubs if she didn't act soon.

She hadn't always lived here in this secure and hidden wilderness. There were vague memories. The thunderous crash of the rifle. Her mother's sudden death. The hunger that had grown worse and worse until she was found by a park ranger, who had stuffed her into his jacket and taken her back to his plane. Ultimately she had been introduced to a new life on the Kenai National Wildlife Refuge, where she had never again encountered a human being.

She was the only true Kodiak living among hundreds of "lesser," brown bears, but it did not matter. She had found a mate, a huge brown male nearly equal to her in size and ferocity; and their union—a rare and unlikely event—had produced a pair of late-born cubs that were now, according to her deep-seated instincts, the primary reason for her existence.

The other things that she understood were equally instinctive: her cubs were still small compared to the others; the weather was turning cold; the salmon run was almost finished; and the competition for the remaining fish was becoming increasingly fierce.

That, and the knowledge that a hungry brown bear—especially the males, and even her mate—would eat anything available during those last desperate days before hibernation.

Standing just over nine feet in height and weighing nearly seventeen hundred pounds, the mother Kodiak knew that she could take on and defeat any one of the males face-to-face. But she also sensed that a battle might leave her cubs undefended for a few precious moments, and she could not accept that kind of risk. She would have to move her cubs away from the Killey River spawning beds.

Thus, intent on finding the food, shelter, and isolation they would need in the coming months, she led them north along Benjamin Creek, slowly working toward the rocky southern shore of Skilak Lake, where her fate, and the fate of Operation Counter Wrench, would be irrevocably entwined.

CHAPTER TWENTY-EIGHT

MONDAY, SEPTEMBER 13TH

Henry Lightstone and Marie Pascalaura ended up with almost an hour and a half to kill before their long-awaited flight to Anchorage. They had been sitting quietly next to each other in the main concourse of the Seattle-Tacoma International Airport, holding hands and lost in their own daydreams, when Lightstone suddenly felt a momentary wave of fear that seemed terrifyingly familiar.

Jarred by the sensation, but too self-controlled to give in to panic, he remained absolutely still in his seat.

"Henry, are you all right?" Marie asked in a calm and quiet voice. She had been startled by the sudden tension in Henry's arm. Her hand slid gently over to his wrist, casually feeling for his pulse. He started to tell her that he was fine, that there was nothing to worry about.

"Henry? What is it?"

"I don't know," he said softly, forcing himself to relax as his trained eyes began to scan the crowded concourse once again, searching for the one object, or entity, or thing that had jarred him to attention. He checked his watch, noting that it was eleven twenty-five, West Coast Time, and that they had forty-five minutes before it would be time to board another plane for the third time that morning.

Forty-five minutes, he nodded in satisfaction. Plenty of time to get up and stretch his stiffened leg muscles, pick up a local newspaper, grab a cup of coffee, find a rest room, and spot a killer.

Still willing himself to relax, Lightstone closed his eyes for a brief moment, taking in and releasing a deep breath. Then he forced himself to turn his head slowly and scan the immediate terminal area for one more time, continuing to search for the out-of-place element—a person, an article, whatever it was—that had jarred his mental alarms.

There were a lot of factors to be considered, Lightstone reminded himself. The real bad ones were rarely stupid enough to try to take someone out in a public place. Especially if that someone was likely to be armed. Far better to run the tail, maintain a reasonable distance, and watch for the opportune moment.

"Listen," he said quietly, "don't look around, but I think there may be somebody here in the concourse watching us."

Marie Pascalaura's eyebrows furrowed in bewilderment, but she was alert and thoughtful enough not to move her head.

"Watching us? Why?"

"I don't know," Lightstone shrugged easily. "It happens occasionally. Somebody you worked on a few years back spots you in a public place, wants to make sure it really is you, and then maybe sticks around just to see what you're doing."

That was one of the built-in hazards of working covert investigations, Lightstone thought as he continued to scan every adult male in the SEA-TAC main concourse, searching for a face out of his past. A face to justify that ever-present edge of self-serving paranoia that you never quite escaped when you worked undercover.

"I thought you said you didn't have to worry about that sort of thing anymore," Marie Pascalaura said softly.

"I didn't think I did. The U.S. of A. is a hell of a lot bigger than San Diego County."

"Oh."

Presumably a familiar face, Lightstone told himself reassuringly. Male, most likely, because through his entire law-enforcement career, he could remember working only two women sufficiently aggressive and dangerous to worry about. So figure twenty-five to forty, with a vindictive personality, he told himself. And considering his current occupation, maybe even a hunter. Which would make it male, white, middle-aged, tough, and deadly.

Wonderful, Lightstone thought as he continued to scan the sea of faces moving back and forth beneath the large, internally illuminated blue sign that directed people to the "C", "D" and "N" terminals.

"Are we in danger?" Marie Pascalaura asked, trying not to react to the goose bumps crawling on her arms and the cold chill starting to travel down the back of her neck.

"No, I don't think so." Lightstone shook his head. "An airport's too public, too many witnesses."

"Too many witnesses for what?" she whispered, but Lightstone ignored her as he continued his scan of the concourse.

Then it occurred to her. "Do you have your gun with you?" she whispered.

"No."

"Where is it?"

"Packed away in one of the suitcases."

"Oh, great."

"It doesn't matter." Lightstone shrugged with what he hoped was a reassuring smile. "Nobody's going to be stupid enough to try something with a gun in a major airport like this."

"So what are we supposed to do, just sit here and wait for this character to show his face?" she asked after a long minute went by.

"Until I can get a better idea of who or what and where, that's exactly what we're going to do," Lightstone said emphatically.

Which wasn't going to be easy, he thought to himself, because the huge main concourse of the Seattle-Tacoma International Airport was literally teeming with groups of energetic and self-assertive white males of every age and description.

Lightstone's trained eyes had been categorizing them with almost monotonous ease during the half hour that he and Marie had been sitting there daydreaming. He'd done it mostly out of habit and amusement, because he'd been mildly bored then, even though he thoroughly enjoyed sitting next to Marie's warm body and holding her hand.

But he wasn't bored now.

"This is crazy," Marie Pascalaura said quietly.

"Yeah, I know," Lightstone nodded as he absentmindedly stroked a relaxed hand along his girlfriend's tensed arm, vaguely aware that they had switched roles: he was starting to relax, while she was becoming increasingly nervous and uneasy.

Eventually his eyes returned to the group of four men and one woman waiting in line to pass through one of the metal detectors that led into the "C" concourse, where he and Marie would be catching their Alaska Airlines flight. He realized that they were the ones who had caught his attention when he first felt that warning tug from his subconscious. He'd ignored them at first, because he was absolutely certain that he'd never seen any of them before. But this was the third time now that his attention had been drawn back to them. Two members of the group, the woman and one of the men, were Asian—possibly Japanese, he guessed—and three were Caucasian, one of whom looked vaguely European, although Lightstone wasn't sure why he thought so. All of them were casually dressed in jeans and short-sleeved shirts. And all were carrying traveling bags that would easily fit in the overhead rack or under the seat in front.

"Do you see anybody?"

"I'm not sure," Lightstone said. "Maybe."

He watched the group more closely as it moved forward in the long line. As far as Lightstone could tell, the only visual element that set these five apart from all the other nameless entities wandering around the airport terminal was a pair of hiking boots worn by one of the white males.

From a distance of about twenty feet, the boots looked like they were made of a dark-gray leather with a rough, grainy texture that seemed vaguely familiar.

"Listen," he said quietly, "I'm going to get up and walk around for a couple of minutes."

"Why?"

"Just to move around a little bit, see what happens."

"Are you sure that's a good idea?"

"Good as any," Lightstone shrugged as his eyes continued to scan the concourse.

"Mind if I come with you?"

Marie Pascalaura was not a timid or fearful woman. But she knew Henry Lightstone well enough by now to be thoroughly unnerved by the idea that someone or something in the concourse had spooked her certifiably crazy and seemingly fearless special-agent lover.

"Probably better if you didn't." Lightstone shook his head. "You'll be a lot safer sitting right here, where I can keep an eye on you."

"But what about you?"

"I'll be fine, too. I just want to check something out."

Bothered and encouraged at the same time by the fact that there was something oddly familiar about those boots, Lightstone got up and walked over to a nearby row of newspaper boxes. There he fed a quarter and a dime into the slots, pulled out a paper, folded it under his arm, and began walking in a circuitous route that ultimately took him past the group of four men and a woman waiting in line.

After pausing to look at an oddly twisted piece of sculpture, he wandered back to his seat with a relaxed smile on his face.

"*Ceratotherium simum,*" he said to Marie as he settled back into his chair, feeling more relaxed now.

"Cera what?"

"*Ceratotherium simum,*" Lightstone repeated. "That's the scientific name for white rhino."

"You think that we're being watched by a white rhino?" Marie Pascalaura asked suspiciously.

"No, not watched. More like we just happened to cross paths." Lightstone winked. "No big deal."

"I see," Marie nodded skeptically.

Probably a felony because the boots looked brand new, Lightstone told himself, vaguely proud of his knowledge of wildlife parts and products. But even so, he wasn't about to arrest someone for wearing a pair of rhino-hide boots. Not today anyway, he smiled, watching casually as the group shuffled up to the baggage-screening area. They stood just under the split-view overhead TV monitor that showed the two X-ray scanner screens and the flow of people through the two rectangular metal detectors.

Then, as Lightstone blinked in surprise, two of the men in the group did something completely unexpected.

Walking around to the side of the hand-carry X-ray unit, they casually displayed small, black-leather badge cases to the security officer standing in front of the walk-through metal detector. Then, as Lightstone continued to watch, all five of them walked around the side of the X-ray machine, past the metal scanner, and proceeded to the desk of the "C"-concourse duty officer, where they presented their three-page forms.

"Well, I'll be damned," Lightstone whispered.

"What is it?" Marie Pascalaura asked.

"I think I just figured out what it was that jarred my antennas. The five people I pointed out to you are cops."

"Are you sure?"

"I'm positive that at least two of them are," Lightstone nodded. The other three members of the group took the yellow and pink copies of their forms back, then picked up their bags and started walking down toward the "C" concourse.

"I'm pretty sure the other three are carrying concealed weapons, but I'm not sure that they're any kind of law-enforcement officers," Lightstone added.

"How do you know that?"

"They were careful to walk around the metal detector, as if they didn't want to set it off. But then they didn't show the security guards any badges. That's the first thing you've got to do when you try to bypass the screening system," he explained. "Otherwise, everybody gets real upset."

"Who would they let on an airplane carrying a gun except a cop?" Marie asked curiously.

"I don't know," Lightstone shrugged. "Maybe drug dealers, snitches, CIA agents, terrorists, people like that."

Marie Pascalaura stared at him for another long moment.

"Anybody ever tell you that you've got a warped imagination?" she finally asked.

"Just about every supervisor I ever had," Lightstone admitted.

"Are you *sure* you're mentally fit to get married?"

Henry Lightstone blinked in surprise and then smiled. "You mean you changed your mind?"

"Not necessarily," Marie Pascalaura hedged as she stood up and reached for her carry-on bag. "Let's see if anybody starts shooting at us before we get on that plane. We probably ought to worry about getting married *after* we get to Anchorage."

"I just talked to the pilot," Shoshin Watanabe said as he watched the attractive woman on the other side of the security check stretch to give her boyfriend a long, lingering kiss. "The plane is refueled and ready to go."

"How much time?" Gerd Maas grunted as he dropped his carry-on bag next to his expensive rhino-skin boots. He stared out through the window at the approaching private jet that they would be boarding. The pilot had received special permission to pick up passengers at the Horizon gate while the plane was being refueled for the long flight.

Standing beside his team leader, Shoshin Watanabe continued to watch Marie Pascalaura and Henry Lightstone as they picked up their carry-on bags and walked to the end of the security check-in line. Typical Americans, he thought. No sense of shame when it came to fondling each other in public.

Then he looked down at his watch and smiled. "In about four minutes," he said, "it will all begin."

CHAPTER TWENTY-NINE

MONDAY, SEPTEMBER 13TH

The call came in at seventy-thirty that Monday morning. Carl Scoby tried to beg off because he had planned to spend the day with the resident-agent staff of the Marana Law Enforcement Training Center on a tour of the Fort Apache Indian Reservation.

But the woman was insistent that *someone* had to show up. She knew where twenty-four bear carcasses had been buried after their paws had been cut off, and she could show him where at least fifty bear gallbladders were being dried in preparation for sale.

Scoby tried to explain that he was new to the area, already had plans for the Indian reservation, and would much rather make an appointment to talk with her on the following day.

"But don't you see," the informant said, "the bears are from the reservation." The woman, who sounded like she might be German, added with a nervous edge to her voice: "My boyfriend is planning on making a big sale this evening, and if the bastard ever finds out I've squealed on him, he'll *really* beat me up bad the next time."

Scoby finally agreed to meet the woman at ten-thirty that morning at her cabin on the Simon River. If it turned out to be something worthwhile, he told himself, he and the other resident instructors at the Marana Training Center could always set up a surveillance and track the boyfriend back to his customers.

So at exactly ten-thirty that morning, Carl Scoby drove his

Jeep to the cabin, got out, and looked around briefly at the surrounding forest.

"Mrs. Hoffstedler?" he asked when an attractive young woman opened the door slightly and looked out over the stretched chain latch.

"Yes, I am Carine Hoffstedler," Carine Müeller acknowledged in a thickly accented voice. "Who are you?"

"I'm Special Agent Carl Scoby of the U.S. Fish and Wildlife Service, ma'am," Scoby said, holding out his badge and credentials to the visibly nervous woman. "Is your, uh, husband home?"

"No, my boyfriend and his friends, they are not here," Müeller said as she unlatched the chain and then stepped far enough outside for Scoby to see the large, purplish bruise on the side of her cheek. "But I was afraid you might be one of their friends, checking up on me. Please, come in."

Responding to well-ingrained habits, Scoby entered the cabin cautiously, but it was immediately apparent that they were alone in the small two-room structure.

"Would you like some coffee?"

"No, thank you." Scoby smiled.

"Then let me take you there right now to show you the bears," she said as she strapped a small pack around her slim waist. She grabbed up a jacket and led Scoby out the back door to a narrow trail.

"This is one of my favorite places," Carine Müeller said as she carefully moved branches aside so they could pass. "I'm going to hate to leave it."

"Have you been here long?" Scoby asked, trying to concentrate more on the forest and less on the woman's tight jeans.

"You mean at this house?"

"No, I mean in the United States."

"Oh, not so long," Müeller shrugged.

"You speak English very well, but I couldn't help noticing your accent," Scoby said.

"Oh, yes. You like the way I speak?"

"Yes, I do," Scoby smiled. "It's very, uh, flavorful," he said, searching for the word.

Carine Müeller laughed, looking back at the agent. "I have never heard anyone say that before."

"Well . . ."

"My boyfriend thinks I am very sexy when I talk English, but then he is not so shy as most of you Americans," Müeller said. Scoby thought she had a great deal of composure for a supposedly nervous and abused woman.

"You think Americans are shy?" he asked.

Müeller nodded. "You Americans know the big talk, but not so much the gentle words. I think it is because you are too shy, and that is no way to impress a *Fräulein*."

"You're German, then?" Scoby asked.

"No, not German, but you are very close," Müeller said as she continued to push forward through the narrow trail. "I was born in Germany, but my father is Swiss and my mother is French, so I am what you Americans would call a hybrid. Is that the right word?"

"I think we would call you someone who shouldn't allow her boyfriend to give her black eyes," Scoby said seriously.

"Yes, you are right. It was stupid of me to let him do that," Carine Müeller nodded, glancing back at Scoby again. "Sometimes we hybrids are foolish about our men. But did I not convince you to come here to take my boyfriend and his friends away so that I can have the cabin all to myself? So maybe I am not so stupid after all, yes?" With that, she turned her attention back to the trail.

After about five minutes of hiking through the dense woods, they came to a small clearing alongside the riverbank.

"Over there," Müeller said, pointing to the opposite side of the clearing. "See those shacks? The one on the right is where he stores the paws and the gallbladders until they're dried. The one in the middle is their processing shed. And the larger one on the left, the one with the chimney, is where they drink and have their poker parties."

"How many people usually work here?"

"Usually it is my boyfriend and his three partners. But sometimes there are one or two others when they decide to play cards."

"But you're sure none of them are here now?" Scoby asked as he scanned the wooden structures with his binoculars.

"I am very sure they are not here. If they were, we would have seen one of their cars back at the cabin, or one of their boats tied up at the riverbank."

"Is that how they come here, by boat?"

"The buyers always arrive by boat, but then they go away somewhere else to make the exchange," Carine Müeller told him. "Do you think you can follow them to the place where they do that?"

"I'm sure we can come up with something," Carl Scoby smiled. "Shall we take a look at the galls and the burial site?"

"Oh, yes, of course," she nodded. "But first I wanted to ask you something. How will you prove that they are doing something illegal if you don't actually see them killing the animals?"

"When we make arrangements to buy wildlife parts or products from a suspect, sometimes we can get them to brag about how they're outsmarting all the law-enforcement people," Scoby explained as they walked to the storage shed. "If there happens to be a hidden tape recorder nearby, we can always play the tape back to a judge or a jury."

"Would *you* do something like that?"

"It depends on the situation," Scoby said as he surveyed the three shacks.

"I think it is so strange that a person like you could do something like that."

"Oh, really? Why's that?" Scoby asked as he moved cautiously up to the side of a door, slipping his left hand inside his vest and releasing the safety strap on his shoulder holster.

"Because you look so much like a policeman."

"Yeah, I know," Scoby nodded as he reached for the door with his right hand. "A lot of people tell me that."

"Which I find fascinating, because I hate policemen so much," Carine Müeller said softly as she stepped forward into a semicrouched position with a .357 Magnum revolver she had withdrawn from her jacket extended out in two steady hands.

"What?" Scoby said, starting to come around when the first

of six semijacketed hollow-points caught him square in the center of his chest.

As Scoby crumpled backward, Müeller continued to follow him with her sight pattern, smoothly triggering off five more high-velocity rounds into the rib-cage area of the agent's falling body.

None of the six bullets had actually penetrated Carl Scoby's Kevlar vest, but the sledgehammer-like impacts of the mush-rooming .357 Magnum projectiles had cracked or broken at least half of his ribs, and the agonizing pain made it almost impossible for him to draw the heavy SIG-Sauer automatic from his shoulder holster.

Stunned and nearly unconscious, Carl Scoby might have given up then. But the sight of Carine Müeller calmly dumping the expended brass out of .357 Magnum, then reaching into her pack for one of her speed-loaders, gave him all the incentive he needed.

Functioning on instinct and training alone, Scoby had just brought his heavy automatic to bear on the blurry figure and was starting to squeeze the trigger when Kiro Nakamura stepped out of the shack and fired a single .357 round right into the side of his exposed head.

"I can't believe it," Marie Pascalaura whispered as she slid her head up against Henry Lightstone's shoulder and closed her eyes.

"What don't you believe?" Lightstone mumbled, nearly asleep because they'd been up half the night before, packing and chasing each other around the bedroom.

"That you and I are actually flying to Alaska to see if we want to live there," she whispered against his ear. "And that you're willing to give up undercover work so that we can live almost like normal people."

"And we're going to get married?" Lightstone mumbled drowsily.

"Nope. After you get those transfer papers signed, and after you've worked for McNulty as a senior resident agent for a few months, *then* we can get married," Marie Pascalaura said firmly. "Until then, you're just going to have to get used to being shacked up."

"Nice trusting attitude," Lightstone said as he moved his head around to give her a gentle kiss.

"Attitude nothing," Marie Pascalaura smiled. "I just want to be sure you can do it."

"Do what, leave undercover work?"

"Uh-huh."

"You really don't think I can?" Lightstone asked, lifting his head and staring into the beautiful dark eyes of his girlfriend.

"I have my doubts."

"Well, I'll tell you what," he said as he settled his head down against the soft, aromatic mass of her long, dark hair. "I'll probably miss Scoby, and Paxton, and Stoner, and maybe even that crazy Takahara, but I don't think I'm going to miss the work at all."

At eleven-fifteen that morning, Special Agent-Pilot Larry Paxton was cruising over the Everglades National Park, looking for baited ponds and illegal shooters, when a scratchy voice broke in over his scrambled radio system.

"Super Cub November Two-Two-Seven-Four, do you read me?"

"This is Super Cub Two-Two-Seven-Four," Paxton acknowledged into his helmet mike. "Go ahead."

"Two-Two-Seven-Four, this is Florida State Fish and Game Officer Al Cousins. You that new federal agent-pilot we heard about?"

"I guess that depends," Paxton replied. "What'd you hear about him?"

"Well, to tell you the truth, we heard a lot of things," the voice chuckled. "But ol' Brian Jacobs seems to think that the guy just might be okay anyway, if he's really as good with that airplane as he's supposed to be."

Paxton nodded and smiled. Brian Jacobs was the senior resident agent assigned to the Miami office, and also the man that Paxton was going to have to impress if he wanted to stay assigned to that office. But it wasn't going to be easy. Paxton had a lot of ground to make up.

Predictably, the idea of a black agent getting the Miami slot over the long-standing transfer requests of five other agents with higher seniority had not pleased the rest of the Southern Florida law-enforcement staff. Paxton knew he would have felt the same way if *he'd* been shoved aside by a political appointee with less seniority, regardless of the underlying reasons.

"Uh, did Brian happen to mention anything about how I ended up getting this assignment?"

"Yep, sure did. Told us a real interesting story about how you guys got bushwhacked and broken up by some hotshot political types. Course, to tell you the truth, nobody down here was all that surprised. We kinda expect that sort of thing out of the federal government."

"Well, maybe you can understand why I wouldn't mind getting the chance to show my stuff with this bird," Paxton said after a moment's pause. "Think you might have a target I could play with for a while?"

"Kinda hoping you'd say that," the voice over the radio drawled. "And, as a matter of fact, we sure do. Just got a report sayin' there's a couple of poachers out near Big Lostmans trying to nail themselves one of our Florida panthers. Now just between you and me, I really wouldn't much care if they shot every one of them hybrid bastards, but I guess if that ever happens, we're gonna have ourselves a mess of pissed-off Indians around here."

"If it's all the same to you, I'd just as soon stay out of an Indian war for the first couple of weeks," Paxton commented.

"You and me both," the voice agreed.

"Listen, I'm pretty close to Big Lostmans right now," Paxton said. "What do you want me to look for?"

"Supposed to be two hunters in a pirogue, working their way north toward Alligator Bay," the voice said into Paxton's earphones. "We got ourselves a floatplane waiting down at Whitewater, but we're still about a half hour out, and that's gonna make it a long way to go for a couple of poachers that ain't there. Thought maybe you could make a pass or two around that area for us, see if there's anybody worth talking to down there. You get lucky and then guide us in, maybe we can share the credit, make it one of them fancy state and federal joint investigations," the voice suggested.

"Tell you what," Paxton said as he banked the Super Cub. "If we get lucky, why don't we just keep it a state case, and then you and I share a couple of beers afterward?"

"Son, you *sure* you're an honest-to-God federal agent?" the voice drawled dubiously.

"Yep, that's what the badge says," Paxton chuckled.

"Well, Ah guess Ah'm willing to be convinced."

"Super Cub Two-Two-Seven-Four, be back at you in just a minute." Humming cheerfully, Paxton dropped the nose of the Super Cub down and roared in low over the edge of Alligator Bay.

"This is Two-Two-Seven-Four," Paxton spoke into his helmet mike as he looked back over his shoulder at the irregular shoreline. "Negative on the first pass. I'm going to . . . ooops, what have we here?"

Turning his head quickly, Paxton tried to focus on the blurry dark spot that had suddenly appeared and then disappeared under his left vertical stabilizer.

"Two-Two-Seven-Four, I think I've got something. Hold on a minute," Paxton said quickly as he pulled the Super Cub around into a sharp turn and then came back in low over the water. This time the dark, blurry spot was much easier to locate and identify.

"Two-Two-Seven-Four," Paxton spoke as he continued to scan the shoreline. "Confirming one pirogue located on the west shore of a small cove at the far south end of the bay. Looks like somebody tried to hide it in the tall grass."

"Two-Two-Seven-Four, we copy one pirogue, south end of the bay. You see anybody down there?"

"Uh, that's a negative, but I'm going to make another pass soon as I get a little more altitude," Paxton said as he throttled the Super Cub up into a steep climb and then brought the agile plane around to the left in a tightly banked turn.

On the ground, the two men in the concealed blind waited

until the Super Cub was halfway through its turn and perfectly silhouetted on its side against the blue sky before they brought their M-14 rifles up to their shoulders.

The roar of carefully aimed semiautomatic gunfire was lost in the noise of the Piper Super Cub's engine as the ejected casings began to splash in the water. But the red flashes of tracers fire were clearly visible as the camouflaged riflemen sent round after round of 7.76mm ball tracer ammunition into the cockpit and engine cowling of the Super Cub, until the small, slow plane finally nosed over and dove straight down into the glistening blue water of Big Lostmans Bay.

High over the western shoreline of British Columbia, Henry Lightstone had finally managed to drift off into an uneasy sleep when Marie Pascalaura nudged him awake.

"Hummmph?"

"I've been thinking," she whispered softly.

"Yeah, me too," Lightstone nodded sleepily, keeping his eyes tightly closed as the heavy plane shuddered through a brief stretch of turbulence.

"Oh? How could you be thinking when you were snoring?"

"Um-hum, that too," Lightstone mumbled.

"What I've been thinking," Marie went on as she rubbed her fingers gently over the nicely healed scar tissue on Lightstone's left temple, "is that you and Scoby and Paxton and Stoner really got into helping each other out. You know what I mean?"

"Um-hum."

"So won't you miss that? That adrenaline rush when you guys get into trouble, help each other out, and then joke about it afterward?"

Henry Lightstone yawned and then shook his head slowly into the pillow resting against Marie's shoulder. "Scoby, Paxton, and Stoner are big boys," he whispered as he readjusted the pillow into a more comfortable position. "They can take care of themselves just fine. Don't need me as a baby-sitter."

"So you really don't think you're going to miss all that crazy undercover stuff if you and I decide to settle down, grow carrots, and have kids?"

"Nah, just a game," Lightstone mumbled softly. "Shit-pot full of rules. No referee. Last one standing wins."

"That sounds pretty dumb, if you ask me," she said quietly after a long moment.

"Uh-huh. Exactly what it is," Lightstone mumbled as he drifted back asleep. "Nothing serious. Just a dumb game."

Fifteen minutes after Alligator Bay was once again glistening like a blue, reflective mirror, one of the camouflage-dressed riflemen slipped into the hidden pirogue and slowly paddled out to collect the few pieces of wreckage that had bobbed to the surface from the Super Cub. As he did so, he kept a close eye on the half-dozen alligators that had begun to investigate the floating debris.

Back on shore, the second rifleman removed his ear protectors and slipped them into his jacket pocket. Then, after carefully changing the frequency setting on his scrambled radio, he brought the small electronic instrument up to his camouflage-painted face.

"Charley Whiskey Seven to Charley Whiskey Four," he spoke quietly into the radio microphone.

"Charley Whiskey Four, go," Paul Saltmann, the voice of "Al Cousins, Florida State game officer," responded.

"Charley Whiskey Seven, mission completed."

"Can you see him?"

Günter Aben looked out across the bay as Felix Steinhauser cautiously reached over the side of the pirogue and retrieved the bullet-punctured lid of a foam ice chest.

"That is negative. We can see nothing except the debris and the alligators."

"Charley Whiskey Four, copy. They can have him," Paul Saltmann said. "Two down and four to go."

CHAPTER THIRTY

Lightstone had been expecting to see McNulty waiting for them at the gate. Instead, he saw a young Eskimo man standing off by himself, holding up a sign labeled "LIGHTSTONE." Pulling Marie off to the side, Lightstone watched the young man with the long, dark brown hair and dark features.

"Is something wrong?" Marie Pascalaura asked, still looking around for Paul and Martha McNulty.

"See that young guy over there to the right, the one holding the sign?"

"Yes, I . . . oh, that is odd, isn't it?"

"What do you say we sit over there for a while and see what he's up to?" Lightstone said, gesturing toward a group of empty seats at the opposite gate.

They walked over to a pair of seats that would give them a good view of the young Eskimo man. Lightstone dropped his carry-on bag at his feet and settled into the chair.

"So what are we looking for?" Marie asked calmly. "Somebody else named Lightstone?"

"Tell you the truth, I'm not sure," Lightstone said.

They waited until the first group of stewardesses came through the ramp gate, signaling the end of the deboarding process. The Eskimo walked over to one of the stewardesses as Lightstone rose and walked around and behind him.

"Yes, sir, I *am* certain that all the passengers on this flight are off the plane," Lightstone heard the stewardess say. "You might try down at the baggage-claim area."

"But—" the young Eskimo started to say as he turned to follow the stewardess.

"Maybe I can help you," Henry Lightstone said in a neutral voice.

"Uh . . . you, are you Henry Lightstone?"

"I know a guy named Henry Lightstone. Any reason why he might know you?"

"Oh, yeah, right," the young man nodded as he quickly reached inside his jacket, unaware that Lightstone had almost delivered a takedown kick to his groin as he pulled a black folding badge case out of his pocket.

"I'm Special Agent Thomas Woeshack," he said, holding the opened credentials out for Lightstone's inspection. "Paul . . . I mean Special Agent in Charge Paul McNulty was supposed to be back in the office by now, but we got a call this morning about somebody shooting at bears down around Skilak Lake. He was going to be flying by the area, so he asked me to come out to the airport and pick . . . uh, you up."

"Henry Lightstone," Lightstone nodded, relaxing and smiling as he accepted the eager young agent's firm handshake. "And this," he said, putting his hand on Marie's shoulder, "is my fiancée, Marie Pascalaura."

Thomas Woeshack smiled and shook her hand also. "Happy to meet you, too. Welcome to Alaska."

"It's nice to be on the ground again," she said.

Woeshack picked up one of the two carry-on bags and led the way out of the deboarding area.

"Man, I can't tell you how glad I am to see you," Woeshack said.

"Oh, really? Why's that?" Lightstone asked.

"Because McNulty said that if I wanted to learn how to do undercover work, I'd have to wait until you got here to teach me." Woeshack smiled with bright enthusiasm.

"You're coming up here to *teach* covert work?" Marie asked, looking over at Lightstone with mixed amusement and disbelief.

Lightstone shrugged as he looked down at the young agent's hands. "As a start, if we're going to do any covert work within a hundred miles of this airport, you might want to ditch that sign and put your badge away."

"Oh, yeah, right," Woeshack nodded as he returned the badge case to his jacket pocket and stuck the crudely lettered sign in a nearby trash can.

"I can't believe it," Marie said, shaking her head in amazement. "You really *are* going to give it up, aren't you?"

"As it was explained to me by a wise fellow named Carl Scoby," Lightstone said, "once you accept a promotion to senior resident agent, the fun's over. Nothing but paperwork and headaches until you retire." He looked over at Marie and grinned. "Sound good to you?"

They took the stairway down to the lower level, entered a tunnel with red and blue neon tubes arched over the ceiling, took a short escalator back up to baggage claim, and then worked their way over to the third carousel.

"Speaking of fun," Woeshack said, "Special Agent in Charge McNulty—"

"It's okay to call him Paul," Lightstone interrupted. "He won't mind."

"Yeah, okay, that's sort of what he said, too, but I wasn't sure . . ."

"Paul's a real easy guy to work for. Just don't try to bullshit him too much and you'll be fine."

"I'll remember that," Woeshack said solemnly. "Anyway, Paul suggested that I take you two out for an orientation trip. I thought we might go down to the Kenai Peninsula, put you in one of the cabins, see some wildlife, and then maybe take one of the patrol boats out to do some lake-trout fishing on Skilak Lake." The young agent grabbed up the two larger bags that Lightstone pointed out. "He said you could either do that or sit in his office and do his paperwork until he gets back."

"Orientation trip," Marie Pascalaura said enthusiastically.

"Sounds a lot better than paperwork," Lightstone nodded agreeably as they started for the parking lot.

"Okay, we'll get you checked into the hotel and then, unless you want to rest up some, we'll head on out."

"We can rest up later," Marie said as she watched the two men toss the luggage into the back of the government Suburban. "I want to see my new backyard."

* * *

At the opposite end of the ground-level Anchorage Airport parking lot, Gerd Maas climbed into a van, tossed his duffel bag to the back, and pulled the door closed. He turned to Kimiko Osan.

"What has happened so far?" he asked.

"Aben and Müeller reported in two hours ago," she replied in a controlled, respectful voice. "Phase One and Phase Two were completely successful. The teams are currently repositioning for Phases Four and Five."

"Excellent," Maas nodded as his cold eyes surveyed the parking lot. "Tell me about Phase Three."

"Everyone is in position. They have been waiting for your arrival."

"What about our diversion?"

"We are monitoring his movements right now," Kimiko Osan said. "Shoshin says that he has been alert and uneasy for the past few hours, as if he senses that we are out there."

"Oh?"

"But that is of no concern," she quickly added. "We can take him at any time."

"And the female?"

"There is no indication that she is aware of our presence or our movements," Kimiko Osan said. "She will be easy, I think."

"In most species, the female is often considered the most dangerous," Maas suggested with a slight smile.

"Yes, I have been told that several times," Kimiko Osan said with a straight face.

"And what about Mr. Chareaux? Has he been cooperative?"

"No, not at all. And because of that, it was necessary to be more explicit with our instructions."

"So I see," Maas nodded as he looked at the cut on Kimiko Osan's swollen lower lip. He had already noted the bruising on the knuckles of her lethal right hand.

"It is nothing," Osan said, holding her hands steady on the steering wheel of the van as she watched another group of travelers pass by.

"Of course," Maas agreed. "How badly is he hurt?"

"His internal injuries are of no consequence. He fought against the wrist lock, however, and hit his mouth on a rock when he finally went down. A front tooth was broken."

"Unavoidable?"

"He was very fast," she said matter-of-factly. "I did not see the rock until it was too late."

"The wrist is broken also?"

"I regret to say, yes."

"It had been my intention to handle Phase Three myself," Maas said.

"Yes, I understood that," Kimiko Osan said quietly, looking down at her lap, "I realize that I have failed you."

"Perhaps not," Maas said as he stared out through the spotless windshield in quiet contemplation. "As a matter of fact, I think that you may have provided me with a more interesting option."

Talking in his characteristically low and chilling voice, Gerd Maas outlined his plan for the modification of Phase Three.

"I would be honored to do my part," Kimiko Osan said quietly, still unable to turn and face the man that she alternately worshiped and feared.

"The timing would be critical," Maas said, struck by the irony that he would be entrusting his life to this small, slender young woman.

"Yes, of course," Kimiko Osan nodded, her eyes filled with pride as she finally turned her head and looked into the cold blue eyes of Gerd Mass. "I will not fail you again."

At three-fifteen that afternoon, Special Agent Thomas Woeshack turned off the Old Seward Highway onto Tudor Road, turned right into the first driveway, and then drove around to the rear of the U.S. Fish and Wildlife Service's regional office building. There had been an early winter storm, but most of the snow had melted, leaving only sporadic patches of dirty snow and ice that made Marie Pascalaura shiver in spite of her warm coat.

"This is *fall*?" she said to no one in particular.

"Just wait until you see winter," Lightstone nodded.

"I've got to run inside for a minute and pick up some of my gear," Woeshack said to Lightstone. "Want to come in and say hi to Sally and Jennifer?"

"Sally and Jennifer?" Marie Pascalaura asked, curious.

"Sally's our lead secretary," Woeshack explained. "She's the only one around here who knows how to find anybody in the field any time of the day or night. McNulty says that makes her indispensable."

"And Jennifer?"

"One of the wildlife inspectors. She's very nice, *and* very pretty," Woeshack added helpfully.

"I'd like to meet them," Marie Pascalaura said cheerfully.

"That might not be such a good idea," Lightstone suggested.

"Oh, really?" Marie said, raising her eyebrows questioningly. "Don't you want me to be able to find you when you're 'out in the field'?"

"Of course," Lightstone said solemnly. "I want you to know exactly who I'm with and what I'm doing at all times. Especially when you're cuddled up in front of a fire in a nice warm blanket while Woeshack and I are freezing our asses off in ten feet of snow trying to arrest some guy for shooting a frozen duck out of season."

"Ah."

"And besides," Lightstone added, ignoring the strange look that he was getting from Woeshack, "wives and girlfriends are always getting jealous. To tell you the truth, it can get kind of embarrassing."

"God, you men are hopeless," Marie Pascalaura said as she got out of the Suburban and followed Thomas Woeshack to the side door of the building.

Fifteen minutes later, Marie Pascalaura, Jennifer Alik, and Sally Napaskiak—who, in spite of being in her mid-sixties and decidedly overweight, happened to be a very attractive woman of Canadian and Native Aleut Eskimo extraction—were chattering away happily in the office of Special Agent in Charge Paul McNulty.

"Uh, I really hate to break this up," Lightstone said, "but if we're going to get out to the lake before it gets dark . . ."

"Oh, all right," Marie Pascalaura said with a sigh as she got up out of the chair. "But I still have a lot of questions for Sally and Jennifer."

"I'll have you all over for dinner," Sally Napaskiak said as she walked Marie to the door. "I'll be happy to tell you everything I know about Anchorage."

"Uh, Sally," Thomas Woeshack broke in, "I wonder if you could drop them by their hotel to check in and then take them over to the base? I need to go ahead and get things ready."

"Yes, of course. Go on, go on." Sally Napaskiak waved impatiently and then chuckled as the young special agent disappeared down the hallway.

"He is always so on the go," she said, smiling.

"Have you known him for long?" Marie asked as she and Henry followed the older woman back out into the main office.

"Oh, for all his life," Napaskiak laughed. "His mother and I were children together," she explained as she picked up a set of keys from her desk drawer, grabbed her coat, and then motioned for Henry and Marie to follow her down the hallway to the back parking lot. "Loo-chook, my friend, is a full-blooded Athabaskan, but she thought that my hair was so pretty because my mother was Caucasian, and she was always saying that she wanted a daughter just like me.

"So," Sally Napaskiak smiled as she unlocked the doors to the dirt-covered Ford Bronco, "being the very stubborn person that she is, Loo-chook disobeyed her mother and father, went out and found herself a handsome young Swedish gold miner to marry, and then had five boys. Thomas is the youngest, and my favorite," Sally confided in a lowered voice. "Loo-chook says he has hair just like mine."

They continued to talk as they drove, and Lightstone, sitting in the backseat of the Bronco, his head back and eyes closed, found himself so caught up in the front-seat conversation that he didn't realize where they were when the Bronco came to a slow, sliding stop.

Until, that is, he looked to his right and saw the row of planes.

"What . . . ?"

And then looked to his left and saw Special Agent Thomas Woeshack loading bags of gear into the back storage compartment of a float-mounted, orange, single-engine Skywagon II Cessna. The plane was tied down in one of the three ten-by-twelve slips that had been cut into the rocky shoreline and lined with thick boards to prevent water erosion.

"Oh, my God!" he whispered.

"Marie, this will be your first true adventure in Alaska," Sally Napaskiak predicted. "And all because you have found yourself a very brave fellow for a husband." She reached back and patted Henry Lightstone's leg.

Marie and Sally opened the doors of the Bronco, leaving a numbed Henry Lightstone to pull himself out of the backseat.

"I usually prefer bigger planes," Lightstone said mostly to himself as the women started walking toward the floatplane. He grabbed the duffel bags.

"Big plane, small plane, it is all the same thing." Sally Napaskiak waved her hand in a dismissive manner. "You take off, you fly, you land. What else is there?" she asked, bringing her large hands out in a broad shrug as they stopped about fifteen feet from the plane.

"Yeah, but the guys who fly the big planes . . ." Lightstone said. "I mean, who . . . ?"

Then the light suddenly dawned. "You mean *he's* a pilot?" Henry Lightstone rasped in a horrified voice, pointing an unsteady finger at the youthful-looking special agent who, to Lightstone's disbelieving eyes, suddenly looked even younger.

"Who, Thomas?" Sally Napaskiak laughed. "Yes, of course he's a pilot. Didn't you know? Everyone was so proud of him when he finally got his license, too. You should have seen the family gathering," she said to Marie. "We had so much food—"

"When?" Lightstone asked in a dulled voice.

"When what?" Sally Napaskiak asked, a puzzled look on her face.

"When did he get his license?" Lightstone said slowly.

"Oh, not so very long ago," Sally Napaskiak beamed. "It was such a party. And we were all so proud of Thomas because he had worked so hard. I mean, you could not believe how hard he had worked. Hours and hours he had to practice because they are so picky, those licensing people, about how they want you to land these little toy planes. Can you believe it? I mean, really, these planes are so simple that even a child could— But you're not afraid to fly, are you?" Sally Napaskiak suddenly asked Marie.

"Who, me? God, no, I *love* to fly," Marie Pascalaura laughed. "I can't wait."

Lightstone walked slowly to the plane. Woeshack quickly took his bags and stuffed them into the back storage compartment.

"Going to be a little tight in there, but Marie looks pretty small, so we should be okay on weight," Woeshack said as he finished stuffing in the last bag and then stood up, a pair of long broom handles in his hand.

Lightstone started to say something, but his attention was caught by a reflection off the overhead wing.

"You've got ice on the fucking wings?"

"Oh, yeah, sure. We got a lot of that up here." Woeshack shrugged as he handed Lightstone one of the broom handles. "Believe me, it's no big deal. All we've got to do is get it off." He grabbed the edge of the wing with his left hand for balance, brought the broomstick up over his shoulder with his right, and then slammed the stick down hard on the wing surface, sending small chunks of ice flying in all directions.

Henry turned and walked back to Marie and Sally Napaskiak.

"You know, we're going to crash," he said in a strangled voice. "Either we're going to be too heavy to take off, or we're going to ice up, or the fucking wings are going to fall off because our pilot has been pounding on them with a goddamn broom handle."

"Oh, don't you pay any attention to him," Sally Napaskiak advised Marie, shaking her head. "You two are going to be just fine. Thomas has been a federal government pilot for three whole weeks now, and he hasn't killed anyone yet. So why should you two happy people be the first?"

CHAPTER THIRTY-ONE

TUESDAY, SEPTEMBER 14TH

To virtually any other resident of the southern shoreline of Skilak Lake, the sudden cracking of a dried branch would have been immediate cause for alarm. But in this remote and isolated area of the Kenai National Wildlife Refuge, the fiercely protective Kodiak had no natural enemies. With her cubs close by, she was completely engrossed in the alluring clumps of lush, ripe, raspberry-like salmonberries and low-bush cranberries. She had every intention of seeing her small cubs develop the fatty tissue necessary to carry them through the cold Kenai winters.

Relaxed, confident, and only mildly curious about the source of the crackling noise, the mother Kodiak grunted her annoyance as she rose up to her full nine-foot height. Once upright, so that she could see over the interwoven salmonberry stems and alder branches, she quickly focused on her young male cub, who had wandered too far. More branches snapped as he awkwardly tried to work himself in closer to an especially sweet-smelling loop of fibrous material that seemed to be drenched in berry juice, and the repetition of the familiar sound caused the last of the mother Kodiak's residual concerns to vanish.

The Kodiak bellowed a long, grunting *whooof* to warn the cub back, then dropped down again to continue foraging. She was reaching out toward a particularly enticing clump of red salmonberries when the sudden, terrified yowl of her cub erased all thoughts of eating from her instinct-regulated brain.

In an instant, seventeen hundred pounds of furious mother-hood exploded through the mass of interwoven branches and stems that would have hopelessly trapped any lesser mammal. Charged with adrenaline, her eyes bulged as she saw her tortured baby cub dangling from a rope held by a relatively small and mostly hairless upright creature.

Had the sow possessed any sense of what it meant to have natural enemies, she might have hesitated. But in nature, the desperate urge to protect the young at any cost is always the dominant instinct.

Exposing her huge teeth in a savage snarl, the enraged sow brought her massive shoulder muscles down in preparation for attack. In her fury, she paid no attention to the shiny, long-barreled pistol that suddenly appeared in the creature's hand, nor did she ever actually hear the gunshot that tore into her right shoulder. The fractured joint gave way, sending the roaring bear tumbling muzzle-first into the soft earth.

Mindless of anything but the sound of her squalling cub, she staggered up onto her three functional legs, her right foreleg dangling useless. She tried to make the uphill charge once more . . . only to go down again when the carefully aimed second bullet ripped into her left shoulder socket.

There was another momentary flash of pain, so severe this time that it threatened to eclipse her awareness. But then the white-haired predator yanked on the rope, causing her cub to cry out again, and the mother Kodiak suddenly rose up on her hind legs like a demon out of hell, her neck bowed like a huge striking snake as she lunged upward, her fearsome teeth bared for the kill.

The third high-velocity bullet shattered the knee joint of her right rear leg, and she came down heavily on her side. But this time she was only a dozen feet from her tormentor, and the furious churning efforts of her left rear leg—as well as the swiping motions of her damaged but still functional left forearm—brought her to within six feet before the fourth bullet slammed into her left hip and completely broke her down.

She might have stayed there then on that rocky hillside, having done all that could possibly have been expected of an animal limited to the fearless use of muscle, bone, and heart in trying to protect its young from the most savage species on earth.

It would have been reasonable, and understandable, and even just.

But her cub was squalling steadily now, fighting against the rope to reach its mother, while the white-haired man simply laughed.

Which was all it took to send the tortured Kodiak roaring forward one last time, slashing out at the leg of her tormentor with her one functional paw even as Gerd Maas sent the fifth bullet from Sonny Chareaux's single-action .357 Magnum Ruger revolver into her brain and silenced those unyielding maternal instincts forever.

"Look at them," she whispered in amazement.

Henry Lightstone and Marie Pascalaura were sitting together in the bow of the twenty-five-foot patrol boat, bundled up in thermal underwear, sweaters and windbreakers under their life vests to ward off the chilling offshore breezes. They watched in silent fascination as the now-familiar pair of bald eagles continued to perform their aerobatic twists and turns over the glistening turquoise surface of Skilak Lake.

The graceful raptors had been performing for the past half hour, probably, as Refuge Officer Sam Jackson suggested, because it kept their human competitors from concentrating too much on trying to catch *their* fish.

Sam Jackson, a twenty-two-year veteran at the Kenai Refuge, and longtime friend of Thomas Woeshack, had shown up in a patrol boat an hour before. Wearing his reddish-orange "Mustang" survival suit and carrying his golden retriever pup, he had been more than happy to pull out his own fishing pole and join them.

"I think they're the most beautiful things that I've ever seen in my life," Marie said, cradling the golden retriever pup in her arms now and laying her head back against Henry Lightstone's shoulder. "I think I could get used to days like this."

"It isn't bad," Lightstone agreed. "But I'm not too sure about that idea of saving on grocery bills by catching our own food," he added thoughtfully as he stared out at the gently bobbing lure. Although they had already hooked and released several two- and three-pounders, the ten- to-fifteen-pound "keepers" had shown no interest whatsoever in the Grey Mosquito fishing fly. Their Alaskan guide had apparently overestimated the rainbow trout. Just like he overestimated his flying skills, Lightstone thought, recalling the young agent-pilot's two aborted attempts to put the Skywagon's twin floats down on the wind-rippled lake surface, attempts that Lightstone had privately described to Marie as "probably how a stone feels when it gets skipped across a lake."

"Hey, Woeshack," Lightstone said as they watched one of the eagles swoop down toward the water and then tumble wildly in the air, narrowly escaping disaster as one of its talons locked onto and then lost a glistening and thrashing sockeye salmon. "Is that your flight instructor up there?"

Jackson laughed. "I saw him try to make a landing out on Lake Hood just like that a couple of days ago."

"Don't let them pick on you, Thomas," Marie Pascalaura said, holding onto her pole and the pup as she looked back over her shoulder. "I think you fly just fine."

"That's okay, I don't mind," the young native Alaskan agent shrugged easily. "In fact, they're right. The eagles have always been my inspiration. As a child, I often watched them catching their food from the water and dreamed that I would fly just like them one day." He cast his line with an effortless flick of his wrist out toward a swirl in the water about thirty feet away.

"Well, you've just about made it as far as I'm concerned," Lightstone said, ignoring Marie's warning elbow to his ribs.

Trying to concentrate on the gentle swirls around his slowly drifting fly, Lightstone heard but chose to ignore the sharp, distant explosion that suddenly echoed across the huge Alaskan lake.

Instead, he continued to breath in a slow, steady rhythm, his muscular hands rock-steady on the eight-foot rod. His feet were solidly braced against the tightly secured backpack that contained a pair of 7x40 binoculars, a 2½" stainless-steel Smith & Wesson revolver fully loaded with .357 hollow-points, and his special agent's badge and identification, all of which Henry Lightstone had no intention of using on this bright, crisp, peaceful Alaska fall day.

"Come on, you picky bastards," he whispered. "Go for it. What the hell are you waiting for?"

"Don't worry, lover," Marie Pascalaura whispered. "There's always the fish market."

The second echoing gunshot caused Lightstone to blink, but his eyes never strayed from the gently bobbing fly. In the murky depths of his subconscious, Henry Lightstone had already categorized the shots as having come from a high-velocity pistol somewhere along the southern shore of the lake, probably at least a mile and a half away. Fine, he thought to himself, moving the tip of his rod slightly. I don't care about gunshots today, just as long as the bullets aren't coming in our direction.

Off to the right, a large, slow swirl broke the reflective blue surface about fifteen feet away from the lure.

"There, did you see that?" Marie asked as she clutched Lightstone's arm anxiously.

"Just be patient," Woeshack advised quietly as he stared out over Lightstone's shoulder at the glistening water. "They think they are the hunters, but you're the one who has the bait they want. Watch for the next one. It will come to you."

It was the timing of the third explosion, as much as anything else, that jarred at Henry Lightstone's peace of mind.

Paced shots, cool, deliberate aim, he thought, unable to resist the urge to count off the interval.

Not a hunter.

. . . thousand and three, one thousand and four.

"What's the matter?" Marie Pascalaura whispered, but he ignored her.

Now.

Crr-rack . . . booom!

Henry Lightstone slowly turned his suntanned face toward the distant southern shore, aware that the soaring eagles had instinctively drifted away from the echoing explosion. He waited . . . and then winced six seconds later when the fifth shot echoed across the water with a discernible sense of finality.

"You have many hunters out here?" Lightstone asked.

"A few," Sam Jackson said with an edge to his voice. "Never heard any shoot like that, though." He, too, had detected the unlikely pattern of the gunshots.

"Someone doing some target practice, maybe?" Thomas Woeshack suggested, but the tone of his voice suggested that he didn't really believe it. He slid his rod down against the gunwale of the aluminum boat and reached for his backpack.

Lightstone could hear Woeshack at the rear of the boat, opening up the waterproof equipment box that had been bolted to the cross structure of the sturdy patrol craft. At the same time, Sam Jackson slowly and carefully climbed back into his smaller patrol craft and opened up his own equipment case.

For a good five minutes, the two federal agents and the refuge officer scanned the distant rocky, tree-lined shore with their binoculars, searching for some sign of the individual who seemed much too methodical—much too *precise*—to be a hunter, while Lightstone tried to hold back the harsher reality that threatened to overwhelm the serenity of the glistening, smooth water. Memories of grisly crime scenes and deadened eyes. And of terrified victims, and of nervous suspects on the edge of panic, ready to run or fight or kill again, because they were never sure of exactly how much you knew.

"Anybody see anything?" Woeshack finally asked in a hushed voice.

"Nothing here," Sam Jackson answered from his boat.

"Nothing here either." Lightstone shook his head. "You're probably right. Just some guy out—"

There was another splash nearby, and the fly rod suddenly clattered violently across the bottom of the patrol boat.

"Hey!" Marie Pascalaura cried as she lunged across her fiancé's lap and grabbed her fishing rod just as it was about to go over the side.

The sudden pull on the line as the thirteen-pound, hooked rainbow trout dove for the rocks pulled Marie forward, causing her to squeal in surprise as the rod bent down toward the water like an eight-foot bow.

"Hold on to it!" Lightstone yelled as he yanked the binocular strap up over his neck and reached for the waterproof case.

"What do I do?" she gasped as she tried to get back into her seat.

"Give him some line and watch out for those rocks," Sam Jackson advised, quickly securing his binoculars and reaching for his net. Thomas Woeshack got ready to pull up the light anchor and kick in the motor if the fish pulled them anywhere near the rocks that protruded from the water about fifteen yards away.

"I knew your luck would change," Woeshack said cheerfully from the back of the rocking boat.

"I hope you're right," Lightstone nodded as he looked one more time toward the distant southern shoreline.

CHAPTER THIRTY-TWO

"Do you see anyone?" Gerd Maas asked over the loud, angry roar of the bear.

Up in the hills surrounding the southern shore of Skilak Lake, and about half a mile from the thick berry patch where the Kodiak sow had fought and died, the male grizzly bear had started to growl and slash at the cage again. But Maas was ignoring it, because he was still on a high from his more recent encounter with the enraged mother bear, and because he was much more concerned about getting the setting exactly right.

"Just some fishermen. Four of them, in two boats," Kimiko Osan replied as she continued to scan the distant northern shore with the powerful spotting scope.

"How far out are they?"

"About a mile," she estimated. "Due north, just outside Doroshin Bay. One of them is wearing an orange survival suit. I think he's the refuge officer we've been monitoring. The one with the small dog. They are very busy. Three of them have fish on their lines, and at least two of the lines seem to be tangled."

"Good. They shouldn't be too interested in what we are doing here," Maas nodded as he pulled on a pair of thin leather gloves over his muscular hands. Then he turned to Shoshin Watanabe.

"What about the plane?"

Watanabe spoke into his radio, listened for a reply, and then looked back up at Maas. "He is flying in a circle pattern approximately thirty kilometers to the south."

"And the diversion team?"

"Parker and Bolin are in position, approximately five hundred meters to the east. They are also ready."

"Excellent."

Twenty feet away and partially concealed in a clump of spruce and alder, the male grizzly roared out his anger as he continued to tear and bite at the aluminum crossbars of the portable cage. Several of the bars had already been bent by his furious mauling.

Ignoring the bear for the moment, Gerd Maas walked over to where the two men had been secured to individual trees with lengths of wide medical gauze and hospital tape to eliminate the possibility of telltale bruising.

Kneeling down before the younger of the two, Maas placed the long serrated edge of his belt knife against the man's neck—causing his eyes to bulge wide open—and then, with a savage twist of his wrist, he cut the gauze and tape wrappings away from Butch Chareaux's mouth.

It took the younger Chareaux only a few moments to recover his composure, whereupon he began to curse wildly in his fluent Cajun dialect until Maas dealt him a savage backhanded blow to the side of his bearded face.

"You will remain silent," Maas ordered in a raspy whisper as he cut the bindings away from Chareaux's legs. Then he looked up at Kimiko Osan, who was standing a few feet away with Paul McNulty's .45 SIG-Sauer automatic and Sonny Chareaux's stainless-steel .357 Magnum revolver in her small hands.

"Are you ready?" he asked.

"Yes. Are you comfortable with his boots?" Kimiko Osan responded. She was hesitant to question Maas, but she knew that timing would be crucial and that Chareaux's boots were two sizes too big.

"They are fine," Maas nodded with icy-cold indifference.

"Then I am ready also," she said calmly.

"And you?" Maas turned to look at Shoshin Watanabe, who was standing next to the tree where McNulty was tightly secured with gauze and tape.

"*Hai!*" Watanabe acknowledged with a sharp forward nod of his closely shorn head.

"Good, then we begin," Maas said as he cut the last of Butch Chareaux's ties. Maas held him on the ground with a knee pressed into his lower spine and his unbroken wrist twisted tightly against his upper back.

After dragging the Cajun about ten feet in front of the rocking cage, Maas took the .357 Ruger revolver from Kimiko Osan and slipped it into the back waistband of his jeans. Then he looked up at his young, attractive, and absolutely lethal assistant and gave her the nod to proceed.

Moving with a smooth, almost feline stride, Kimiko Osan returned to the tree where Paul McNulty was secured and slid the heavy SIG-Sauer into the front waistband of her jeans. As she did so, Shoshin Watanabe—a small man with exceptionally strong arms and hands for his size—cut away the gauze and tape restraints from McNulty's mouth, wrists, and legs.

"Goddamn it, what the hell are you— *Aaggghh!*"

Watanabe immediately caught McNulty in an extremely painful reversed wrist lock and then allowed Kimiko Osan to step in and take over the control hold.

"Listen to me, goddamn you!" McNulty raged, but to no avail.

Pausing only to be certain that Osan had McNulty fully in her control, Shoshin Watanabe walked over to the cage and placed his hand on the release lever, ignoring the fearsome thrashing and roaring and clattering of the cage sections as the infuriated grizzly tried to get at its tormentors.

"I am ready," Watanabe said, allowing himself a brief glance at the dangling rope ladder behind him.

Gerd Maas used a wrist lock on Butch Chareaux's broken but unbandaged left wrist and an arm across his throat to drag the cursing and kicking Cajun up to his feet and over to the cage. There, Maas shoved his frantically struggling and screaming victim against the cage door several times, causing the male grizzly to lunge and tear at the restraining bars.

In one quick movement, Maas pulled Chareaux ten feet

back from the cage door, took a last confirming glance at Kimiko Osan, and then yelled out one word:

"Now!"

Moving with the speed and precision of a trained gymnast, Shoshin Watanabe tossed Butch Chareaux's rifle out on the ground in front of the cage, released the locking lever, threw the door open, and then turned and ran for the dangling rope ladder as the grizzly burst out of its prison.

For a brief moment, it looked as though the bear might go for Watanabe, but then Maas yelled out something in guttural German over the high-pitched screams of Butch Chareaux, and the bear lunged toward the two men just as Maas shoved Chareaux forward.

The bear's slashing right paw tore open the sleeve of Maas's jacket in the instant before the four-inch claws slashed deep into Butch Chareaux's shoulder and chest muscles. But Maas had thrown himself backward as he was reaching for the .357 Ruger revolver tucked against the small of his back. And in the brief moment it took for the enraged grizzly to fling Butch Chareaux's now lifeless body aside and lunge toward its white-bearded nemesis, Kimiko Osan had thrown Paul McNulty forward onto the ground, smoothly drawn McNulty's .45 SIG-Sauer out of her waistband, and squeezed the trigger.

The first two .45-caliber jacketed slugs caught Butch Chareaux in the rib cage and the side of the head as he was going down. The shots were only for effect, since Chareaux was already dead.

The next round ricocheted off the surface of the bear's skull, sending blood and small gouged chunks of furry tissue in all directions and causing the bear to turn away from its murderous charge toward Maas to focus on its new tormentor. Kimiko Osan unflinchingly stood her ground and continued to aim and fire at the oncoming bear.

In that instant, from a distance of less than five feet, Gerd Maas sent two .357 Magnum bullets ripping through the rib cage and heart of the huge beast. Both of these wounds would prove to be fatal, but not yet. The huge grizzly turned once again to lunge at its white-haired tormentor.

From five feet away, Gerd Maas had less than a second to live when he coolly triggered off a .357 round straight into the bear's wide-open mouth—partially severing its spinal column—and then swiftly cocked and fired the powerful handgun two more times, sending a pair of the high-velocity projectiles through the deep eye sockets of the suddenly paralyzed grizzly.

Calmly turning his back to the huge falling beast, he felt one heavy lifeless paw strike against his shoulder, drawing five bloody streaks down the side of his jacket. Maas coolly aimed and fired the final .357 round from Sonny Chareaux's single-action revolver into Paul McNulty's throat at a point just above the agent's Kevlar vest.

Over a mile away, and distracted by Marie Pascalaura's excited screams as he struggled to untangle the two jerking lines, Henry Lightstone never heard the first three shots fired through Paul McNulty's .45 SIG-Sauer.

But all of them certainly heard the two booming explosions from Butch Chareaux's .357 echo across the bright turquoise water.

"Henry! Watch out, he's going under the boat again!" Marie Pascalaura warned as she tried to bring the tip of her rod around the cover of the outboard motor. But then she gasped in surprise as Lightstone quickly reached for his belt knife, snapped the sharply honed blade open one-handed, and severed both lines.

"*WHAT*—" Marie Pascalaura started to yell, but Lightstone silenced her with a wave of his hand while he and Woeshack and Jackson listened as the steady gunfire continued to reverberate across the water and off the surrounding mountains.

Nine more echoing shots later, the lake was silent once again. Henry Lightstone tossed his backpack into the bottom of Sam Jackson's patrol boat and crossed over to the smaller craft as the engines of both outboard motors were started up.

"Soon as you get in the air, get on the radio," Lightstone said to Woeshack. "Try to raise Paul, let him know we've got a situation out here. After that, put yourself over the south side of the lake, see if you can spot a boat or a plane. Sam and I will work our way in from the shore."

"Got it," Woeshack acknowledged.

Working quickly, Lightstone secured his two-and-a-half-inch .357 Magnum revolver into the hip holster and then transferred the three cylindrical, hollow-point-filled speed-loaders from the backpack into the deep front pocket of his jacket.

"What about me?" Marie asked, looking anxious and concerned as she clutched the puppy to her chest.

"Sam, have you got a portable with you?" Lightstone asked quickly, noting that the refuge officer was also armed with one of the standard Fish and Wildlife Service handguns.

"Sure do."

"Okay," Lightstone nodded as he reached into his backpack and handed Marie his packset radio and the pair of binoculars. "You're going with Thomas to the refuge dock. Once you get there, you lock yourself in the boat house, go upstairs, and watch for anyone in a boat or on foot heading toward the public launch ramp. You see anybody heading that way, especially anyone moving fast, you get on that radio, okay?"

"Got it," Marie acknowledged as she secured the radio in her jacket. She hunched down as Woeshack cast off Sam Jackson's line and headed the patrol boat toward the distant northwestern shore.

"You got anybody else in the area?" Lightstone asked Jackson as he braced himself in the seat next to the refuge officer.

"Couple of biologists tracking some moose on the north side, and a trainee down at the dock working on one of the boats," Sam Jackson replied. "Nobody with law-enforcement authority."

"Okay," Lightstone nodded, picking up the refuge officer's binoculars and beginning to scan the distant shoreline again as Jackson started the small patrol craft toward the southern shore, "let's just hope these people are halfway friendly."

* * *

It was Shoshin Watanabe who first spotted the approaching craft.

"It is the refuge officer with one of the other fishermen," Kimiko Osan confirmed, focusing the spotting scope on the rapidly moving outboard.

"How are they armed?" Maas asked.

"I can't tell." Osan shook her head, frustrated by the distance and the narrow focusing field of the scope. "The other boat is heading back toward the landing very fast," she added.

Gerd Maas surveyed the bloody kill site one last time, noting that the now empty .45 SIG-Sauer lay in the blood-splattered weeds a few feet away from Paul McNulty's out-stretched hand. He was pleased to see that Shoshin Watanabe had already collected all of the cut tape and gauze and placed the materials in one of the backpacks.

As far as Maas could tell, the scene looked perfect.

Walking over to the sprawled body of Butch Chareaux, he placed the empty stainless-steel Ruger revolver in the Cajun poacher's bloody palm, and with gloved hands, wrapped Chareaux's lifeless fingers around the rubber grip and trigger guard of the gunpowder-and-blood-smeared weapon. Then, after tossing the still-warm pistol a few feet away from Chareaux's limp hand, Maas looked up at Shoshin Watanabe with his deadly cold-blue eyes.

"Tell Parker and Bolin to be ready."

CHAPTER THIRTY-THREE

Apart from the cries of distant eagles, there was no sound.

And no movement.

Nothing.

"Why don't we hold it right here for a couple of minutes?" Henry Lightstone suggested quietly as he lowered the binoculars and stared out across the glistening turquoise water at the still, quiet, and seemingly unoccupied landscape. Set before a backdrop of snowcapped mountains, low cliffs stretched out across the long, rocky, tree-and-shrub-covered shore.

"Sounds good to me," Refuge Officer Sam Jackson nodded as he throttled the powerful outboard motor down to a rumbling idle.

"What's the name of this place again?" Lightstone asked as he readjusted the binoculars and continued his methodical search.

"Lupus Island, though it's not actually an island. There's a narrow spit of shale-covered sand that connects it to the shore."

To Special Agent Henry Lightstone, it looked like the point of land could easily conceal several hundred drunk, camouflaged, and potentially trigger-happy hunters. But if all of that shooting had been done by legitimate hunters, there should be at least an occasional flash of camouflage clothing. A hat, or a vest, or laughter, or loud voices.

But there wasn't.

The idea of being a sitting duck out on about twenty-four thousand acres of glassy-smooth, subarctic water didn't appeal to Lightstone.

"Still nothing?" Jackson finally asked.

"Nope. Nothing at all." Lightstone shook his head. "What do you say we try that little cover straight ahead, work our way west?"

"Sounds good to me," the orange-suited refuge officer nodded as he throttled the thin-skinned aluminum boat on a new course roughly parallel to the shoreline. When they reached the shallow cove, Sam Jackson turned the small patrol craft perpendicular to shore and then gave it one last nudge with the powerful outboard engine.

"How deep do you figure the water is?" Lightstone asked, setting aside the binoculars and getting ready to jump out and protect the boat from the sharp-edged rocks.

"Well, out here we usually go by the rule of ten," Jackson said as he cut off the engine and brought the prop up out of the water. "About ten feet out from shore, you can figure that you're going to be standing in about ten feet of water that's just about ten degrees Celsius."

"Christ," Lightstone muttered as he held his hand in the ice-cold water for a moment, then quickly brought it back out.

"Personally, if I was you," Sam Jackson advised in his slow Georgia drawl, "I'd stay in the boat until we run up on shore. We can always get the government to spring for a new boat every now and then."

Taking the bearded refuge officer at his word, Lightstone remained in the bow of the boat until the thin, insulated hull scraped loudly against the shale-covered shore. Jackson double-tied the bowline to a pair of tire-sized boulders.

"No one in his right mind ever goes swimming after a loose boat in these waters," Jackson said as he pulled a packset radio out of his backpack and looked over at Lightstone.

"Ready?"

"I am, but you might want to get out of that Day-Glo suit first."

Sam Jackson looked down at the bright orange Mustang suit that was supposedly guaranteed to keep him alive for at least an extra four or five minutes if he ever had the misfortune to get dunked into the frigid subarctic waters of Skilak Lake.

"You really think we're going to get into some kind of confrontation with these folks?"

Lightstone hesitated for a moment. "Let's put it this way," he finally said. "Given the choice, I'd rather swim halfway across this lake after your boat than try to sneak in on some trigger-happy idiots in a getup like that."

Lightstone waited while Jackson worked himself out of the bright survival suit, then led the way as they climbed to the top of the fifteen-foot cliff. Once there, they slowly worked their way through a nearly impenetrable barrier of waist-high scrub brush, irregular moss-and-lichen-covered outcroppings, and ten- to fifteen-foot spruce trees.

"Christ, how the hell can anybody hunt in stuff like this?" Lightstone muttered as he noisily pulled himself through a tightly grouped clump of white spruce trees, only to find himself blocked by the sharp, poking branches of a dead and partially dropped cottonwood.

"What they do is look for the bare spots, usually around the big patches of salmonberries," Jackson said. "Saves a lot of wear and tear."

"Like those over there to the right?" Lightstone asked hopefully.

Sam Jackson looked up, squinting against the glare of the low sun. "Yeah, I'd say that's a likely spot."

Two minutes later, the two federal wildlife officers were kneeling down beneath a large clump of berries, examining the still-warm carcass of the maliciously killed mother Kodiak. One of the first things that Lightstone observed was the radio collar around the bear's thick neck.

"You know this one?"

"Oh, yeah." Sam Jackson nodded sadly. "We named her Molly. Found her as an orphaned cub over on Kodiak Island. Poacher killed her mom. Decided to transfer her over to the Killey Valley as an experiment. It seemed to be working out just fine, but I guess some goddamn bastard just couldn't wait to get his bear."

"Out of season?"

"Huh? Oh, yeah, I guess that, too," Jackson confirmed. "Not that it really matters in a situation like this."

"Why's that?" Lightstone asked, distracted by the curious details that his homicide-trained eyes were starting to pick up.

"Number-one rule in bear hunting out here. Can't hunt a female with cubs, no matter what. Christ, look at those teats. It should have been obvious to anybody with eyes that she was still nursing. She had two, and they're probably not far away. They'd stay fairly close to their mother," Sam Jackson muttered in frustration as he stood up and looked around. "Not that any of that will matter much, even if we find the guy. He'll just claim it was self-defense, like they always do."

As Jackson started to poke around in the nearby brush, Henry Lightstone pulled a sharp folding knife out of his pocket and began to cut and probe the massive left front shoulder of the huge bear.

"The cubs were late-born," Jackson said half to himself as he slowly extended his search out into the surrounding brush and trees. "Probably running around here, scared half out of— *Oh, for Christ's sake!*"

"What's the matter?" Lightstone brought his head up from where he had been examining the bear's massive front paws, instinctively reaching for his pistol as he looked around quickly.

"Well, at least the bastard didn't leave the poor damn thing out here to starve," Sam Jackson muttered as he reached into the brush with gloved hands. Using the length of berry juice-soaked rope that was still looped around its neck, he pulled out the carcass of the young male cub.

"Must be a hell of a sport, tying up baby bears and taking potshots at them." Lightstone shook his head, checking the surrounding hillside one more time before he resecured the .357 in his hip holster and went back to examining the huge mother Kodiak.

"Potshots, my ass. Take a closer look," the furious refuge officer said.

"They cut its throat?" Lightstone blinked in surprise. Using his bare hands to move the rope and the blood-soaked fur aside, he exposed the deep, cleanly cut wound. "Why the hell would somebody do that?"

"I don't know *why*, but I can sure as hell tell you they did it after they killed *her*," Sam Jackson replied, nodding down at the mother Kodiak. "No way in the world a bear like that would ever let a human get in *that* close to one of her cubs."

Henry Lightstone spent a few more moments looking back over the scene from his kneeling position before he spoke.

"Actually, I think maybe she *did* let somebody get that close and was trying as hard as she could to correct her mistake," Lightstone said quietly. He felt around the stiffening body of the small cub to confirm the absence of any other wounds.

"What do you mean by that?"

"Take a look at her front shoulders, at the main joints. And then at the back legs, around the knees."

"Yeah, what about—" Jackson started to ask as he knelt down by the sprawled carcass of the huge female. Then he muttered a series of heartfelt curses as he examined each of the four massive wounds.

"Remember how evenly paced the shooting was?"

Sam Jackson nodded.

"Well, the way it looks to me, whoever did this probably broke her down progressively as she was coming uphill," Lightstone explained, pointing to the trail of dislodged rocks, broken trees, and wide splatters of blood. "First shot was probably right down there by that rock, maybe twenty yards away at the most. You can see where she went down each time, and then kept on coming back up. If I had to make a guess, I'd say he was standing right about there," Lightstone added, motioning to a spot about three feet away from the bear's massive head where a partial boot print was just barely visible in the rocky soil.

"How can you tell all that?"

"Used to work a lot of homicides down south," Lightstone replied. "Basically the same thing. If you look close, right around there, you can see the powder burns on the forehead and some of the effects of the muzzle blast." He pointed in the general area of the partially blown-out wound. "Coup de grace. Just stood there waiting for her to get close enough."

"The guy used the cub as bait," Jackson whispered, shaking his head slowly in disbelief.

"Oh, yeah? Why's that?"

"Bears are afraid of people. She would have done anything she could to avoid a human, unless her cub was involved."

Lightstone nodded after looking around the scene again. "You can see some smaller claw marks in that tree right there next to where the guy was standing. Cub was probably trying to get away. Get back to Mom."

"I'll tell you what," Sam Jackson said. "If you're reading this whole thing right, and this guy deliberately drew *this* bear onto himself, using that cub as bait, then I don't care what kind of rifle he's carrying, the man's got to be crazy."

"What would you say if I told you he used a pistol?" Lightstone asked as he dropped two chunks of bloody metal in the refuge officer's hand.

"I'd say he was out of his goddamn mind," Sam Jackson said as he stared down at the badly mangled bullets.

"I dug them out of the knee and shoulder joints, left side, front and back legs. The way they're torn up, it looks like they were probably from a .357 Magnum. I'll send them down to our forensics lab in Ashland for confirmation, see what they can tell us about the make and model from the land and groove ratios."

"A three-fifty-seven *pistol*?" Jackson still didn't want to believe it.

"Three-fifty-seven's one hell of a weapon if you want to take out a human being," Lightstone shrugged. "But it sure wouldn't be my choice for hunting a grizzly bear."

"Yeah, no shit."

"And as long as I'm sending things down to the lab, I'll probably include this." Lightstone showed the refuge officer a tiny strip of hide about an inch long and less than a sixteenth of an inch wide.

"What's that?"

"Not sure. I found it stuck in one of her front claws."

Lightstone shrugged as he pulled three small Zip-loc bags out of his flotation vest. He discarded the fishing flies and carefully transferred the mangled bullets and the strip of hide to separate bags, then put them back in his vest pocket.

"So now what do we do?" the enraged and frustrated refuge officer asked.

"You said these bears were killed out of season?"

Sam Jackson looked at his watch for confirmation. "Yeah, sure. Today's the fourteenth of September. Season doesn't start until the fifteenth, even if these bastards had a tag, which they probably didn't."

"So let me run this by you," Lightstone said. "The guy could always claim that the bear charged him, and that he just didn't have a chance to see the cub. And the fact that he used a pistol to put her down would probably back up the self-defense angle. I'm assuming that it's legal to shoot a bear out of season to protect yourself."

"As long as he didn't provoke the attack," Jackson nodded. "But you don't think this guy—"

"No, of course not." Lightstone shook his head. "But the point is, it doesn't matter what I think. It's what a jury's going to think that counts. On the other hand," he added with a smile, "you'd think the person who did this would have one hell of a time trying to explain to a jury why he had to rope a little sixty-pound cub by the neck and then cut its throat to protect himself."

"*I* sure as hell wouldn't believe it," Sam Jackson growled.

"Well, in that case, seeing as how there's a set of boot prints moving up over in that direction," Lightstone said, motioning with a blood-smeared hand, "what do you say we take ourselves a little hike, find this certifiably crazy bastard, and see what he has to say for himself?"

"Can you see them?" Gerd Maas demanded, speaking quickly into his scrambled radio as he crouched down in the concealing brush.

"Affirmative. Two subjects, approaching cautiously from the south." Roy Parker, one of Paul Saltmann's ICER protection-team members, watched the approaching law-enforcement officers as he spoke into his headset microphone.

"How far away?"

"A couple hundred yards."

"Do you have a clear shot?"

"Doubt it. These guys are staying in pretty tight with the rocks. Let me check with Arturo."

"Why can't he answer for himself?" Maas demanded.

"Antenna link on his com-set's malfunctioning," Parker replied calmly. "Hold on."

Turning his head carefully so as not to lose the limited cover of the small spruce, or to allow the stabilizer on his 5.56mm Colt Commando automatic carbine to disturb the surrounding brush, Parker looked over at a position about twenty yards away, where his headset radio-equipped and camouflage-covered partner, Arturo Bolin, was lying in a prone position with a U.S. Marine Corps 7.62mm bolt-action, bipod and Redfield telescopic-sight-mounted M40 sniper rifle extended out and ready. The camouflage patterns on the fiberglass stock and the clothing had been specifically selected for the Kenai Peninsula area. And when combined with the brown and dark green greasepaint, the wiglike hat made out of shredded brown and dark green rags, the rag netting, and the clumps of rubber-band-attached local foliage, the overall silhouette-concealing effects were so successful that Parker had to look carefully to see his partner's hand signals.

But in doing so, the professionally trained mercenary failed to notice the movement of the small, terrified female grizzly—the mother Kodiak's surviving cub—who, alerted by the sound of the human voice, had quickly crouched down in the surrounding brush.

"Negative on the clear shot." Parker spoke into his own headset radio mike. "Maybe another thirty seconds."

Maas cursed. He knew they had to hurry, because the dark orange floatplane had already made one low run across the west end of the island and was starting to come back around for another pass.

"You want to call it now, or wait?" Parker's electronically scrambled voice asked with calm, professional patience.

"Can you identify them?"

"The tall one with the beard is Sam Jackson, one of the senior refuge officers out here. No make on the second guy."

"Are they armed?"

"From what we can see, it looks like both of them are carrying stainless-steel handguns, short barrels. Probably standard-issue Model Sixty-sixes. No long guns."

"Then the second man is either another refuge officer or a special agent," Maas said as he watched the orange floatplane sweep back around over the eastern end of Skilak Lake.

"That's the way we read it," Parker agreed. "Thing is, we figure you'd better make a call one way or the other pretty damn quick. That guy up there in the Cessna makes another pass, he's bound to spot either us, you guys, or the plane."

"You deal with the two on the ground, we will deal with the plane," Gerd Maas said, the chill in his voice still evident despite the electronic scrambling.

"That mean we have clearance?"

"Yes," Maas said. "Put them down."

CHAPTER THIRTY-FOUR

In reaching to grasp the top edge of the shale outcropping so that he could pull himself up, Henry Lightstone almost put his forehead right in the cross hairs of Arturo Bolin's extremely accurate rifle.

But the deafening roar of the Cessna Skywagon's single engine as it passed over caused Lightstone to drop back at the last second. He took the packset radio from Sam Jackson.

"Woeshack, can you read me?"

There was a long pause, then Thomas Woeshack's excited voice came over the air.

"Ten-Four, I think I saw something!"

"Where?"

"Hold on, I'm coming back around for a better look!"

"Woeshack, what the hell did you see?" Lightstone demanded.

No answer.

"Woeshack!" Lightstone yelled into the radio mike, but it was already hopeless. He could see the small orange floatplane coming around in a tight turn just barely above the treeline, the roar of the powerful engine increasing as the special agent-pilot fought to maintain his precarious altitude.

"Jesus Christ, I think he's going to crash!" Sam Jackson whispered.

"Goddamn it, Woeshack, get your ass back up in the air!" Lightstone raged into the radio as the Cessna Skywagon appeared to stall but then recovered as Woeshack banked the wings of the floatplane and opened the throttle to maximum power.

"I can see—" Woeshack yelled into his mike.

At that instant, the resounding overhead roar of the airplane completely overwhelmed the survival instincts of the Kodiak bear's surviving cub and it broke from the shelter of the dense scrub brush.

Roy Parker reacted out of pure instinct, triggering a quick burst of 5.56mm rounds that threw fountains of dirt, rocks, and twigs into the air as the multiple impacts of the high-velocity bullets sent the frantic cub tumbling back into the brush in an explosion of dirt, torn hair, and blood.

"What the hell!"

Enraged by the agonized cries of the horribly wounded cub, Sam Jackson started to scramble up and over the shale outcropping and was immediately thrown backward as a 7.62mm copper-jacketed bullet tore through his upper shoulder and blew a bloody hole out the back of his down vest.

Henry Lightstone dropped the packset radio, reached for his

hip-holstered .357 Magnum and lunged forward against the protective surface of the shale outcropping. He took a quick, cautious look over the edge, then pulled himself up fast to trigger off three concussive rounds with his short-barreled .357 revolver. Sensing that he hit the first crouched figure, Lightstone then whirled to his right and fired the last three rounds at the barely visible figure that lay prone, a sniper rifle pointed at the dead cub.

Using a pistol with only a 2½" barrel at a distance of over a hundred yards, Lightstone had little hope of making a hit. But that didn't concern him, because all he really wanted to do was to keep everybody down long enough for him to get to Sam Jackson.

After firing the last shot, he ducked down behind the outcropping and only narrowly avoided the second bullet that exploded in a stinging shower of lead, copper and shale fragments just a few inches above his head.

Cursing to himself, Lightstone crouched down with his back against the rocky cliff, quickly dumped the empty casings out of the stainless-steel revolver and fed one of the six-round speed-loaders from his jacket into the open chambers. Then he scrambled down to the lower ledge to where the bearded refuge officer was sprawled out on his back, with his blood-covered left hand clenched tightly against his upper right shoulder, his eyes glazed in shock.

"Henry, can you read me?" The voice of Special Agent-Pilot Thomas Woeshack was muffled because Jackson's radio was facedown in the brush.

Ignoring the discarded radio, Lightstone knelt down and gently pulled Jackson's trembling hand away from the bleeding wound. He used his folding knife to cut and peel back the blood-soaked layers of vest, shirt and long underwear.

After taking a brief look at the exposed entry point, Lightstone tried to gently move the refuge officer's severely injured shoulder so that he could examine the exit area, and then winced inwardly at the sound of shattered bone ends grinding against each other as the refuge officer groaned in agony.

Lightstone began to use his folding knife to cut the cotton lining out of his own jacket.

"What—" Jackson whispered.

"Trying to keep you from getting the refuge all messy," Lightstone said, glancing up and listening for the sound of anyone moving in their direction as he began to tear the jacket lining into long strips.

"Hurts like hell," Sam Jackson mumbled.

"Yeah, I bet it does," Lightstone muttered as he began to pull handfuls of the synthetic fill from the lining of his thick jacket. "You're losing a lot of blood out the back, but I think I can get it stopped. Looks like a straight through-and-through punch, no expansion. Must be using ball ammo."

"Military?" Jackson whispered weakly, blinking his eyes in response to the pain of each shallow breath. "Nobody . . . uses that stuff out here anymore."

"Henry, this is Woeshack. Can you read me?"

"Yeah, well, somebody is today. By the way, you're not going to like this next part, but I've got to do it." Lightstone held chunks of the synthetic fill on either side of the wound. "You ready?"

"Yeah, sure," Jackson nodded, blinking his glassy eyes as he looked up at Lightstone. "Hurry up, get it over . . . *Oh, shitttt!*" he screamed. Then his eyes rolled back into his head and he went limp as Lightstone used the tips of his fingers to jam the filler material deeper into the gaping wound.

"Yeah, hell of an idea. I'd faint too if it were me," he muttered to himself as he quickly used the strips of cotton lining to tie the blood-soaked filler in place.

Lightstone scrambled back up to the top edge of the outcropping, the .357 Magnum back in his hand, just in time to watch the man in shredded-rag camouflage gear kneel down beside his prone partner. He set the bipod-mounted sniper rifle in place, dropped the ammo belt with the extra 7.62mm clips next to the scoped weapon, slipped into the green nylon harness rig that held eight extra thirty-round magazines in snap pouches, and then picked up the 5.56mm Colt Commando automatic carbine.

"Oh, shit," Lightstone whispered.

"Henry!"

Cursing, Lightstone scrambled back over to the clump of brush where he had dropped the small packset radio. In the background, somewhere off to his right, he could hear the echoing roar of the Cessna Skywagon's powerful engine as Woeshack circled the floatplane high over the center of the huge lake.

"This is Henry, go ahead," he said, bringing the radio up to his mouth and keying the mike as he cautiously peered around the edge of the outcropping and saw the figure with the short-barreled automatic weapon start to move forward from tree to tree in their general direction.

"Jesus, I thought you— What's going on down there?" Woeshack demanded.

"Couple of shooters about a hundred yards south of us," Lightstone explained, watching as the rag-camouflaged figure proceeded to move in closer, covered by his wounded but still very functional partner, who had taken over the sniper rifle.

"They're both wearing military cammo gear." Lightstone spoke into the radio mike again. "One of them's armed with an automatic weapon. The other one's got some kind of bipod-mounted rifle with a scope."

"You mean they're soldiers?"

"Sure as hell look like it to me," Lightstone muttered.

There was a momentary pause.

"I thought I saw one of you guys go down," Woeshack said hesitantly.

"You did. Sam caught a round through the shoulder."

"Is he okay?"

"He's alive, but he's out cold and losing blood pretty fast," Lightstone said as he continued to watch the still-distant but rapidly approaching figure, not happy with the idea that the man really *did* look and act like a soldier.

"What about the suspects?"

"The one with the automatic weapon's heading our way right now," Lightstone said in a cold voice. "The other guy's staying in place with the rifle. Looks like I might have hit him. Can't tell."

"Jesus, what the hell are they—"

"Listen," Lightstone interrupted, "we're going to need some help down here. Can you contact Anchorage on that radio?"

"Sure, if I get up high enough."

"Then get up there and try to get ahold of Paul," Lightstone ordered. "Tell him to get us some backup out here, pronto. After that, come back down and help me keep track of these guys."

"That's what I was trying to tell you," Woeshack said. "I spotted Paul's plane down by that island. It's tied up in the cove on the northwest side."

"Can you see him?"

"No. I tried to raise him on the radio, but there wasn't any answer, and there's nobody back at the office."

"Shit," Lightstone snarled.

"What do I do?"

"Get ahold of the tower. Tell them to call the FBI or the Coast Guard or the goddamned Boy Scouts, for all I care," Lightstone growled into the radio mike, watching from the protective shale edge as the rag-camouflaged figure cautiously moved forward another seven or eight yards. "Just get somebody out here."

"Christ, those FBI guys are way downtown at the Federal Building. It would take them a good two or three hours to get here."

"Well, tell them to fucking *hurry*."

Lightstone listened to the changing pitch of the Cessna's engine as Woeshack sent the floatplane climbing up and around the back of the island.

"Okay." Woeshack's excited voice came back on the air in less than thirty seconds. "I got ahold of the tower. They're calling the FBI and the— Hey, what's that?"

"What's the matter?" Lightstone demanded.

"Just a second. I thought I saw something," Woeshack exclaimed excitedly and then went off the air as he brought the dark orange floatplane down in a sweeping low pass across the far north side of the island.

"Woeshack, what the hell are you doing?" Lightstone demanded.

"There's somebody down— Oh, shit!"

The roar of distant gunshots almost blocked out Woeshack's panicked scream. From his position below and behind the shale outcropping, Lightstone could hear the roar of the straining engine and see the dark orange overhead wings of the Cessna wobble frantically as Woeshack sent his aircraft almost straight up in a desperate effort to escape the ballistic onslaught from the ground.

"Woeshack, get the hell out of there!" Lightstone yelled into his radio.

"Two bodies!"

"What?"

"Two— Jesus, I've been hit!"

"Woeshack, what the hell—"

Dead silence.

"Woeshack!"

". . . okay . . . not hit . . . airplane's been hit," Woeshack managed to stammer out. "Jesus, they shot this thing full of holes!"

"What about the bodies?" Lightstone demanded, watching the rag-camouflaged figure carefully because he was almost close enough now.

"I saw two bodies on the ground, in a clearing near the spit," Woeshack answered in an audibly shaken voice. "I think one of them's McNulty."

"You *assholes*!" Lightstone whispered.

Then, after one last glance to make sure he had the approaching figure positioned correctly, Lightstone lunged out from behind the protection of the shale outcropping, dove to the ground and then rolled behind another smaller mound of rocks and brush as a jackhammering stream of 5.56mm rounds tore up the surrounding landscape.

Rolling quickly to his left, Lightstone fired two rounds in the general direction of the rag-camouflaged figure, then dove forward on his hands and knees to the relative security of a nearby spruce just split seconds ahead of a second burst of wildly ricocheting copper-jacketed slugs.

Working hard to control his breathing, Lightstone tucked himself in tight against the moderately protective tree trunk as a third burst of the small but deadly 5.56mm bullets shredded brush and tree branches all around his new position.

Then the much louder *crack-pow!* of the sniper rifle echoed through the trees, and Lightstone threw himself flat and rolled to his right across rock and moss and lichen-strewn ground as a 7.62mm rifle round tore a huge chunk of wood out of the tree trunk less than two inches over his head, sending sap-filled fragments flying in all directions.

Lightstone brought the short-barreled .357 Magnum up in an instinctive point-shoulder position and fired two rounds at the running figure just as it disappeared behind a tree. Then, eyes fixed in a murderous rage on the concealing tree, Lightstone remained in his dangerously exposed, extended-arm position for two more heartbeats as the other man faked a move to his right with his back against the tree. Lightstone triggered the last two rounds at center-chest level just as the man came back around to his left with the Colt Commando automatic carbine firing in the full auto position.

Henry Lightstone had less than a second to enjoy the sight of the rag-camouflaged figure staggering backward from the double wallops of the mushrooming hollow-point slugs when the glancing impact of the 7.62mm copper-jacketed bullet knocked the .357 Magnum out of his hand.

The fourth incoming bullet from the 7.62mm sniper rifle, deflected by a mass of spruce and birch-tree branches, still had enough power to rip through the front panels of Lightstone's jacket and leave a shallow, bloody gouge across his chest in its wake.

Staying as close to the ground as possible as he retrieved his pistol, and then fumbling around in his jacket pocket for one of the remaining speed-loaders, Lightstone frantically crawled and twisted away from the explosive sprays of metal, wood, and rock fragments. He heard the crunching sound of boots moving quickly through downed tree branches and dry brush . . . and then the metallic click of the Colt Commando carbine's bolt as it ejected the last expended casing and snapped into the open position against the spring-operated feeder of the empty thirty-round magazine.

He's wearing a vest, Lightstone told himself.

Functioning now on pure training and instinct, and driven by a blinding and mindless fury, Lightstone rolled over to his side, hurriedly fed the six rounds into the empty chambers of the .357, released the speed-loader, slapped the cylinder shut, and came up firing alongside a much too narrow birch tree. He sent three rounds at the rag-camouflaged figure—who had instinctively lunged toward a much larger tree while reaching for another loaded magazine—and then three more at the wounded sniper. He reflexively dumped the expended .357 casings from the hot pistol one-handed while he reached into his jacket pocket for his last speed-loader . . . and found nothing.

Blinking in shock, Lightstone started to look around on the ground for the lost speed-loader. But then, hearing the metallic clack of a carbine bolt nearby, he dropped the useless .357 and scrambled desperately for the shale outcropping.

"Henry, he's coming, behind you!" Thomas Woeshack yelled unnecessarily, and then sent the unarmed floatplane diving down in a low, strafing run.

But Woeshack's heroic maneuver was still effective because it caused Arturo Bolin to duck down long enough for Henry Lightstone to throw himself forward over the edge of the outcropping. He landed hard on his side against the rough-surfaced shale and was scrambling toward the sprawled body of Sam Jackson when the sound of oncoming boots and Woeshack's static-filled voice warned him.

"Henry!"

Diving forward, Lightstone was reaching for the holstered .357 on Sam Jackson's hip when the rag-camouflaged figure of Arturo Bolin appeared over the top of the outcropping.

Laughing maliciously, the professional mercenary stepped forward to the edge of the rocky cliff with the intention of immediately triggering a fatal burst of 5.56mm bullets into Henry Lightstone's exposed back when his boot came down on a loose rock.

Lightstone heard the cold laughter, the clatter of dislodged rock, and then the grunt of surprise as Arturo Bolin winced in pain, trying to regain his balance. Lunging forward, Lightstone wrapped his fingers around the black rubber grip of Sam Jackson's pistol, pulled the weapon loose, rolled onto his back, and instinctively fired three rounds up at the greenish-brown blur. Then he twisted desperately away from the jackhammer roar of the automatic carbine and stared up wide-eyed as the lifeless body of Arturo Bolin pitched forward and struck the rocky base of the outcropping.

Gasping for breath as he lay on his back, Special Agent Henry Lightstone tried to blink the sweat and dirt out of his eyes. Then, straining to listen over his own labored breathing, he heard a strangely quiet and muffled voice coming from . . . somewhere. It took him almost thirty seconds to locate the commset that had been knocked loose from Arturo Bolin's bleeding head. He picked up the still-functioning earphones, wiped off some of the blood, and listened for a brief moment to the voice of Roy Parker, who first demanded to know what was going on, then called for additional backup in a distinctly cold, furious, and professional voice.

Jarred by the prospect of more assailants, Lightstone took the nylon harness containing the loaded magazines for the carbine from Arturo Bolin's lifeless body and snapped it around his own aching chest. He scooped up the automatic weapon then, loaded it with a full thirty rounds, and confirmed that a round was in the chamber and that the selection switch was set to auto.

He reached over then and picked up Jackson's scarred but still functional radio.

"Woeshack, can you hear me?"

"Yeah, I hear you!" the shaken special agent-pilot answered. "Jesus, I thought you guys were—"

"Good. Pick us up at the water, by the cove," Lightstone interrupted. "Right now."

"Is Sam—"

"He's still alive, but he isn't going to be much longer if we don't get him out of here."

"I'm on my way in," Woeshack said quickly. "But listen, there's another plane heading our way that won't answer my calls. And there's a boat—"

"Woeshack, I don't give a shit if the fucking Spanish Armada is out there. Get that plane down on the water and meet me at that cove!"

"Ten-Four, on my way."

Muttering to himself, Lightstone fit the radio into one of the empty ammo pouches, then slung the Colt Command over his shoulder. He reached down, scooped up the limp, unconscious Sam Jackson in both arms and started to carry him down through the brush toward the distant cove.

From way out to his left, he heard an airplane engine and saw a flash of blue metal low on the horizon. But Lightstone didn't care about other planes right now. He was determined to get Sam Jackson into the Cessna Skywagon and out of the area as quickly as possible.

Halfway down to the rocky shoreline, Lightstone thought he could hear voices near the outcropping. He propped Jackson up beside an uprooted birch tree and paused to listen. But the echoing roar of the Cessna Skywagon's single engine prevented him from hearing anything as Special Agent-Pilot Thomas Woeshack banked the floatplane around in his approach for a water landing.

Lightstone scanned the wide overhead expanse of rocks and trees and brush, searching for any sign of movement. When he didn't see anything, he reached down and picked up Jackson one more time, then stumbled the rest of the way down to the rock-strewn cove, where he found Thomas Woeshack, waiting for him on shore, and Marie Pascalaura.

"What the hell are you doing here?" Lightstone demanded in a voice that was hoarse and filled with disbelief. Shaken by his narrow escape from death, and nearly exhausted from his awkward and painful descent down the cliffs, Lightstone could only consent as Woeshack and Marie ran forward and took the still-unconscious refuge officer from his aching arms.

"I heard you call for help on the radio, so I got in the boat and came back," Marie said matter-of-factly as she and Woeshack put Sam Jackson down on the rocky shore. Then Marie looked at the blood that had soaked through the front of Lightstone's torn jacket.

"Are you all right?"

"I'm fine," Lightstone rasped, looking back over his shoulder at the surrounding cliffs. "But—"

"Well, Sam's not," she said firmly. "We've got to get him to a hospital."

"The controllers at the Kenai Tower picked up my call to Anchorage," Woeshack said, looking up. "They're sending a paramedic team and state troopers from Soldotna out to the docks right now."

"Okay," Lightstone nodded weakly as he forced himself to start moving again. "Then let's hurry up and load him in the plane. We've got to get out of here before—"

"Uh, I think we've got a problem," Woeshack interrupted.

"What's that?"

"I don't think we can take off with four people on board."

"There're four seats in the damn thing. Why the hell not?" Lightstone demanded, looking over his shoulder again as he slid his right index finger over the trigger of the automatic carbine.

For a brief moment, he thought he'd seen something move near a large bolder up on the cliffs, but now he wasn't sure.

"We got a bunch of bullet holes in the floats, and some of the chambers are filling up with water," Woeshack explained. "The plane's still floating now, but if we don't—"

Crack-pow!

Lightstone had just turned around to look at the bullet holes that seemed to pockmark the dark orange floatplane when the 7.62mm bullet whipped past his head and exploded through the right-side bubble window of the Cessna Skywagon.

"Shit!" Lightstone cursed as he triggered a long, piercing burst of 5.56mm rounds into the trees surrounding the boulder where he'd sensed movement. Expended casings flew over his shoulder, and Marie Pascalaura screamed and dropped to the rocks. Woeshack rolled to the ground and fumbled for his shoulder-holstered .357 Magnum.

"Get that prop going!" Lightstone yelled at Woeshack. Then he and Marie dragged Sam Jackson over to the water and up into the boat.

"What do I do?" Marie Pascalaura yelled as she fumbled with the starter and got the outboard running, while Lightstone spun around and emptied the rest of the carbine's magazine in the general direction of the distant boulder.

"You still have the radio?" he asked as he turned to push the open aluminum boat out into the water.

"Yes."

From behind his back, Lightstone heard the Cessna Skywagon's starter whine as Woeshack tried again and again to kick the engine over. Finally the floatplane erupted into a loud, rumbling roar.

"Then go like hell for the dock, and let them know you're coming. State troopers should be on their way," he yelled over the deafening sounds of the plane and the outboard motor as he replaced the short-barreled carbine. "We'll meet you there."

"But—"

"Get going!" he ordered as he aimed and fired another short burst at a sudden movement of green camouflage next to the distant boulder and then ran toward the plane, vaguely aware that his lower legs had started to turn numb in the icy water.

Lightstone pulled himself into the front passenger seat, yanked the door shut, and began to put on his headset when the sharp crack of a high-powered rifle echoed across the water once again. He started to duck down, but then, out of the corner of his eye, he saw a broad splash of water about ten feet to the far side of Marie Pascalaura's rapidly accelerating patrol boat.

"Goddamn it!" Lightstone screamed. "Those sons of bitches are shooting at *her*!"

Then he turned to Woeshack, his eyes widened with rage. "Get this thing between her and that boulder, *right now*!" he yelled as he pulled himself into the narrow backseat area, braced himself against the right side of the plane and used both feet to kick out the left-side rear Plexiglas window.

As Special Agent-Pilot Thomas Woeshack throttled the dark orange floatplane forward, Lightstone switched the Colt Commando carbine over to single shot, aligned the open sights of the short-barreled weapon as best he could inside the bouncing and vibrating plane, and began to methodically fire round after round at the pair of cammo-clad figures barely visible on one side of the tree-covered boulder.

He completely ignored the loud clatter of torn metal as an incoming stream of 5.56mm bullets ripped into the float-plane's left pylon, and the loud *clang!* as another 7.62mm bullet punched through the thin-skinned aircraft in the space equidistant between Lightstone's stomach and the back of Woeshack's pilot's seat.

Thomas Woeshack continued to accelerate the bouncing and rattling floatplane in an effort to keep up with the rapidly moving patrol boat. He had to leave the Cessna's wing flaps locked in the full-up position to keep the plane down on the water.

But all too soon, the forward speed of the plane, the bullet damage to the waterlogged floats, and the counteracting force of the wind against the torn metal fabric started a rattling vibration that threatened to tear the small plane apart.

"Feels like the left pylon is going to tear loose any second now! Either got to go up or slow down!" Woeshack shouted over his shoulder.

"She's clear. Go up!" Lightstone yelled as he set the smoking carbine aside and reached for the headset in the back of the plane.

"Can you hear me?" Woeshack asked as he readjusted the wing flaps and started the Cessna up into a steady, roaring climb.

"Christ, I think I'm deaf," Lightstone muttered, the headphones making him aware for the first time of the high-pitched ringing in his unprotected ears.

Marie Pascalaura waved her hand and continued to accelerate the small patrol boat toward the distant western shore.

"You sure that was Paul you saw on the ground back there?" Lightstone called loudly into his mike.

"Yeah, pretty sure," Woeshack acknowledged. "He had on that red-and-yellow vest that his wife made for him. Real easy to spot."

Lightstone didn't say anything for a long moment.

"You get to know Paul very well?" he finally asked.

"Well enough," Woeshack said, his voice taking on a bitter tone. "He got me through flight school when everyone else was trying to have me grounded."

"Then what do you say we go back around, then come in low over that goddamned boulder?" Lightstone said in a cold, deadly voice as he wrenched another loaded magazine out of the nylon harness and reached for the carbine.

Woeshack looked back at Lightstone for a moment. Then he smiled. "How low do you want it?" he asked, banking the vibrating aircraft around to the right.

"Low enough that if I miss, you get to take them out with the prop," Lightstone replied as he loaded the automatic carbine and set the selector back to automatic. He waited with cold, murderous patience for Woeshack to bring the aircraft to an altitude of about twelve hundred feet.

"You ready?" Woeshack asked.

"Absolutely." Lightstone set another loaded magazine between his legs.

"I'm going to go up high and then drop us in fast. I don't think they're going to be expecting something like that."

"Good."

"Okay," Woeshack nodded. "Here we go."

True to his word, Woeshack put the Cessna in a steep dive that caused the no-longer-streamlined airframe to shake and rattle and vibrate all the way down, leveling out just in time to clear the trees as Lightstone held the trigger down and sent all thirty 5.56mm rounds streaking into and around the boulder area.

Chunks of trees and dirt and rocks went flying in all

directions as one of the camouflaged-dressed men spun away and then tumbled down the cliff, while the other scrambled for the safety of a narrow ditch.

"Nice job, Woeshack," Lightstone whispered into his mike, not caring that his hands were shaking as he released the empty magazine and let it drop to the floor. "One down and one running."

"I think he's running for that plane that landed over by Paul's," Woeshack said. "You want to cut him off?"

"Damn right I do," Lightstone said evenly as he reloaded the carbine, ignoring the dozens of empty casings that were rolling around on the floor of the aircraft. "Take her around again, and we'll see if we can get an ID on that plane while we're at it."

"Okay, but don't forget we've got gas tanks in our wings," Woeshack reminded.

"Why, did we take any hits there?" Lightstone asked, never having thought—much less cared—about where the gasoline was stored in a Cessna Skywagon.

"I think we caught a bunch more in the floats, and at least one in the left wing flap that I can see," Woeshack said as he banked the plane in a long, looping turn. "Doesn't look like we're leaking any gas. Long as they don't hit one of the control cables or us, we're probably okay," the Native Alaskan special agent-pilot shrugged.

"Wonderful," Lightstone muttered.

"Hey, there's another one!" Woeshack suddenly yelled into his mike as he banked the plane to the right.

"Where?"

"Off to the right side."

Lightstone quickly shifted over to the right rear seat, suddenly aware of an all-too-familiar queasy feeling in the pit of his stomach.

"Can't see him."

"There were two of them. Both in the same cammo gear. Come back up front, you'll have a better view," Woeshack advised.

Lightstone forced himself to ignore his growing nausea and

climbed back over into the front seat as Woeshack brought the small floatplane around in a tight circle.

"See, over there." Woeshack pointed over to the right. "Two of them. Looks like they're going for the plane, too."

For a brief moment, Henry Lightstone saw a flash of white hair, and what looked like a gun. He was starting to bring the automatic carbine up for a shot through the shattered right passenger window when the right front cowling of the plane was suddenly hit with three successive *thunks*. Black smoke started to pour out of the engine on Lightstone's side, effectively blinding his shot and causing him to choke and cough as a thick fog began to fill the cockpit.

"We're hit!" Lightstone yelled into his mike.

"Yeah, no kidding," Woeshack grunted as he reached down between the seats for the fuel shutoff valve and then used the stick to nose the plane down into a moderately steep dive.

"What are you doing?"

"Gotta maintain air speed or we'll stall out."

"Yeah, but we're going to crash."

"That's right," Woeshack nodded. "Listen, there's a couple of sleeping bags in the back with the survival gear. Can you get them?"

"Sleeping bags?"

"Yeah, I think we're gonna need them real bad in about thirty seconds or so. Better hurry."

As Lightstone scrambled back over the front passenger seat again, this time fighting the force of gravity, Woeshack quickly switched over to the 121.5 standard emergency frequency, keyed his outside radio transmitter, and then spoke calmly into his mike. "Mayday, Mayday. Kenai tower, this is November Six-One-Four-Seven-Seven. We've lost our engine and we're going down, eastern shore of Skilak Lake. Do you copy?"

"November Four-Seven-Seven, we copy that you have lost engine power, going down, eastern shore of Skilak Lake." The Kenai tower controller came on the air immediately as Lightstone scrambled back into his seat clutching both sleeping bags. "Help is on the way."

"Kenai tower, advise Foxtrot Bravo India that we need immediate assistance. Suspects escaping in a— *Oh, shit!*"

The Cessna shuddered and seemed to start to fall backwards in the air, which forced Woeshack to quickly concentrate on his flying and increase the angle of the dive. From Henry Lightstone's horrified point of view, the ground seemed to be coming up at them at an incredibly fast speed. Then it suddenly occurred to him.

"Hey, you're aiming for land. What about the lake?"

"I can't swim," Thomas Woeshack said. "Besides, it feels like that left float is starting to go. We hit the water like that, we're gonna break up and then probably freeze to death before anybody can get to us."

"But—"

"You got that safety belt on tight?"

Lightstone quickly fastened his belt and shoulder harness, trying not to look at the mass of trees coming up at them fast now.

"Yeah, it's as tight as I can get it."

"Okay, put your hands in through the sides of the bag and hold it up in front of your face," Woeshack said as he grabbed the other sleeping bag and put in in his lap.

Then he waited until the last moment before pulling the stick back and dropping the wing flaps to send the orange Cessna plummeting floats-first into a dense clump of spruce trees, looking for all the world like a huge orange eagle flaring its wings as it swooped in to grasp its prey with its talons.

The initial impact of the crash was absorbed by the two floats as they buckled and then crumpled up into the cross pylons. But all Henry Lightstone knew at the time was that the front windshield was suddenly filled with tree branches, and the safety belt tore into his body, and his head was slammed forward toward the instrument panel, with the sleeping bag absorbing most, but not all, of the impact.

Barely conscious, Lightstone was vaguely aware of the plane starting to shift in its precariously wedged position in a clump of broken spruce trees about ten feet off the ground.

He was trying to reach for the seat-belt release when he felt a hand pulling on his arm and a sharp knife blade sawing through his safety harness. Then somebody pushed him out the door and he tumbled to the ground through what seemed like a thousand broken spruce branches that smelled like a curious mixture of fresh pitch and gasoline.

Then he and Woeshack ran as fast as they could until the concussive force of the plane exploding knocked both of them off their feet and into the darkness.

Even after he regained consciousness, it took Henry Lightstone several seconds to recover to the point that he could turn his head and throw up.

Then, after what seemed like an eternity of gasping and coughing, he finally found the strength to crawl over to where Thomas Woeshack was lying on his back, using his cut and bruised forearms to block the sun from his bloodied face.

"You alive?"

"Must be," Woeshack mumbled after a moment. "My whole body hurts."

"Good sign." Lightstone nodded weakly as he slowly rolled over on his back and lay next to the sprawled-out pilot.

"Well, you finally did it, kid," he said quietly after a few moments.

"Did what?"

"You finally figured out how to fly just like one of those goddamned birds."

"Yeah, you really think so?" Woeshack smiled through his split and bloody lips.

"Absolutely. No question about it."

It was only then, as the two special agents lay there in the rock and spruce and lichen-covered clearing, bruised, bleeding, and covered with black soot, that they first heard and then saw the large blue floatplane that appeared overhead at an elevation of about a thousand feet.

"You read the number?" Lightstone asked.

Woeshack tried to focus his blurry eyes on the moving blue object and then slowly shook his head. "No."

"Me neither."

"Maybe they'll try to land."

"Yeah," Lightstone smiled. "That'd be nice."

The plane made three complete circles over the crash site. Then, apparently satisfied that his team had caused sufficient damage to their unexpected adversaries, a tired, blood-smeared and mildly irritated Gerd Maas directed the pilot to rock the wings of the plane in a mock salute before turning away.

For a long time, neither agent spoke, until finally Woeshack said: "They just gave us the finger, didn't they?"

Henry Lightstone continued to watch the large blue float-plane until it finally disappeared off in the distance. Then he nodded his head slowly. "Yeah, I'd say so."

Woeshack thought about that for a few more seconds. "So what do we do now?" he asked.

Then Henry Lightstone turned his head to stare straight into the dark, questioning eyes of his thoroughly bruised, battered, and bleeding partner, and said:

"Find us another airplane."

CHAPTER THIRTY-FIVE

"Understand you're still the senior law-enforcement officer here representing your agency."

There were at least eight of them on the scene, and they'd been working diligently for three hours now: chalking the locations of the bodies; taking measurements; making sketches; filling paper bags with pieces of neatly tagged evidence; photographing everything at right angles at least twice; and videotaping the whole thing. They worked with such methodical thoroughness that Lightstone found it easy to accept that the "new" FBI was really something else.

The only trouble was, they still hadn't put it all together yet. And based upon what Henry Lightstone was seeing with his own CSI-trained eyes, he wasn't sure that they were going to. At least not right away.

Which was beginning to worry him, because if there was ever a time when he wanted a crime-scene team to come in, pick up the clues, and get back to their desks with plenty of time to complete all the paperwork, it was right now.

"Apparently," Lightstone answered in a carefully neutral voice. "I don't think we've met." He felt like his body was a mass of cracked bones and torn muscles.

"Al Grynard, assistant special agent in charge of the Anchorage office," the gray-haired man said politely, offering his hand. He was dressed in a neatly pressed sport shirt, new blue jeans, and gray Gor-Tex hiking boots that looked like they'd just come out of the box.

"Henry Lightstone. Senior resident agent, on special-duty assignment to *our* Anchorage office," Lightstone responded equally politely, making a mental note that the ASAC's light gray eyes seemed just a little too intense and skeptical to have any serious connection with that infamous FBI smile. "And this is one of our agent-pilots, Tom Woeshack."

"You must be the fellow who made that fancy emergency landing back there," Grynard said as he turned to shake Woeshack's hand. "What is it you pilots say? Any landing you can walk away from must be a good one?"

"Uh, yes sir, that's about it."

"Nice landing any way you look at it," the FBI agent smiled. "Too bad you couldn't have made it to water, though. Probably would have been a lot easier on you two, and you might have been able to save the plane. Gets rough on the budget when you lose an expensive floatplane like that."

Feeling every bit as bruised and battered as his new senior-agent partner, Thomas Woeshack was suddenly finding it difficult to remain composed in the face of the FBI agent's comments. He had no idea of whether they were rooted in interagency camaraderie, warped amusement, or simple accusation. Woeshack recognized him as the man who had arrived in a fancy executive helicopter and who had waited until the rotors had shut off before he opened the door.

Being new at the game, of course, Thomas Woeshack had no way of knowing that the elaborate helicopter incident had just been the opening move in a very intricate game. By arriving at the scene in such a way that the subjects in question would naively focus on the FBI agent's perceived arrogance and vanity, they would presumably fail to notice later the signs of his carefully contrived traps.

Henry Lightstone, however, had seen this sort of thing many times in his earlier police career, and he was very interested in seeing where this particular interrogation was headed.

"In my opinion, Agent-Pilot Woeshack simply made the best choice he could under what I judged to be extremely difficult circumstances," Lightstone interjected in a courteous but firm voice.

"Ah," the FBI agent nodded noncommittally.

Woeshack glanced over at Lightstone, who gave him a steady look and a barely perceptible shrug that basically said: "Don't let him bug you, kid." A glance that Al Grynard observed.

"Gave it my best shot, sir," Woeshack shrugged.

"Yes, I'm sure you did. And I'm sure that your Accident Review Board will take that into account. Ah, I assume your agency does maintain a standing AR Board?" Grynard asked, turning to Lightstone.

"Far as I know, we've got every kind of bureaucratic committee imaginable, so we probably have one of those, too. But to tell you the truth, I'm kind of new up here, so I really haven't the slightest idea," Lightstone replied evenly. He was finding it increasingly difficult to keep from telling the FBI agent that one of the bodies under those tarps was their senior agent, as well as a cherished friend, and that he really didn't give a flying fuck about overspent equipment budgets or Accident Review Boards right now.

But he didn't tell ASAC Al Grynard anything of the sort, mostly because he'd interrogated more than his share of homicide suspects in his previous career, and he knew exactly what the FBI agent was doing.

"You have already given your statement for the records," Grynard said to Lightstone. "Now I would like to try to fill in the gaps. I understand that you were injured in the shooting, as well as in the airplane crash." The FBI agent glanced down at Lightstone's torn and bloody jacket. "Are you sure you wouldn't like to continue this conversation back in Anchorage, where we can get you some first-rate medical attention?"

Lightstone smiled and shrugged. "I'm fine right now."

"Okay, well let us know if either of you change your mind and decide that you'd like to be medivaced out of here."

"Appreciate the offer. We'll let you know if either of us starts feeling bad."

"Fair deal. Rough having something like this happen your first day on at a new duty station," the FBI agent offered. "Guess you Fish and Wildlife guys don't run across this kind of thing very often, do you?"

"What? Oh . . . you mean the human bodies? No, not really."

"I'm sure you see some really gory stuff," the FBI agent said in a tone that somehow didn't quite cross the line of being patronizing, "but as far as I'm concerned, there's nothing I hate worse than working a scene where a fellow law-enforcement officer's been killed. Especially over something as senseless as this."

"Yeah, he knew better than to work by himself," Lightstone nodded. "But I guess we all do it. Part of the game when you're short on agents."

"Yeah, well, it's too bad you guys don't have some kind of portable computer system so you could run makes on your contacts in the field," Grynard suggested. "If your buddy there had known who he was up against, he might have backed off and tried to find you guys first."

"Oh, yeah? Why's that?"

"See the guy lying there next to the bear? Well, we just ran a make on him. Name's Butch Chareaux. Turns out he and his brothers were part of some poaching ring, whatever the hell that is, back in Louisiana. They all have outstanding felony warrants related to the murder of two—" Grynard glanced down at his notebook—"Louisana Department of Fish and Game officers. You'd think that some of your agents would have run across one of these characters during the last few months." Grynard shook his head sadly. "Too bad they didn't. Might have given your buddy a fighting chance."

"You sure none of us ever did?" Lightstone asked carefully. "We're pretty well spread out, and it's a big county."

"I don't know," the FBI agent shrugged. "According to your Records Bureau back in D.C., nobody in your agency has ever worked these guys. Or at least the name Butch Chareaux doesn't show up in any of your computerized case files."

"So Paul stops by to check on a couple of hunters and runs into a buzz saw," Lightstone nodded in apparent understanding. "Any idea what they were doing out here?"

"Probably setting up what you guys call a 'canned hunt.' According to the folks back in Louisiana, that was one of their favorite tricks. Irony of the whole thing, of course, is that our friend Chareaux seems to have been killed by the bear that they had in that cage. Must have gotten loose during the ruckus when your buddy showed up.

"By the way," Grynard added casually, "I meant to ask you something. Did you ever work with McNulty before?"

Lightstone hesitated, trying to remember exactly what Paul McNulty had told him about his file. Something to the effect that he'd gotten it cleared through Washington for Carl Scoby to hand-carry it over from Customs to the Anchorage office, so that he could still function—to a much lesser extent—as a wild card within the region. Although he hadn't told Marie or anyone else yet, he'd already told McNulty that he'd take the job, which meant that his transfer orders had presumably already gone through to the regional office.

The question was whether ASAC Al Grynard or his men had managed to locate and talk with Carl Scoby or any of the very few senior agents in the D.C. office who knew about McNulty's plans for a regional undercover team. Given that they'd been working the scene for only three hours, Lightstone didn't think that too likely.

"I ran across him a couple of times on previous duty assignments," Lightstone said. "Guess I figured we'd have plenty of time to get to know each other after Tom and I got back from the fishing trip," he added, giving Woeshack—who was looking thoroughly confused now—a meaningful glance. He turned back to Grynard. "You mind if I ask you a question?"

"Sure, go ahead."

"You have any idea who killed him?"

"You mean McNulty?"

"Yeah."

"It's a little hard to tell just yet. Could have been Chareaux, of course, or one of his brothers. Or even one of the people they were working with out here. Apparently you got to see at least one of them close up. The guy you thought you killed."

Lightstone blinked.

"Thought?" he asked, incredulous. "The guy's brains were all over the rocks."

"Well, if he was dead, then apparently somebody made off with the body *and* the brains." Al Grynard looked down at his notebook again. "We found a lot of blood, of course, some of which probably belonged to this guy Jackson, the refuge officer. And a couple of expended .357 and 5.56mm casings."

"A *couple?*"

"That's right, but no body."

"Oh."

"And we did happen to notice that there was what appears to be a 5.56mm Colt Commando rifle in the debris of your airplane, along with a considerable number of expended casings. I guess some of them could have cooked off in the fire—"

"I explained all of that to your agent," Lightstone said calmly. "We got fired on from the ground when we took Jackson's boat in to check on all the shooting we heard. I ended up killing one of the men who was shooting at us, and

I took his weapon because I didn't want to leave it there for the other guy—"

"The one with the sniper rifle?" Grynard interrupted.

"Right."

"And you were more concerned about a small-caliber automatic weapon than what you've described as a larger-caliber scoped rifle with . . . what did you say . . . ?" Grynard looked down at his notebook. "A tripod?"

"Bipod. Two legs. Military type. And to answer your question, I would have been concerned about guys with slingshots if they were aiming the damn things at me," Lightstone said evenly.

"Yes, of course," Grynard nodded sympathetically. "Please go on."

"And then we were fired on when we went back up in the Cessna, so we fire back—"

"With the Colt Commando?"

"Because I'd lost my .357 back at the outcropping when I ran out of ammunition. I don't suppose any of you guys have managed to find it yet?"

"No, we haven't found your duty weapon, or Refuge Officer Jackson's, or any larger-caliber casings, or any evidence of a bipod-mounted weapon being fired in the general area you described to our agents." Al Grynard shook his head regretfully. "Nor have we been able to confirm your statement that your plane was hit, as you and Special Agent Woeshack put it . . ." Grynard referred to his notebook again ". . . several dozen times. Unfortunately, as you undoubtedly realize by now, thin aluminum panels seem to burn very quickly when—"

"Hey, wait a minute. I *know* we got hit because—" Woeshack started to interrupt, but Lightstone waved him off.

"I'm sure that if we search long enough," the clearly unperturbed FBI agent went on, "we will undoubtedly find both duty weapons, *and* some evidence of the other rifle, *and* possibly even some brains of the individual that you claim to have killed. And perhaps, if you . . . excuse me, I meant if *we* are real lucky, our laboratory just might be able to verify your contention that there were a large number of bullet strikes on what little remains of your plane. But there's a great deal of very rugged country out here—"

"And right now, you don't believe much of anything we've told you?" Lightstone finished.

"I *do* understand that we are all fellow law-enforcement officers," Al Grynard smiled easily as he put away his notebook, "but I have to tell you that I find this case—and you, in particular, Mr. Lightstone—to be quite vexing."

"Oh, really?" Lightstone smiled. "And why is that?"

"Because I find it difficult to understand why the Chareaux brothers, assuming that at least one or two of them are still alive, would remove the body of one of their associates but leave their own brother's body here.

"Nor can I understand," Al Grynard went on, "why it is that when we query *your* background, we can easily retrieve your police records from San Diego. However, when we try to follow up on your transfer to the federal government, we discover that aside from your fairly impressive training records at FLETC, no one at the U.S. Customs Service seems to remember you."

"I told your agents—"

"That you were placed on a covert assignment because of your previous police experience," Al Grynard nodded, no longer making any pretense of needing to refer to his notebook. "Which does make a certain amount of sense. Unfortunately, you declined to describe the nature of this assignment—"

"As I told your agent, it's my understanding that the investigation is still ongoing."

"—or the name of your immediate supervisor, which I suppose is reasonable for someone working a deep-cover assignment." Al Grynard smiled. "But what we found to be far more difficult to understand was why you failed to mention the fact that approximately one year ago, Special Agent Paul McNulty booked you into the Anchorage Police Department jail on suspicion of dealing in illegal ivory."

"Uh . . ."

"Oh, no, that's quite all right," ASAC Al Grynard said, holding up his hand. "I'm sure that you could provide me with an explanation that would keep my staff busy for the next three or four weeks. And under normal circumstances, I wouldn't really mind, because that's what they get paid for."

Lightstone tried to interrupt again, but Al Grynard would not have it.

"You see, we're shorthanded, too, and we're awfully busy right now trying to figure out who *did* kill Special Agent McNulty. So I'll tell you what. Why don't you take that helicopter ride back to Anchorage and get that wound of yours looked at, then start becoming acquainted with your new job as—what was it?—senior resident agent of the Anchorage office? I'm sure you'll find that sufficiently distracting that you won't see any need to leave the Anchorage area for, oh, let's say for about three or four weeks. How does that sound to you?"

"Like you and I aren't going to be getting along very well for the next few days," Henry Lightstone said evenly, nodding his head in appreciation of the senior FBI agent's interrogative skills.

"I think that's probably a fair statement," Al Grynard agreed, his light gray eyes taking on that glint of amusement again. He started to turn away, then stopped and turned to face the two agents once more.

"Oh yes, I almost forgot to mention one other fascinating bit of information," he said calmly, his penetrating gray eyes staring straight into the eyes of Henry Lightstone. "It seems that two other Fish and Wildlife Service Special agents who happened to be working with Paul McNulty at the time of your, uh, booking incident last year have recently turned up missing."

"*What?*" Lightstone blinked in shock.

"Special Agent-Pilot Larry Paxton and Assistant Special Agent in Charge Carl Scoby," Grynard recited from memory. "Those names mean anything to you?"

"What happened?" Lightstone demanded in a cold, hard, and unforgiving voice.

"Paxton's plane has been overdue from a routine patrol

flight over the Florida Everglades since Monday afternoon. And Scoby hasn't checked back in from a routine contact with a female informant somewhere in southern Arizona. That also took place last Monday. I don't suppose you know anything about either of these two incidents?"

"No, I don't," Henry Lightstone whispered, his eyes glazed with barely suppressed rage.

"Then why don't you and your associate get on that helicopter, while I'm still in the mood to be friendly to a fellow law-enforcement officer?"

Then Al Grynard turned and walked back over to the camouflaged tarp that covered the lifeless body of Paul McNulty.

CHAPTER THIRTY-SIX

"Is she okay?" Thomas Woeshack asked quietly when Lightstone finally came out of the room.

"Yeah, pretty much. They gave her something to help her relax," Lightstone said with a discernible edge to his voice as he gently pulled the door to the hospital room closed.

"What about tonight?" the Native Alaskan special agent asked as they started walking down the linoleum hallway to the central nurses' station.

"Marie's going to take her back to the house," Lightstone replied, his manner suggesting that his mind was far away. "Said she'll stay there with her until her sister gets here tomorrow afternoon."

"Do you think she would mind if my family brought food tomorrow?" Woeshack asked after a moment. "It's a tradition among our people, but . . ."

Lightstone blinked and then seemed to refocus himself as he looked over at the still-shaken young agent.

"I think Martha would really appreciate that," he nodded.

"Good. I'll tell them."

Woeshack was silent for a long moment as he continued to match Henry Lightstone's steady strides. Then, when they finally stopped in front of the nurses' station, Woeshack turned to Lightstone again.

"You know, I think being in that room when you told her about Paul was one of the toughest moments in my life," he whispered, his voice tight with emotion. "We Eskimos are a very fatalistic people, and we are . . . taught, I guess that's the right word, to accept death as a natural part of life. But she—"

"It's a rough deal any way you look at it," Lightstone nodded sympathetically. "They were married a long time. You put in that many years together, and get that close to retirement, you've got a right to hope that nothing like this is ever going to happen."

"Yeah, well, I'll tell you," Woeshack said seriously, "if we ever lose an agent like this again, I want to be the one kicking the door instead of the one who has to notify the family."

"I know a lot of homicide investigators who'd agree with you wholeheartedly," Lightstone nodded as he stepped to the front counter of the nurses' station.

"Yes, may I help you?"

"Special Agent Henry Lightstone," he said in a carefully polite voice, having to work at keeping his own tumbled emotions in check as he held out his badge and credentials. "Would it be possible for me to use your phone to make a couple of long-distance credit-card calls?"

"Yes, of course." The nurse set the phone on the counter, then discreetly moved her chair to the far side of the enclosed area.

"Fish and Wildlife, Law Enforcement," the pleasant voice answered. "How may I help you?"

"Mike Takahara, please."

"I'm sorry, but he's not available right now. May I take a message?"

"Can you tell me when he *will* be available?"

"No sir, I can't, but perhaps—"

Frustrated and distracted, Lightstone was about ready to hang up when he suddenly remembered.

"I'm sorry, I forgot to identify myself," he interrupted. "This is Special Agent Thomas Woeshack from the Anchorage office. Mike and I used to work together. I need to talk with him regarding an urgent matter."

The voice on the phone hesitated.

"Just a second, I have his home number," Lightstone said, mentally decoding and then reciting the confidential phone number from the folded piece of paper he took out of his badge case. "I just need to know when he'll be home so I know when to call."

The voice hesitated and then said: "There's a young Eskimo woman who works out of the Anchorage LE office."

"Jennifer Alik," Lightstone responded, forcing himself to remain calm and controlled. "Wildlife inspector. About twenty-five years old. Five-six, black hair, brown eyes, and very pretty."

"Have you ever gone out with her?" the receptionist asked in a friendly voice.

"Uh, no, but I'd sure like to," Lightstone guessed, remembering Woeshack's description of her.

"You should ask her out. I think she'd like that," the receptionist said cheerfully. "And to answer your question, Mike left early to do some work on his patio. He should be home in half an hour or so, unless he decides to stop by a computer store on the way."

"In which case he could be there the rest of the day," Lightstone finished.

"You obviously know Mike."

"All too well. Listen, if he happens to come back to the office in the next hour or so, could you tell him to call home and check his messages? It's very important."

"I sure will."

"Okay, thanks," Lightstone said as he disconnected.

"Now you're *me*?" Woeshack asked, his eyebrows furrowed in confusion.

"Had to be," Lightstone shrugged. "She wouldn't know anybody named Henry Lightstone, because I'm not in the Fish and Wildlife Service directory yet."

"So what does that have to do with Jennifer?" Woeshack demanded suspiciously.

"You ever date her?"

"Ah, no, not exactly. I was planning to ask her out, though."

"You should," Lightstone advised as he picked up the phone and began dialing again. He let the first number in San Diego ring eight times and then got Mike Takahara's answering machine with the second.

"Mike, this is, ah . . . your wild-card buddy," Lightstone said after a moment's hesitation. "Listen, I think the Chareauxs are coming after the team, and they've got some help. We found Paul shot to death this morning out on the Kenai Peninsula, and Butch Chareaux lying dead a few feet away. The rest—presumably including Alex and Sonny, and at least a couple of unknowns in cammo gear—got away in a blue floatplane."

Lightstone hesitated again, wondering how much he dared say over the phone, and then decided that if anyone would have their answering machine protected like a bank vault, it would be Mike Takahara.

"Something else I just learned," Lightstone went on. "Carl and Larry have apparently been missing since Monday, which is why I think they're coming after us. See if you can get ahold of Stoner, let him know what's going on, and in the meantime, watch your back. I'm heading his way right now."

Then he hung up and turned back to the nurse.

"Could I borrow a phone book? Thanks."

"So what do we do now?" Woeshack asked as Lightstone quickly thumbed through the Yellow Pages and then reached for the phone.

"Exactly what they expect us to do," Lightstone muttered, listening to the ringing in the background.

"Alaska Airlines," a cheerful female voice answered.

"Hello, this is Thomas Woeshack," Lightstone said calmly. "I'd like to see if you have two seats available for a flight from Anchorage to Tucson, Arizona, government fare."

"We can get you on Alaska Flight Eighty-four, leaving Anchorage at seven A.M., transferring to Alaska Flight Six-oh-six at SEA-TAC, and arriving in Tucson at four-forty P.M."

"That would be fine. The name is Woeshack, W-O-E-S-H-A-C-K, first name, Thomas."

"And the second passenger?"

Covering the mouthpiece, Lightstone looked up at Woeshack. "What's your brother's name?"

"Which one?"

"Any one."

"Timothy."

"My brother Timothy," Lightstone said into the phone. "Yes, government Diner's Card. Thank you very much."

Thomas Woeshack looked bewildered as Lightstone hung up. "I thought the FBI guy told us we couldn't leave Anchorage."

"That's right, he did."

"So what if he decides to put one of his agents on us, to see what we're doing?"

"He already has," Lightstone shrugged. "One of them's waiting in the lobby and the other one's outside, circling the hospital in a blue Ford Explorer." He reached for the phone again.

"Oh."

"Alaska Airlines," an equally cheerful male voice answered, causing Lightstone to wonder momentarily what they fed people who answered phones for a living.

"Hello, this is Robert LaGrange. I'd like to make reservations for a flight from Anchorage to San Diego as late as possible tonight or as early as possible tomorrow morning. One-twenty tomorrow morning? And what time would I arrive in Seattle? That would be perfect. LaGrange. L-A-G-

R-A-N-G-E. First name Robert. Thank you." Lightstone smiled as pleasantly as he could as he returned the phone to the duty nurse.

"I take it I'm going to be the decoy?" Woeshack asked as he and Lightstone walked down the wide hallway toward the main lobby.

"Woeshack, you're starting to think like a cop."

"I watch a lot of TV when I'm not busy crashing airplanes," the Native Alaskan special agent shrugged. And then, after a pause: "You're going after these guys, right?"

"Something like that."

Woeshack hesitated. "So how come I don't get to help?"

Henry Lightstone stopped at the double doors, turned to the young agent and stared straight into his dark, concerned eyes. "You're going to get involved in this, buddy. You can count on it. But the first thing you've got to do is to help break us loose."

For a moment, it seemed that Woeshack might argue, but Lightstone's gaze never wavered. Finally Woeshack sighed and nodded his head.

"Okay, so how are we going to do it?"

"Ideally, with you and a couple of your brothers. Are any of them close to my height and weight?"

"Joe's about your size," Woeshack judged, cocking his head as he looked up and down at the tall agent. "Maybe a little shorter. But the hair—"

"I'll start wearing a hat and shades this afternoon," Lightstone said. "Think you guys can make it look good if I give you some of my clothes?"

"Sure, if they don't get in too close."

"They won't."

"So how do we do it?"

"Your truck has tinted windows all around, right?"

"Yeah, sure."

"You and I are going to eat dinner about eight o'clock tonight at the Hilton. Afterward we go over to the bar, have a couple of beers, and reminisce about Paul until about ten. Then you're going to leave me at the hotel, go home, go to bed, and come back with your truck at precisely five in the morning. You'll pick me up in the back parking lot."

"Except that it'll be Joe I pick up, because by then you're already halfway down to San Diego on the one-twenty flight, right?"

"That's right."

"So how do we make the switch?"

"Joe's going to be in the bar, too, but he'll stay completely away from us. Around ten, when we get ready to pay the tab, Joe gets up and leaves ahead of us, takes the elevator to the sixth floor and waits for me in the hallway outside Room Six-seventy-two. I give him the key, the hat, and the sunglasses. He goes in, turns on the lights and calls down to the front desk for a four-thirty wake-up call. He turns on a pay-TV movie because he can't sleep. You can figure the Feds will be monitoring all · that with hotel security. Around midnight, he turns everything off, goes to sleep, and then gets up at four-thirty, takes the stairs down to the back entrance, and meets you in the parking lot at five."

"Remembering to put the hat and shades on before he leaves the room."

"Right."

"How long do you want us to keep it going?"

"My plane lands in Seattle at five-thirty in the morning, and I've got an hour layover until the next flight," Lightstone said. "If you guys keep them from getting suspicious until at least five-thirty, ideally six-thirty, then I'm home free."

"No problem," Woeshack smiled. "I'll have Joe drop me off at the main terminal and drive around while I go in and pay for the tickets. No luggage, just carry-ons. Then I'll go back out to the truck and we'll drive around for a while, make it look like we're going to hold back, and then make a dash for the gate at the last minute."

"That ought to do it," Lightstone nodded.

"You really think they're going to be watching the parking lot at five in the morning?"

Lightstone paused before answering.

"What I think is that Grynard's going to have three or four

guys on us twenty-four hours a day, working eight-hour rotating shifts."

"Christ! I thought he said he was short on agents."

"He is," Lightstone replied knowingly, remembering the intense and skeptical look in the FBI agent's light gray eyes. "Otherwise, he'd be using six or eight."

"Yes?"

"This is Maas."

"Where are you?"

"Do we have a clear line?"

"Just a moment."

Dr. Reston Wolfe punched a series of three buttons on his phone, then waited until the green light at the lower right corner of the receiver began to blink.

"Okay," he said, "go ahead."

"We are in Soldotna. Phase One and Phase Two were completed successfully, but we ran into complications with Phase Three."

"What happened?" Dr. Reston Wolfe asked quickly. He could feel his chest starting to constrict.

"We lost a man."

"*What?*"

"A small group of Fish and Wildlife law-enforcement officers happened to be fishing on the lake," Maas said in his distinctively calm and chilling voice. "They heard the shots and came over to investigate. They had access to a floatplane, and one of them turned out to be very proficient with weapons."

"Who did we lose?" Wolfe whispered.

"Bolin got careless and was killed. Parker was wounded in the left leg, below the knee, and in the right arm. We have sent him back to the base for treatment. Watanabe received superficial wounds in the buttocks and lower legs, but indicated that he is perfectly capable of continuing on with the mission. I sent him down to assist Günter and Felix."

"My God, what about the scene?" Wolfe asked, numbed

and horrified by the thought that Operation Counter Wrench could possibly start to come apart *now*.

"We were able to cause their plane to crash, which gave us time to retrieve Bolin and clean up."

"And the other, ah . . . bodies?"

"They were left in place, precisely as we planned."

"Then we're okay?" Wolfe whispered, hardly daring to hope.

"Yes, I believe so," Maas replied. "The survivors of the crash saw our plane, but we were able to land quickly on Tustumena Lake, dispose of the plane and Bolin, then leave in the backup plane without being observed."

"How deep is the water?"

"Approximately three hundred meters, and the water is very cold and murky. He will not be found."

"What about the investigation?"

"The FBI is on the scene, as we expected. They will be intrigued by the physical evidence, and confused by the statements of the survivors. In the end, they will have no choice but to believe that the Chareaux brothers are seeking their revenge on these federal agents."

"Then all we have to do is wait until it's over," Wolfe said, almost limp with nervous relief.

"No," Maas said coldly. "First we go and kill the last three, as we planned. *Then* we wait for it to be over."

CHAPTER THIRTY-SEVEN

"Jennifer?"

"Yes?" the voice mumbled sleepily.

"This is Henry Lightstone. Sorry to call you this late, but I need to ask you a question about airplane cargo inspections."

"Ah, *yes sir*, go ahead," the young wildlife inspector said, blinking herself awake.

"The question is, would you normally inspect the cargo shipments coming into Anchorage on Alaska Flight Ninety-nine, the one that lands at eleven-fifty this evening?"

"Uh, no sir, not normally. That flight comes in through SEA-TAC, so there usually aren't any foreign import declarations. Those would have been checked at Seattle."

"But you would inspect occasionally if you thought there was something illegal in one of the shipments?"

"Oh, yes, certainly, especially if we got some kind of tip."

"Such as a single passenger trying to bring three untagged trophy grizzlies in from British Columbia, listing Anchorage as his final destination?"

"We would definitely search on something like that," Jennifer Alik said emphatically. "Of course it would help if that tip came from a reliable source."

"Then I guess the next question is, do you think I'm reliable enough?"

"Yes sir, of course," the young wildlife inspector laughed. "Do you have any idea of when this passenger might be coming in?"

Lightstone looked at his watch. "Far as I know, in about an hour and twenty minutes."

"Tonight?"

"I'm afraid so."

"Okay," Jennifer Alik sighed. "I'll be there, but it'll take me a couple of minutes to get dressed."

"Ah, listen," Lightstone said, "I'm staying here at the Captain Cook. Do you think you could pick me up on the way?"

Making full use of her connections with the operations staff at the Anchorage airport, it took Jennifer Alik less than twenty minutes to get Lightstone's bag checked onto Flight 394 and then return to her small, shared office at Alaska Air Cargo, where Henry Lightstone was waiting.

"Any problems?" he asked as she handed him the ticket packet with the red "Checked Firearms" tag stapled to the front.

"I had to verify that the gun in the locked case was unloaded," the cheerfully smiling wildlife inspector nodded. "McNulty's been saying some nice things about you the last couple of weeks, so I assumed that it was."

"Yep, all safe and sound," Lightstone nodded, wishing that he had the heart to tell her about McNulty, and wishing also that he could have carried the new 10mm Smith & Wesson automatic pistol—the one he'd checked out of the Anchorage property room—with him on the plane. But he knew that it wasn't beyond Al Grynard to have his agents monitoring the issuance of weapons passes by the airlines. And there was no way to avoid having to show his real credentials if he tried to go through the checkpoint armed.

Something about that whole weapons check-through procedure was tugging at the back of Lightstone's brain, but he didn't know why, and then Jennifer Alik interrupted his thoughts before he could figure it out.

"Anything else I can help you with?" the young Eskimo woman asked.

"Well, for the next twenty minutes or so," Lightstone said, "why don't you show me how you really *would* have inspected a shipment from Flight Ninety-nine had that tip come from a more reliable source."

CHAPTER THIRTY-EIGHT

At exactly one o'clock that Thursday morning, Special Agent Henry Lightstone went through the motions of suddenly remembering that he had a flight to catch. The assistant manager at the Alaska Cargo office—who was apparently willing to do just about anything for Jennifer Alik—stepped in and offered to drive him out on his baggage cart to the loading ramp for Alaska Flight 394.

Entering the plane via the emergency access stairway, Lightstone managed to bypass the surveillance teams that FBI Agent Al Grynard *had* placed at the security checkpoints.

Eight hours and twenty minutes later, at precisely 10:20 A.M., after passing through one time zone, and two more security checks without incident, Lightstone approached the Budget rental-car counter at San Diego International Airport. He signed for a small sedan in the name of Henry Allen Lightner, using one of his undercover credit cards that he hadn't gotten around to canceling.

Forty-five minutes later, Lightstone entered the Federal Building on "C" street, took the elevator up to the seventh floor, and walked into Dwight Stoner's office . . . completely unaware that he had been followed all the way from the Budget parking lot.

"Henry Lightstone. I'm here to see Dwight Stoner," he said, holding out his badge and credentials for inspection by the young blond receptionist.

"I'm sorry, sir," the young woman smiled apologetically,

"but Agent Stoner left the office a little while ago. Was he expecting you?"

"Uh, no, not really. Do you know when he'll be back?"

"No, I don't. He received a call from an informant, and then he left right away."

"An informant?" Lightstone blinked. "Are you sure?"

"Well, uh, yes, I guess so. I mean—"

"When exactly did he get the call?"

"Oh, uh, earlier this morning," the receptionist said, looking flustered.

"I mean, what *time?*" Lightstone said impatiently.

"Oh, sure, let's see here," she said as she turned back the top page in her telephone memo book. "Yes, here it is. The call came in at exactly nine forty-six, a little over an hour ago."

"Did you happen to get the name of the informant?" Lightstone asked as he tried to read the barely legible script upside down.

"No, I didn't. She wouldn't give me her name. I asked her twice, but she said that—"

"She?" Lightstone's head came up. "Are you sure it was a woman?"

"Oh, yes, it was definitely a woman's voice," the young woman nodded. "She had a real strong accent. Sort of Germanic, I think."

Lightstone forced himself to remain calm. "Do you remember what was it, *exactly*, that she said to you?" he asked, feeling his blood pressure starting to rise as he remembered Al Grynard's words: *And Scoby hasn't checked back in from a routine contact with a female informant somewhere in southern Arizona.*

"Well, let me think. Humm, first of all, when I asked who she was, she said that she didn't want to give me her name because it was not a big deal and she didn't think—"

"Listen, uh, Tracy," Lightstone interrupted as he quickly read the nameplate on the front of the desk, "this is very important. Do you have any idea of where Agent Stoner was to meet this informant?"

"No, he didn't say, but he might have written it down in the notebook on his desk. He usually—" she started to add, but Lightstone was already sprinting to Stoner's small office, where he rummaged around the top of the cluttered desk and then in the lower file drawer.

"Uh, sir, I'm really not supposed to let you do that," the young woman said as she came in through the doorway with a determined look on her face. But Lightstone already had the spiral-bound notebook opened to the last entry. A moment later he was out the door and running down the wide corridor to the elevator.

At six-foot-nine, and three hundred and ten pounds, Special Agent Dwight Stoner had long since become accustomed to the fact that his presence tended to intimidate people.

And while that sort of thing was perfectly okay when facing down defensive linebackers like Lawrence Taylor and Carl Banks, or malicious biker punks like Brendon Kleinfelter, it was often a disadvantage when the formidable special agent tried to interact with the general public.

Thus, when Dwight Stoner saw the momentary look of fear in the very attractive young woman's eyes, he immediately tried to compensate by relaxing his guard.

"I didn't mean to frighten you, ma'am," Stoner said with what he hoped was a reassuring smile as he held out his badge and credentials. "I'm Special Agent Dwight Stoner with the U.S. Fish and Wildlife Service. I believe you called me this morning about an illegal rack?"

"Oh yes, Officer. Please come in." Carine Müeller said in a shaky voice, genuinely startled by the immense size of the federal agent. She decided immediately that she wouldn't let Sonny Chareaux draw the game out with this man the way he wanted to. "I was afraid that you might have changed your mind."

"Had to stop for gas, and then I made a wrong turn back at the junction." Stoner shrugged his massive shoulders apologetically. "Took me a while to find somebody who knew this part of the country well enough to give me directions."

"It was very kind of you to drive all the way out here," Müeller said as she led him in through the kitchen and out the back door, then started walking toward a large, decrepit barn at the far corner of her acre-sized lot. "My neighbor was so frightened."

"Is that Mr. Nakamura?" Stoner asked, observing the slender, nervous-looking Oriental man who stood next to the partially opened side door of the barn.

"Yes," Carine Müeller nodded. "He's such a nice man, and he and his wife are wonderful neighbors. But they haven't been in this country very long, and he was afraid that he'd be arrested if he kept it at his house. And he didn't know what to do, so I told him that he could keep it in our barn until you got here."

"Mr. Nakamura, I'm Special Agent Stoner, from the U.S. Fish and Wildlife Service," Stoner said as he walked up and slowly extended his large hand.

"Yes, I thank you very much that you come to help me," Kiro Nakamura—a Shotokan fourth-degree black belt—said in broken English, taking professional note of Dwight Stoner's limp as he returned the agent's handshake with his deliberately relaxed right hand.

"I understand you had a run-in with a poacher out here?"

"Yes," Nakamura nodded with wide-eyed enthusiasm. "He say that for very little money, I can have big animal trophy and family name in record book. I say yes, but now he want more money, and I not want," Nakamura stuttered, forcing his lethal hands to tremble visibly. "I am visitor in your country. Not want to go to jail."

"It's okay, Mr. Nakamura," Dwight Stoner said soothingly. "I'm here to help you, not to arrest you, okay?"

"Yes, okay, I like that." The Asian man smiled happily as Stoner turned back to Carine Müeller.

"You said the rack is in the barn?"

"Yes, let me show you," Müeller said as she led the way into the dark, cobwebby barn that was filled with stacked boxes, trunks, gasoline cans, and a vast array of farm equipment that looked like it hadn't been touched in years.

"Ugghh, this place gives me the willies," she shuddered as she fumbled around in the semidarkness. "I almost never come out here. I hate spiders, and I can never remember where the light switch is."

"Is this it?" Stoner asked as he stepped between two head-high stacks of old cardboard boxes and looked down at the huge, eight-point elk rack that had been propped up against a pair of wooden ammo crates.

"Yes, that is what he want to sell to me," Kiro Nakamura said in an excited voice as he moved up past Stoner. "But then he say I no have papers, so I must pay more."

"What did you say the man's name was?" Stoner asked as he bent down to examine the record-sized rack more closely.

"Chareaux," said a familiar voice to Stoner's right.

"What—"

Dwight Stoner started to come up and around just as Sonny Chareaux lunged forward and swung the baseball bat square across Stoner's right knee, causing the surprised special agent to roar in agony as he collapsed on the concrete floor.

As Stoner went down, Kiro Nakamura immediately moved in to grab for his shoulder-holstered .45 SIG-Sauer automatic. Pulling Stoner's jacket aside with his right hand and reaching in his left, Nakamura unsnapped the restraining strap and had the heavy weapon halfway out of its holster when Dwight Stoner brought his head up with a savage look in his pain-filled eyes and closed his huge right hand around Nakamura's left wrist.

Reacting with blinding speed, Nakamura yelled out a guttural *"Ki-ai!"* as he drove the heel of his right palm into Stoner's nose, slamming the agent's head backward in a spray of blood. Yelling out again, Nakamura brought his tightly closed right hand around in a vicious back-fisted strike that caught Stoner square across the right eye and snapped his head around to the left. He then delivered a knife-hand thrust to the agent's exposed throat.

Stunned and nearly unconscious, Stoner dropped hard onto his knees with an agonized gasp, but somehow he managed to find the strength to snap Nakamura's wrist, causing the Asian to release the SIG-Sauer pistol, which clattered to the floor.

Then, using the broken wrist for leverage, Stoner sent the injured karate master stumbling into Carine Müeller just as she was reaching into one of the boxes for her .357 revolver.

"Get him . . . *agghhh!*" Müeller cried out in pain as her head struck the metal edge of a table saw, splitting the skin over her left eye. She cursed in her native German as she fumbled around under the boxes, searching desperately for her weapon.

Dwight Stoner was still trying to recover from the savage blows to his nose and throat, and the agonizing pain in his shattered knee, when he saw movement out of the corner of his rapidly swelling eye. He barely managed to turn away in time to absorb the impact of the bat against his upper arm and shoulder rather than against his head. But the blow jarred him backward, and all he could do was to try to twist around and bring his massive forearms up to ward off Sonny Chareaux's next swing when . . .

Ka-booom!

. . . the sudden concussive detonation of a high-velocity pistol round going off in the contained area seemed to send ice picks through his eardrums. The 180-grain jacketed hollow-point bullet tore through the back of Sonny Chareaux's right hand and sent pieces of the bat flying in all directions.

Stunned by the impact of the expanding 10mm projectile, and groaning from the terrible pain of shattered bones and torn nerves, Chareaux stumbled forward. Then, turning around in a daze, one bloody hand clutched tight against his stomach, the Cajun poacher found himself staring into a very familiar face.

"I'd kill you right now," Henry Lightstone whispered as he centered the sights of the stainless-steel automatic between Chareaux's blinking eyes, "but I'd rather see you rot in jail."

"You!" Chareaux rasped, his eyes widening in disbelief. Then, in an incredible display of rage, the Cajun poacher lunged forward, his lips bared back, looking for all the world like the wounded Kodiak whose only thought had been to move forward and destroy.

Lightstone had already dropped the sights of the S&W

automatic and was starting to squeeze off the first point-blank shot into the center of Sonny Chareaux's chest when Carine Müeller suddenly sprinted off across the debris-covered floor.

Reacting instinctively, because Chareaux was already crippled and thus presumably a lesser threat, Lightstone spun around in a crouch and triggered three concussive shots in the direction of the disappearing figure just as Dwight Stoner threw himself forward at Chareaux's legs and Kiro Nakamura came in fast with a spinning kick that sent the fifth 180-grain bullet streaking over Sonny Chareaux's head and through the main door of the barn as the stainless-steel automatic was knocked out of Lightstone's hands.

For a brief moment, the two bare-handed fighters paused to stare at each other in the dust- and debris-strewn semidarkness while Dwight Stoner and Sonny Chareaux continued to twist and grunt and roll across the cement floor, sending boxes and tools flying as they hit and elbowed and bit and tore at each other's throat.

Then, sensing an advantage, Nakamura suddenly stepped forward, missed with a lunging, high jump kick, absorbed and then spun away from Lightstone's combination block and punishing side elbow strike to his upper rib cage, came back all the way around with a roundhouse heel kick to the side of Lightstone's head . . . and then went down hard when the Okinawan-trained agent recovered, shifted his feet and twisted his hips sharply as he drove a punishing left-handed punch into his assailant's floating ribs and then immediately followed with a reverse-direction right-elbow strike that caught the Skotokan black belt square in the mouth and nose.

Behind his back, Henry Lightstone heard a horrible crunch of breaking bones—and then an agonized scream—but he didn't have time to look around because his seemingly indestructible opponent was already back on his feet and smiling in apparent amusement through bleeding lips and nose as his flickering eyes searched for yet another advantage in the dust-filled semidarkness.

Lightstone had instinctively brought his feet back into a balanced defensive stance, ready to counter Nakamura's next move, when the far side door of the barn burst open and a curly haired body-builder type appeared, holding a short-barreled H&K 9mm submachine gun.

"Come on, let's blow this place!" the body-builder yelled, putting a stream of 9mm bullets ripping through the rotten wooden walls of the barn—sending Lightstone and Nakamura diving for the floor . . . before he and Carine Müeller disappeared through the far side door.

Looking around frantically, Lightstone finally spotted the reflective stainless-steel finish of his 10mm Smith & Wesson on the floor about ten feet away and was starting toward it when he heard, and then saw, Kiro Nakamura coming in fast.

The full-powered front kick would have caught Lightstone square in the face—and either knocked him unconscious or broken his neck—had it not been for Dwight Stoner, who pulled himself up out of the semidarkness on one leg, caught Kiro Nakamura by the shirt in midair, and then slammed the Shotokan master back into the rough six-by-six support beam, with his feet dangling a good sixteen inches above the floor.

Reacting out of pure instinct, Nakamura drove his left fist into the huge agent's exposed neck and then shrieked in pain as the broken bones of his wrist grated against torn nerves.

"Shithead!" Dwight Stoner screamed, glaring into Nakamura's agonized eyes. Then, holding the struggling Shotokan black belt up and out with his left hand, the infuriated agent drove his huge fist into Nakamura's chest, sending him crashing into the wall in a shower of loose boards and flying tools. He landed facedown on the hard concrete.

But then, to the astonishment of both Stoner and Lightstone, the crippled Shotokan black belt slowly pushed and pulled himself back up to a sitting position against the wall and smiled once again through his now profusely bleeding mouth as he brought Henry Lightstone's stainless-steel automatic up in both trembling hands.

The splintered end of Sonny Chareaux's bat was lying on the cement floor about six feet away, and Lightstone was already going for it—knowing that he'd be too late, but trying anyway—when the roar of new gunfire reverberated through the barn.

In quick succession, three .45-caliber jacketed hollow-point bullets caught Kiro Nakamura in the chest, neck, and forehead, slamming him backward into the broken and splintered wall boards like a rag doll.

As both Lightstone and Stoner spun around, they saw Larry Paxton standing on one crutch and braced against the doorway, a smoking SIG-Sauer pistol in his outstretched right hand.

"Karate, mah ass," the cut, bruised, battered, and seriously wounded agent grinned through his broken teeth.

"Where—?" Lightstone started to ask, looking around quickly as he crawled over and retrieved the stainless-steel automatic from the lap of the now-dead black belt. Then he remembered what the curly haired body-builder with the submachine gun had yelled:

Come on, let's blow this place!

"How the hell did you get here?" Dwight Stoner rasped through his swollen and bleeding lips as he stared up at Paxton.

"Thought you candy-asses might need help," Larry Paxton shrugged, wincing from the pain as he moved his left shoulder cautiously, "so I dragged my ass out of the swamp and—"

Then, in the light from the far open door, Lightstone saw the wires running to sticks of dynamite that had been taped to three of the ten-gallon gas cans sitting next to the tractor.

"This place is wired! Get out of here, now!" Lightstone yelled, and then frantically helped Paxton pull and drag their partner out of the barn and across the grass until, suddenly, the monstrous explosion behind their back sent the agents tumbling to the ground in a shower of shattered wood, broken tools, flaming gas cans, and the bloody remains of Sonny Chareaux and Kiro Nakamura.

"Okay, Lieutenant, here's what we've got so far," Sergeant Peter Balloch, senior homicide investigator for the San Diego

County Sheriff's Department, said as he spoke into the phone. "You got the recorder on?"

The tired voice at the other end of the line muttered something affirmative.

"Okay," Balloch sighed, "at approximately eleven twenty-five hours, this date, a Mrs. Wanda Perkins reported what she believed was a gunshot fired in the vicinity of her next-door neighbor's home. According to the informant, the neighbors were on vacation and the house was supposed to be vacant. A two-man car was dispatched to check it out. However, before the patrol got to the scene, the informant called back to say that she had just heard numerous gunshots—some of which she thought came from an automatic weapon, because they sounded like what she watched on TV—in or around her neighbor's barn. According to dispatch, she was still on the line when they heard one hell of an explosion in the background that basically blew the neighbor's barn all over the fucking neighborhood.

"What? Yes, Lieutenant, of course I know you're recording this. I *asked* you to, remember?" Balloch said, rolling his eyes skyward as he asked himself for perhaps the five hundredth time how the man had ever managed to pass the lieutenant's exam.

"Anyway," Balloch went on quickly before he said something on tape that he might actually regret, "when our guys arrived, they found four bodies. One of them has been positively identified as Sonny Chareaux. C-H-A-R-E-A-U-X. There should be some kind of warrant on file for him out of Louisiana."

Balloch paused as the man on the other end of the line apparently said something.

"Yes, I think that would be a real nice idea to call Louisiana and let them know," Balloch said, wondering if there was any chance that one of the captains might listen to the tape some day.

"Anyway," the homicide sergeant went on, "at least two of the other bodies have been tentatively identified as Dwight Stoner and Larry Paxton, federal agents of the U.S. Fish and

Wildlife Service. Yeah, right. As far as suspects go, we've got witnesses who saw two Caucasians—one male, short, curly blond hair, armed with an automatic rifle of some kind, and one female with shoulder-length blond hair—take off in a silver van, no plate, in one direction. Yeah, right. And one Caucasian male, six feet plus, running away on foot in the opposite direction. Yeah, go ahead and put it out on the wire. I'll keep you posted if we pick up anything else."

Shaking his head sadly, Homicide Sergeant Peter Balloch hung up and then looked over at the man who was sitting in his favorite lounge chair.

"That about what you guys want?" he asked.

"I think so, buddy," Henry Lightstone nodded. "How long do you think you can keep it running?"

"The way that asshole handles things, probably not very long," Balloch said. "Probably depends on how much cooperation we get from your head honchos."

"John Marsh, Chief of our Law Enforcement Division, promised me that he'd be on a plane heading this way within six hours. And if he can pull it off, he'll have the director of the Fish and Wildlife Service with him."

"They know who you are?"

"Marsh knows my name, but we've never met," Lightstone shrugged.

"What about the big guy?"

"The way I understand it," Lightstone said, "all he knows is that he authorized Marsh and McNulty to run a wild-card agent completely outside the parameters of the federal government's personnel rules and regulations."

"And seeing as how your entire operation has apparently gone headfirst right down the toilet, I assume that means both their asses are hanging out a mile?" Balloch guessed.

"Yeah, I imagine so," Lightstone nodded.

"So let me see if I understand this right," Balloch said as he settled back in the overstuffed chair and massaged a throbbing temple. "What you're trying to tell me is that the only people who can vouch for you being a real, honest-to-God federal agent—as opposed to someone who probably ought to be

locked up for his own good—are these two basket cases here?"
He gestured with his head over at the sprawled bodies of the
two men.

Dwight Stoner was stretched out on Balloch's living room
couch with his badly swollen leg tightly strapped into a
temporary cloth brace. Larry Paxton lay semicomatose in the
other chair, his left arm in a sling, his left leg tightly
bandaged, his head back and eyes closed. He looked *exactly*
like someone who had been shot out of the air, crashed his
airplane into an alligator-infested swamp, then escaped an
exploding barn with a three-hundred-and-ten-pound human
anchor on the end of his one good arm. All within the past
forty-eight hours.

"Outside of Snoopy—uh, Mike Takahara, the tech agent we
haven't been able to contact—and maybe Scoby, if *he's* still
alive, yeah, that's about it."

"Okay," Balloch nodded after a minute of quiet contemplation. "I can probably guarantee you twenty-four hours on my
say-so, just 'cause I'm getting old and slow and grouchy, and
nobody really wants to screw with me too much if they can
avoid it. But after that, somebody like my lieutenant is liable
to start counting on his fingers and wondering how come
we've got only two bodies in the freezer instead of four.
What'd you say the FBI guy's name was?"

"Al Grynard. Assistant special agent in charge of their
Anchorage office."

"What's he like?"

"Old, slow, grouchy *and* curious as hell about anything that
even looks halfway suspicious," Lightstone said. "You two
ought to get along just fine."

A pained expression appeared in Pete Balloch's eyes. "And
you figure this guy's probably going to be down here checking
up on all this?" he asked.

"Yeah, I'd bet money on it."

"Why?"

"Because as soon as he gets the word that Stoner and Paxton
are dead, he's gonna think I'm the one who's responsible,"
Lightstone said.

"Oh."

"Ain't gonna blame him none, either," Larry Paxton muttered through his badly split lips. "Ah'm just about convinced of that mahself."

"Yeah, no shit," Dwight Stoner agreed from his sprawled position on the couch. "We shoulda hired Kleinfelter instead. Guy like that woulda caused us a whole lot less trouble."

"As it is, this Al Grynard is already half convinced that I killed McNulty," Lightstone added, "because he found out Paul had me booked for buying illegal walrus ivory up in Anchorage when I was supposed to be buying dope. Told me not to leave town until he got everything straightened out."

"When was that?" Balloch asked.

Lightstone looked at his watch. "About twenty-four hours ago."

"He get everything straightened out?"

"I don't know, I didn't ask. Too busy trying to sneak out of town."

The veteran San Diego County sheriff's sergeant stared at Lightstone. "Jesus, I'm glad you work for somebody else. I'd hate like hell to be your supervisor." He paused. "So what're you guys going to do now?"

"First thing we've gotta do is find Mike before Alex does," Lightstone said.

"You really believe that these Chareaux assholes are going to try to take out a six-man federal-agent team, just because they got busted for illegal *hunting*?" Balloch asked in a disbelieving voice.

"It sure looks that way, except that it's brother, singular, now," Lightstone corrected. "Butch and Sonny are dead. But good old Alex, the one who's still running around out there, is the real freak. Likes to cut people up and watch them die. We know he's good for at least two Louisiana game wardens. Probably a whole lot more we don't know about."

"So you figure that if this Alex thinks you guys are out of the picture, then he— Hey, wait a minute." Pete Balloch's head suddenly came up. "How come only two names on the wire, instead of three?" the veteran homicide sergeant demanded suspiciously.

"Because I want him to think I'm still out there, or to at least wonder about it for a while," Lightstone said matter-of-factly.

"You *want* this asshole coming after you?"

"Not especially," Lightstone shrugged. "But Paul's dead, and if Mike and Carl are too, and he believes he got all three of us, then he's just going to take off. This way, if he thinks I'm the only one left, then maybe he'll leave his commando girlfriend at home and come after me himself."

Sergeant Peter Balloch blinked and then stared curiously at his longtime friend.

"You call *that* a plan?" he finally asked.

"You got a better one?"

"Yeah, I sure do," Balloch nodded. "Put out an APB and then sit back and let a couple hundred thousand cops hunt this bastard down."

Lightstone shook his head. "He'd just run off to Louisiana and hide out in the swamps for a few years, wait until everything cooled off, and then come back for me when I'm not paying attention. I don't want to be looking over my shoulder for a guy like Alex the rest of my life."

"So what are you going to do? Sit around like a piece of mangled bait, wait for him—and maybe his buddies with the dynamite and the H&K—to show up, and then take them all on by yourself?"

"Not exactly." Lightstone smiled as he glanced over at Stoner and Paxton. "I've got a couple of ghosts here to help out."

"No offense," Balloch said dubiously as he looked at the three nearly crippled agents, "but right now, you three guys don't look like you could defend yourselves from a couple of pissed-off Girl Scouts."

"If we find Mike or Carl, we'll be fine," Lightstone shrugged. "Besides, we've got some backup on the way. Eskimo kid named Woeshack. One of our rookie agent-pilots who can't fly worth a shit."

"That the guy you said crashed the plane up in Alaska?"

"Uh-huh."

"So what the hell is he going to do, outside of getting you all killed?"

"He's going to be our pilot," Lightstone smiled. "As soon as he manages to steal another plane."

"Ah."

Then, before Sergeant Pete Balloch could say anything more, the phone rang next to his hand.

"Yeah?" Balloch answered, and his voice dropped an octave as he said: "Ah, shit. Are they sure? When?" A long pause. "What about the other guy?" A longer pause. "Yeah, okay, thanks." He sighed as he put down the phone.

"Scoby?" Lightstone asked quietly.

"He's dead," Balloch nodded. "Some of your guys found him this morning. Six rounds in his vest and one in the head, execution style."

All three agents were silent until Lightstone finally said: "What about Mike?"

"No answer at his place, no sign of forced entry, and the neighbors haven't seen anything." Balloch shrugged. "The guys out there are willing to help, but they don't want to bust in and look around unless we can fax them a warrant."

"Tell them not to worry about it, we're heading that way anyway." Henry Lightstone shook his head as he slowly pulled himself to a standing position. He watched as a shaky Larry Paxton helped Stoner up onto one foot, then handed him the set of crutches. "Snoopy likes to cheat when he busts into computers, so I don't think he'll mind too much if we don't bother to get a warrant."

CHAPTER THIRTY-NINE

Washoe County Sheriff's Sergeant Clinton Hardwell took one look at the cut, bruised, and swollen faces of the three men who had hobbled off the Southwest Airlines plane, and then immediately asked to see some identification.

"Sorry about that," Hardwell apologized as he returned the badge cases to the agents, "but honest to God, you guys don't look like any federal raid team I've ever seen before."

"New Washington Office concept," Lightstone said as he and the plainclothed sergeant started walking slowly toward the baggage claim area, giving Paxton and Stoner a chance to keep up on their crutches. "Anybody sees us coming, they're not going to be expecting us to kick in the door."

"Yeah, I guess not," the homicide sergeant nodded as he glanced down at Dwight Stoner's horribly swollen knee and then at Larry Paxton's tightly bandaged leg.

After passing the first set of slot machines, the agents took a right turn to the baggage claim area. Their bags were waiting for them, stacked in a neat row next to the stainless-steel carousel and a uniformed sheriff's deputy.

"Uh, listen, you think you guys might be able to stick around a while and give us a hand, in case we run into any trouble?" Lightstone asked as he and Hardwell picked up the bags. They walked through a sliding glass door out into the blazing heat of Reno, Nevada.

"Buddy, let me tell you something," the deeply tanned homicide sergeant said as three of his detectives helped Stoner and Paxton into the back of two of the unmarked detective units. "Pete Balloch vouched for you, and he and I go back a long way, so I really don't care who you guys are, or who you're going after. But I can tell you one thing for sure—" he pointedly looked around at all three agents "—I wouldn't miss this operation for the world."

Just as the Washoe County homicide sergeant had described, the Japanese-style house that Special Agent Mike Takahara had recently purchased in Spanish Springs Valley—a rural development about fifteen miles north of downtown Reno—looked pretty much like all of the other widely scattered ranch-style homes in the quiet and peaceful hillside area.

From their concealed position about a hundred yards down the road, Henry Lightstone listened to the hissing sound of empty tape for another five seconds and then put the cellular phone down on the seat as Hardwell continued to scan the windows with his powerful binoculars.

"Nothing?" the homicide sergeant asked as he lowered the binoculars and looked over at Lightstone.

"No." Lightstone shook his head.

"You sure you got the right number?"

"Yeah, absolutely sure."

"Maybe he forgot to check his machine?" Hardwell shrugged.

"Not Snoopy," Lightstone said as he stared out across the sand-and-sagebrush landscape at the closed garage door. "Guy's a communications freak. Damn near religious about that sort of thing."

"Maybe he's found himself a girlfriend," the homicide sergeant suggested. "They could be down in the basement, where it's cooler."

"Yeah, that's always a possibility," Lightstone conceded, "but it doesn't sound like him. You *sure* your guys saw a red Four-Runner in that garage?"

"Pretty sure that's what they said," Hardwell nodded. "I'll find out. Need to check in with those guys anyway."

"Yeah, where the hell are they?" Lightstone asked, looking around as he realized that he hadn't seen any other vehicles with the distinctive police radio antennas in the area.

"Up in the hills, where they've got a better view," Hardwell said, glancing toward the upper slope. "The way Pete described these characters, I figured we ought to maintain some distance until you guys got here."

"Yeah, probably a good idea," Lightstone said absentmindedly.

Reaching over to the dash-mounted console, Hardwell unhooked the coiled cord mike and brought it up to his mouth. "Delta Seventeen and Delta Twenty-two, request confirmation you spotted a red Four-Runner in the subject's garage."

"If it's like our place," Hardwell said as he put the mike down on the seat next to his leg, "it's hard to hear the phone in the basement."

"I don't know," Lightstone said uneasily. "Last place this guy had, he put a phone in the john and one at both ends of his workbench so he wouldn't have to get up."

"Oh."

Two of Hardwell's detectives cautiously approached the house from the blind garage side, shotguns out and ready, while Larry Paxton and Dwight Stoner slowly worked their way down the road on their crutches.

"Couple of characters like that, I'm surprised we haven't heard from every housewife in the neighborhood," Hardwell commented dryly. He started to say something else, but then realized that he hadn't received any response from his surveillance team.

"Delta Seventeen and Delta Twenty-two, *check in*," Hardwell repeated into the mike in an irritated voice.

Silence.

Lightstone and Hardwell looked at each other briefly, and then Hardwell brought the microphone up to his mouth again.

"Delta Fifteen."

"Fifteen, go."

"Did you spot Kenny or Jim on your way in?"

"Negative."

"Shit," the Washoe County homicide sergeant cursed.

"You give them authorization to follow if anybody left the house?" Lightstone asked, watching Larry Paxton readjust the miniaturized radio speaker in his ear as the two injured agents began to move at a faster pace toward the house.

"Standard procedure is that one guy follows while the other stays in place and calls for backup," Hardwell replied in a distracted voice. "Dispatch, this is Delta Three. Any call-ins from Delta Seventeen or Twenty-two during the past hour?"

"Negative, Delta Three," the dispatcher's raspy voice came out over the car speaker. "No radio contact."

"Delta Fifteen," Hardwell ordered, "break off, get up the hill and check on those two."

"Ten-four, on my way," the detective acknowledged.

"Delta Twenty and Twenty-one, move in on that garage window, tell me what you see," Hardwell directed his other two investigators. Then he and Lightstone watched as one of the shotgun-armed detectives knelt down to provide a cover while the second casually dressed investigator ran forward in a low crouch to the garage, flattened himself upright against the cream-colored stucco, and quickly peered in through the side window.

"It's empty," the detective's voice echoed clearly over the radio static.

Hardwell swore again as he looked over at Lightstone.

"Let's get in there," Lightstone said, releasing his seat belt and drawing the 10mm Smith & Wesson automatic from his shoulder holster.

"All units, move in *now*!" Hardwell said and then dropped the mike on the seat and accelerated the unmarked detective unit toward the distant driveway as Larry Paxton dropped his crutches and limped toward the far side of the house and Dwight Stoner hobbled furiously up the brick walkway toward the front door.

Henry Lightstone was out of Hardwell's detective unit and running up the brick walkway when Stoner lifted a huge decorative rock out of Mike Takahara's carefully landscaped garden and heaved it through the wood-and-glass door.

Lightstone lunged forward past Stoner with the 10mm Smith & Wesson automatic clenched tightly in both hands.

"Oh, my God!" one of the detectives coming in behind Lightstone and Stoner with a shotgun whispered when he saw the blood.

Even to Henry Lightstone, who had worked over three hundred homicide cases during his police career, the sight of the blood splatterings that seemed to cover every square foot of the off-white walls jarred at his soul. But he kept on moving through the living room, searching the doorways, because the body that lay facedown in the middle of an irregular pattern of congealed blood on the white carpet did not belong to Mike Takahara.

Not unless the Japanese-American agent had started to dye his hair blond, lose weight, and take hormone shots, Lightstone told himself, noting the insignia on the uniform of the sprawled female figure as he continued to search for movement.

"Mike, where are you?" Lightstone yelled, even though he knew that anyone within fifty yards who hadn't heard the rock going through the front door was either deaf or dead.

They found the second body in the kitchen. The coal-black hair gave Lightstone a momentary scare until he realized that the victim was still a good fifty pounds lighter and three or four inches shorter than Takahara.

Hardwell came in with a .357 Magnum in one hand and a packset radio in the other. He glanced down at the body of the Asian, who had lost massive amounts of blood from deep and gaping slashes in his arms, face, and chest.

"That him?"

"No." Lightstone shook his head.

"Then what the hell—" Hardwell started to say when the radio in his hand began to squawk.

"Clint, I found Jim and Kenny," the choked voice said. "They're up here on Twin Springs Road. Both of them dead. Small-caliber shots to the side of the head."

Homicide Sergeant Clinton Hardwell was still cursing when they heard the crashing sound of wood breaking.

"Where——" Hardwell demanded, his eyes widened with rage, but Lightstone was already out of the kitchen and heading toward the basement stairs. He got there just as Dwight Stoner lunged at the door with a savage roar. His full-body forearm shot tore the door completely off its hinges as the half-crippled agent staggered forward. But the impact of a vicious side-thrust heel kick just below his left ear sent him tumbling to the floor.

When Henry Lightstone came through the splintered doorway right behind Stoner, he saw the reverse kick coming and blocked it with his left forearm. He started to bring the butt of the 10mm Smith & Wesson around in a deadly variation of a palm-heel strike that would have shattered Mike Takahara's jaw if Lightstone hadn't recognized the blood-smeared and swollen face that looked down at him.

Lightstone quickly reholstered his pistol and stepped forward to support the agent's dangling body while Larry Paxton used a sharp-edged pocketknife to cut away the medical gauze and tape that tied the Japanese-American agent's hands and wrists to the three-inch cast-iron pipe overhead.

Once loose, Mike Takahara dropped down in front of Stoner, who was just starting to come up on one knee.

"Dumb-ass jock . . . told you . . . supposed to wear a helmet when you kick a door," Takahara said between deep, gasping breaths.

Stoner glared at his ex-partner. "Before I go ahead and stomp the shit out of you," the huge agent rasped, "you mind telling me *why* you had to do that?"

"Over there, to your right," Mike Takahara said weakly. The ex-Oakland Raider tackle turned his head back the other way and stared at the dangling and horribly mutilated body of ICER team-member Felix Steinhauser.

"I don't understand. You *sure* these guys weren't working for Alex?" Lightstone asked as the four agents sat in Mike Takahara's blood-splattered living room. The homicide investigation team was working around them, trying to reenact the sequence of events that had led to the death of two of their detectives, before the state investigators got here and took over the scene.

"Hey, all I know is that when I opened the door to get a package from this Federal Express delivery girl, the guy over there in the kitchen kicked me in the groin and then hit me with something hard," Takahara said. He nodded toward the body of Shoshin Watanabe and then winced as he gently touched the swollen and bruised right side of his head.

"Don't know what his problem was, but he had a hell of an attitude. Kept mumbling something in Japanese about being pissed off 'cause he'd gotten shot and it hurt. When I woke up, I was hanging from the pipe down in the basement and Alex was hanging there next to me."

"So how'd that bastard get loose?"

"The tall blond guy and the little shithead with the attitude were playing with one of my kitchen meat knives and working me over with pressure points, trying to get me to tell him who you were and what that phone message of yours was all about, when the broad in the Federal Express uniform comes running down the stairs yelling something about a couple of cops being outside."

"Washoe County sheriff's deputies," Lightstone explained. "They were supposed to be keeping an eye on your place until we got here."

"Makes sense," Mike Takahara nodded. "Anyway, the German guy takes off and—"

"You said German?" Stoner interrupted.

"I guess," Takahara shrugged. "Had a pretty convincing accent if he wasn't. So after he's gone and we're still down there in the basement, the little Jap guy pulls out this shit-ass *kodachi*—uh, short sword," the Japanese-American agent explained, "—and uses it to cut Alex down. Then he tells the gal in the uniform, who's got a forty-five SIG-Sauer out now— probably mine—to give Alex the knife."

"They *gave* that freak a knife, on purpose?" Lightstone asked, disbelieving.

"Yeah. The two of them argued about it for a little bit, but she finally did it," Mike Takahara nodded. "Something about him being in charge when the team leader was gone. Real bad mistake on her part."

"What the hell were they doing?" Lightstone asked, thoroughly perplexed now.

"Beats the shit out of me," Takahara shrugged. "The way they were talking, it sounded like they were planning to make it look like Alex and I got into a fight.

"Anyway, the broad finally tosses this meat knife of mine over to Alex and then puts the SIG on him right away, which was smart. So here's Alex. First he looks down at this knife like he can't believe it either. Then he looks up at the Japanese guy, who's standing there in a ready stance with that fucking sword up over his head, looking like he wants to get even with the whole world for something. Then, all of a sudden, Alex flings the meat knife backhanded right into the throat of the broad with the SIG, picks up about a five-foot piece of two-by-four off the floor, and goes after the little guy with the sword. The little guy backs up the stairs, because I guess he really was shot after all, and that two-by-four was a hell of a lot longer than his sword."

"Hey, wait a minute. How come the woman in the Federal Express uniform ended up dead on the living-room floor instead of in the basement?" Lightstone asked.

"Must have missed her carotids," Takahara shrugged. "All I know is, one minute she's standing there holding her throat with blood all over her hands, and the next she's going up the stairs with the meat knife after her buddy and Alex."

"Jesus!" Paxton whispered.

"She should have shot the bastard right on the spot when she had the chance," Dwight Stoner muttered, shaking his bruised and battered head slowly.

"Probably would have," Takahara nodded, "except that she lost the gun when the knife hit her. It landed behind me and she tried to get at it, but I caught her a good one in the face, so I guess she figured she'd come back down and take care of me after she and her buddy finished off Alex."

"Only they never did."

"Naw." Mike Takahara shook his head. "After about five

minutes, I didn't hear any more ruckus upstairs. Then about twenty minutes later, something like that, I hear it all start up again, only it doesn't last very long. Then Alex comes back down the stairs, dragging the blond guy, and spends another ten or fifteen minutes trying to find out who *they* were. You saw his technique."

"Did he get any answers?" Paxton asked.

"Something about they had to kill all six of us. Those were their orders."

"*Whose* orders?" Lightstone demanded.

"I don't know," Mike Takahara shrugged. "Alex worked on him some more, and then I guess he must have said something else, because all of a sudden Alex just cut the guy's throat. Then he turned around, stared at me with those freaky red eyes of his, smiled like he knew something funny that I didn't and then disappeared up the stairs. I heard my garage door open and close, so he probably took off in my truck."

For a long moment, nobody said anything. Then Henry Lightstone spoke up. "Somebody's using the Chareaux brothers to get to us. It's the only thing that makes any sense."

"Sure looks that way," Mike Takahara nodded.

"So what the hell did we do to deserve that?" Dwight Stoner asked.

"Pissed somebody off *real bad*, that's for damn sure," Larry Paxton commented. "Maybe—"

"And speaking of pissing people off," Homicide Sergeant Clinton Hardwell said as he walked up to the huddled group, "apparently that teletype you asked me to send out had the desired effect. Anybody here know an FBI agent named Al Grynard?"

"ASAC out of Anchorage?" Lightstone asked.

"Sounds right," Hardwell nodded. "Know anything about him?"

"I think he's probably a damn good investigator," Lightstone said after a moment, "but a little too focused for my tastes. What'd he do, call all the way down here from Anchorage?"

"Nope, from San Diego," Hardwell said. "However, in

addition to being thoroughly pissed and overly focused, he also seems to be a little confused. Said something about you being a suspect in the murders of four other Fish and Wildlife Service special agents, two of whom were—" Hardwell looked down at the piece of paper in his hand, "—Dwight Stoner and Larry Paxton. I assume he's talking about you two guys?" The homicide sergeant looked over at Stoner and Paxton.

"Most likely," Paxton nodded.

"I see," Hardwell said, hesitating for a moment before going on. "Anyway, Special Agent Grynard is apparently heading this way on the next available flight. However, in the meantime, he would like me to take you into custody until FBI agents from the Reno office can get here and take over the scene."

"Sounds reasonable," Lightstone said equably. "Mind if I ask what you told him?"

"Said that I thought you might have been seen in the area and that we'd start looking around immediately."

"You planning on taking him in?" Dwight Stoner asked with a curiously polite expression on his bruised and battered face.

"I'll do anything I can to help a fellow law-enforcement officer," Clinton Hardwell said as he checked his watch. "Just as long as they don't get too pushy and try to horn in on one of my investigations.

"Trouble is," he added with a tired smile, "I'm already way overdue for my coffee break, so I was thinking we might take a little ride down a back road I know before these FBI types get here. Stop by the Reno Sky Ranch Airport, get us a cup of coffee, and maybe introduce you to one of your retired agent-pilots who runs the rental operation down there."

"Rental operation?"

"Planes by the hour, day or week, with or without pilot. Understand you have to have decent credit, though."

"Think he'd take a government credit card?" Larry Paxton asked.

"Wouldn't be a bit surprised," Hardwell shrugged. "Last

time I talked with him, he still had a pretty good sense of humor."

"Then maybe we'd better get going," Lightstone said as he pulled his aching body out of the chair.

"Before we do that," Hardwell said, looking as if he hadn't quite made up his mind about something, "mind if I ask you a question?"

"Sure, go ahead."

"The guy who got his nuts sliced off. You figure he's the one who shot Kenny and Jim, right?"

"Looks that way to us," Lightstone nodded.

Clinton Hardwell considered the answer. "Okay," he said finally. "Anything you'd like my detectives to tell them FBI folks when they get here?"

"Yeah, as a matter of fact, there is," Lightstone said. "Tell them that the Asian guy on the floor has been positively identified by one of our agents as Special Agent Mike Takahara."

CHAPTER FORTY

After all of the certificates were verified, the gas tanks filled, the credit-card slip signed, and a couple of wildlife law-enforcement war stories exchanged, the retired special agent-pilot and his mechanic at the Reno Sky Ranch Airport finally got around to estimating that it would take them another fifteen minutes to remove two of the six seats from the cabin of the Cessna Golden Eagle.

Which was cutting it awfully close as far as Henry Lightstone was concerned.

But Homicide Sergeant Clinton Hardwell reassured him

that during that time, his detectives were perfectly capable of keeping a team of FBI agents busy with questions of jurisdiction and procedure. The extra room in the cabin *would* make it possible for Dwight Stoner to stretch his injured knee out into a halfway comfortable position, so Lightstone just nodded and said sure, go ahead.

Twenty minutes later, he and Stoner were strapping themselves into a pair of spacious cabin seats while Special Agent-Pilot Larry Paxton taxied the Cessna down to the end of the runway, with Trainee Pilot Mike Takahara in the copilot's seat.

After bringing the twin-prop plane around to face the runway, Paxton turned and looked back into the cabin.

"We're set to go. Next stop Ashland?"

"Yeah, I'd like to drop the evidence off at the lab," Lightstone said. "But what about those teletypes? Isn't that going to raise a flag if we show up there when you three are supposed to be dead?"

"No problem," Mike Takahara said over his shoulder. "I know the chief electronics guru out there. Guy named Ed Rhodes. He'll help us keep everything low-key."

"He know we're coming?"

"I sent him an e-mail message from the house before we left; asked him to pick us up at the airport. Figured we didn't want to alert anyone else yet, just in case."

"Okay, Ashland it is," Henry Lightstone nodded agreeably. Finding himself able to relax for the first time in many hours, he closed his eyes for a few moments, and then opened them up to find Dwight Stoner staring at him.

"You know, Henry," Stoner said over the muted roar of the twin engines, "if anybody had tried to stick you in a plane a few months ago where you knew that the pilot had a messed-up arm, a torn-up leg, and probably a concussion to boot, and the copilot didn't even have a license, you'd have gone ape-shit."

"Yeah, I probably would have," Lightstone conceded. "But that was before I flew with a guy named Woeshack."

"Woeshack? You mean that new guy up in Anchorage? Eskimo kid, looks like he's about sixteen?"

"That's the one."

"So what's the matter with him?"

"As a rookie agent, not much," Lightstone shrugged. "In fact, from what I've seen so far, I'd say he's smart, aggressive, and has a hell of a lot of guts. On the other hand, as a pilot, he's pretty much an air crash waiting to happen."

"Yeah? How so?"

"Well, I can give you three reasons right off. First of all, his idea of a takeoff is to go like hell to the end of the runway and then pull up at the last second before he hits something. Second, I don't think he has any idea of what a compass is for. And third, he acts like he doesn't know how to land the goddamn plane once he's up there."

"Sounds like a government pilot to me," Stoner observed. "But isn't he also the guy that buzzed those bastards who were shooting at you, and then hauled your ass out of the plane after he dumped it into the trees?"

"That's Woeshack all right," Lightstone nodded.

"Sounds like good covert agent material to me," Stoner said.

"Yeah, I know." Lightstone smiled as Larry Paxton received clearance from the tower and began to roll the twin-engine airplane down the runway. "I've been thinking the same thing myself."

Senior Electronics Specialist Ed Rhodes stood inside the small Ashland Airport terminal building and watched through the window until the twin props of the Cessna Golden Eagle stopped turning, the door opened, and one by one, the four men made their way down the stairs.

Sighing in relief as the last man stepped down onto the asphalt, Rhodes walked outside and strolled across the tie-down area. Two of the men were standing around on crutches, while the other two were busy removing from the small plane what luggage they had.

"Hey, buddy, you aren't going to believe the LEMIS messages we got just after you called," the bearded scientist said as he came up behind Takahara and slapped him on the shoulder. "For a minute there, I thought—"

Then Rhodes blinked in shock when Mike Takahara turned around and showed his badly damaged face. "Jesus! What the hell happened to *you*?"

"Long story," Takahara shrugged. "Tell you all about it after we've had a couple of beers. These are the guys I told you about. Ed Rhodes, meet Henry Lightstone, Larry Paxton, and Dwight Stoner."

Rhodes tried to hide his shock when he looked at the badly bruised and swollen faces of the three men as he shook hands.

"Did you say Stoner and Paxton?"

"That's right," Takahara nodded.

"Uh, did anybody mention to you guys that you're supposed to be dead?" the scientist asked. "Though I don't recall seeing anything in either of the messages about an agent named Lightstone."

"Henry's one of our deep-cover agents in Special Ops," Takahara explained. "In fact, the only people so far who actually know he's a Fish and Wildlife agent are the director, the chief, a U.S. Attorney, the four of us, and now you."

"I see," Rhodes nodded thoughtfully. "Uh, you want to be introduced by some other name when we take you through the lab?"

"How about Lightner? Henry Allen Lightner," Lightstone said.

"Henry Lightner it is," Rhodes said easily. "Man, you guys must be into something heavy."

"Well, we're hoping that the people who caused us all this grief will continue to think that Mike and Larry and Dwight *are* dead," Lightstone explained carefully. "For the moment, they may think I'm still alive, which we're planning to use to our advantage."

"That's an interesting twist," Rhodes said.

"Yeah, we think so. Is that going to cause any problems if I give you some evidence using the name Lightner?"

"No, no reason why it should." The bearded scientist shook his head as he led the three men over to the white government-plated Suburban. "We get a lot of evidence in from agents and game wardens working undercover, so we're used to keeping our mouths shut about what we see and hear. Whatever name they give us is what we put down on the chain."

"Good," Lightstone nodded approvingly.

"I guess the thing is," Rhodes added, his jaw tightening as he unlocked the back doors of the Suburban and began to stow away their luggage, "everybody at the lab knew Paul and Carl pretty well. So as far as we're concerned," he added as he closed the doors, "it really doesn't matter *who* or *what* you guys are. All we want to know is how we can help."

"Fair enough," Lightstone nodded, "because help's exactly what we came here for."

During the five minutes it took Rhodes to drive them to the new four-and-a-half-million-dollar wildlife crime laboratory securely nestled in the Rogue Valley of Southern Oregon, it became obvious to Lightstone, Paxton, and Stoner that they had an interesting new ally in the bearded scientist.

"The boss is out of town, but he told me you guys could have anything here you want, including his desk," Rhodes said as he led them into an amazingly clean and shiny evidence-control area of the lab, where a lab technician and another scientist were working around a bar-code scanning computer disassembling packages of evidence.

"This is Tim, one of our lab techs, who's helping Joe log in some evidence for Serology," Rhodes said. "Henry, Mike, Larry, and Dwight, from Special Ops. You guys about done there?"

"Yeah, just got some stuff in from the Army Crime Lab over in Georgia," Joe Biggs, the serologist, said and then looked at Lightstone more closely. "Hey, aren't you that guy who was involved in the bear case we got from Yellowstone a few months ago?"

"That's right," Lightstone nodded cautiously. "How'd you know that?"

"They sent us some photos taken at the hospital. Somebody had the bright idea of trying to match the claw marks on your arms and shoulder against one of the bears claws to tie you to the scene."

"Were you able to do it?" Lightstone asked, curious.

"Naw. That's the kind of thing these guys get from watching too much television. What we *were* able to do, though, was work up the blood on your clothes. Basically proved that you were covered with bear blood, which I guess you already knew," the serologist smiled. "Then we used our computerized DNA system to match up the stains on your clothes with the two bears in that guy's truck. No big deal, but it might help corroborate your testimony if it ever goes to trial."

"Don't count on it," Lightstone said grimly. "That case is just about over with."

"Yeah, that's what I heard," the serologist said, sounding vaguely disappointed. "Oh well, guess I'd better get back at it."

"Okay, Henry," Rhodes said, waiting until Tim and Joe left with their evidence and closed the door, "so what have you got for us?"

"This," Lightstone said as he handed the forensic scientist a small plastic bag containing the strip of hide he'd removed from the claw of the mother Kodiak.

Rhodes held the plastic bag up to the light and began to write notes in a new case folder as Lightstone explained the significance of the collected material, verified the seal on the package, and then signed the chain-of-custody forms.

"Not sure how much we're going to be able to tell you on something that small," Rhodes said as he reached for a nearby phone, "but we'll give it a try. Hey, Margaret? This is Ed. Yeah, listen, can you come down to Evidence and Property? Yeah, right now. I've got something interesting for you."

Two minutes later, after listening to Ed Rhodes' concise summary of the information Lightstone had provided, the white-coated mammalogist disappeared down the long hallway in the direction of her lab section with the evidence in hand.

"Want to see the rest of the lab while we're waiting?" Rhodes asked.

"Sure," Lightstone said agreeably.

"Okay, why don't we first go see what Joe's doing," Rhodes suggested as he led the four agents down the narrow hallway and into the main door on the right. "Then I'll take you around to morphology, criminalistics, the photo-video lab, graphic arts, and save the best part of the lab for last."

"Electronics and computers, the critical stuff," Mike Takahara nodded with a cheerful smile as Paxton and Stoner rolled their eyes.

"Christ, is this place all ours?" Lightstone asked in disbelief as they entered the modern serology lab, where he could see at least a dozen white-coated figures working in and around the red oak cabinets and black epoxy countertops.

"Yours, and about seven thousand other state and federal wildlife officers, not to mention a hundred and thirteen countries that signed the CITES treaty," Rhodes said. "Only lab of its kind in the world. Here we basically look at blood and tissue samples, and try to figure out what species is involved." Rhodes led them over to the serologist he had introduced earlier. "Maybe Joe here can explain what he's working on."

Joe nodded. "This is some bloodstain evidence that the Army Crime Lab guys sent over to us." Two sets of blood-stained, camouflaged clothing were laid out on a low examination table. "They're trained to work up human crimes, and these samples had both human and animal specificity. They sent them to us to see if we could work it out a little further. There are at least twenty or thirty separate stains on that one pair of pants alone. But with our new micro-separation system, the tagged probes, and one of Ed's computers hooked up to the scanners, we can work this kind of stuff ten times as fast as we used to."

"What he's saying is that he wants you to bring him more evidence so he can justify stealing another one of my computers," Rhodes interpreted as they thanked the serologist and continued on.

"And over here," Rhodes said as he stopped at the far end of the long room, "is probably the most important piece of equipment in the serology lab." He stood next to what looked like a large freezer, with temperature gauges on the front and a stainless-steel tank of liquid nitrogen hooked up to the side.

"A freezer?" Dwight Stoner asked dubiously.

"Yes, but not just any freezer," Rhodes smiled. "This one can keep blood and tissue samples down to minus eighty degrees Celsius. Which is cold enough that if you stuck your hand inside and kept it there for, oh, maybe about a minute or so, you could take it out, smack it against the wall, and then pick the pieces up off the floor.".

"No shit?" Stoner whispered, moving in cautiously to take a closer look at the apparently lethal machine.

"Actually, what it *is* is their library of tissue samples from all over the world," Rhodes explained. "For example, if these guys are going to try to figure out the genetic code of a wolf, they're going to have to start out with samples from a pure wolf, not eighty-percent wolf and twenty-percent dog. The question, of course, is how do they know?"

"Because one looks like a wolf and the other—" Paxton started to guess.

"What did you say?" Lightstone interrupted, puzzled, because something in the scientist's comments had triggered his memory. Something about . . .

At that moment a woman's voice came over the loudspeaker.

"Ed Rhodes, can you come to morphology, right away please?"

Rhodes walked over to a nearby wall phone, picked up the handset, and punched in a three-digit code.

"Hi, Margaret. What have you got? Oh, yeah? *Really?* We'll be right there."

The morphology section of the lab consisted of three semicircular workbench areas and two freestanding layout tables, both of which were situated under wide skylights. When they got there, they found Margaret Kuo sitting in front of a comparison microscope that was equipped with a ten-inch-square split-view screen.

"Well, what do you think?" the Korean-born mammalogist asked as she moved aside to make room for Rhodes and the four agents.

"Looks good to me," the electronics engineer commented as he glanced casually at the two pieces of hide that had been magnified several times and then brought together side by side in the split screen. "What are we looking at?"

"You know, you computer guys are really pretty useless if you can't recognize a classic match of *Ceratotherium simum* hide when you see it," the white-coated mammalogist grinned as she reached into one of the nearby drawers and brought out a pair of boots made of dark gray leather with a rough, grainy texture.

"Here's an example. Got this pair out of a shipment going to West Germany," Margaret Kuo said, unaware that Henry Lightstone, standing right beside her, was staring down at the boots as though seeing a ghost for the second time.

"*Cera*-what?" Ed Rhodes started to ask, but Henry Lightstone already knew the answer.

"White rhino," he rasped, blinking in confusion as his mind flashed on an identical pair of boots, and the white hair, and the white beard and . . . that same white-bearded face as it flashed beneath the plane.

"Oh, Jesus!" he whispered in pure disbelief.

"Hey, that's right—" the white-coated mammalogist started to say, but Lightstone wasn't listening because he'd already turned to Mike Takahara.

"SEA-TAC Security," he said insistently, grabbing at the agent's muscular arm. "We've got to get ahold of them, *right now*!"

Exactly twenty-three minutes later, Ed Rhodes was working quickly to connect cables from the back of a multifunction VCR to the back of one of the overhead monitors in his electronics lab, while Mike Takahara was talking on the phone to the technical coordinator for the Seattle Tacoma International Airport's security office.

"Yes, that's right, Monday the twentieth, 'C' terminal,"

Takahara said, and then looked over at Lightstone. "What time?"

"Umm . . . " Lightstone had to stop and think. "About ten o'clock in the morning. Maybe a little after."

"Ten o'clock," Takahara repeated, and then turned to Rhodes. "You ready?"

"Just a second," Rhodes said as he reached over and set three switches on the jury-rigged communications board and then watched the computer screen as he punched in a series of command codes on the keyboard.

"How are you doing this?" Lightstone asked, not sure that he'd understand, but wanting to ask anyway.

"Two land-line connections with a satellite uplink at Bellevue," Rhodes said as he continued to work at the computer.

"You mean telephone lines?"

"Yeah, exactly," the intent electronics engineer nodded.

"So why not use the phones all the way down instead of screwing around with the satellite?" Paxton asked.

"Need a fiber-optic line for the quality. Haven't managed to get one run down to Ashland yet," Rhodes replied, and then suddenly smiled brightly. "*All right*, we're locked onto the satellite, transponder eighteen, and we *are* recording. Tell them to go ahead and transmit."

"We were pretty damn lucky on this," Mike Takahara said to Lightstone as he and Rhodes and the other two agents watched the flickering screen. "They're required to maintain the tapes for only seventy-two hours. Probably would have reused this tape sometime this evening."

"Far as I'm concerned, it's about time we had some luck on this deal," Paxton growled.

"Yeah, no shit," Stoner said in agreement.

"Come *on*, guys, where are you?" Rhodes muttered as he glanced down at his watch. "We've only got this transponder for . . . *there*!"

The monitor suddenly flickered to life, displaying a montage of four smaller screens—two screens showing people walking through metal detectors, the other two displaying the same images as viewed by the X-ray units.

"Christ! They've got those things focused right on the metal detectors." Lightstone shook his head in frustration.

"Yeah, so?" Rhodes asked.

"These guys didn't go through the detectors. They were carrying, so they walked around."

"That's okay. We can see about eighteen inches on the left-hand side of each one," Rhodes said as they watched progressive sets of travelers walking slowly through the detectors, several of whom had to back up, empty their pockets, and try again.

"What did you say these assholes looked like?" Larry Paxton asked as they watched one overweight man make four successive trips back and forth through the scanner.

"Three Caucasian males, one Asian male, and one Asian female," Lightstone recited, his eyes fixed to the flickering quarter-screen on the right. "Guy with the boots had white hair and white beard, both closely trimmed. The woman—"

"There!" Mike Takahara yelled. "Left screen, guy with white hair and a white beard just went through. Is that him?"

"I don't know, went by too fast." Lightstone shook his head. "Have them run it back."

"No, that's okay. Let it run, we've got it recorded," Rhodes said as they watched a young-looking Asian man and then a very attractive Asian woman walk around the scanner.

"What about him?" Lightstone asked Mike Takahara.

"Yeah, that could have been him," the Japanese-American agent said hesitantly, "but he had his head turned, saying something to the girl."

"It has to be . . . *oh, yeah*," Lightstone whispered as he watched the tall Caucasian male with the close-cropped, curly dark hair and mustache walk past. He remembered the startled look on Arturo Bolin's distinctive face when the three .357 hollow-point bullets had caught him in the head and throat and caused him to drop onto the rocky base of the shale outcropping.

"You sure?" Mike Takahara asked, covering up the mouthpiece of the phone.

"Yeah, I'm absolutely sure," Lightstone nodded. "Now let's see if we can find out who they are."

Forty-five minutes later, Ed Rhodes dropped five blurry but still legible eight-by-ten color photographs in front of Lightstone.

"There're your bad guys," the electronics specialist said, watching over Lightstone's shoulder as the agent spread the five head and upper- torso photos out on the table.

"Al Grynard doesn't believe it, but that one's dead," Lightstone said, pointing to the blurred image of Arturo Bolin. "The other one there," he pointed to the profile shot of Roy Parker, "could be the one I hit first. The guy with the H&K. Looks right, but they were wearing cammo-grease and I never got that close to him."

"What about this one?" Larry Paxton asked, pointing to the photo of the Asian man who had his head turned away from the camera.

Lightstone stared at the side view of Shoshin Watanabe for several seconds. "He could have been the one who got nailed next to the boulder, up at Skilak Lake, but I can't tell. We were too far away. I don't think I ever saw *her*," he shrugged, pushing aside the photo of Kimiko Osan.

"But this one," Lightstone whispered as he held up the photo of Gerd Maas and stared at the man's cold, pale eyes, "this is the guy I want to find."

"Looks like a real freak, doesn't he?" Larry Paxton commented appraisingly.

"Yeah. Now all we need is a name," Lightstone said as he looked around. "Hey, where's Mike? He should have gotten the scoop on their credentials by now."

"Right here," Mike Takahara said as he came into the small conference room.

"Well?"

"Negative," the Japanese-American agent shook his head. "The two Caucasian males were carrying Federal Protective

Service badges and credentials, but there's no record of their ever being issued to anybody."

"Federal *Protective* Service?" Lightstone blinked. "Shit, these people don't need any protection."

"Hey, I'm just relaying the message," Takahara shrugged. "Security people at the airport confirmed the IDs."

"They could have been faked."

"Yeah, maybe, but that'd be rough to do," the Japanese-American agent said. "They'd have to get a hold of that new Treasury paper, which is real easy to confirm under a crossed-polar light."

"Did those security guys at the airport check?"

"They said they did."

"But if these guys had legitimate federal credentials, then *somebody* with authority had to sign them," Paxton said.

Takahara shrugged his muscular shoulders. "No way you can expect anybody to remember three days later what a scrawled signature looked like, especially when he sees dozens of those things every day."

"Shit," Lightstone cursed.

"Come on, guys, there's *got* to be a link here," Mike Takahara said insistently. "What is it that we know for sure? That we got shut down on an investigation and then scattered all over the country. And now a bunch of assholes are trying to hunt us down, and the Chareaux brothers are involved somehow, only maybe these guys have had a falling out, because we also know that Alex killed at least two of them."

"And we know for sure that *these* guys here went after Paul," Lightstone said, nodding at the photos, "and that Butch Chareaux was killed in the process."

"Paul shoot him?" Takahara asked.

"It looked that way at the scene," Lightstone shrugged, "but who the hell knows?"

"And then I got a call from that female informant," Stoner offered.

"Just like Carl did," Lightstone reminded.

"Yeah, and then the little broad lures me into this barn,

where Sonny and some karate asshole try to bust my knee," Stoner finished.

"Only Sonny ends up getting killed, which would sure as hell piss Alex off if he knew about it," Mike Takahara added.

"Which he obviously didn't, or he wouldn't have walked away when he had you hanging there," Lightstone said. "And which also means that he probably didn't know about Butch, either."

"Maybe he isn't after you guys at all," Ed Rhodes suggested. "Like you said, he had Mike right there. No reason to walk away."

"Well, if *he* isn't after us, then who the hell is?" Lightstone demanded.

"I don't know, man, but every time we try to figure this thing out, I keep coming back to that hunt you went on with Alex and Butch," Paxton said. "That and the fact that everywhere we look, some Asian guy is popping up into the picture."

"You mean those three idiots with the hundred-thousand-dollar guns?"

"One of whom you described as Japanese," Paxton reminded.

"Whoever's been doing this had enough influence with the Department of Interior to get us reassigned," Lightstone nodded. "And they had to have *some* connection with the Chareaux brothers if they were willing to spend that much money to pop them loose."

"Three hunters, filthy rich, lots of influence, who think that they're about to get in serious trouble with the law," Paxton smiled.

"Or maybe worse, worried that they might get embarrassed?" Lightstone suggested.

"How could we possibly embarrass them if we don't even know who they are?" Stoner asked.

"Henry could ID them, they know that," Paxton reminded.

"Yeah, and I know somebody who could help me find them," Lightstone said with a slight smile.

"Alex," Stoner whispered in a soft voice.

"Jesus Christ! Paul was right," Lightstone said quietly. "We tripped over something big, and the Chareaux brothers were involved."

"And it's big enough to make it worth sending a bunch of multinational commandos out after us. The Chareaux brothers were supposed to be left behind to throw everybody off," Paxton said.

"Except that one of their commandos was dumb enough to give Alex a knife, and now *he's* on the loose, too," Mike Takahara added.

"Tell you what," Paxton said, looking at the picture of Gerd Maas. "I think we better find those three hunters of yours before this white-haired bastard finds us."

"Or Al Grynard," Lightstone reminded as he looked around the room. "Anybody have any ideas?"

"You're looking for three wolves in sheep's clothing," Ed Rhodes said to no one in particular. "How the hell are you going to find them?"

Henry Lightstone sat motionless as an image exploded in his mind. "Guns," he rasped as he turned to Ed Rhodes, his eyes blazing with intensity.

"What?"

"Who knows about guns around here?"

"Uh, Gary. He's our firearms examiner."

"I want to talk to him, *now*."

CHAPTER FORTY-ONE

THURSDAY, SEPTEMBER 23RD

At precisely sixteen minutes after midnight that Thursday morning, the phone in the firearms examination area of the National Fish and Wildlife Forensics Laboratory in Ashland, Oregon, rang loudly.

Ed Rhodes picked it up on the first ring.

"Forensics Laboratory, Rhodes."

And then: "Yes, sir. He's right here," Rhodes said as he handed the phone over to Lightstone.

"Hello?"

"Special Agent Lightstone?"

"Yes."

"This is Nigel Hooper from Holland and Holland. I understand that you've been inquiring about one of our rifles?"

"Yes, sir. A double-barreled African Hunter, chambered for the .416 Rigby cartridge. We're trying to find out the name of the individual who purchased the weapon."

"Do you happen to know when he might have made his purchase?"

"No, I don't."

"Perhaps a serial number, then?"

"Uh, no, sir," Lightstone said, speaking loudly over an annoying hiss in the telephone line. "All I have is a description of the etching on the receiver, and the fact that the weapon was sold to an American."

"I see. Well, perhaps we could start with the etching," Nigel Hooper said politely. "That might help narrow things down a bit."

"The etching is of a single wolf standing on a rock."

"Umm, I'm afraid that's a rather common design request," Nigel Hooper said. "Is there anything else about the etching that might be distinctive?"

"I'm afraid that I'm doing this from memory," Lightstone said, recalling in his hallucinatory dream how the first point of light had become a slowly rotating disk and then the face of a dog that really wasn't a dog after all.

"I see. Are you certain that the creature *is* a wolf?"

"I assume it is," Lightstone said. "That's what was etched in script just below the rock. W-O-L-F-E."

"Oh, really?"

"Would you have any idea of how many rifles Holland and Holland might have made with that particular etching?"

"Yes, I think I can tell you exactly how many," Nigel Hooper said. "But first, perhaps I should explain that while we Brits may use the English language a bit, uh, differently than you Yanks, we still spell wolf 'W-O-L-F.'"

Henry Lightstone sat in absolute silence as he listened to Nigel Hooper explain the background of a certain .416 Holland and Holland African Hunter with the picture of a wolf etched into its receiver.

"Yes, you've been a wonderful help, Mr. Hooper. Thank you very much," Lightstone said as he hung up the phone and turned to the four haggard individuals who had been hanging on every word.

"Dr. Reston Wolfe," Lightstone said with a tired smile. "Special executive assistant, U.S. Department of Interior, Washington, D.C."

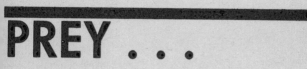

PREY . . .

CHAPTER FORTY-TWO

FRIDAY, SEPTEMBER 24

At precisely quarter past twelve on that Friday afternoon, Lisa Abercombie set Dr. Reston Wolfe's summary report aside and slowly began to flip through its accompanying sheath of police reports, interagency teletypes, and press clippings.

Three minutes later, having satisfied herself that the names and numbers in Wolfe's report seemed reasonable, she went back and read the entire four-page summary report one more time.

Having done that, she sat back in her beige-leather executive chair and stared incredulously at the three men sitting across from her desk.

"Five of *our* people are dead?"

"That's right," Paul Saltmann said matter-of-factly. "Arturo, Corrie, Felix, Shoshin, and Kiro. Roy, Carine, and Kimiko were wounded. Of the three, Roy's injuries are the most serious."

"And Alex Chareaux is . . . *loose?*"

"Apparently," the curly-haired weight lifter and intelligence specialist nodded.

For a long moment Lisa Abercombie simply stared at the three ICER team leaders.

"Three months ago, in one surgical operation," she said, her voice hoarse with disbelief, "Operation Counter Wrench created absolute havoc among five of the top environmental activist organizations in the world. Since then, we have conducted seven follow-up operations, which have literally set these extremists at each other's throats, without a single one of our people being so much as scratched.

"But then," Abercombie went on, "when we send you out to deal with six Fish and Wildlife Service officers—not Delta Team members, or Secret Service agents, or U.S. Marines, but *wildlife* officers—none of whom have the slightest reason to suspect that you're coming, you come back and tell me that not only have we lost half of our effective team, but also that an *incredibly* dangerous individual, one in a position to cause us *immense* grief, has been allowed to get away from us?"

For a brief moment, Abercombie allowed her gaze to fall on each of the men individually. "Can any one of you please tell me," she asked in a glacial voice that matched the cold fury in her eyes, "how we could *possibly* have gotten ourselves into such a position?"

For approximately ten seconds, all three men simply stared back at her with varying degrees of casual indifference. Then, out of no apparent sense of intimidation or urgency, Paul Saltmann spoke up again.

"I can explain it very simply," he said. "You and your bureaucrat buddy tried to make it too cute."

"*Cute?*" Lisa Abercombie rasped, her eyes almost bulging with rage. "You call the endangerment of a hundred-million-dollar operation *cute?*"

"We could have taken every one of them out with long-range weapons," Saltmann responded with icy calm. "We told you that. And if you had allowed us to handle it that way, we would have left appropriate evidence at the scenes and then disposed of the Chareauxs separately, without the slightest difficulty. It was only when we tried to integrate the Chareaux brothers directly into the situation that we ran into complications."

"However," Dr. Morito Asai reminded, "five of these agents are now dead. Also, we are following the sixth agent right now, and we may have located Chareaux."

"You *know* where Alex is, right *now?*" Lisa Abercombie asked quickly.

"We believe so, yes."

"Where?"

"In a remote cabin approximately three miles northeast of us," Paul Saltmann said. "We recognized this location as a possible jump point for an intruder, so we had it wired into our security system. The sensors detected one individual moving in there last night."

"You mean he's *here,* close by?" she asked with undisguised panic in her voice.

"Not so close, but not so far away either," the Japanese technical specialist said. "From our point of view, he is accessible."

Abercombie hesitated, trying to maintain her icy demeanor. But the thread of fear was there, and they could sense it now.

"Do you anticipate that he will be coming after us?" she finally asked.

"Alex Chareaux is a proud and vengeful man, and we have sacrificed his two brothers for our purposes," Asai shrugged. "Why would he not?"

"How did he know to come here?" she asked.

"Probably because Felix told him," Paul Saltmann said.

"What do you mean, Felix *told* him?" Abercombie demanded. "Why in the world would he do that?"

"An individual under torture can be made to say almost anything," the curly-haired intelligence specialist said coldly. "Even someone like Felix is not immune. Read the Reno sheriff's report. It's fairly descriptive."

Abercombie looked at Saltmann quizzically, then quickly flipped through the sheath of papers until she came to the report filed by Homicide Sergeant Clinton Hardwell. One third of the way through the report, her tanned face turned pale.

"My God, he—" Then she blinked in sudden realization and turned her attention to Gerd Maas, who was seemingly bored by the drift of the conversation. "Why haven't you gone out there and killed this bastard?" she demanded, her voice harsh and unforgiving.

"Because it is essential that we dispose of the sixth agent

first," Gerd Maas responded, his deep and foreboding voice causing Lisa Abercombie to pull back from her aggressive posture. "It must look like Chareaux is determined to complete his mission."

"But . . . but the risk," Abercombie started to argue as she stared down at the report, seemingly unable to take her eyes away from the descriptive paragraphs.

"Chareaux is emotional, and therefore does not represent a significant risk to this operation," Maas said with cold indifference. "The cabin is under constant surveillance, and he will not be allowed to approach this facility until we are ready for him to do so."

"But what if he eludes all of you again?"

"Mistakes were made when we had him in our possession at Reno," Maas said coldly. "Such mistakes will not be made in the future."

"Mistakes? What do mean by that?"

"For example," Maas replied, "it was a foolish mistake to send Günter away and leave Alex in the hands of Felix and the others. Felix was a tactician whose primary concern would have been to carry out his assignment, whereas Günter would have killed Alex the moment he tried to escape, and not given him the opportunity to harm the others."

"But you were in charge—" Abercombie started to protest.

"Gerd was monitoring the situation in the Kenai," Paul Saltmann interrupted. "He left orders for all of us to maintain our positions until he returned. However, your bureaucratic buddy, who didn't have the balls to stick around, decided to change the program."

"Dr. Wolfe had two appointments in Washington that he couldn't reschedule," Lisa Abercombie retorted. "But what do you mean, he changed the program?"

"The sixth agent had disappeared, and we didn't want to finish off Chareaux until we had located him," Saltmann explained. "Wolfe found a lead through the Fish and Wildlife Service personnel records that turned out to be useful; but instead of waiting for one of us, he ordered Günter to follow up on the lead, leaving Felix, Shoshin, and Corrie in Reno to monitor Chareaux and Takahara."

"And I might add that Dr. Wolfe issued those orders knowing that Shoshin had been injured, and therefore was certain to be less effective," Asai said accusingly.

"*Wolfe* did that?" Lisa Abercombie blinked in astonishment.

"That's right," Saltmann said grimly, "which is why Felix, Shoshin, and Corrie are now dead."

The Bronx-raised politician muttered a curse under her breath.

"All right," she whispered. "I will deal with Wolfe when he returns. Now, what about Nakamura?"

"I was there on that one," Saltmann nodded. "Everything was going according to plan until Paxton and his buddy showed up."

"Larry Paxton, the black agent whom you and Felix and Günter supposedly killed in Florida?"

"That's right," Saltmann conceded. "The plan was to go down and confirm the body, but the lake was filled with alligators that were acting aggressive, like they were down there chewing on fresh meat. There was blood in the water, so we decided it wasn't worth the risk."

"But obviously it would have been."

The chilling voice of Gerd Maas stopped Abercombie.

"Other than Wolfe's mistake, the decisions in the field have been correctly made," the assault-group leader said. "In this kind of operation, casualties are to be expected."

Lisa Abercombie started to interrupt, but Maas waved her off.

"These six agents have had some luck," he said. "But we can replace our losses, they cannot. This Paxton was clever enough to avoid death in Florida, but then he died in the explosion along with Stoner. And Chareaux was helpful enough to kill Takahara before he escaped, so now there is only one left to deal with—one agent, and then Chareaux—before we have resolved our problem."

Lisa Abercombie considered this; then, her cold bureaucratic facade back in place, she turned to face Dr. Morito Asai.

"You said that you know the location of this sixth agent right now?"

"Yes."

"Where is he?"

"At the moment, he is on board a small, private, twin-engine airplane enroute to Washington, D.C."

"You are certain of that?"

Dr. Morito Asai maintained a stony expression as he absorbed the insult. "He is on that plane, along with several others. Yes, I am certain."

Lisa Abercombie glanced down at her watch. "It's twelve-thirty now. In approximately five and a half hours, the Committee is expecting me to call in with a full report on our progress. When I do so, I would like very much to be able to tell them that—in spite of the horrible cost—the entire situation has been completely resolved. Is that possible?"

Asai turned to Gerd Maas, who nodded his head.

"Günter has been following the plane for the past eight hours in one of our jet helicopters," the assault-group leader said.

"By himself?" Abercombie asked.

"Yes, of course." Maas shrugged indifferently. "Günter will not need assistance in this matter. The helicopter can follow this plane wherever it goes, and he can complete his mission at any time, even with an air-to-air missile if necessary."

"Then what is he waiting for?"

"There are others on the plane, and Chareaux would not logically have access to such weapons," Maas said. "They are scheduled to land at D.C. National in approximately one hour. It is better to wait until then."

"But when they land?"

"Then Günter will not fail, and the last agent will be dead," Maas said matter-of-factly.

"Good," Lisa Abercombie approved. "I will meet all of you in the conference room at five-thirty, and I will be expecting good news when I get there."

After waiting until the door closed behind the ICER team leaders, Lisa Abercombie pressed two buttons on the underside of her desk. The outer door of her office automatically locked, and her phone console was set to record. Then she retreated to her private quarters, accessible only from the inner sanctum of her underground office.

Once inside this luxuriously furnished sanctuary, Abercombie treated herself to a long, hot bath, and then to a two-hour nap, which had become a physical necessity to the hard-driving and late-working politician-turned-counterterrorist.

At four P.M., her alarm went off and she woke refreshed and ready to begin again. Thirty minutes later, she was dressed and back in her office, where she turned her full attention to the sheath of reports and clippings on her desk.

By five minutes past five that afternoon, Lisa Abercombie was halfway through the Washoe County coroner's autopsy report on Felix Steinhauser when the private line on her phone console rang.

"Abercombie," she answered in her characteristically gruff, no-nonsense voice.

"Mrs. Abercombie, this is Gwen Fletcher, Dr. Wolfe's secretary at the Main Interior Building in Washington, D.C."

"Yes?"

"You asked me to let you know if anyone attempted to contact Dr. Wolfe at his office."

"Yes, go on," Abercombie said, impatient to get back to the autopsy report.

"There have been three such contacts this afternoon. One at two-fifteen. One at three fifty-five, and one at a quarter to five."

"Oh, really?" she said. "And what did they want?"

"They all wanted to speak to Dr. Wolfe, of course. I explained to them that he had several appointments today and wouldn't be back in his office until tomorrow morning."

"How would you describe these people?"

"One of them was a white-haired, older gentlemen in his sixties. I believe he is a biologist interested in Dr. Wolfe's grizzly bear research. The other two were much younger men, in their mid to late thirties, I suppose. One of them—"

"Did you make the recordings, as I asked?" Abercombie interrupted.

"Yes, of course. That's why I'm calling. I dropped the tape off at K-Link Communications. They said to tell you that they would be ready to transmit whenever you called."

"Thank you, Mrs. Fletcher," Lisa Abercombie said in a neutral voice as she hung up the phone. She began humming to herself as she picked up her reports, stepped out of her office, closed and locked the door, and then walked quickly down the long, narrow hallway toward the command-and-control room.

When she entered the glass-walled room, Gerd Maas was just hanging up the phone.

"It is done," he said abruptly. "The last agent is dead."

"Are you *certain* that it was him?" she asked.

"They were going out to eat in a rented automobile. Günter verified his presence with his binoculars, using the photograph you provided, and then waited until they came out of the restaurant before he detonated the device," Maas replied. "Everyone in the vehicle was killed instantly."

"Fine," Abercombie nodded after a moment. "Then all we have to do is dispose of Alex Chareaux and we are home free." She smiled as she sat down at the main control console, reached for one of the phone handsets, and dialed a memorized number.

"Marlene, this is Lisa. Yes, fine, thank you. I'm ready to receive. Which transponder will you be using? All right, fine, just a moment."

Looking up at the main video screen, Abercombie keyed in a series of commands, then watched the control board until the screen read:

DISH ONE
SATELLITE: K-16
TRANSPONDER: 33
LINK VERIFIED
SYSTEM READY
DO YOU WISH TO TRANSMIT OR RECEIVE?

Abercombie pressed "R" and then "Enter" on the keyboard before speaking into the phone again.

"We have a verified link at our end. Please begin transmitting now," she said. She watched the screen as the computer controlled the receipt of the digitalized video signal. After approximately two minutes had passed, the screen went blank for a brief moment, and then a new message appeared:

> SIGNAL PACKET DOI-DD-OO162 RECEIVED.
> DURATION 117.32 SECONDS
> STORAGE: DRIVE 13
> FILENAME: WC0008.VID
> SYSTEM READY
> DO YOU WISH TO TRANSMIT OR RECEIVE?

Abercombie punched the "N" and "Enter" keys, waited until the main menu display reappeared on the screen, and then turned to Maas.

"In five minutes," she said, "As scheduled, we will all meet again in the first-floor conference room."

CHAPTER FORTY-THREE

It was dark and raining, and the two agents could still hear the sirens in the background as they climbed into the front seats of the rented van. Whatever it was, it had happened in Georgetown, at least a mile away, and so they figured they probably wouldn't get caught up in the confusion.

"Well?" Dwight Stoner asked from the far backseat as he adjusted his sprawled-out body to take full advantage of the legroom created by Mike Takahara's unauthorized removal of the middle seat.

Henry Lightstone had tried to talk the rental company people into removing the middle seat themselves, but the clerk at the counter had balked, and the manager of the maintenance facility had said it was against company policy, and the employees in the shop had mumbled something about it not being in their job description. So Lightstone and Takahara had finally given up, gone back to the maintenance area parking lot and pulled it out themselves.

"Guards were a piece of cake," Lightstone said. "We gave them some bullshit story about getting into an accident on the Beltway, which was why we were late, and how we needed to use the Y-band transmitter on the roof to send an emergency message to South Africa before the government shipped any more of their elephants to the Saudis. Don't think they even looked at our credentials."

"Pretty sad performance for a couple of D.C. brothers." Paxton shook his head.

"So what's a Y-band transmitter?" Stoner asked.

"Beats the hell outta me. Ask Captain Marvel up here." Mike Takahara, in the front passenger seat, shrugged. "I just do locks."

"Yeah, so how did the locks go?" Paxton asked.

"Easy. Typical government low-bid stuff. But we did discover something else that was interesting," Takahara said. "Somebody set up a remote video unit to monitor the secretary's desk outside Wolfe's office."

"Oh, really?" Paxton said. "Any kind of surveillance system inside the office?"

"Nope, just a wire to his phone that he had hooked up wrong," Takahara replied. "Doesn't look like he's the technical type."

Larry Paxton thought about that for a moment. "Which would lead a suspicious person to think that somebody else wants to know who stops by to see our little piss-ass bureaucrat."

"Looks that way," Lightstone agreed. "We'd better not lose

track of him tomorrow, because he's about the only lead we've got."

"Yeah, no shit," Paxton nodded. "So what do we do now?"

"According to his secretary," Lightstone said, "if he's in town, Wolfe almost always goes to the office on Saturday, either late in the morning or early in the afternoon, to catch up on his paperwork. Said I could probably catch him there tomorrow because he's got some kind of report due."

"Unless he decides to come back tonight and sees what we've left him," Takahara reminded.

"Yeah, right."

There was a brief silence, then Dwight Stoner cleared his throat.

"Don't know about you guys," he said, "but *I'm* starting to get hungry."

Lightstone looked at his watch. "We have a choice, guys," he said. "We can either set up in the van outside this asshole's apartment, eat cold hamburgers, pee in cans, and take turns staying up all night watching it rain on the off chance Wolfe might drag his ass out of bed and stop by his office before noon tomorrow; *or,* we can bribe his doorman to give us a call on the pager when he starts to move, go out and have a decent meal, check into a first-class hotel, get a good night's sleep, and go after the potbellied little wimp in the morning."

"We know where he lives?" Stoner asked.

"Yep," Lightstone told him. "Got his address out of his secretary's Roledex, so all we've got to do is go find the building and talk to the doorman."

"If I gotta eat a cold hamburger and sleep in this thing all night, I'm gonna be hard to live with," Stoner warned.

"I know a good rib joint out near Lincoln Park," Larry Paxton said. "Little Joe's. Slow-cook pork and beef, all you can eat, and draft beer."

"Mike?"

"Personally," Mike Takahara smiled, "I'm getting to where I like eating cold hamburgers and peeing in tin cans, but if that's what it takes to keep Stoner happy . . ."

"All right, Paxton," Lightstone nodded. "Let's go find that doorman."

Lisa Abercombie waited until Roy Parker had maneuvered his wheelchair into the huge conference room, then motioned for Asai to shut the door.

Standing behind the podium at the head of the hexagon-shaped table, Abercombie allowed her eyes to sweep across the six individuals—Osan, Asai, Maas, Müeller, Saltmann, and Parker—who, aside from Günter Aben, were now the surviving members of her incredibly talented and aggressive counter-terrorist team.

"I wanted to bring you all together this evening to give you a status report on an operation that, to date, has cost us the lives of five of your comrades," Abercombie said solemnly. "Special Agent Len Ruebottom died in a car-bomb explosion in Georgetown approximately forty-five minutes ago."

There were general mutterings of approval around the table.

"We thought that this would be the end of it, and that we could get back to the primary mission of Operation Counter Wrench," Lisa Abercombie went on. "But, as it turns out, we have one loose end remaining."

The room went silent.

"When Dr. Asai and I took part in the hunt that Dr. Wolfe arranged with the Chareaux brothers," Abercombie explained, making it clear that she did not consider either herself or Dr. Asai to be guilty of any wrongdoing, "there was another man involved, one Henry Allen Lightner."

"The man who was accidentally shot during the killing of the first bear," Asai nodded.

"Yes, that's right," Abercombie said. "We were concerned at the time that Mr. Lightner might reveal our identities if he was ever threatened with prosecution. But fortunately," Abercombie smiled, "we were able to divert the case against the Chareaux brothers, and we have never heard from Mr. Lightner again . . . until now." She reached down to the controls on the podium, dimmed the conference-room lights slightly, and then turned on the VCR and the overhead monitors.

"Our concern was that Mr. Lightner might try to use his knowledge of our involvement with the Chareaux brothers to blackmail one of us." Abercombie continued to speak as the videotape showed the white-haired scientist who had spoken with Wolfe's secretary.

"So when we learned that Lightner made an attempt to contact Wolfe this afternoon," Abercombie went on as the white-haired man was suddenly replaced by a second, much younger man with a terrible bruised and swollen face, "I decided that we—"

"Wait a minute, that's him!" Roy Parker yelled out from his wheelchair, causing Abercombie to jab at the pause button, freezing the blurry face of Henry Lightstone in the center of the stilled monitor.

"Yes, of course, that's—" Abercombie started to say, but Parker ignored her as he turned to Maas.

"No, I mean that's *him,* the guy Arty and I were shooting at out there on the island."

Gerd Maas turned slowly to face the injured ICER team member.

"Are you certain?" he asked.

"Yes, goddamn it, *of course* I'm sure," Parker said emphatically. "I had that bastard in the cross hairs at least three different times. He's the one who shot Arty and then opened up on us from that goddamned plane."

"Lightner was up there in Alaska? That doesn't make sense." Lisa Abercombie shook her head in confusion. "Why would they let a—"

Then she blinked in shock. "Oh, my God, he's not a businessman. He's—"

"—a special agent," Gerd Maas finished in his cold, hardened voice.

"He's also the one who took out Nakamura hand-to-hand," Carine Müeller nodded slowly.

"Yeah, I think Carine's right," Paul Saltmann added. "I got only a quick look, but—"

Gerd Maas turned to stare at Carine Müeller, then brought

his head back around to scrutinize the blurry image of Henry Lightstone.

Then he smiled.

"Ruebottom was not the sixth agent we were looking for," he said, speaking to Abercombie in his glacial, calm voice but keeping his eyes fixed on the monitor, as if fascinated by what he was seeing. "This is the one they were hiding."

"But—"

At that moment, one of Abercombie's aides stuck his head in through the door, gulped nervously, then hurried in and whispered something in Abercombie's ear.

Lisa Abercombie frowned and waited until the aide disappeared back through the door before she turned to Maas.

"It's Reston," she said, staring down at the blinking button on her phone console.

"Put him on the speakerphone," Maas directed.

Numbly aware that she had somehow managed to lose control of the meeting, Lisa Abercombie complied.

"Reston? This is Lisa."

"Thank God!" Dr. Reston Wolfe's excited voice burst out into the still room.

"What's the matter?"

"They know! Listen, you've got to help me. They know all about us!"

"Who knows all about us?" Abercombie demanded.

"They . . . they do. The ones . . . they . . ."

"Reston!" Abercombie snapped. "Listen to me!"

"But—"

"Reston, *where are you?"*

"In my office, M-M-Main Interior," he stuttered. "Forgot my attaché case. Nothing in it, but didn't want to leave it there, so I came in. Found it just like that, all over the walls. I'm telling you, they *know,* so I've got to get out of here quick, before they—"

"Reston, I want you to listen to me very carefully," Lisa Abercombie said. "The only one who knows anything at all about us is Henry Lightner. Nobody else, just him."

"But he . . . he's just—"

"Lightner is a federal agent," Abercombie explained calmly. "He's the one who came to see you today."

"An agent?"

"That's right."

"But . . . but he *can't* be. I mean, I *checked*. Honest to God . . ." The man was almost whimpering now.

"Reston, it's all right," Lisa Abercombie said soothingly. "He doesn't know anything at all about what we're doing, so he can't possibly do anything to harm *any* of us, as long as no one panics. Do you understand?"

"I . . . yes, okay, I understand," Wolfe said, taking in a deep, shuddering breath. "Just send the plane out here immediately. I'll wait at National."

Lisa Abercombie looked up and saw Maas slowly shaking his head.

"Reston, we can't send anybody out to get you right now," Abercombie said. "It's too dangerous."

"Oh, yeah. Right. Uh, that's okay. I'll just take a commercial flight to Denver, and then—"

Abercombie saw Maas shake his head again.

"Reston, listen to me. You've got to stay where you are until we can get you some help," Abercombie said, watching as Maas nodded his head slowly in agreement.

"But—"

"Reston, go back to your apartment *immediately*," Abercombie ordered in her firm "don't-give-me-any-shit" voice. "I'll take a red-eye flight and be there first thing in the morning with our legal team. You and I will go to my apartment and stay there, and Koles will see to it that no one can possibly touch us. All right?"

There was a long pause, and then Wolfe seemed to partially recover his composure.

"Yes, that's good, a good idea," he rasped shakily. "How soon will you be here?"

"I'll have one of the helicopter pilots take me over to Denver Stapleton right now," Abercombie promised. "What you need to do is to have one of the guards call you a cab and then go home *right now,*" she emphasized. "I'll see you tomorrow morning. All right?"

"Yes, okay, tomorrow morning," Wolfe agreed, and Abercombie hung up before the thoroughly unnerved executive director could say anything more.

For a long moment, Lisa Abercombie and Gerd Maas simply stared at each other.

"You understand that they are trying to make him panic and run to us," Maas finally said calmly.

Lisa Abercombie nodded.

"Then you realize, also, what we must do." It was not a question.

Lisa Abercombie nodded again, this time with her lips tightened.

"You call your Committee and advise them of the situation, and then find out who this Henry Allen Lightner really is," Maas directed, his pale eyes gleaming with amusement. "I will deal with Wolfe."

Five minutes after they finished talking with Dr. Reston Wolfe's doorman, the cursing agents were back in the van and heading down Connecticut Avenue in the direction of Eighteenth and "C" Streets.

"What the hell's the *matter* with this bastard?" Dwight Stoner grumbled as he held on to the armrest to balance himself against Lightstone's frenzied driving.

"I don't know," Larry Paxton growled, "but I'm telling you, if this guy makes us follow him all night, and we have to eat cold, fucking hamburgers instead of Little Joe's barbecue, I'm gonna—"

Before Larry Paxton had a chance to describe his intentions in greater detail, Lightstone brought the van to a tire-screeching stop in front of the "C" Street entrance of the Main Interior building.

Moments later, he and Paxton were in a heated conversation with the federal security guard.

"Hey, look, man, it ain't my job to keep track of all the people who come in and outta here." The guard shook his head emphatically. "All I do is watch the building, you know what I mean?"

Larry Paxton was just about to rip into the self-righteous uniformed guard when the duty sergeant came up to the door.

"Anything I can help you gentlemen with?"

"I'm Special Agent Lightstone, and this is Special Agent Paxton," Lightstone said as he displayed his credentials, not trusting his more volatile partner to speak. "We're looking for Dr. Reston Wolfe. He was apparently dropped off here by a taxi about a half hour ago."

"Wolfe? Oh, yeah, sure. He just left a couple of minutes ago," the uniformed sergeant nodded.

"He say where he was going?" Lightstone asked, looking around quickly at the surrounding buildings.

"Hell, that man don't never say nothing to us peons," the uniformed sergeant shrugged. "All I know is, he went out the westside door and . . . hey, isn't that him down there? Yeah, there he goes, right there, guy in the blue raincoat heading down Nineteenth Street toward the gardens!" The guard pointed to a hunched figure walking hurriedly down the dark, wet sidewalk.

"Get in the van," Lightstone yelled back at Larry Paxton. "See if you can cut him off." Then Lightstone took off in a sprint.

Lightstone was within fifty yards of Wolfe when the distraught executive director apparently heard the slapping sound of Lightstone's shoes on the wet cement, looked back, then broke into a frantic run out across Constitution Avenue right into oncoming traffic.

The driver of a Mercedes, trying desperately to avoid hitting Wolfe head-on, jammed his brakes hard, sending his car sliding sideways on the wet asphalt, across the main divider, and into the path of a brand-new BMW.

Incredibly, in the midst of the ensuing jumble of swerving vehicles, screeching tires, shattering windshields, and dull crunches of chromed steel and sheet metal, all punctuated by the screams and curses of enraged and frightened drivers,

Reston Wolfe somehow managed to stumble across all six lanes of traffic without once being hit.

Running frantically and gasping for breath, Wolfe could hear Lightstone yelling behind him. Through the darkness and rain, Wolfe saw the three agents coming around in the van to his left, and he started to run to his right. But he found himself blocked by the Reflecting Pool. He staggered from the impact of the first bullet as it caught him high in the chest and punctured his right lung.

Lightstone was already yelling *"don't shoot!"* at Paxton and Stoner and Takahara before he realized that he hadn't heard a gunshot.

Instinctively, Lightstone dove to the ground and rolled to a prone position, his 10mm automatic extended at he searched hopelessly for a target.

Reston Wolfe was still on his feet when the second, third, and fourth bullets ripped through his thoracic cavity, tearing through his heart and both lungs. He died before his limp body touched the ground.

"Goddamn it," Lightstone whispered as he watched the elimination of their one and only link to the men and women who had mercilessly executed Paul McNulty and Carl Scoby. He was still breathing heavily from his run when the area in front of the Reflecting Pool was suddenly crisscrossed by six pairs of headlights.

"Henry Lightstone, this is the FBI. Put your weapon down on the ground, and put your hands up in the air, right now."

CHAPTER FORTY-FOUR

SATURDAY, SEPTEMBER 25

"I'd really appreciate it, Ed," Henry Lightstone said and then handed the phone to Assistant Special Agent in Charge Al Grynard, who had a decidedly unpleasant expression on his unshaven face.

As Al Grynard stood behind the dark wooden desk in the borrowed office he listened to the senior forensics specialist describe the significance of a recovered .416 Rigby bullet that had almost certainly been fired through a Holland and Holland rifle, the unique etching of a wolf that was spelled "W-O-L-F-E," and the strip of hide that Lightstone had recovered from the Kenai Peninsula.

Larry Paxton leaned over and whispered in Lightstone's ear, "Don't think I've ever seen an FBI man look that pissed before."

"You can see his point, though," Lightstone nodded, speaking quietly as he observed the gradual change in Grynard's expression. "He's got a hell of a case. Only trouble is, three of the guys I'm supposed to have killed at least once are sitting here in this room."

"Think he's gonna hold that against us?" Paxton asked after a moment.

"If I were you, I wouldn't piss him off any more right about now," Lightstone advised.

"Yes," Al Grynard was saying into the phone, "I would appreciate that. Yes sir, thank you very much."

As Henry Lightstone, Larry Paxton, Dwight Stoner, and

Mike Takahara watched in respectful silence, Al Grynard stood for a moment with his finger on the disconnect button in apparent indecision.

Then, seeming to nod to himself, he dialed a four-digit number, spoke softly into the mouthpiece, hung up and then sat down in the padded executive chair. He turned around to face the four agents.

"In my entire law-enforcement career," Grynard said after a moment, "I don't think I've ever come across a case quite like this."

"It *is* a little unusual," Lightstone conceded agreeably, waiting to see which way the veteran FBI agent would decide to play it.

"Did I tell you that we located your duty weapon?"

"In the water?" Lightstone guessed.

Al Grynard nodded. "About fifteen feet offshore, pretty much in a straight line from where you claimed to have shot the one suspect. Two Model Sixty-sixes, yours and the refuge officer's, as well as a bipod-mounted M-Forty sniper rifle and one H&K nine-millimeter submachine gun, along with three or four handfuls of expended brass."

"Brass?"

"We sent a diver down," the FBI agent explained. "He found over a hundred and fifty expended casings before we finally made him come out. We've got him at Lake Tustumena right now. We received a report from a couple of fishermen who saw a blue floatplane land and then sink out there. One of our technicians picked something up on sonar about a thousand feet down. May have to use a submersible to get to it."

"Clean up the scene and dispose of the evidence." Lightstone shook his head slowly. "These guys are thorough."

"Yes, they are," Al Grynard agreed as the door behind the four wildlife agents opened and two FBI agents entered the room carrying a pair of cardboard boxes. After receiving a confirming nod from Grynard, they carefully placed a stainless-steel Rolex watch, three .45 SIG-Sauer automatics, a 10mm stainless-steel Smith & Wesson, four shoulder rigs, and four sets of credentials on the table, then left as quietly as they entered.

"Your equipment, gentlemen," Grynard said. Takahara, Paxton, and Stoner gladly reached for their weapons and IDs. Grynard looked over at Lightstone, who was staring at the Rolex. "Mrs. McNulty said her husband would want you to have his watch," he said quietly.

Henry Lightstone started to speak, but just blinked and nodded instead. He held the Rolex in his hand for a moment, then slipped it into his pocket.

"Special Agent in Charge Paul McNulty was killed with a .357 Ruger that was left at the scene," the FBI agent went on. "Prints on the weapon belong to Butch Chareaux, who was shot with McNulty's SIG-Sauer, which was also left at the scene. And whoever killed Scoby used a couple of Model Sixty-sixes, but definitely *not* the ones issued to you and Jackson. So what it all comes down to, Henry," Grynard said with a tired smile, "is that while we think the scenes were rigged, we don't think you did it."

"I see," Lightstone said noncommittally.

"You haven't gotten anything on the fingerprints?" Mike Takahara asked quietly.

"No, nothing." Al Grynard shook his head. "Far as Interpol's concerned, those four individuals do not exist."

"Shit," Larry Paxton murmured.

"So now what?" Lightstone asked, watching the FBI agent carefully.

"We're digging into Reston Wolfe's background right now," Al Grynard replied, "and we seem to be hitting a lot of brick walls. He was supposedly just a junior-grade political appointee. He'd been out of the office on travel a lot, but his secretary didn't seem to know where he's been, or why, and there weren't any travel vouchers or plane reservations to trace. Nobody at Interior seems to know much about him or, for that matter, to particularly care."

"Whoever's running this thing decided to cut him loose," Lightstone shrugged. "That's what he was there for."

"Right," the FBI agent nodded. "So now all we have to

figure out is who these people are and what the hell they're up to."

For a long moment, the two special agents stared at each other.

"All we know for sure is that we tripped over something big when we went after the Chareaux brothers. Somebody with a lot of influence went after us, and Wolfe was our only lead," Lightstone said carefully.

"No idea what it was you tripped over?"

"No, none at all."

"Oh, by the way," Grynard added as he stood up. "There's a sergeant from the Louisiana Department of Fish and Game out in the lobby. He'd like to ask you some questions about Alex Chareaux."

"Oh, really?" Lightstone said as he and the others followed Grynard toward the door.

"Tell you the truth," Grynard said as he accepted Henry Lightstone's handshake, "I'm not sure where our jurisdiction lies with this thing anymore, but if this sergeant from Louisiana knows anything, or you happen to run across another lead—"

"You'll be the first guy we call," Lightstone promised solemnly.

"I'd appreciate that," the FBI agent nodded without the slightest change of expression in his dark, brooding eyes.

A half hour later, Larry Paxton, Dwight Stoner, and Mike Takahara introduced themselves to the five somber-faced Louisiana State Fish and Game officers in the lobby of the J. Willard Marriott Hotel on 14th Street. Henry Lightstone was at one of the lobby phones dialing a long-distance number.

"Forensics lab, Rhodes."

"You guys ever go home?" Lightstone asked.

"Doesn't seem like it some days," the senior electronics specialist chuckled. "I was beginning to think you weren't going to call back."

"What have you got?"

"It's not me. Biggs. Hold on just a second."

"Hi," the familiar voice came on the line. "This is Joe Biggs."

"The guy with the DNA probes," Lightstone said, remembering the term but having no real idea of what a DNA probe was.

"Yeah, right," the serologist chuckled. "Hey, listen, we happened to trip across something weird down here and I thought you might want to know about it."

"Oh, really? What's that?"

"You remember those sets of camouflage gear we got in from the Army Crime Lab when you guys were here? The ones that had blood all over them?"

"Yeah, sure."

"Well, we ran the stains with those new probes I told you guys about, and guess what? The computer popped up with a match."

"A match with what?" Lightstone asked.

"You."

Lightstone blinked. "What?"

"To be more accurate," Joe Biggs said, "you *and* the bear. Your blood on one set and the bear's on both."

"*My* blood was on those clothes? Are you *sure*?"

"The odds against it are about one in a hundred million for you, and maybe one in fifty thousand for the bear," Biggs replied. "That makes it . . . um, fifty thousand times a hundred million . . . about five trillion to one that another bear and another human, both with the exact same DNA patterns, put that blood on those cammies. I'd say that makes it a pretty decent match."

Suddenly the entire thing crystallized in Henry Lightstone's mind. Reston Wolfe and the woman, Lisa something, dressed in brand-new camouflage clothing and armed with incredibly expensive rifles, and the bear chasing him . . .

Can you hear me?

I'm going to try to move your arm.

Holding his head in her lap, knowing it was her because he could smell her perfume over the smell of the blood. His and the bear's.

Jesus!

"Joe," Lightstone asked in a voice as calm and quiet as he could manage under the circumstances, "do you have *any idea* where the Army Crime Lab got those clothes?"

"Kinda thought you might want to know that," the forensic serologist chuckled. "Got a pencil?"

It was eleven-fifteen that evening when the phone in Paul Saltmann's carefully locked and secured underground room rang softly.

"Saltmann," he rasped sleepily, and then became wide awake as he listened to the familiar voice describe exactly what it was that it wanted done.

"Yes sir, Mr. Bloom," the curly-haired weight lifter and intelligence specialist finally said when the voice finished. "I understand completely. You can count on me."

CHAPTER FORTY-FIVE

SUNDAY, SEPTEMBER 26TH

Lisa Abercombie was furious.

"*They can't do that!*" she screamed into the phone.

"My dear, they not only *can* do it, they *will* do it if you don't find Chareaux and this Agent Lightstone immediately," Albert Bloom warned.

"But—"

"Lisa, listen to me. The FBI is beginning to probe into areas that we do not want examined. And if they ever manage to discover what you and Wolfe have done, there will be nothing we can do to protect you. Nothing."

The words "you and Wolfe" jarred at Lisa Abercombie's soul, but she forced herself to ignore their lethal implications.

"Albert, that's not fair," she protested in a raspy voice, finding it difficult to believe that she was actually using those words. "You provided the Chareaux brothers with the best legal team in D.C."

"Yes, but they had absolutely no connection to any of us," Bloom reminded. "You do, and we cannot allow it to go beyond you. Not something this big. You, of all people, should understand that."

"Albert, you *have* to tell them——" Abercombie started in, but her mentor and lover would have none of it.

"Lisa, listen to me," Bloom said in a calm, cold voice. "I can't tell them anything right now. They are telling me."

"But——"

"Find Lightstone and Chareaux, and dispose of them immediately," Bloom repeated. "It's the only thing you can do."

The phone disconnected with a loud click.

"Goddamn you, Albert, you spineless bastard!" Abercombie screamed, her face ashen with fury as she slammed the phone down on her desk and stormed out into the hallway.

"Where's Maas?" she yelled at the first person she saw. She followed the aide's stammered directions until she burst into the central conference room on the lower level to find Maas, Günter Aben, Carine Müeller, and Kimiko Osan standing around the sprawled, dirty, and blood-splattered body of Alex Chareaux.

He was lying facedown on the floor, his wrists hooked together with nylon ties behind his back. Around his neck, a long chain was fastened, the end of which was held by Carine Müeller. Abercombie could see that Chareaux's eyes were blackened and swollen and that blood was dripping from his mouth, nose, and ears.

As she came forward, Abercombie also noted that Günter Aben had what appeared to be a recently bandaged cut on his left forearm, and that Kimiko Osan had a similar wound across

her left cheek. Of the four, only Gerd Maas seemed to b
amused by the situation.

"Thank *God* you found him," Lisa Abercombie said fer
vently as she stepped into the loose circle formed by the fou
ICER team members, and then leaped backward in shock a
Alex Chareaux suddenly brought his knees up to his chest
rolled, came up fast, growled in the depths of his throat, an
lunged at her with his teeth bared like a wild beast . . . onl
to be hammered back to the floor with the butt of the shotgu
in Günter Aben's gloved hands.

"For God's sake, what did you bring him here for?"
Abercombie demanded, shaken by the insane fury that she ha
seen in the Cajun poacher's reddened eyes. "Kill him righ
now, and then go out there and find Lightstone."

"Not yet," Gerd Maas said coldly. "It is better to use him.

"What do you mean, *use him?*" Abercombie's dark eye
widened in disbelief. "The Committee is getting ready to shu
us down, right now, if we don't find this Lightstone bastard.

"There is no need to go after Lightstone," Maas smiled, hi
pale eyes gleaming with amusement. "He will come to us."

"Maas, listen to me—" Lisa Abercombie started to plead
and then the excited voice of Dr. Morito Asai caugh
everyone's attention.

"We have a problem!" he yelled from the doorway leading t
the conference room.

"What is it?" Abercombie yelled back.

"Park service people. They say they have an emergenc
situation. They must land. Injured people."

"For God's sake, no! Tell them they can't land here!"

"I will try, but—"

"*Jesus Christ!*" Abercombie cursed as she looked aroun
wildly and saw Gerd Maas—with a wide grin on his fac
now—step forward and pull Alex Chareaux to his feet.

"*Hey, where are you going with him?*" Abercombie demanded
but Maas ignored her as he and the remains of his ICER assaul
group started walking toward the connecting hallway to th
main training areas, dragging Alex Chareaux along as the
went.

Still cursing and mumbling to herself, Abercombie ran to the command-and-control room and grabbed the microphone out of the hands of the radio-room technician.

"What's their call sign?" she demanded.

"Uh, Two-Five-Poppa-Sierra," the technician stammered.

"Two-Five-Poppa-Sierra, this is Whitehorse Cabin," Abercombie spoke into the microphone. "Do you read me?"

"Two-Five-Poppa-Sierra, that's a roger," the static-filled voice acknowledged.

"Two-Five-Poppa-Sierra, Whitehorse Cabin is a restricted area. You cannot land here."

"Uh, roger that," the pilot responded. "Be advised we have an emergency situation. The Park Service is fighting a brush fire in the southeast sector. I'm transporting three badly injured smoke jumpers to Gardiner, and I'm losing oil pressure. I have to put down, and these guys are in bad shape. We need help from your medical staff."

Abercombie looked up at the helicopter camera monitor that showed a white helicopter with a red cross on the side setting down onto the helipad in a swirl of dirt and leaves. Dark smoke was coming out of one of the engine exhausts. The side door slid open, and men in fire-fighting uniforms jumped out onto the asphalt pad, crouching down to avoid the swirling blades as they pulled the first stretcher out.

Abercombie turned to the technician. "Close and lock tne emergency doors," she ordered.

"But they—" the technician started to protest, only to wither under Lisa Abercombie's rage as she screamed, "Do what I tell you, and do it now!"

The technician reached for the five levers that controlled the two upper-level and three lower-level emergency exit doors to the underground facility.

"What's the matter with you? Hurry up and close those doors!" Lisa Abercombie yelled when nothing happened. The technician began to tug frantically on the individual levers.

"I can't! They're stuck. Somebody must have locked them open!"

"*What?*" Abercombie screamed as she watched the secon and third stretcher being unloaded.

"Call MacDonald," Asai advised. "He will know what do."

"Sergeant MacDonald, call the command-and-control roo immediately," the technician spoke hurriedly into the inte com mike. "Repeat. Sergeant Clarence MacDonald. Call th command-and-control room *immediately.*"

Abercombie and the technician waited expectantly, bu there was no answer.

"For Christ's sake, I'm going to the training area to ge Maas," Lisa Abercombie snarled, and then started for the do when the first shots rang out in the underground trainin facility.

The first stretcher team was waved through by Comman Sergeant Major Clarence MacDonald and Master Gunner Sergeant Gary Brickard, both dressed in full combat gear an armed with M-16 assault rifles.

As soon as they were inside, Paxton rolled off the stretche The carriers, both officers of the Louisiana Department of Fis and Game, let the stretcher drop. All three men, armed wit shoulder-holstered pistols and wearing Kevlar vests unde their fire-fighting jackets, took up defensive positions. Günte Aben took one look and cut loose with a stream of 9mr submachine gun bullets that caught one of the Louisian officers across the chest and throat. Aben immediately twiste away then and disappeared as a burst of 5.56mm ball amm from MacDonald's M-16 and three evenly spaced hollow-poin rounds from Paxton's SIG-Sauer shredded wood and plaster board around his head.

The second stretcher team, consisting of Lightstone an Takahara as the bearers of a stretcher loaded with assault rifles shotguns, stun grenades, ammo pouches, and first-aid gea hit the floor to avoid the first flurry of gunshots. The disappeared then down the sloping helipad access tunnel followed by MacDonald and Brickard and the Louisian sergeant as the third stretcher team—consisting of the fou remaining Louisiana officers and Stoner—moved into defensive positions and immediately went to the aid of the injured officer.

By the time they got to the end of the tunnel and were positioned to cover the swinging access doors to the conference room and the stairwell, MacDonald was already forming a plan.

As Brickard, Lightstone, Takahara, the Louisiana sergeant, and three of his officers crouched against the angled walls, their weapons out and ready, watching for the first sign of movement at either of the doors, MacDonald nodded at Lightstone.

"I'm Clarence MacDonald," the veteran combat soldier said, and then motioned with his head. "The gunny over there is Gary Brickard. You Lightstone?"

"Yeah," Lightstone nodded as he continued to scan the opposite corridor.

"Anybody else on the way?"

"Eventually there'll probably be a couple hundred FBI agents surrounding the park," Lightstone replied, "but right now, we're it. How many of them are there?"

"Seven," MacDonald said, "and they're all damn good."

"Which one's the white-haired asshole with the rhino-skin boots?" Lightstone asked.

"That's Maas," Brickard said. "He's the one you *really* gotta watch out for," the gunny sergeant advised. "Man's got reflexes like a cat. You see him, you better put him down fast."

"What about Chareaux?" the Louisiana sergeant asked quickly.

"They brought him in about a half hour ago on the end of a chain," MacDonald said, "beat to shit, and now they're hauling him around like a goddamn dog."

"We want him alive," the Louisiana sergeant said.

"Fine with me," MacDonald shrugged. "Okay, here's what we'll—"

At that moment, a pair of crashing gunshots rang out, followed by the sound of a loud, pulsing alarm that echoed through the huge underground facility.

* * *

The volley of gunfire in the distant corridor sent Lis
Abercombie running back into the command-and-contro
room, where she found Dr. Morito Asai trying to follow th
movements of the invading law-enforcement officers on a banl
of monitors as he spoke into his headset microphone. Th
communications technician had long since disappeared.

"Who are they?" Abercombie demanded as she closed an
locked the glass-paneled door behind her.

"I don't know yet." Asai shook his head as he continued t
adjust one of the security cameras.

"Look, there!" he said, pointing to the main screen.

"Who . . . wait a minute!" Lisa Abercombie's eye
bulged. "That's Paxton! He's supposed to be dead!"

"And Agent Stoner, too," Asai said as he switched over t
the outside helipad camera. He focused on the huge agent wh
was guarding the entry into the facility.

"And Takahara, and . . . oh, my God, Lightner, he
here!" Lisa Abercombie whispered as Asai focused securit
camera number twelve on his easily recognizable face.

"Yes, definitely him," Asai smiled as he hit a button wit
his foot and spoke into his headset microphone.

"Maas, I can see eight intruders outside the lower-leve
stairwell. One of them is Lightner."

"Ah, *gut*!" The German assault-group leader's voice echoe
over the speakers.

Then Asai and Abercombie whirled around with a start
Asai going for his shoulder-holstered automatic pistol, as Pau
Saltmann entered the control room with a Smith & Wesso
.44 Magnum revolver in his muscular hand.

"Christ! You scared the shit out of me," Lisa Abercombi
gasped as she glared at her intelligence specialist. "What th
hell is going on out there?"

"Looks to me like MacDonald and Brickard changed sides,"
Saltmann said as he glanced over at one of the monitors an
saw the two combat-uniformed soldiers. "How many of ther
are there?"

"Not so many," Asai shrugged as he took his hand awa

from the grip of the small automatic. "Maybe ten at the most."

Saltmann smiled and shook his curly head sadly. "Those poor bastards. Maas can handle that many by him— Oh, shit!" The intelligence specialist blinked, his eyes widening in surprise as he stared at one of the far monitors.

"What's the matter?" Abercombie demanded, and then stared in horror at the row of camera monitors that showed the expanse of land surrounding the facility. Each of the six small screens showed at least two assault-type helicopters landing and unloading armed combatants.

Saltmann shook his head and turned to Asai. "Can you tell who they are?"

Dr. Morito Asai made several rapid adjustments to the control panel. The camera lenses zoomed in until all three of them could easily read the lettering on the raid jackets and the sides of the helicopters.

"FBI and U.S. Army," Lisa Abercombie whispered. "My God, what are we going to do?"

Dr. Morito Asai turned to look at Abercombie, and she realized that he was waiting for her to make a decision.

It occurred to her then that she might have a chance, after all, if she could tell her story to the right people . . . to someone who would appreciate the significance of what they had tried to do and the magnitude of the risks that were necessarily involved.

Someone who would understand.

"Tell Maas that we must surrender immediately. There are too many of them for us to fight," she said to the Japanese team leader, who nodded solemnly and turned back to his control board.

Paul Saltmann raised the .44 Magnum and triggered off a high-velocity round that blew Dr. Morito Asai out of the console chair like a rag doll. The concussion sent Lisa Abercombie staggering back against the glass wall in shock, her hands clenched tightly over her ears.

"Why did you do that?" she shrieked, deafened by the explosive force of the contained gunshot, unable to hear the words even as she screamed them.

"Sorry, folks, but we are *not* going to surrender," Saltmann said evenly. He shifted the aim point of the powerful handgun in his two-handed grip and fired a second expanding .44 bullet. The creator of ICER, hit square in the chest, was flung backward through the shattering glass wall.

Paul Saltmann checked to make sure that no one else was around, moved up to the control board and called up the menu on the computer screen. He selected "Security," typed in his password, and selected "Destruction," typed in a second password, checked his watch, typed in the numerals 45, selected "Activate," and then "Confirm."

Then, after working through a similar set of commands to cancel all other passwords out of the system, Paul Saltmann ran out into the tunnel corridor leading to the ICER team's quarters while red warning lights began to blink overhead and a blaring alarm began to pulse and echo through the building.

No one had bothered to tell Command Sergeant Major Clarence MacDonald that the engineers who created the Whitehorse Cabin training facility had incorporated an interesting twist into the design of the lower-level command-and-control center: namely, the destruct sequence overrode the manual settings and automatically closed the five exterior emergency doors that provided access to the secured facility.

Dwight Stoner discovered this when a heavy concrete door suddenly started to roll across the twelve-foot opening. The crippled agent took one last look at the rapidly approaching helicopters, shrugged, and barely managed to jump inside the access tunnel before the leading edge of the six-inch-thick panel slammed into the locking mechanism on the opposite side, effectively sealing off the facility from outsiders.

Shaking his head and mumbling to himself, Dwight Stoner grabbed his crutch in one hand, a twelve-gauge shotgun in the other, and began hobbling down the sloping corridor toward the sound of distant gunfire, barely audible over the pulsing alarm.

The stairwell leading to the upper level of the training facility had become a free-fire battle zone.

As the agents, state wildlife officers, and military instructors moved up the stairs to the upper level behind the concussive blasts of flash grenades and directed gunfire, and the ICER counterterrorists continued to retreat, both sides shot out lights to conceal their position and their intended movements. As a result, most of the available light in the smoke-filled stairwell and upper-level hallways came from red emergency lights pulsing in a synchronous rhythm with the echoing alarm.

And thanks to the frenzied antics of Günter Aben and Carine Müeller, who delayed the raid team's advance with bursts of 9mm submachine gun fire, the bullet-pocked stairs and hallways were now slippery with blood and expended brass casings.

Of the ten men who had begun the raid from the deceptive landing of the white-painted helicopter, two Louisiana officers were dead and four others—Brickard, Lightstone, Paxton, and the Louisiana sergeant—had been wounded.

On the ICER team side, Carine Müeller was now bleeding from the nose—the result of being too close to the stairwell door when a flash grenade went off—and limping from a ricocheting chunk of buckshot in her upper thigh. Günter Aben had sustained at least four or five minor wounds, which hadn't slowed him down at all. He continued to dive and twist and roll from one barricade to another, sending three- and four-round bursts of 9mm ball ammo at anything that moved in the reddish-streaked darkness.

Farther back in the forestlike Hogan's Alley, Gerd Maas worked with cool, calm, and deliberate movements to set the stage for his latest, and possibly his most exhilarating, brush with death. He ignored the curses and screams of Alex Chareaux as Kimiko Osan guarded her assault group leader's back with careful sweeps of her laser-aimed Colt Commando submachine gun.

When Command Sergeant Major Clarence MacDonald and Special Agent Mike Takahara burst into the lower-level command-and-control room, they first spotted the bloody, lifeless body of Dr. Morito Asai, then looked out through the broken glass and discovered Lisa Abercombie, equally dead.

Both men looked up when the curly-haired man in the distinctive blue FBI raid jacket stepped into the room. MacDonald tried to bring his M-16 up in time, but the .4 round caught him high in the chest and slammed him backward into one of the steel pillars just as the second .4 slug mushroomed into Mike Takahara's solar plexus and sent the shocked technical agent stumbling backward through the broken glass wall and atop the sprawled body of Lisa Abercombie.

Then, humming contentedly to himself, Paul Saltmann checked his watch, glanced at the flashing red numerals on the control board that had changed from forty-five to thirty-six, and walked through the destruction he'd caused toward the lower-level conference room and stairwell.

As he did so, Saltmann was unaware that wheelchair-bound Roy Parker, blocked from escape by the six-inch-thick emergency doors, was rapidly working himself toward the command-and-control center from the opposite direction.

It was Lightstone who picked up on the pattern first, noting that as the returning ICER members worked their way back into the first of the Hogan's Alleys, designed to look like two floors and the open plaza of an indoor shopping center, Carine Müeller had started to conserve her energy by waiting for the explosion of the flash grenade and then running immediately to the position vacated by Günter Aben, invariably using the cover of her previous position to protect herself from the raid team's directed gunfire.

"Hey, Brickard, Paxton," Lightstone hissed as he holstered his pistol, pulled one of the flash grenades off his belt, and then signaled with his hands what he intended to do.

They waited until Günter Aben suddenly rolled away to a new position under the covering fire of Carine Müeller's H&K submachine gun.

Then, after Paxton heaved one of the canister grenades at Müeller's position, and Brickard and the remaining three

Louisiana wildlife officers opened fire on both positions, Lightstone took three lunging steps forward, pulled the pin and flung the grenade toward the barricade position that Günter Aben had just vacated.

At that point, Henry Lightstone had less than a second to roll forward and cover his ears as the detonation of the first grenade sent shock waves through every inch of his exposed body.

Dazed by the concussive force of the blast, Lightstone was still reaching for his shoulder-holstered 10mm automatic when Carine Müeller broke from cover, lunged toward her new position, and then saw Lightstone out in the open.

Hesitating in mid-stride, the beautiful young counter-terrorist started to come around with her finger tightening on the trigger of her H&K when her eyes caught the motion of the rolling canister out in front of her. Reacting instinctively, she turned away just as the grenade exploded and sent her tumbling to the floor, the H&K clattering away in the red-tinged semidarkness.

Nearly unconscious and bleeding from the mouth, ears, and nose, Carine Müeller's right hand fumbled for her belt-holstered Model Sixty-six .357. Henry Lightstone centered the sights of the 10mm automatic on the young German woman's hand, because they had all agreed that they wanted to take *someone* out of here alive.

But then the words of Al Grynard flashed through his mind: *Whoever killed Scoby used a couple of Model Sixty-sixes.*

Without thinking about it further, Henry Lightstone shifted the sights of the heavy automatic, sent five 10mm hollow-point rounds into Müeller's upper chest, throat, and head, then rolled away from the stream of 9mm slugs that tore the wooden floor into splinters right where he had been lying . . . and Günter Aben screamed out his rage in his native German tongue.

Continuing to twist away from the furious 9mm assault, Lightstone fired one round at the German's exposed head, missed, felt the jarring *clack* as the receiver jammed open on an empty magazine, and was reaching for one of the loaded

magazines on his belt when Günter Aben came back aroun
the corner fast, the H&K leveled, a sneering smile on his face

The impact of the first .44 bullet nearly severed Günte
Aben's arm as it ripped through bone and tissue, punche
through the gap where his thick Kevlar vest didn't quit
overlap, splintered a rib, and then buried itself in th
counterterrorist's heart.

The second bullet that slammed his back into the wall wa
unnecessary. The ICER team member, who could never qui
control his temper when he tried to outwit Clarence MacDon
ald's simulators, was dead before his knees hit the floor.

When Dwight Stoner hobbled into the lower-level conferenc
room, he saw Mike Takahara trying to push himself up on h
hands and knees, coughing out blood in the process. As h
moved to the doorway of the command-and-control cente
Stoner saw the sprawled bodies of Clarence MacDonald, wh
was starting to moan and move around a little, and Morit
Asai, who wasn't doing either, and a man in a wheelcha
working frantically at the keyboard of the control console.

Roy Parker didn't see or hear Dwight Stoner coming unt
the agent's huge body suddenly filled the doorway and blocke
out the incoming light from the adjoining conference room
Parker turned to look and then drew back in shock as he sav
the huge form pointing the barrel of the 12-gauge pum
shotgun directly at his head.

"Move away from that desk," Stoner ordered in a cold, deep
and unfeeling voice.

"It wasn't me, buddy. I didn't shoot any of them," Parke
said carefully, trying to keep his voice steady as, out of th
corner of his eye, he saw the red numerals on the control boar
change from thirty-three to thirty-two.

"Shut up and keep your hands in the air," Stoner ordered

"I'm carrying a Beretta nine-millimeter in a shoulde
holster, right-hand draw, under my jacket," Parker sai
quietly as Stoner moved slowly around to his back. "It's clean
It hasn't been fired." Then Parker took a deep breath as he fel
the shotgun barrel against the base of his skull.

"Look at the blood splatters on that wall," Parker continued in a voice as steady as he could manage. "No nine-mil in the world could do that. That's Saltmann. He carries a forty-four mag with hot loads. Like a fucking freight train when they hit."

The barrel of the shotgun dug deeper into Parker's neck, and he immediately realized that he had said the wrong thing.

"Hey, no, wait a minute!" Parker whispered frantically. "You gotta listen. They wired this place to blow, and it's—"

"It's okay, man. He's not the shooter," Mike Takahara gasped in a pain-filled voice, holding his right arm tight against his severely broken rib cage as he slowly reached into Roy Parker's jacket with his left hand and pulled out the loaded and locked 9mm pistol. "Big curly-haired bastard wearing an FBI raid jacket."

"That's Saltmann," Parker nodded, nervously aware that the barrel of the shotgun was still pressed tight against his neck. "He's the cutter on this deal. He's supposed to shut the whole operation down and blow the place if something goes wrong."

"Keep talking," Mike Takahara directed in a painful whisper. He stuck the 9mm Beretta in the back of his belt, brought Parker's hands down, one at a time, and handcuffed them through the left wheel of the wheelchair. Then he wiped the blood from his mouth and tried not to cough or breathe any more than he had to as he placed his shaky left hand on the console for support. He tried to blink his eyes clear enough to see how the control board had been designed.

"The guys on top wanted to make sure they didn't end up with another Watergate or an Iran-Contra deal blowing up in their faces," Parker went on carefully, sensing that the two agents were beyond the point of caring about rules and regulations. "So they put Saltmann, Arty, Corrie, and me in as a safety valve. Something goes wrong, we're supposed to make the whole thing go away."

In the background, Command Sergeant Major Clarence MacDonald clutched both forearms to his chest in the area where the hot-loaded .44 Magnum expanding round had mushroomed against his Kevlar vest, breaking several of his ribs and causing massive bruising all the way to the pericardial covering of his heart. He tried to bring himself up to a sitting position.

"That what happened to the little guy in the doorway, and to the broad out there on the floor?" Stoner growled.

"Yeah. We're supposed to take everybody out so they don't get any ideas about talking," Parker nodded. "Only, Arty and Corrie are dead, and I'm pretty much out of it, so Saltmann's on his own."

"So who takes you guys out?" Mike Takahara asked in almost a whisper as he motioned for Stoner to drag the wheelchair out of the way. Then he sat down gratefully in the console chair and used his left hand to call up the menu on the screen.

"Yeah, we talked about that," Parker said nervously as he felt the shotgun barrel dig into the back of his neck again. "We've got FBI and DEA credentials that're supposed to look good enough to let us talk our way out, but we figured—"

Then the red numerals on the console board changed from a thirty-two to a thirty-one, and Parker started to panic.

"For Christ's sake, man," he pleaded, "we've *gotta* shut this damn thing down. It's gonna blow in thirty-one minutes, and I can't do a goddamn thing to stop it."

Mike Takahara had already discovered that "Security/Destruction" was locked out of the menu. He tried to go in through the operating system and found himself blocked there also.

"What's your access code?" Takahara whispered.

"'Sunshine,' but it won't do you any good," Parker said. "I already tried. It doesn't work."

Mike Takahara tried a series of machine language instructions that should have given him access to the back door of the processing chip, but they didn't.

The red numerals changed from thirty-one to twenty-nine.

"How's it wired?" Mike Takahara finally asked.

"It's a dual system," Parker said. "First series of explosions takes out the internal cross-support walls, and probably kills everybody inside. The second series goes off fifteen seconds later and basically blows the two main side walls into each other like a couple of fucking bricks."

Dwight Stoner muttered something under his breath, but Takahara ignored it.

"What's the explosive?" he asked.

"They said C-Four, but I don't know," Parker said. "They never showed any of it to me."

"Come on, Snoopy, how long's it gonna take you to break into this thing?" Dwight Stoner demanded uneasily as he listened to the sound of automatic gunfire in the distance.

"The long, safe way, probably a couple of hours," Takahara whispered, wincing as he readjusted himself in the chair.

"For Christ's sake, we haven't *got* a couple of hours!" Roy Parker exploded, and then froze as the shotgun barrel pushed harder against his neck. "Come on, man," he pleaded quietly. "We can't get out of here, because the goddamned doors are blocked off. Do it the fucking short way."

"Right," Mike Takahara nodded, groaning in pain as he reached around behind his back and drew out Parker's 9mm Beretta. Then, before Dwight Stoner could say or do anything to stop him, the technical agent fired five 9mm pistol rounds pointblank into the main processing unit of the command-and-control computer.

The handcuffed counterterrorist looked on in horror as every light on the command-and-control console seemed to increase in intensity and the red numeral display went haywire. Then, in the space of a single heartbeat, the console board went dead, the red numerals blinked out, the pulsating alarm was suddenly silent, and the red warning lights stopped flashing.

As Roy Parker and Dwight Stoner turned to stare at Mike Takahara with expressions that ranged from absolute horror to stunned disbelief, the technical agent looked up at the two men and said with the smallest shrug possible, "I cheat."

Shaking his head and muttering another heartfelt curse, Stoner hobbled over to where Sergeant Clarence MacDonald had managed to pull himself up into a sitting position. Judging from the stunned expression on the combat instructor's face, Stoner figured that MacDonald was alert enough to realize what Mike Takahara had done.

"Here," he said as he set the 12-gauge shotgun in MacDonald's lap. "Far as I'm concerned, you can shoot both of them any time you want."

Then, drawing the .45 SIG-Sauer from his shoulder holster, Dwight Stoner started hobbling on his single crutch toward the distant stairwell.

CHAPTER FORTY-SIX

"All right!"

"Yes, sir. Way to go, FBI!"

The sight of the man in the FBI raid jacket taking out Günter Aben in two quick shots brought a rousing cheer from Larry Paxton and the Louisiana wildlife sergeant, the only two, apparently, with enough breath or energy to yell.

After verifying that Carine Müeller and Günter Aben were dead and that no more ICER counterterrorists were in the immediate area, the raid team pulled together into a defensive position and began to treat their wounded.

As they did so, the pulsing alarm and the flashing-red warning lights suddenly went out, leaving the area illuminated only by the pale yellow glow of the battery-powered emergency lights.

"What the hell's going on now?" Larry Paxton demanded, but Henry Lightstone and the others just shrugged, intent only upon finding Alex Chareaux, the infamous Gerd Maas, and whoever else remained of his counterterrorist team.

Then, as the seemingly impatient blue-jacketed figure followed them from the catwalk above, Henry Lightstone,

Larry Paxton, Gary Brickard, and the Louisiana sergeant slowly and cautiously moved forward into the mock forest of the mountain cabin simulation area.

They left behind the remaining Louisiana officer—who had caught a 9mm round in the knee from Günter Aben's last flurry—to stay with his far more severely wounded buddy and to provide rear-guard support.

Spreading out and moving as carefully and quietly as they could through the amazingly lifelike concrete and plastic trees, brush and rock, the four men never saw Kimiko Osan pop out of the concealed trapdoor, and were aware of her presence only when she opened up on Brickard and the Louisiana sergeant with a burst of 5.56mm rounds from her laser-sighted Colt Commando submachine gun.

Both men went down, and Kimiko Osan was running for her next position when a concussive *ka-boom!* echoed throughout the cavernous simulation area. The impact of the .44 round sent the small, young, and incredibly fast counterterrorist tumbling to the floor as her laser-sighted weapon clattered away in the semidarkness.

"Nice shot, buddy," Gary Brickard, the veteran gunny sergeant muttered, grateful for the overhead cover as he quickly set his M-16 aside and knelt down beside the groaning Louisiana sergeant—vaguely aware of the pain in his lower hip from the one 9mm round that he *hadn't* absorbed with his vest—and began to apply a field dressing to the wildlife officer's shattered upper thigh.

Ka-boom!

Ka-boom! Ka-boom!

The first .44 bullet caught Master Gunnery Sergeant Gary Brickard full in the lower throat just above his vest and smashed him back into the trunk of a concrete tree. The second and third bullets exploded chunks of concrete off of an adjoining tree trunk just above Larry Paxton's rapidly ducking head as Henry Lightstone recovered and sent a half-dozen 10mm rounds up at the blue-jacketed figure, who immediately twisted back behind one of the armored glass panels that had been installed to protect observers from an accidently deflected round.

"What the hell?" Larry Paxton screamed . . .

Ka-boom! Ka-boom! Ka-boom!

. . . and then dove behind a much larger concrete trunk as Paul Saltmann took advantage of his overhead position to come around to the edge of an armored glass panel and send three more .44 rounds streaking down at the two scrambling figures.

Dumping the expended casings and pulling a heavy speed-loader out of his jacket pocket as he ran forward to the end of the walkway where it extended out over the middle of the "forested" simulation area, Paul Saltmann quickly reloaded and extended the powerful handgun around the edge of another glass panel in a two-handed grip. He fired two rounds down at the fleeing figure of Gerd Maas, and three more at Henry Lightstone, who was unsuccessfully trying to shoot back up through the armored glass at the silhouette of Paul Saltmann.

The ear protectors that Paul Saltmann wore were more effective than he realized, and it was only the clattering sound of a .44 brass casing knocked by Dwight Stoner's single crutch that made him spin around and trigger off one more concussive round.

The stunning impact of the .44 round sent Dwight Stoner staggering backward, knocking the .45 SIG-Sauer out of his hand and down into the concrete-and-plastic forest as his wrist struck the leading edge of one of the armored glass panels.

Paul Saltmann was certainly aware that the raiding agents were likely to be wearing vests capable of stopping the penetration of his .44 expanding bullets, and he was skilled enough with his deadly weapon to have gone for a head shot every time. But he also knew that the center of the body was the easiest shot, and that his hand-loaded rounds really *did* hit like a freight train. The impacts were so devastating that no one had ever gotten back up from one of his shots, anyway.

Thus the fact that Dwight Stoner was still standing after being shot from only twenty feet away shocked Paul Saltmann so thoroughly that for the first time in his professional life, he actually tried to fire a seventh round from a six-shot revolver.

The loud *click!* of the firing pin striking the base of the empty casing jolted Saltmann back to reality, and his right hand dropped down to his jacket pocket for another speed-loader as he broke open the heavy cylinder of the revolver and dumped the casings . . .

"*Yeeeeeeeeaaaaaaaahhh!*"

"No!"

. . . and then both Saltmann and Stoner screamed in rage as the ex-tackle for the Oakland Raiders threw aside his crutch and lunged forward into a bruising heads-up tackle that sent both men crashing through the gap in the armored glass panels and falling to the concrete-treed floor far below.

Lightstone and Paxton saw the two bodies plummet toward the trees, and both men started to run forward when a mechanical figure suddenly swung around one of the massive tree trunks and fired three rounds straight into the middle of Larry Paxton's fire-fighting jacket.

Caught off guard and wincing against the shock he should have felt, Paxton blinked and then looked down at the three bright yellow splotches of paint in the center of his chest.

"Whaaat?"

"Robotic simulators. Ignore them," Lightstone said as they began to move through the concrete trees again, heading toward the clearing where Dwight Stoner and Paul Saltmann lay sprawled facedown.

They had taken only ten steps when the next simulator came around the tree to Paxton's right and fired three more shots.

The first impact left a bright yellow spot on the black agent's muscular upper arm. The second shattered both bones in his forearm, causing him to drop his SIG-Sauer. The third caught him just as he was turning away, so that the bullet went under his vest from the side, tearing into the muscle and fatty tissue of his stomach.

"*Shit!*" Larry Paxton screamed, rolling away and fumbling

for his lost SIG-Sauer as two more simulators popped up behind a nearby bush.

Snarling with rage, Henry Lightstone dropped both simulators with head shots before they could fire off a single round, started toward Paxton, saw three more simulators come around trees and dropped all three in a series of movements that were pure instinct before he managed to roll away behind a protective concrete tree trunk.

Looking down at his jacket, he saw a single yellow paint splotch in the center of his chest.

"Larry, you okay?" he hissed.

"Ain't good, but I'm okay," the shaken agent responded.

"Listen, *don't move.* These things respond to movement, and they're programmed to go for the center of mass."

"Ah ain't moving nowhere," Larry Paxton promised. "You just get that sucker."

"All right. Stay there, and I'll—"

"Are you enjoying my interesting game, Agent Lightner?" the cold, mocking voice, magnified by the overhead speakers, boomed out through the cavernous simulation area. "The real bullets are loaded randomly. Even I do not know the order in which they will be fired."

"Maas?" Lightstone called out, having no idea of where the man was.

"Yes, of course. I waited for you because I knew you would come."

"I didn't come here to play games, Maas," Lightstone responded as he started to move forward, out of the corner of his eye saw the simulators coming, put 10mm rounds between both sets of mechanical eyes and got behind the next tree trunk without getting any more yellow splotches on his chest.

"*Zehr gut!* You improve!" the booming voice chuckled.

"*Maas,*" Lightstone yelled out, "*My name is Lightstone. Henry Lightstone. I'm a federal agent, and you're under arrest. Come out with your hands up.*"

"Ah, but you are wrong, my friend. You cannot arrest me, because I have done nothing wrong that you can prove."

"Maas, this is *not* a game!"

"Don't be foolish. Of course it is a game. And you must play it, or I will come and kill all of your friends."

"Take him, man. Don't let that jive-ass fuck with you," Larry Paxton whispered shakily, his face streaked with sweat as he carefully tried to get a grip on his recovered SIG-Sauer with his injured left hand.

There was a long pause, and then the booming voice echoed through the public address system once again.

"Perhaps I should make it more interesting, yes?"

Looking out around the side of the cabin, Gerd Maas opened the razor-sharp folding knife that he had taken away from Alex Chareaux and tossed it between the legs of the bound and furiously thrashing Louisiana poacher.

Staring at the white-haired assassin through deeply reddened eyes, Chareaux grabbed the knife with his bound hands, then cut away the rope that tied him to the concrete tree.

Coming up to his feet, Alex Chareaux glared at Maas with a fury that promised death. But Gerd Maas held up the .22-caliber target pistol in his hand and shook his head.

"The man out there is named Henry Lightstone. He and his friends are the undercover agents who killed your brothers."

Alex Chareaux blinked, then turned to stare out into the darkened concrete-and-plastic forest before turning back to stare at Maas with a hatred that had not diminished at all.

"No, you must deal with him first," Maas said, shaking his head slowly. "Then it can be you and me."

For a brief moment, it appeared as if Alex Chareaux would go straight for Maas anyway. But he looked around at the darkened forest again, grinned madly, then turned and disappeared.

Smiling in anticipation, Gerd Maas reached for the microphone one last time.

"It is Alex, Henry. He comes for you now."

Lightstone saw Alex Chareaux charging through the trees and reacted instinctively, moving forward with the 10mm Smith & Wesson in both hands.

The first two shots were paint to his chest; then suddenly Lightstone found himself surrounded by simulators that popped up from behind rocks and bushes and swung around trees. Lightstone kept on moving, turning and firing, sensing the thumps of two more paint balls, then staggering under the impact of a .357 hollow-point against his vest. An incredibly fast simulator suddenly popped up out of a concealed "trapdoor spider" hole and was stopped by the last two 10mm bullets out of Henry Lightstone's pistol. Then Alex Chareaux lunged out of the trees like a nightmare, the razor-sharp knife slicing at Lightstone's exposed leg.

Gerd Maas stepped out into the clearing with the .22 target pistol in his hand, waiting to see which of the two would eventually come forward: his prey. He smiled as the two men thrashed and screamed and grunted, fighting for their lives in the simulated darkness.

So absorbed was he that Gerd Maas almost didn't see Dwight Stoner slowly bring his muscular hands to his side and steadily push himself up into a crouched position in the middle of the clearing.

As Gerd Maas watched in fascination, the huge agent somehow managed to get himself into a fully upright, though shaky, position.

From thirty feet away, Gerd Maas could see, and even feel, Stoner's determination as the ex-Oakland Raider started forward, and he smiled as his mind went back to the moment when the mother Kodiak had first begun her determined but inevitably futile charge.

Maas was smiling when, from twenty feet away, he sent the first .22-caliber bullet into the kneecap of Stoner's already crippled left leg, causing the huge agent to crash to the floor with a hiss of suppressed pain and rage.

Maas was still smiling, his eyes gleaming with the sensory rush, as Dwight Stoner started to pull himself back up, his eyes fixed on the face of the man he fully intended to take apart with his powerful bare hands, if he could ever get close enough.

The second .22 projectile shattered Stoner's right kneecap, and he crashed to the floor again. The sole sound in the entire chamber was that of Dwight Stoner as he forced himself up onto his hands and knees, only ten feet away now, as he started forward again.

Gerd Maas was lost in the adrenaline rush, and he never noticed the red dot that appeared on his right shoulder as he brought the .22 target pistol up again to carefully place the third shot . . . but he certainly felt the impact of the single 5.56mm bullet that tore through his shoulder and caused the target pistol to clatter to the floor.

Reacting with catlike instincts, Maas reached for his belt knife with his left hand. The red dot traveled to his left shoulder, which the second 5.56mm bullet hit, tearing through bone and muscle and sending the knife clattering to the floor, where it lay next to the pistol.

Then Gerd Maas looked up as Henry Lightstone stepped out of the shadows, a stainless-steel Rolex on his wrist and Kimiko Osan's laser-aimed Colt Commando in his bruised and bloody hands.

"You know, Maas," Lightstone said as he walked slowly toward the still-standing ICER leader, "that guy on the floor who was coming after you told me about a game once. It was called bunnies and guppies. Big playing field, shitpot full of rules, no referee."

Then Lightstone smiled pleasantly. "You know what else he said?"

Gerd Maas blinked his pale eyes, but didn't say anything.

"'Last man standing wins.'"

"You can't—" Maas started to say, and then the red dot swung down and two 5.56mm bullets tore through the legs of the ICER counter-terrorist, sending him sprawling to the floor within a few inches of Dwight Stoner. The ex-Oakland-Raider-tackle-turned-wildlife-agent looked at the shining red dot that was now focused between Gerd Maas's glassy eyes and smiled.

"Henry, don't do it," the voice of Al Grynard said behind Henry Lightstone's back, but the red dot never wavered.

"I'm not going to kill him," Lightstone said after a moment. "I'm going to arrest the bastard."

"But I told you . . . you can't arrest me," the counter-terrorist leader rasped. "You can't prove—"

"I can't prove that you killed Paul McNulty or Carl Scoby. And I can't prove that you blew up a bunch of environmentalists, or cut the throat of a little bear cub, or shot an airplane out from under a guy who can't hardly fly to begin with," Lightstone nodded.

"But what I can prove," the coldly smiling agent said huskily as he shifted the red dot of the laser sight to a thin strip where the skin had been gouged out from Maas' rhino-hide boot, "is that you killed a mama Kodiak on a National Wildlife Refuge, and that you killed her illegally, which is going to get you ten years in a federal penitentiary.

"And while you're serving those ten years," Henry Lightstone added as FBI agents moved in to assist Dwight Stoner and take the crippled ICER assault group leader into custody, "if I can ever prove that you so much as plucked a tail feather from a goddamned duck, then I'm going to charge you with that, too."

BESTSELLERS FROM TOR

HIGH-TENSION
THRILLERS FROM TOR

☐ 52222-2　BLOOD OF THE LAMB　　　　　　　　　$5.99
　　　　　　Thomas Monteleone　　　　Canada $6.99

☐ 52169-2　THE COUNT OF ELEVEN　　　　　　$4.99
　　　　　　Ramsey Campbell　　　　　Canada $5.99

☐ 52497-7　CRITICAL MASS　　　　　　　　　　$5.99
　　　　　　David Hagberg　　　　　　Canada $6.99

☐ 51786-5　FIENDS　　　　　　　　　　　　　$4.95
　　　　　　John Farris　　　　　　　Canada $5.95

☐ 51957-4　HUNGER　　　　　　　　　　　　　$4.99
　　　　　　William R. Dantz　　　　Canada $5.99

☐ 51173-5　NEMESIS MISSION　　　　　　　　$5.95
　　　　　　Dean Ing　　　　　　　　Canada $6.95

☐ 58254-3　O'FARRELL'S LAW　　　　　　　　$3.99
　　　　　　Brian Freemantle　　　　Canada $4.99

☐ 50939-0　PIKA DON　　　　　　　　　　　　$4.99
　　　　　　Al Dempsey　　　　　　　Canada $5.99

☐ 52016-5　THE SWISS ACCOUNT　　　　　　　$5.99
　　　　　　Paul Erdman　　　　　　Canada $6.99

Buy them at your local bookstore or use this handy coupon:
Clip and mail this page with your order.

Publishers Book and Audio Mailing Service
P.O. Box 120159, Staten Island, NY 10312-0004

Please send me the book(s) I have checked above. I am enclosing $ _____
(Please add $1.25 for the first book, and $.25 for each additional book to cover postage and handling.
Send check or money order only—no CODs.)

Name _____
Address _____
City _____ State/Zip _____
Please allow six weeks for delivery.　Prices subject to change without notice.

THE BEST IN MYSTERY

☐ 51388-6 THE ANONYMOUS CLIENT $4.99
J.P. Hailey Canada $5.99

☐ 51195-6 BREAKFAST AT WIMBLEDON $3.99
Jack M. Bickham Canada $4.99

☐ 51682-6 CATNAP $4.99
Carole Nelson Douglas Canada $5.99

☐ 51702-4 IRENE AT LARGE $4.99
Carole Nelson Douglas Canada $5.99

☐ 51563-3 MARIMBA $4.99
Richard Hoyt Canada $5.99

☐ 52031-9 THE MUMMY CASE $3.99
Elizabeth Peters Canada $4.99

☐ 50642-1 RIDE THE LIGHTNING $3.95
John Lutz Canada $4.95

☐ 50728-2 ROUGH JUSTICE $4.99
Ken Gross Canada $5.99

☐ 51149-2 SILENT WITNESS $3.99
Collin Wilcox Canada $4.99

Buy them at your local bookstore or use this handy coupon:
Clip and mail this page with your order.

Publishers Book and Audio Mailing Service
P.O. Box 120159, Staten Island, NY 10312-0004

Please send me the book(s) I have checked above. I am enclosing $ _____
(Please add $1.25 for the first book, and $.25 for each additional book to cover postage and handling.
Send check or money order only—no CODs.)

Name _____

Address _____

City _____ State/Zip _____

Please allow six weeks for delivery. Prices subject to change without notice.